Hákon konungr Aðalsteinsfóstri lagði undir sik allan
Nóreg, þá er Eiríkr, bróðir hans, hafði brot flýit.
Hákon konungr sótti inn fyrsta vetr vestr í landit,
eptir þat norðr í Þrándheim ok sat þar. En fyrir þær
sakir, at eigi þótti friðligt, ef Eiríkr konungr leitaði
vestan um haf með her sinn

When King Eirik Bloody Axe had left the country,
King Hakon, Athelstan's foster-son, took the whole of
Norway. The first winter he visited the western parts,
and then went north… However no peace could be
looked for so long as King Eirik with his vikings could
come to Norway from the Western Sea.

The Saga of Hakon the Good, Part 6

skeggjöld, skalmöld,
skildir klofnir,
vindöld, vargöld,
áðr veröld steypisk.
An axe-age, a sword-age,
shields shall be cloven;
A wind-age, a wolf-age,
before the world falls.

Völuspá, 'The Prophecy of the Seeress'

Prologue

Frodisborg in the folksland of Gandvik, Norway

AD 935 – Late Summer

Einar wondered if he was drowning. Like a man sunk deep underwater, he felt like he was wrapped up in coldness. All noise was muffled and indistinct and he had the sensation he was sinking into darkness. When he closed his eyes strange dreams took over his mind. When he woke, pain throbbed in his eyes and head. He felt freezing cold one moment then boiling hot next. All the strength in his body had drained from him leaving him weak, tired and sick. Confusion fogged his thoughts. Where was he? Why did he feel this way? What had happened to him?

He heard voices.

They seemed familiar but very far away. With an effort he found similar to the one that he had once needed to swim clear of a sinking ship, Einar forced his mind to wake.

He opened his eyes and felt the stab of pain behind them. He was in a gloomy room and it was dark, though a whale oil lamp burned somewhere nearby. Its glow cast an orange light on the faces of the people gathered around him and its stench caused his stomach to lurch.

There was a man leaning over him. He had his hand on Einar's sweat-soaked forehead. The man's skin was dark, almost black. For a moment Einar thought he was back in one of the weird dreams that haunted him, then remembered it was the man they called Surt, King Eirik Bloody Axe's former ring fighter and slave who now sailed with Ulrich's crew of *úlfhéðnar*, the wolf-coated warriors of Odin.

Behind Surt loomed the figure of an old man with long white hair and beard that cascaded around his chest and shoulders. As he regarded Einar he leaned his chin on the backs of his hands that were placed on the top of a long walking staff. Einar wondered if he were dead and perhaps this was Odin himself, come to take him to the next world. Then his reasoning mind saw that unlike the one-eyed God of the Gallows, this man had two good eyes. It was Grimnir, the wise old man from Gandvik who had sailed with Einar and the Wolf Coats on several of their expeditions.

'His wound has festered,' Surt said, looking down at Einar's right hand. He spoke the Norse tongue, but with an accent that came from the hot, burning lands that lay far to the south.

Einar's right hand was maimed, the little finger gone and the palm sheared off. The wound was purple and black. Puss oozed from where his finger had once been. The flesh of the rest of the hand was swollen and angry red.

'How do you know?' Grimnir said.

'Warriors of al-Andalus all have some training in the crafts of healing,' Surt said. 'Armies lose more men to wounds that rankle than to killing blows.'

'We know wound craft too,' another voice said. The sharp featured face of Ulrich, the short, wiry leader of the úlfhéðnar crew came into view. He wore the pelt of a wolf as a cloak around his shoulders. His dark brown hair was shorn short, revealing that, even though he was not an old man, it was receding from his forehead. 'Surt is right. The wound has gone bad.'

Surt lifted his hand away from Einar's forehead. It was slick with the young man's clammy sweat.

'The poison runs throughout his blood, making him sick,' Surt said. 'It's clouding his mind and has already stolen his strength.'

'I knew there was something wrong when we sailed away from Orkney,' a woman's voice said. She stepped into the light of the lamp. Like Ulrich she wore a wolf pelt cloak around her shoulders. Even in the soft glow of the oil lamp, her skin appeared so pale it seemed pure white. Her red-gold hair was tied in a short braid. A pair of very dark eyebrows arched over eyes so green they would not have looked out of place on a cat. Einar knew her too. Though she had all the appearance of a Valkyrie, she was not one of the shieldmaidens Odin sent flying over battlefields to pick those who had died in the bravest of ways. She was Affreca, daughter of the King of Dublin and a Wolf Coat like him and the rest of Ulrich's crew.

'He went very quiet and huddled by himself under the prow of the ship,' she said. 'I thought he was just angry and brooding.'

'That's understandable,' Grimnir said. 'He fought his own father to the death. He won but got that wound in the duel. Then he was forced to leave the High Seat of Jarls Gard just after having won it. It must all have been hard to take.'

The others all nodded.

'And you know what Einar's like,' Affreca said. 'He always over thinks everything. Will he get better?'

Her eyes flicked towards Surt.

The dark-skinned man shrugged.

'Perhaps,' he said. 'Perhaps not. Who can say? Only Allah knows the answer to that. But he's a young, strong lad. He has a lot to fight the poison with. With time, care and attention he might pull through.'

'Those are the three things we can least afford to give him,' Ulrich said. 'We have to leave him here.'

Einar tried to speak but his throat felt dry and swollen. All that came out was an incoherent croak.

'Einar is one of our wolf pack, Ulrich,' Skar, the big prowman of the úlfhéðnar crew and Ulrich's right-hand man, said. 'He is an oathsworn brother. We can't just leave him behind.'

'Right now, he's also too sick to travel,' Surt said, meeting Skar's intense gaze with his own. 'If we take him with us we'll kill him for sure.'

'Why can't we wait here until he's recovered enough to move?' Affreca said.

'Because, your high and mightiness,' Ulrich said, glaring at Affreca over clenched teeth, 'In case you haven't noticed, the world is at war with itself. The powers of chaos are loose. Brothers fight brothers, sons fight their fathers.

Towns are being put to the sword and the flame, whole folk lands are being ravaged.'

'What's that to us?' Wulfhelm the Saxon with his long, straight moustache asked. Like Surt, he too spoke the Norse tongue with an accent, but his was of the West Saxons who lived in Britain.

'There are vikings pillaging along the western coast of Norway. They were sent here across the northern whale road by Eirik Bloody Axe,' Ulrich said. 'We may have helped Hakon chase Eirik out of this land but if we don't do something more, Eirik will be back and Hakon will lose the kingship again.'

'Then we're all dead,' Skar said, pursing his lips.

'War is our work,' Ulrich said. 'It's what we do and King Hakon has need of our skills. We cannot waste time sitting around waiting for Einar here to either get better or die. Eirik Bloody Axe will not be sitting on his arse I can assure you of that.'

'But Eirik is in Orkney now,' Affreca said. 'He ran there like a whipped dog when he was driven out of Norway.'

'Do you think a man like Eirik will just accept that?' Ulrich said. 'No. He's in Orkney now, licking his wounds, yes. But I know Eirik. After all, we were his sworn warriors for years until the bastard betrayed us. He'll be rebuilding his strength and when he's ready he'll be back. I don't want to be sitting here playing healer-woman to a sick lad when he comes. He's too dangerous a foe to allow him to come to us. We need to make sure Hakon is safe from him too.'

The members of his crew nodded, stroked their chins or otherwise showed their assent.

'Besides all that,' Ulrich said. 'Can you not see what is happening? Any of you?'

He looked at those around him. The short man's eyes were now wide, bright and glittering.

'There has been no summer,' he said when no one answered him. 'Winter has just continued on when summer should have come; rain, cold wind, grey skies and no warm sun to ripen the crops. The harvest will fail. That will cause more war. Think about it. War and back- to-back winters. What do three winters with no summer herald?'

Again no one responded.

In the resulting silence, Einar finally managed to find his voice.

'*A time of axes, a time of swords. Shields will be sundered,*' he chanted, his voice hoarse and croaking. '*A time of howling winds, a time of wolves. Then the world falls. No man has mercy for another.*'

The effort was too much for him. Einar groaned and closed his eyes once more.

'Even this dying lad knows what I'm talking about!' Ulrich said, a look of fervid triumph on his face. 'Don't you see it yet?'

'*Ragnarök,*' Affreca said. Her voice was hushed, little more than a whisper.

'The end of the world,' Skar said, his tone equally daunted.

'The final battle is coming,' Ulrich said. 'Time is running out. Soon Odin will send his Valkyries to pick those who will fight with him on the last day. We only have a little time to make sure we've done deeds great enough to be chosen for his army.'

Affreca smiled and shook her head.

'This company have already done more than enough to grab Odin's attention,' she said.

'But what if someone does something to outshine everything we've done?' Ulrich said. 'In times of war folk have no end of opportunities to impress the Gods, and the benches in Odin's Valour Hall only have room for a certain number of heroes. I don't intend to let someone take mine.'

'Perhaps you're right,' Grimnir said. 'And King Hakon needs your help regardless. It's best you go. I will stay here in Frodisborg and look after the lad, Einar, here. My house is here and besides, you must travel fast. I'm an old man and will only slow you down.'

'If Einar survives,' Ulrich said, 'he can rejoin us. But in case he doesn't, leave him his *Ulfberht*. If he has one of the best made swords in the world in his hand when he dies, perhaps Odin will turn his good eye blind to the fact the lad died in bed instead of on the battlefield.'

He left the room. The others began filing out after him.

Affreca lifted Einar's sword from beside his bed and unsheathed it. The blade shimmered in the lamp light as she ran her finger along the runes set into the middle of the blade, spelling out +ULFBEHRT+, the name of the wizard-smith who forged it. She stooped over Einar. Even in his daze he could sense it was her. He felt the back of her fingers stroke down his cheek. Then she pushed the hilt of the sword into his uninjured left hand. Einar's fingers closed around it in a feeble grasp. Affreca closed her eyes.

'As Odin took nine rune sticks and cut the poisonous serpent into nine parts,' she said in a whisper. 'May this poison be driven from you and nevermore enter the house of your body. Get better Einar, son of Thorfinn the Skull Cleaver. If you don't, I'll come back here and kill you myself.'

Then she too was gone.

Too weak to move or speak, Einar drifted off once again into the nightmare-haunted darkness.

Part One

Norway

One

Frodisborg

Six weeks later

The fight was lost and Einar knew it. His opponent knew it too.

Einar cursed, spat and moved sideways, hefting his shield so it was still between him and the warrior facing him. Sweat stung his eyes. His breathing was heavy. His shoulders were sore and his arms felt as if the shield he bore was made of stone.

His opponent had not even broken sweat. He crouched, peering over the top of his shield at Einar. His sword was ready. The eyes behind the helmet visor were alert and eager, watching for the opportunity to strike.

The warrior sprang forwards.

Their shields collided with a crash of linden wood. Einar felt his left foot, braced behind him against the impact, skid backwards.

The other man swung his sword in an overhead blow, scything through the air in an arc intended to finish somewhere about halfway through Einar's head. Einar threw his own sword up to block it. With a clang of metal on metal the blades met.

Einar felt the hilt of his sword twist in the weakened grip of his injured right hand. A cry of dismay escaped his lips as the weapon fell from his grasp. It bounced off the rim of his shield and clattered to the ground.

With a heavy sigh, he lowered his shield. What was the point in continuing?

His opponent gave a low chuckle. The warrior drew his sword back to strike. He stepped closer, then pushed the blade forwards, poking Einar on the chin with the tip.

'You're dead,' he said, his face breaking into a grin.

Einar cursed again, tossing his shield to the ground with a petulant shrug.

'I'm useless, Bersi,' he said, shaking his head. 'With this injured hand I can't grip anything properly.'

'Don't be too hard on yourself,' Bersi said. He pulled his helmet off, revealing the face of a young man whose blond hair was plastered to his head with sweat. 'You did well, considering.'

Einar shot a sharp glance of reproach in his direction. He looked down at his maimed right hand. The thumb and first three fingers were fine and he had recovered from the poisoning from his festered wound, but the hand was now ended after his ring finger. Grimnir, the wise old man who had nursed him through his sickness, had been forced to remove more septic flesh to save Einar so now not only was his little finger gone but his palm was sheared off almost to the wrist. Grimnir had been forced to cut away some of the flesh at the bottom of Einar's ring finger, making it hard to move.

The wound was now covered by new, clean skin which at least was a healthy pink instead of the rotting purple that had been there before.

They stood in the meadow beyond Frodisborg, the little village on the edge of the fjord of Gandvik in western Norway. Both Einar and the other man's helmets and shields were usable war gear but the swords were blunted practice weapons. They were little more than flattened iron bars used in training for real combat.

Einar opened and closed what was left of his right fist.

'Considering your wound, I mean...' Bersi said. He was a young lad from the village who Einar had asked to spar with him to test if his war craft capabilities had recovered yet.

Einar made a face.

'Did your father grant you a legacy, Bersi?' he said, then realised it was a stupid question. The lad's father, one of the village fishermen, was still well in the prime of life. The lad returned Einar's gaze, confusion portrayed all over his face.

'Well *my* father bequeathed this to me,' Einar said, spreading his remaining fingers. 'It was his parting gift. I killed him just after he dealt me this blow.'

Einar saw the shock in the young lad's eyes and knew he had to explain further.

'He killed my mother,' Einar said. 'He tried to kill me several times. We weren't what you might call a close family.

When I killed him I took the right to sit in his high seat as Jarl of Orkney. Then I lost that too.'

Bersi shook his head.

'You know what, Einar?' he said, a smile of admiration on his lips, 'When I listen to your tales, I sometimes think I'm hearing the saga of some legendary hero like Sigurd Volsung or Hrolf Kraki, not the life of a lad who's only a couple of years older than me. I'm nearly eighteen winters old. I've lived all my days in this sleepy little village where nothing ever happens except fishing and harvest. You've experienced so much more. You've sailed the whale roads, been to cities, met with jarls and kings, fought in battles.'

'It's not true that nothing happens here,' Einar said. 'There was a battle in this very meadow not that long ago. We fought Eirik Bloody Axe's bastard son here when he came to burn down the village.'

'And I even missed that!' Bersi said. 'I was away at sea on a fishing voyage with my father.'

'Well, be careful what you wish for, lad,' Einar said, aware that all of a sudden he was talking to someone almost his own age as if he himself was an ancient, wise man. 'Just over a year ago I was on my mother's farm in Iceland. I was just like you, thinking I was at the very edge of Middle Earth where nothing ever happens. Then I got into a fight, was exiled from my homeland and found out I had a father I never knew about who also wanted me dead.'

'You became Jarl of Orkney,' Bersi said, his eyes wide. 'And you became a great warrior: an *Úlfhéðinn*, one of Odin's own warriors. What man doesn't want to be one of those?'

'And now I'm nothing once again!' Einar said with a snarl. 'I had barely time to warm the high seat of Orkney with my arse when Eirik Bloody Axe arrived with an army and stole it away from me. Then my wound rankled and I ended up like this—'

He held up his injured hand once again.

'And what use is a Wolf Coat warrior who cannot hold a weapon properly?' he said, heaving a heavy sigh. 'Apart from that, as our bout just showed, the sickness has taken away all my stamina. You beat me easily. Einar, son of Thorfinn the Skull Cleaver, bested by a fisherman's son! So much for the *great warrior*.'

He caught the look of consternation on Bersi's face and knew he should not let the dark bitterness that clouded around his own heart taint the other's young spirit.

'Sorry,' Einar said. 'I don't mean to belittle your own effort in the fight. It's just that when you rise so high, so fast, coming back down to earth again is hard to take.'

'Einar, this time a few weeks ago you were flat on your back in bed, in the depths of sweating and sickness,' Bersi said. 'We thought you'd never rise again. But here you are back on your feet. You should be happy just to be alive. Who knows where you will be in another few weeks?'

Einar did not reply. He had a horrible feeling that the answer to that question was that he would still be stuck right here in Frodisborg.

Bersi looked at the practice sword.

'I still have your real sword,' he said. 'The princess, Affreca, gave it to me to keep for you until you got better. Do you want it back?'

'The Ulfbehrt?' Einar said clenching his teeth. 'Keep it.

Knives are fine but any long blade just twists out of my grasp.'

'Are you sure?' Bersi said, eyebrows raised. 'An Ulfbehrt sword is worth more silver than a jarl's treasure hoard.'

'I'm sure,' Einar said. 'What good is it to me? I may as well have died the straw death in my sickbed. If I can't wield a sword or axe I'm nothing.'

'I'll look after it until you're better then, as Affreca asked me to,' Bersi said. 'How about we agree on that? I just might have need of it too. Eirik Bloody Axe has sent vikings to ravage Norway. They say he's punishing us for driving him out of the kingship. Frostvik was burned to the ground only last week. That village is not far south of here. If Eirik's vikings come to Frodisborg then with this sword I'll be ready to stand against them.'

'I won't be much help if that happens,' Einar said.

'You're still the best skald I've ever heard,' Bersi said. 'The way you chant the old songs, Einar, I've never seen anyone who could captivate an ale hall the way you do.'

Einar grunted, looking down at his injured hand again.

'The same wound means I can't pluck the strings of the harp properly,' he said. 'It all sounds wrong. Notes are missing because of the missing finger. What use is a poet who cannot play his harp?'

Bersi frowned. It was clear that the lad was beginning to get annoyed at Einar's black mood.

'Einar, I can see why you're angry at what has happened to you,' he said. 'But what good will this anger do you? You can't use it to fight anyone. The *Norns* who govern all our fates have put you where you are now. Do you think you can fight them? No. Even the Gods fates are determined by the Norns.'

Einar gaped, open-mouthed, astonished that words of such insight had come from a lad younger than him who had never left his home village except to go fishing.

'Now, you want to try again?' Bersi said, hefting his sword and shield into the defensive position. 'Maybe you'll beat me this time.'

Einar shook his head.

'Maybe if you let me win,' he said. 'Besides, I've work to do. I should go back to the smithy.'

Einar stomped off across the meadow, leaving Bersi to tidy up the fighting gear as the first drops of a rain shower began to fall from a sky as grey as wolf fur. As he walked he tried his best to dispel the black feelings that swirled inside him but it was hard. The younger lad's words had disturbed Einar more than his beating him in the practice duel. Ulrich's úlfhéðnar company had left him behind here in a little village in the back end of nowhere. He had no idea where they had gone and if Eirik's vikings really did come, how could he even defend himself?

Two

Einar walked out of the meadow into the line of houses that made up the village. He was heading for a round building with a low, thatched roof which stood in contrast to the other long, rectangular houses. It was the forge of Tostig, the smith.

At home in Iceland they had a name for idle folk who liked to sit by the fire instead of working to help everyone else: *kolbítur*. A coal biter. It was not a compliment.

This was why, as soon as the old man Grimnir had nursed Einar with his herbs and potions through the worst of the sickness brought on by his poisoned wound, Einar had sought work. Tostig, the ageing village blacksmith, had offered him employment doing odd jobs and Einar had accepted. He was far from happy at being stuck in Frodisborg but like any settlement in rough country where life was a constant struggle against weather, earth and tides, he knew if he did not start to contribute in some way the hospitality of the local folk would soon wear out.

And right now, Einar had nowhere else to go.

He had been in Frodisborg for many weeks now and was beginning to worry that he would be stuck there forever. Einar should be Jarl of Orkney now. Instead, here he was, left behind in a sleepy village by Ulrich's Wolf Coat company and Orkney was Eirik Bloody Axe's new high seat of power, not Einar's.

Ulrich's plan had been to sail to Norway and offer the services of his Wolf Coats to the new king, Eirik's younger brother and usurper, Hakon. They had, after all, common cause; Eirik wanted Hakon dead as much as Hakon wanted Ulrich and his company dead. That was why they had arrived in Frodisborg on the fjord-riddled western coast of Norway. It was the last place they had seen Hakon. Only now he was no longer there and had moved further north.

Then they had left Einar behind, due to the sickness brought on by his festering wound. The old man, Grimnir, with his wisdom of arcane lore, had eventually returned Einar to the land of the living but the trouble was, now Einar had no idea where Hakon was or how he might find him and Ulrich's crew. Even if he did, the wound poison had left him feeling weak as a child and with his maimed hand, would the Wolf Coats even want him back? Did he even deserve to call himself one of them any more?

Over this last week or so, Einar had soon learned that the 'odd job' Tostig had said he wanted him for actually meant doing most of the old man's work for him. After teaching Einar the basics of smithing, Tostig had taken to spending his days away from the hot, darkness of the smithy, fishing and sleeping on the banks of the fjord at Gandvik while Einar was left alone to finish the old man's tasks.

Einar walked into the dark warmth of the forge, glad to be out of the ever-drizzling rain. He dropped his helmet and shield to the floor and prepared to get to work.

Inside, the fire glowed, pouring out heat like the breath of a dragon. Before wandering off to his fishing that morning, old Tostig had left Einar a pile of broken tools to fix. Einar had left two shovel bales in the fire before he had gone to spar with Bersi and now they glowed a hot, cherry red and were ready for working.

He picked up his special hammer and prepared to get to work. At first a hammer had proved as impossible for him to wield as a long sword, but Tostig had taken one of his old hammers and cut the shaft in half. With the weight of the head closer to his hand, Einar found he was able to keep the much shorter tool more firmly in his weakened grasp. It was not totally under control, however. For added grip Einar required a leather strap. Unfortunately the same solution did not work with a full sized sword whose blade could not be cut in half, but at least this allowed Einar to work in the smithy.

He set about winding the leather strap around his wrist, hand and the shaft of the hammer. The final part – binding the strap in a knot – was the trickiest part, especially when he was on his own. He struggled to complete the knot using his left hand in combination with his teeth.

'Do you want help with that?'

A female voice interrupted him. Einar started and looked around. His face flushed a crimson that had nothing to do with the heat of the forge. Standing in the doorway of the forge was a girl with long golden hair which she wore unbound in the custom of unmarried women. She was about sixteen winters old and by any standards beautiful. She held a large clay jug in both hands before her.

'My father said I should bring you some ale,' the girl said, setting the jug down on a nearby bench then joining Einar.

'He said you would get thirsty working in the heat of the forge today.'

'Thank you, Frida,' Einar mumbled, letting go of the strap with his teeth and grinning at the blacksmith's daughter like an idiot. 'Your father has left me quite a lot of work to do.'

He felt as if he were frozen to the spot as Frida took the strap in her nimble fingers and tied it into a tight knot. When she finished, she looked up and smiled at him, locking her blue eyes with his for a moment. As she did so Einar felt like the warm summer sun, something that there had not been much of this year, was shining directly on his face.

'Thanks,' was the best he could come up with to say.

Frida nodded, turned and went to the door.

'I have my own work to do,' she said over her shoulder, 'perhaps we shall see each other later?'

'Definitely!' Einar said, his grin spreading from ear to ear.

Then she was gone.

For a moment Einar stared after her, then he sighed, realising he needed to get to work himself. Pulling one of the red hot, bent shovel blades from the fire, Einar began pounding it back into shape.

Sparks showered from the hot metal as the hammer head crashed into it, sending the clangs of metal on metal through the air. Einar welcomed the work. Each blow of the hammer helped to dispel the clouds of frustration inside him. On top of all that, the work in the forge was helping him regain his strength. The shorter shaft meant the hammer had to be swung harder and though strenuous movement might still leave him breathless, Einar's right arm had grown powerful already, even more than it had been before he was injured.

By the time the shovel blade was knocked back into

shape he felt satisfied enough with his work that there was even a ghost of a smile playing on his lips. He was sweating again and his shoulder ached from the effort but it was a warm, welcome tiredness.

As the clangs of the hammer died away in his ears, Einar became aware of other sounds. Somewhere distant he could hear a horn blowing.

He frowned. Grimnir lived in a house that was up on the mountain. From there he had a view across the river valley and out into the fjord. He kept a horn for alerting the village if he saw any potential danger approaching. Could that be him?

Then other horns were blaring, these much closer; from the village and its surroundings. Each one was insistent and warning. Within moments they were joined by shouts and voices raised in consternation.

He heard a woman scream and felt as though his heart had dropped through the bottom of his chest.

Frida appeared in the doorway once more. Her eyes were wide and pleading. Her mouth worked as if she was trying to say something but no words came out. She had both hands clasped around the blade of a spear that burst from the front of her dress. A huge red stain was spreading through her dress, centred on the spear. The rest of the spear shaft protruded from her back.

She stood for a moment more, then her eyes rolled up into her head and she collapsed to the ground.

Einar felt like a bucket of iced water had been thrown over his head. Frozen by shock he stared down at the dead Frida.

More shouting from outside broke the spell of horror.

He looked to the doorway as a man from the village came running past outside. As Einar watched, astonished, another spear thudded into the man's back. It transfixed his torso, the blood-covered blade bursting from his stomach. With a startled cry he fell, sprawling face forwards into the dirt.

A girl of about eight winters old came running behind the fallen man.

'Vikings!' she shouted. 'Vikings are coming!'

Three

The war craft training Skar, Ulrich and the other úlfhéðnar had drummed into Einar finally took over. The shock at what was happening around him dissolved, loosening his frozen limbs. Amid the commotion outside he saw a shadow fall across the threshold of the forge. Someone was coming. If he did not do something fast, Einar would join the dead lying outside.

He jumped to one side of the door. He pressed his back to the wall. His hair scraped the thatch of the low roof as the rattling of ring mail and thump of a wooden shield came closer.

A warrior burst through the doorway. He wore a visored helmet, his torso was encased by the metal rings of a *brynja* and in his right hand he grasped a sword whose blade shimmered as it reflected the light of the forge. There was blood on the sword and splashed across the shining rings of his brynja. In his left hand he carried a shield. Einar caught a glimpse of a design painted on it but there was no time to work out what it was.

The viking roared a war cry at the top of his lungs, a scream that told of bloodlust and indiscriminate hatred. The man stopped, blinded for a moment as his eyes went from the brightness of daylight outside to the dark of the interior of the forge. Einar did not waste his chance.

He smashed the hammer into the viking's helmet. The heavy metal head crushed a huge dent in it and one equally as large in the man's skull beneath. His war cry came to an abrupt end and he dropped to the ground like a sack of grain whose bottom end had burst. He lay face down, body twitching and jerking in a way that told Einar the man was either dead or at the very least would never rise again under his own power.

Einar peeked out through the doorway. The scene that met his gaze was one of terror and chaos. Village folk ran this way and that, panic written over their faces. Warriors in helmets and shields – viking raiders – ran among them, stabbing and hacking at anyone they could reach. Some were setting fire to the thatch of the buildings. At the little harbour beyond the village two longships were beached, their dragon-carved prows rising high in the air like bloodthirsty *jötnar*, watching with pleasure the killing taking place before them. Grey smoke and the smell of burning was beginning to drift from flames that already licked the houses on the edge of the village.

The sails of the longships and the shields of the vikings all bore the same symbol – the bloody red axe of Eirik Haraldsson.

The little girl was crouched over the body of the man who had fallen outside the door of the smithy. With a jolt Einar realised the villager laying, unmoving, his torso transfixed by the spear, was Torfi one of Bersi's fishing crew. The girl howling and pleading with him to get up was his daughter.

Einar knew he had no time to waste. He grabbed his

helmet with his left hand and plonked it on his head. There was no time to untie the strap that bound the hammer to his right hand or to tie the straps of his helmet under his chin. With the cheek guards flapping loose, Einar lifted his shield and ran out of the forge.

For a moment he stopped, looking down at the corpse of Frida. She lay in a dark puddle of her own blood, her beautiful blue eyes open, fixed and staring forever at the empty sky. Einar's eyes stung with sudden tears and felt a lump sticking in his throat.

Then the cold fires of rage ignited in his heart. Einar felt it coursing through his veins like icy water. He closed his eyes and gritted his teeth. Skar and the other Wolf Coats had taught him he had to control the emotion. At all costs he could not let himself go berserk, lose all control and run, screaming, straight out onto the spear points of the vikings outside.

He took a deep breath, struggling to channel the anger into action. He sensed the blood pounding in his arms and legs, driving away the tiredness. He took one last look at Frida then stepped over her body and out the door of the forge. There would be time for mourning later. Now it was time to fight.

Einar looked around, taking in the calamity and bloodshed around him. A viking was running straight towards the little girl huddled over the corpse of the speared man. His axe was raised to strike. He was screaming incoherently, his spittle flying in all directions.

Einar stepped in between him and the girl. He raised his shield, countering the blow of the axe designed to chop the child in two. As the axe bit into the wood with a solid *thunk*,

Einar swept the shield upwards, pushing the weapon away from the viking's body. Then he struck with his hammer, catching the viking on the right knee with a gut-churning crack of shattering bone. The man screamed in agony as his knee bent the wrong way. His leg collapsed under his weight and he fell face forward onto the ground. Einar raised the hammer again and smashed it into the back of the viking's head. He went limp in an instant.

The little girl was now looking up, her face pale as snow, her eyes wide with shock and terror.

'Get out of here,' he shouted at her. 'Run for the forest. You'll be safe there.'

The girl flinched at his words but did not move. Einar realised that towering over her, his face behind a visored helmet and brandishing a bloody hammer he looked every bit as frightening as the vikings who were running around destroying her village.

There was no time to reassure her, however. He needed to get her away.

Einar roared at her, raised his hammer and shield in an exaggerated fashion and stepped towards her. It had some of his intended effect. The girl, now even more terrified, rose to her feet. Confused and afraid, she half turned to run, then stopped, perhaps thinking he would attack her when she turned her back.

'Go on! Get away!' Einar shouted. He raised his right boot and planted a kick on her backside. Remorse stung him as in his anger and excitement he overdid it and the girl lifted off the ground a little from the force of his kick. When she hit the ground again, however, she was running. This time she did not stop and ran as fast as the wind towards the meadow past the village and, to Einar's fervent hope, the relative safety of the trees beyond.

Einar spun around to cover her flight. A running child would present a tempting, easy target to the vikings. None saw her however and Einar realised that the vikings were now occupied with something else.

The men of the village had got over their initial shock and were gathering at the end of one of the tracks that ran through the village intending to confront the raiders. Their war gear was old, few had helmets, some had shields but many just had farming tools. Only one man wore a brynja and it was an ancient one, with several holes and rusted rings of mail. They had enough shields however to form a wall across the track that led to the meadow.

Behind them the women, children and elderly folk who had been able to get away fled towards the trees on the far side. Einar felt a thrill of excitement.

The men of Frodisborg may have been simple farmers and fishermen, but they had been trained in war craft by Ulrich's wolf warriors. They had held off the army of King Eirik Bloody Axe's son, Rognvald, until Hakon had arrived with the horde of Jarl Sigurd of Hlader. These vikings had picked the wrong village to raid.

Einar ran to join their shield wall. Spotting Bersi, his sparring partner, near the middle of the formation, he took up a position beside him, adding his own shield to the defensive formation.

'Who's this come to help us? Thor?' the man on Einar's right said, catching sight of the blood-splattered hammer strapped to Einar's hand.

Bersi held up a sword. Despite the gloomy weather

the light shimmered across the blade, making it look like countless metal snakes twisting and turning around each other. There were runes used by the Christians embedded down the middle of it, spelling out +ULFBEHRT+, the name of the wizard-smith who made these superb swords.

'Thanks for the sword, Einar,' Bersi said. 'Today it will taste blood again.'

'I didn't think you'd have to use it so soon,' Einar said.

The vikings left off their burning and looting and began to gather into a bunch before the villagers' shield wall. Einar took another look at them, assessing the threat they posed. There were perhaps forty of them, outnumbering the men of the village two to one. If the Frodisborg men kept their discipline, however, they could hold the vikings off long enough at least for the women and children to get away.

As the vikings formed up for attack, Einar noticed that the red axes painted on their shields appeared to have been daubed on in haste. The paint had run on some and many had been splashed on over other existing symbols of stags, wolves heads or ravens. Whoever these warriors were, they seemed to be relatively recent recruits to the cause of Eirik Bloody Axe.

Some of them bit the rims of their shields and all had a fervid look in their eyes. They looked a wild bunch and Einar began to fear that some of them may be berserkers: warriors blessed by the uncontrollable divine rage bestowed by Odin.

A horn blew. With a roar the vikings launched their attack. It was not an ordered advance. Instead it was a wild charge, every man sprinting as hard as he could toward the villagers' line of shields.

'Remember what Ulrich and Skar taught you,' Einar said to those around him in a loud voice as the vikings closed the distance. 'Stand firm and we will force them back.'

Einar crouched behind his shield, setting his right foot back, bracing for the impact to come.

The vikings smacked into the shield wall in a clamour of screaming and the clatter of wood hitting wood. Einar felt the impact on his own shield ripple up his arm and through his left shoulder. The viking on the other side shoved his spear over the top of Einar's shield, the point seeking Einar's face.

Einar ducked left so the blade missed its target and the shaft continued to slide over his right shoulder. Then he smashed the hammer down on the viking's exposed hand where the man gripped his spear. The viking cried out and let go of his weapon. Knowing he was momentarily safe from attack, Einar dropped his shield a little, surged forwards and brought the hammer down again, aiming for the viking's helmet this time.

The viking ducked himself but Einar's blow still connected, delivering a crushing blow to the man's left collar bone. He bellowed with pain and staggered back from the shield wall, his left arm dangling at an odd angle.

Almost immediately another viking took his place. This one had a sword which he put to use slashing and hacking at Einar. Einar countered three hits with his shield or hammer then, when the viking was about to strike a fourth time, raised his shield as the blow fell. The viking's blade thudded into the top rim of his shield and Einar struck it with his hammer. A dull clang rang out and the sword bent, its top half curling down the back of Einar's shield. The viking pulled his sword back, his mouth falling open as he stared in dismay at his now useless weapon. He stumbled back, turned and began to run back, away from the villagers' shield wall.

Einar glanced to his left and right. He felt a swell of pride to see their shield wall still intact and solid, with four dead vikings lying before it. The rest of the raiders, their initial ferocious assault halted, appeared to have lost their initial momentum and were retreating down the track.

'Good work lads!' Einar shouted. 'We're winning.'

Then Einar saw a figure emerge from behind the other vikings. He swallowed, scarcely able to believe his own eyes. By any standards the man was huge. Einar was a big enough lad and Skar, the prowman of Ulrich's crew, was a head taller than him. This man was bigger again. He stomped through the crowd of vikings, towering over them like a mountain ash amid heather bushes. He wore a brynja polished to gleaming, while around his shoulders was a cloak made from the white fur of an animal. That it had been a white bear was obvious as the creature's head formed the hood of the cloak, which the viking had pulled up over a helmet that glittered like silver, even in the dull rainy weather. A wide, brown beard fell from beneath the helmet visor. It was cut straight across, midway down his massive chest so it was shaped like the blade of a shovel. He carried a black shield and alone among the vikings his was not daubed with the red axe of Eirik. Instead the snarling face of a bear, its teeth bared, was emblazoned in white. In his right hand he held a sword. Einar judged that it must have been specially made for this giant of a man. A normal sword held in his meaty fist would have looked like little more than a long knife, but the weapon he carried was in proportion to the rest of him. Its long, wide blade shimmered and glinted in the pathetic sunlight.

'You useless sea scum,' the giant said, haranguing the vikings around him. Einar noticed that a couple of them flinched at the sound of the man's voice. It was clear that the big man was their leader. 'Can't you beat a pathetic bunch of fishermen? Let's finish this now!'

The big viking turned to face the villagers' shield wall.

'Folk of Frodisborg,' he bellowed at the men crouching behind the protection of their shields. 'Eirik Bloody Axe has a message for those who have betrayed him. We are here to deliver it with blades, fire and death.'

He hefted his shield into position and began lumbering towards the line of villagers' shields. As the other vikings began to fall in behind him the huge man in the white bear pelt picked up speed. A thunderous roar of pure rage burst from his lips as he charged.

Einar felt his guts lurch as he realised the big man was running straight at him.

Four

Einar clenched his teeth and prepared for the coming impact. He pushed forward his left shoulder, stiffened his left arm and crouched in the cover provided by his shield. He pushed his right leg back to provide further bracing. He had to keep his head down behind his shield if he did not want to risk presenting a target for the enemy. While it meant he was protected he could not see where the attacker was and could only guess how far away the big man was.

He waited, every nerve in his body feeling like it was stretched to snapping point. What could only have been moments seemed to drag on and on. Even though he knew it was only in his own frenzied imagination, it was hard to dismiss the impression that the ground beneath his feet trembled with every thumping footstep of the giant viking charging towards him.

There was a crack like thunder as the shields met. The next thing Einar knew, he was off his feet and stumbling backwards. Unable to recover himself, he crashed down, landing flat on his back with a teeth-rattling impact. The back of his head struck the ground and despite the protection given by his helmet, the world before him disappeared in a storm of countless multicoloured, spinning stars.

Einar blinked, trying to clear his vision and dispel the astonishment mixed with shock at the sheer power of the man that flooded his mind. Einar had been swept aside like a dog before a charging bull.

He felt cold air on his face and realised that his helmet, its straps untied, had rolled off his head after he hit the ground.

He had a dim awareness of a small voice somewhere deep within his mind screaming to him to get up or he was dead, but for a moment he could not move. Then his sight cleared and he wished it had not. Looming over him was the terrible sight of the huge viking in the white bear pelt, sword reversed, preparing to stab it down through Einar's face.

Einar's paralysis dissolved. He swiped with his hammer at the only part of the viking he could reach – the man's left foot. It connected, the viking grunted and shifted his weight a little but it did not stop him in his killing intent. The blade came down. At the last possible moment Einar wrenched his head to the side. Combined with the viking's change in stance the movement was enough that the sword missed Einar, the point burying itself in the earth instead of his head.

He felt the cold metal running across the side of his neck. His flesh stung where the wicked-sharp edge nicked it and knew the viking had only missed by a hair's breadth.

For an instant Einar had a close up view of the big viking's sword, much closer than any normal person would ever want to have. He saw that like his Ulfbehrt, there were runes set into the centre of the blade. They did not spell out +ULFBEHRT+ however. They were in the runes the Christians called their alphabet and he could not read what they said.

There was no time to try to anyway. Einar rolled to his left, away from the viking and up to his feet again. A quick glance told him that the big man had punched through the villagers' shield wall like it was a line of scarecrows. The disciplined defensive formation was smashed and the villagers were now fighting hand to hand with the vikings who had piled through the gap opened up by their leader.

Einar hefted his shield into a ready position as the viking wrenched his sword out of the earth. To Einar's dismay he saw that the linden wood of his shield was now cracked from the impact of the big viking's charge. To his further consternation the metal band that ran around the rim to hold the shield together came apart with a *ping* and fell to the ground. The shield disintegrated like the villagers' shield wall, leaving Einar gripping only the metal boss.

Several of the villagers recognised that the fight was lost and started to run. Their flight meant they had to get past the viking leader who was now between them and the meadow beyond the village.

The big viking had his sword out of the ground now and swiped at them as they tried to run past. One of the fleeing villagers was the man who wore the old brynja and the viking's blade tore through its metal rings as if they were made of wool. The sword opened up a huge wound in the man, almost cutting him in half at the waist. He cried out, stumbled and dropped to the ground.

Einar heard screaming and turned to see one of the other vikings coming straight at him, axe raised. He hurled his shield boss at the man. The bowl-shaped metal boss caught the viking full in the face. The man's belligerent yelling ceased. He dropped his shield, his left hand going to his smashed teeth and nose as his headlong charge turned into a wobbling stagger. Einar stepped forward and hit him across the head with his hammer. The man went down.

Bersi yelled a war cry and swung the Ulfbehrt at the viking leader. The big man blocked the blow with his shield then counter-attacked with his own sword. The blade swooped through the air, the force of the man's arm and its own momentum causing the steel to flex in the air. It lashed downward like a metal whip and Einar was reminded of one of the kennings the poets used to describe swords as the serpents of battle.

Bersi raised his own sword to counter the attack. The blades met in a tremendous ring like the noise made by the Christians' bells. Bersi's arm was forced down but he managed – just –to stop the deadly blow. Bersi staggered back to create space between himself and his opponent as the viking struck again. Again the blade scythed down and Bersi blocked it once more with his sword. This time the sound when the swords met was a dull clang.

Before Einar's astonished gaze, he saw the Ulfbehrt sword, the finest weapon to be made on this Middle Earth, break in half, leaving Bersi holding only a stump. Bersi's own incredulity froze him and he was still gazing in disbelief at the broken sword in his hand when the viking leader stabbed him through the throat.

Several buildings were now burning and smoke billowed around the fighting men in the village track. Despite this, Einar could see that for the men of Frodisborg, the fight was over and the battle lost. Their shield wall broken, many of them were dead, some were fleeing and the remainder were fighting with the vikings to get the chance to run.

The time had come for Einar to run too. He could stay and make a glorious, futile final stand, but it was against everything Ulrich and Skar had taught him.

If the situation is hopeless but you can get away, do it, Ulrich had said. *Odin teaches us that even a cripple is more useful than a great warrior on his funeral pyre. A corpse is no use to anyone.*

The big viking leader was busy swiping and stabbing at those village men unlucky enough to be within striking distance as they tried to run away. This could be Einar's only chance. He turned and ran for the meadow.

'Einar!'

Amid the throng he heard someone shout his name. He stopped again and looked in the direction the voice had come from. There was a man standing between two of the longhouses that lined the track into the village. He had very long white hair and beard, both of which were combed straight and smooth and flowed like an avalanche over his shoulders. He had a long walking staff grasped in one hand.

It was Grimnir, the wise old man of the village who had sailed with Einar and the Wolf Coats on several of their expeditions and who had nursed Einar back to health. Seeing he had caught Einar's attention, Grimnir cocked his head in a gesture that Einar should follow him, then turned and hurried off between the two houses.

Einar glanced around to see if any of the vikings were watching. By luck a thick cloud of dark smoke drifted over the trackway, hiding him from view. Einar switched direction and ran between the houses after the old man.

With impressive speed for an old man, Grimnir jogged out the back of the houses and hopped into the undergrowth beyond. To his consternation, Einar realised Grimnir was leading him towards the shore of the fjord. Everyone else from the village was fleeing inland, towards the forest on the other side of the meadow and the many hiding places it offered.

'When you're caught by a rip tide or current that is too strong to fight,' the old man said over his shoulder. 'The best thing to do is swim sideways.'

They pushed their way through the ferns and gorse until they entered the short strip of fir trees that lined the edge of the fjord at Gandvik. In a small creek a little sailing boat, a *karfa* capable of carrying five or six people, was beached.

Grimnir clambered in.

'Push us off, if you please Einar,' the old man said. 'I need your strength. Then the oars.'

Einar held up his right hand which still had the hammer lashed to it.

Grimnir nodded and leaned over to untie the leather strap. Einar felt a brief twinge in his heart at the thought that the last fingers to touch the strap had been Frida's. Then his hand was free of the hammer and Grimnir set to work unfurling the sail while Einar shoved the boat out into deeper water. When he had waded up to his waist and the karfa was fully afloat, Einar dragged himself over the side and took a seat on the middle one of the three rowing benches. He pushed the oars out either side and began to strain his shoulders and back as he pulled out long, even strokes that soon had the boat gliding along, out into the waters of the fjord and away from Frodisborg.

'Do you think this is wise?' he said over his shoulder to Grimnir. 'Those vikings have two longships.'

'They'll be too busy burning and looting to bother with us,' the old man said.

Facing backwards, Einar saw the columns of thick black smoke rising from beyond the trees. Frodisborg was ablaze.

'Eirik has delivered his message,' Einar said, remembering the words of the huge viking leader. 'There's no mistaking that.'

'Well you did kill his bastard son here,' Grimnir said. He sat at the back of the boat, one hand on the steering oar and the other tugging on a rope attached to the sail as he tried to catch the wind. 'We shouldn't be surprised he chose to hit back here.'

The sail snapped tight as the wind filled it. The boat surged forward faster than Einar could propel it with the oars so he pulled them back on board. He watched as the burning village receded in their wake, thinking of Frida and all the others who had died there both today and when Eirik's son Rognvald had attacked it earlier in the year.

'What was it all for, Grimnir?' Einar said.

The old man raised an eyebrow.

'We trained the men of Frodisborg to fight. We fought side by side with them in a battle and saved the village,' Einar said with a sigh. 'We killed Rognvald. So many fought and died. Now its burning.'

'It's just buildings that are burning,' Grimnir said. 'They can be rebuilt. A village is the folk who live there, not the daub, wattle and thatch they live in.'

'A lot of those folk died today,' Einar said, his voice laden with bitterness.

'The stand of the men of Frodisborg allowed the rest of the village to escape,' Grimnir said, 'vikings by nature raid and leave. The folk can come back to Frodisborg and rebuild it.'

Einar was quiet for a moment as their boat sailed on down the fjord towards the sea beyond.

'Did you see that man who led them?' he said, after a time, feeling an involuntary shiver at the memory of the big man wrapped in the white bear pelt. 'He was huge. That sword of his broke my Ulfbehrt. It must be a magic weapon.'

Grimnir made a face.

'Often when men don't understand something they call it magic,' he said. 'Perhaps it is. Perhaps it is just very well made.'

'I wonder who will feel Eirik's anger next?' Einar said.

'I suspect many folk along the Norway coast will be raided by these men,' Grimnir said. 'We need to warn King Hakon. We will sail north.'

'You know where Hakon is?' Einar said. 'Why didn't you tell me? Ulrich and the others will be with him. Affreca too.'

'There are still many in Norway who oppose King Hakon,' Grimnir said. 'He's not yet completely secure on the high seat of the land, and we don't want Eirik finding out where he is either. So I thought it best not to let anyone know. Now it seems I have no choice but to let you into the secret.'

'So where is he?' Einar said.

'He is in the north-west part of the country,' Grimnir said. 'He should be at Dale among the Fjaler folk. He is travelling around, meeting the ordinary people so they can see their new king and know he is now in charge. Jarl

Sigurd is paying your wolf-coated friends to keep Hakon safe while he is there. We will sail there and warn him of this danger. I hope Ulrich has done his job and the lad is still alive.'

Five

Dale, in the folksland of Fjaler, north-western Norway

'What I don't understand,' Wulfhelm the Saxon said, pointing a wavering forefinger at Affreca, 'is why a good-looking girl like you isn't married.'

His voice slurred a little and an extra moustache of ale foam sat on top of his usual long, drooping blond one.

Affreca was sitting across the table from him. She was lounging back on her bench, legs crossed at the ankles, feet on the table. She scowled at Wulfhelm's words and looked away, then lifted her own ale horn and took a swig.

'Don't you wonder about this too, Surt?' Wulfhelm, undaunted, used his finger to prod the meaty forearm of Surt who sat, arms folded, beside him.

'It's not a surprise to me,' Surt said. 'Look at her, sitting here in a tavern. Feet up on the table. Drinking ale. Who would marry a woman like that?'

The three of them sat at a table in the ale house of the settlement at Dale. Dale was a little village at the top of a fjord in north-west Norway and although it was currently hosting a visit by the new king, Hakon, very little of consequence happened in this sleepy little backwater. There was not much danger for Ulrich's Wolf Coats to protect Hakon from and Affreca and the others found their biggest challenge was finding enough to do to fill their days before retiring to the settlement's single tavern to dispel their boredom with ale.

Despite supposedly being dedicated to hospitality, the tavern was not the most inviting of places. The floor was covered in filthy straw that bore the sour reek of vomit and spilled ale. The tables were unwashed and sticky. The fire remained unlit. The room was gloomy at the best of times, but as the grey, rain sodden sky outside darkened towards evening, it was becoming almost too hard for the drinking companions to make out the features of their fellows.

Affreca wore the pelt of a wolf around her shoulders while the other two wore heavy wool cloaks. They were all part of Ulrich's crew but only Affreca was an initiated Úlfhéðinn, one of Odin's own wolf warriors.

Affreca swept her feet off the table and leaned forward.

'I am the daughter of the King of Dublin, Serklander,' she said. 'You would do well to remember that.'

'A king's daughter who wears men's boots, leather breeches and a leather jerkin that still bears the rust stains of the brynja she often wears over it,' Surt said, a faint smile on his lips. 'Forgive me, but she does not look like a highborn lady who could run a great man's estate and feasting hall. A lady who might *burn one down* on the other hand? Yes.'

'Ah, but look at that pure skin. The lovely red hair. Those eyes...' Wulfhelm rambled on, his gaze dropping to a point well below Affreca's eyes. 'If she was cleaned up she would grace the hall of any king or thane. She could serve the ale at the table of the highest of kings, don't you think?'

'I think,' Surt said, pulling the drinking horn away from Wulfhelm's befuddled grasp, 'you've had too much ale.'

'Give me that back!' Wulfhelm said, swiping to reclaim his horn, a look of mock dismay on his face.

'Did it ever occur to you,' Affreca said, 'that the idea of being married off to stop some war then spending the rest of my days serving beer to tables full of drunken oafs like you may not appeal to me that much?'

'What else would a noble woman want?' Wulfhelm said, his face clouded by a puzzled expression. 'It's considered the highest honour for a woman.'

'Perhaps I'm just strange,' Affreca said, 'But sailing the whale roads as part of one of the most dangerous crew of warriors in this Middle Earth is somehow more attractive a proposition. Anyway, why would I have to be the one serving the ale instead of being served. Why couldn't I rule in my own right?'

Wulfhelm and Surt looked at her, open-mouthed.

'Erm, because you're a woman?' Wulfhelm said, as if it were the most obvious thing in the world.

'There are women who rule,' Affreca said. 'Not many I grant you. But you Saxons had a queen. One of Aelfred's daughters. Didn't she rule by herself?'

Wulfhelm pursed his lips. Surt looked at him, expectant of a rebuttal but the Saxon shrugged instead.

'Aethelflead, Lady of the Mercians,' he said. 'I grant you

that one. She was quite a lady. She kicked your lots' arses anyway.'

'My lot?' Affreca said.

'The Danes,' Wulfhelm said, taking advantage of Surt's astonishment that a woman had ruled a kingdom to snatch back his ale horn. 'She stopped them taking Cæstir and captured Deoraby from them.'

'You people are so ignorant,' Affreca said, scowling again. 'They weren't even Danes who attacked Cæstir. They were Ostmen from Ireland. My clan: the sons of Ivar. We honour her name as a valiant enemy.'

The door banged open, spilling some of the remaining daylight into the tavern. Starkad and Kari, two of their fellows in Ulrich's Wolf Coat crew, came in. Both were tall and walked with the easy athletic pace of men who spent most of their time rowing, fighting or practising to fight. Starkad's long blond hair and beard were braided while Kari's brown hair was shorn very short over most of his head except for two long tails that were wound around the top of his head and tied in a knot just to the right of his crown. He had runes tattooed across his face in black ink and looked a little like a bird had left its footprints over his cheeks. Both wore around their shoulders the wolf pelt cloak of a Úlfhéðinn.

Starkad's pale blue eyes surveyed the miserable tavern as he sat down at the table with the others.

'Another wild night in Dale, eh?' he said. 'I'm not sure I can live much more with this excitement.'

Kari whistled to the ale wife who ran the tavern. She was a formidable lady in the middle years of life who looked like if pushed to wrestle any of the men in her tavern she would win. The look she shot at Kari as he waggled Wulfhelm's now empty ale horn at her would have curdled milk.

'Are you going to light some torches or lamps?' Starkad said as she waddled over, cradling a large jug of ale before her in both hands. 'It's getting so dark in here we can hardly see enough to bite our own fingers.'

'Torches cost silver,' the ale wife said, pouring horns of ale for all of those at the table. 'Maybe if you lot ate some of the food I sell instead of your own fingers it might be worth my while lighting a lamp.'

She turned to Kari to fill the ale horn he held, giving him a wink as she poured the foaming liquid.

'Though *you* can eat whatever you want in here, big lad, free of charge,' she said.

Despite the gloom, the others noticed Kari turn a shade paler. As the ale wife flounced off, all at the table raised their horns in salute to each other.

'Aethelflead was exceptional though,' Wulfhelm said, resuming the earlier conversation.

'Aethelflead of the Mercians?' Starkad said. 'My grandfather fought against her. A hard-nosed bitch by all accounts.'

'An exceptional woman for exceptional times,' Wulfhelm said, his ale horn wavering before him.

'And these times aren't?' Affreca said. 'Ulrich is convinced that the Ragnarök, the end of the world, is coming.'

'He does, doesn't he?' Wulfhelm said. 'He seems obsessed. I worry he's so desperate for glory that he's going to get us all killed.'

'There's not much chance of that,' Kari said with a grunt. 'This place is quieter than the grave.'

'Maybe Ulrich is right,' Affreca said. 'There's something strange going on. Look at the weather. I don't recall ever a time like this when there was no summer.'

'Hakon clearly doesn't seem worried about it,' Surt said. 'He's travelling around these backwaters like he's going to live forever.'

'Well why wouldn't he?' Wulfhelm said. 'He's a Christian like me. He knows the world will end when Christ returns, not when heathen gods battle monsters.'

'Hush! Don't say such things so loud,' Affreca said, her eyes darting around the room. 'If the locals find out you're a Christian we'll have a fight on our hands.'

'Relax,' Starkad said. 'There's no one here to overhear us. Except maybe Kari's girlfriend over there.'

'I don't know about you,' Wulfhelm said. 'But I'm getting so bored here I would welcome a fight. Why is Hakon wasting time in this place anyway?'

'Hakon is engaged in what they call statecraft,' Kari said, clearly keen to change the subject. 'Skar taught me about it. Eirik Bloody Axe was rightful King of Norway. He was granted power by his father Harald.'

'But rightful heir or not, Eirik was a tyrant,' Affreca said.

'Aye, he was,' Kari said. 'Who knows that better than us, who used to keep that tyrant on his throne?'

He shot a knowing smile in Starkad's direction.

'And what gratitude did he show us for that work?' Starkad said. 'Nothing but betrayal.'

'Anyway,' Kari continued. 'Because Hakon drove the rightful king out of Norway, tyrant or not, his position is still not a strong one. He needs as much support as he can gather and many districts have still not seen him, so if push came to shove and Eirik were to return with an army, why would those folk support Hakon? So he's travelling around the country talking to the common folk and gaining their confidence to ensure their support.'

'And the boy is good at that,' Surt said. 'He's such a likeable person. I've never seen someone with such a gift.'

'The folk who meet him all love him,' Affreca said, nodding. 'They say it's like Harald Fairhair has returned, somehow grown young.'

Starkad tutted.

'Harald was an old bastard too. Every bit the tyrant Eirik was,' he said. 'Anyway, there's no one in this district but bonded labourers and low-born farmers. What use are they to kings? They don't command armies. They can't provide brynjas and swords. We're here to protect him but what danger is he in from the peasants around here?'

'When it comes to war it's these folk who make up most of the army,' Affreca said. 'Hakon's father, Harald, took the ancestral *Odal* rights of inheritance away from the commoners and bondsmen. It was by promising to give them back that Hakon won their support. That was how he chased Eirik Bloody Axe out of Norway.'

'But we're warriors, not nursemaids,' Starkad said. 'And these folk wouldn't lift a finger against Hakon. Everyone loves the lad. He's got a gift.'

'That would change fast if the ordinary folk knew Hakon was a Christian,' Kari said. The expression on his face suggested he was not too happy with the fact either.

'I hope Ulrich knows what he's doing in giving Hakon our support.'

'That's why you need to keep your voice down when you say such things,' Affreca said, glancing around again.

'Kari get your girlfriend over here,' Starkad said holding up his already empty horn. 'I need more ale.'

Kari frowned but the ale wife had already spotted Starkad's gesture and was trundling over with the jug of beer.

'Thirsty lads? That's what I like to see,' she said, refilling Starkad's horn and topping up the others, regardless of whether they were ready for more or not. 'I could do with the custom tonight.'

'So where is everybody anyway?' Starkad said. 'This place isn't exactly lively of an evening but there's usually a few locals in. Tonight it looks like there is a feast or party going on somewhere else that we've not been invited to.'

'Haven't you heard the rumours?' the ale wife said. Her face became serious and she leaned closer, speaking in a low, conspiratorial voice, even though there was no one else to overhear her. 'An old one-eyed man wearing a wide-brimmed hat, long blue cloak and carrying a staff has been seen walking in the forest near the village. Several people have seen him over the last few days. Levi the goatherd saw him only last night. He beckoned to the woods then disappeared.'

Wulfhelm made a face.

'So?' he said with an exaggerated shrug. The others looked at him with a mixture of surprise and recrimination.

'They say Odin himself walks the world dressed just like that,' Affreca said in a hushed voice.

'That's what they say,' the ale wife said, widening her eyes and nodding. 'If Odin is walking the world then great things must be afoot. I expect many of the village folk are out looking for him. He must have a special reason to come to Dale.'

With that she left again. The table of companions fell into silence as each contemplated the ale wife's words.

'If Odin is walking among men,' Starkad said, after a time, 'then strife will follow. Maybe Ulrich is right after all.'

The door banged open again, this time causing most of the group around the table to start. They relaxed again when they saw the newcomer was Sigurd, the only other remaining member of the Wolf Coat crew in Dale except for the leaders, Ulrich and Skar.

Sigurd came over to join the others.

'Have you seen Ulrich?' he said, pushing rain-sodden hair away from his forehead.

'Not since before noon,' Affreca said. The others all concurred.

Sigurd shook his head.

'There's something going on,' he said. 'I think Ulrich should know about it.'

'What do you mean?' Affreca said.

'All the menfolk have left the village,' Sigurd said.

'Apparently Odin is walking the woods,' Kari said. 'The ale wife says they've gone to find him.'

'Odin?' Sigurd said, his eyebrows raised. 'In this shit hole? What would the All Father be doing here?'

'You're guess is as good as mine,' Affreca said.

'It was strange,' Sigurd said. 'The men all left and went to the forest. It was like they got a message or orders or something. I don't like it. Ulrich should know.'

'If he's heard that Odin is in the woods,' Affreca said. 'Then you can guess where Ulrich will be. Ulrich loves nothing more than Odin. He'll be out there looking for old One Eye too.'

Once more the door of the tavern opened. The group at the table turned to see a man standing in the threshold. He was wrapped up in a heavy wool cloak to protect him from the rain and carried a bundle of something made of cloth.

'It's all right. That's the village head man's *dróttseti*,' Starkad said, relaxing his fingers which had twitched towards the hilt of his knife when the newcomer entered. 'He's the steward who runs the head man's household. Hakon is staying there. This man is no danger.'

To everyone's surprise, the steward came over to their table.

'You must come to my master's house,' he said in a loud voice. 'The king wants to see you.'

They all looked at each other then started to get up.

'No,' the steward said. He pointed at Affreca. 'Just her. I was told to just bring the woman back. Hakon sent you this.'

He tossed the bundle of cloth to Affreca who caught it. Standing up she let it unfurl before her. It was a dress; green and white and decorated with colourful, twisting embroideries.

'What am I supposed to do with this?' Affreca said, her

face twisted into an expression of suspicion and growing anger.

'King Hakon requests you put it on and come with me to join him for food,' the steward said. 'He has a proposal for you.'

Six

Skar tramped behind Ulrich along a little animal track that led through the bracken and ferns of the undergrowth in the woods around Dale.

The big prowman was much taller than his leader and slightly skinny. His mousy hair tumbled around his shoulders and was slick with rain. His beard was as long as his hair but plaited under his chin and his moustache drooped down either side of his mouth. Around his shoulder was a cloak of grey wolf fur.

Ulrich was not just shorter than Skar, he was a little shorter than most men. His dark brown hair was shorn short, revealing it was receding from his forehead, though he was not an old man. Like Skar he wore a cloak of wolf fur but his was dark, almost black.

In the dying light of day they could see through the trees the waters of the fjord of Fjaler. The rain continued to drizzle from the darkening grey sky above and both of the wolf warriors wore sealskin jerkins normally worn on board ship under their wolf pelt cloaks to keep out the damp.

'Do you really believe Odin walks in these woods, Ulrich?' Skar said. 'It makes little sense to me.'

'Who are we to question the motives of the All Father?' the wiry little Wolf Coat leader said. 'Is one of his names not *Gangleri*, the Wanderer?'

'But *here*?' Skar said. 'The folk of this district are bondsmen, fishermen and low born farmers. Why would Odin spend time among them? Thralls, *bondes* and farmers honour Thor. Odin is the god of kings.'

'Odin has his own higher purpose that is above that of men,' Ulrich said. He stopped and turned to Skar. The big prowman, Ulrich's right-hand man, was unnerved to see that the strange glassiness that sometimes came over Ulrich's eyes when he talked of religious matters glittered in them now. 'Who can say what he is up to? But if Ragnarök is coming then he will need every warrior he can get for the final battle. If he really is here walking among us then it proves to me that the end of the world really is coming. What better sign could we have, Skar? Time is running out!'

Skar did not reply for a few moments, then nodded.

'Very well,' he said. 'Let's keep going. But I'd rather be sitting by the fire in the ale house on a night like this than out here. At least the trail is easy to follow.'

Jarl Sigurd of Hlader, Hakon's mightiest supporter in Norway, had many warriors but had had to return with them to his own realm in the north to deal with some troublesome nobles. As he left he had engaged Ulrich and his crew to protect the new King Hakon until his return. Ulrich had already decided that Hakon, despite his foreign religion, was the person to back in the war of kings that was tearing the north of the Middle Earth apart, but the silver Sigurd had promised him for looking after Hakon was welcome too.

Ulrich, like the god he honoured, was always alert for news or gossip: Any scrap of knowledge that could mean forewarning of dangers or advantage. Listening in on others' excited whispers in the tavern and around the village, he had overheard the tales being recounted of Odin wandering the woods nearby. When the menfolk had started leaving the village as evening drew in, he knew something was afoot and he and Skar decided to follow them.

Even though it was getting late, as it was late summer and they were in the north of the world, the day stretched on in a twilight that allowed them to see where they were going.

As Skar had pointed out, the path the villagers had taken was obvious. The large crowd of men were wandering ahead into the forest, making no attempt to conceal their progress. Hence the little track was churned to mud by many feet and the surrounding undergrowth was beaten down and trampled.

After some time the general hubbub of many people chattering came from through the trees. Ulrich and Skar slowed down.

'They must be gathering just up ahead,' Skar said.

He and Ulrich picked their way up a rise until they came to the edge of a wide clearing. A broad, circular depression in the forest floor formed a natural bowl which was now filled by the menfolk of Dale. Excited chatter echoed around the trees. Ulrich drew his knife, a broken-backed seax, and Skar pulled a short axe from his belt. They both dropped to a crouch, then took up positions behind the wide trunk of a big pine tree.

Skar peeked out from the left of the trunk and Ulrich from the right, so they could both watch what was going on without being observed themselves.

The crowd in the clearing was a mixture of farmers, woodsmen and fishermen, the ordinary folk of Dale. They were of all ages and dressed in the drab, un-dyed wool jerkins and breeches of the lower ranks of society. Before them stood an outlandish figure in long, white robes. He had shoulder-length black hair and a headdress of bronze from which two curling horns rose above his crown to end in round balls. He held two spears in one hand, crossed mid shaft to form an X. The man pranced and leapt around the edge of the grove, shouting, howling and chanting indecipherable words.

'That's the *Galdr maðr* of this village,' Skar said, referring to the man in the horned helmet who wore the costume of one who conducts the religious customs on behalf of the folk.

Ulrich nodded.

'And isn't that one of the slaves from the household of the village head man?' he said, cocking his head towards a scrawny, miserable looking young man whose clothes were even poorer and drabber than the villagers, if that were possible. He stood at the edge of the crowd, his arms bound by rope behind his back, his mouth gagged with a piece of cloth. Two burly farmers stood on either side of him. From their demeanour it was clear they were there not to support the slave, but to stop him running away.

A third villager stood beside them with a rope, the end tied in a noose, dangling from his hands.

'I doubt this evening is going to go well for the thrall,' Skar said in a whisper.

After some time the magic worker stopped his jerky movements and held both arms up high. The babbling chat of the villagers died away, replaced by an expectant hush.

'Folk of Dale,' the Galdr maðr said in a loud voice, 'By now, you will have heard tell of He who has been seen walking in the forest by night. The Wanderer, the Bale Worker, *Fráríði*, the one who rides forth.'

'All praise to Odin,' several of the men in the clearing shouted.

'Some of you have even seen him,' the Galdr maðr continued.

Murmurs of assent went around the crowd.

'Brothers: tonight we must seek the truth. If the High One really is here in the world of men there must be a reason. We must find out why he has chosen to come to Dale.'

'Indeed,' Skar heard Ulrich say.

The magic worker turned away from the crowd to face the forest.

'All Father,' he cried out to the trees. 'We are your devoted children. Come to us tonight. Accept our sacrifice as an offering to show you our devotion.'

He nodded towards the bound slave. The slave moved as if to run but the two big men on either side of him grabbed him by the upper arms.

The man with the noose tossed it over a stout branch that projected from one of the pine trees that ringed the clearing about twice the height of a man from the ground. The two big farmers lifted the thrall under the arms and hauled him towards the makeshift gallows. The others in the clearing began a loud chanting – a *galdr* – a hymn of praise to the Gods.

The slave was shouting but the gag in his mouth muffled his words. He struggled against the men who held him but his strength was no match for theirs. His head strained this way and that. His eyes rolled as he sought to lock gazes with anyone who might extend fellow feeling for him and intervene but he was surrounded only by iron-hard, pitiless stares.

The hangman slipped the noose over the slave's head and pulled it tight around his neck. The man's knees sagged and he started to drop to the ground, whether in utter terror or a final attempt to escape, Skar could not tell. As the villagers' chanting rose to a crescendo, the two big men grabbed the rope and hauled. The noose snapped shut around the slave's throat and he was trailed back up to his feet and into the air. His legs flailed wildly and his body twisted, swinging back and forth.

Those in the clearing stopped chanting as one. The only sounds were the creaking of the rope and the grunts of the hanged man, his cries strangled by the gag and now the rope that bit deep into his neck.

The Galdr maðr grasped one of his spears in both hands and stood beneath the hanging man.

'Now I give you to Odin!' he shouted.

He drove the spear upwards. The point pierced the slave's chest just below his ribcage. He forced it in further as the slave's body arched and stiffened. Blood poured down the spear shaft from the wound as he hung suspended for a long moment. Then he slumped and went limp.

The Galdr maðr released his spear, leaving the corpse of the slave, still transfixed, to twist and turn on the rope.

'All Father, High One,' the magic worker shouted, holding up his bloodstained hands. 'Accept our sacrifice. Come to us. Speak to us. What message have you for us?'

His words echoed through the trees until they died away in the hushed silence of the pine forest.

There was no response.

For long moments there was no sound but the rain hissing down on the trees and the creak of the rope as the dead slave's body swung back and forth.

'He is not here,' one of the villagers broke the silence at last. 'This is all nonsense. Our sacrifice is in vain. Odin is not here. Why would he come to Dale anyway?'

Skar looked at Ulrich, seeing the look of disappointment that fell across it.

'Hush!' the Galdr maðr said. 'Or your lack of faith will cost us all dear!'

'Wait! Look!' another villager said. He was pointing into the depths of the forest. Gasps came as those around him looked at where he pointed.

A figure was coming towards the clearing through the gloom of the trees. As he got closer, they could see that he was very tall and extremely thin. He wore a dark blue travelling robe that flowed down to his ankles. On his head was a wide-brimmed hat, the sort some wore to keep the sun and rain off their faces and shoulders. He walked with a staff that was almost as tall as he was. Long white hair tumbled from beneath his hat around his shoulders. As he entered the edge of the clearing, all could see that his left eye was covered by a black patch.

Odin had come.

Seven

The awed hush fell on the assembled villagers once again as the newcomer surveyed them all with his one good eye. His upper lip twitched, as if what he saw angered him a great deal.

Almost as one, the men in the clearing dropped to their knees.

'High One, we are your loyal servants. Speak to us,' the Galdr maðr, head bowed, said. 'Why have you come to Dale?'

For several more moments the strange figure just glared at those in the clearing.

'High One, Just as High and the Third,' the Galdr maðr said, his voice now trembling as he spoke the formal titles of the God Odin. 'Why do you cast your baleful eye on us with such a fury? Have we done something to displease you?'

'No, I am not pleased. I am very far from pleased,' the strange figure finally spoke.

At the sound of his voice Skar frowned. He glanced across at Ulrich. To his dismay the little Wolf Coat leader was staring, open-mouthed at the stranger in the hat.

'What is it that has angered you, Lord?' the Galdr maðr said. 'Tell us so we can make amends if we can.'

'Do you really need told what your offences are?' the stranger said. 'The world is in chaos. Loki's monstrous children are loose. The great wolf, Fenrir, looks with hunger at the sun. The walls of Asgard tremble with the feet of marching jötnar and what have the people of the Northern Way done? What have *you people* done?'

The last words were spoken in a thunderous tone. They provoked gasps of fear and little cries of dismay from the men in the clearing.

'You have driven Eirik, the rightful king from his realm in Norway,' the stranger said. 'Eirik, a son of Harald Fairhair: a king who always honoured the Gods and practised all their customs, a man who most pleased me with the many harvests of warriors' souls he sent to me. A king who reddened his axe and bore his bloody sword to many lands. You people drove this lord of vikings from the High Seat that was his right by birth and his strength!'

There were more fearful whimpers from the crowd. The one-eyed stranger stood in dreadful silence for a few more moments, letting the portent of his words sink into the hearts of the villagers.

'And who have you put in his place?' the stranger said after a time. 'A mere boy. A lad brought up in a foreign land, with foreign ways. Hakon. A lad who does not even honour the customs of this land. Who does not honour its Gods!'

Many in the clearing looked at each other, puzzled expressions on their faces.

'What do you mean, Great Lord?' the Galdr maðr said, looking awkward.

'Hakon is a Christian,' the stranger said. He pronounced the word *Christian* as if speaking the name of the most vile worm to slither over the earth. The men in the clearing gasped again, this time in astonished disbelief. Within moments this was joined by angry murmurs.

Skar glanced at Ulrich again. He saw the expression of dismay on his leader's face.

'You're not falling for this are you?' he hissed in a loud whisper.

Ulrich's mouth worked in silence but Skar could guess they formed the words *what have we done?*

'High One we had no idea about this,' the Galdr maðr said, his own voice becoming hoarse with ire. 'Hakon has hidden that from everyone! Not just us. Jarl Sigurd of Hlader is a diligent man for performing the sacrifices. He is Hakon's greatest supporter. If he knew this he would not waste his warriors' lives keeping the lad in power.'

'Like all Christians, Hakon lies,' the stranger said. 'But I have come to this world to tell you the truth. The boy is in your village. Sigurd's warriors are far away to the north. You have the power to right the wrong you have done me. You can do a deed tonight that will make me look favourably on Dale once again.'

'Right. Enough of this,' Skar said, standing up and raising his axe.

'What are you doing?!' Ulrich said, glaring aghast at his prowman as the big man cocked his arm to throw. 'No!'

The little Wolf Coat dived across the forest floor. He drove his shoulder into Skar's side just as the big man launched the axe at the stranger on the other side of the clearing. Ulrich was a lot smaller and lighter than Skar but his impact was enough to knock the axe slightly off target.

The stranger spotted the commotion straight away. He saw the axe coming at him through the air, tumbling end over end, aimed directly at his head. He ducked, one arm flashing up from instinct to protect his head. The axe, making a whooping noise like the beating of swan's wings, flew past, missing him by a hand's breadth. Its flight stopped dead with a loud thump as it embedded its blade in a tree trunk behind him.

The stranger's arm movement knocked the wide-brimmed hat from his head, revealing that the top of his head was completely bald and the long hair that fell around his shoulders was just a ring that remained around his crown.

'Look!' Skar grabbed Ulrich by the scruff of his neck and forced him to look at the bald- headed man across the clearing. 'I thought it was strange that Odin spoke with the accent of an Orkneyman. That's not the All Father. That's Vakir, Thorfinn the Skull Cleaver's *seið maðr*.'

For several heartbeats there was nothing but silence. Vakir froze in his crouch, glaring at Skar in surprise and disbelief. Ulrich gaped at Vakir. The villagers were stunned by all of it. Then Ulrich's face twisted into a snarl of rage. He pulled himself away from Skar's grasp.

'This is sacrilege,' he said. 'How dare that rat pretend to be Odin? I'll make him swing from the noose like that slave.'

Vakir had also recovered from his initial shock. He raised a bony finger and pointed it at Skar and Ulrich.

'Hakon's guard dogs are here,' he said, shouting to the

men in the clearing. 'Those are the men whose swords keep you in your place and the Christian Hakon on the throne! They must be punished with him.'

The crowd of villagers looked at each other in confusion, but it was clear to see this would not last long. Already hostile glances were being cast in the direction of the two Wolf Coats.

Skar assessed the options. They were just a band of farmers and he and Ulrich were elite warriors but neither of them wore any war gear. He had thrown away his axe and Ulrich only had a long knife. They were outnumbered by about forty to two.

'Run,' Ulrich, who had been weighing the same options and was always a faster thinker, said.

They both turned and bolted back the way they had come, running back down the slope and ploughing through the undergrowth once more. Behind them they heard shouts as the villagers broke out of the spell cast on them by shock. Moments later the sounds of many feet crashing through the ferns and bracken told Ulrich and Skar that they were being chased.

They sprinted as fast as they could, dodging in and out of the tree trunks. Their pace was such that they could not sustain it for long, however from years of practice in war and stealth craft they both knew that their first priority was to get as much distance as possible between themselves and their pursuers. With that intent, they tore through the woods, running headlong and praying to the Gods that an unlucky footfall did not send them tumbling to the ground and into the merciless hands of the mob coming after them. They did not dare look round to see how close their hunters were, lest they ran flat out into a tree while their heads were turned.

At the bottom of the slope the forest floor levelled for a bit then it rose again up a small ridge. When they neared the top of the ridge Ulrich shouted to Skar in a loud voice:

'Go right. Make for the fjord waters.'

As they crossed the top of the ridge, still in full view of the men chasing them, they switched direction and began running to the right. Once over the ridge, and momentarily hidden from those behind them, they reversed direction and went left instead.

They ran down the far side of the ridge at an angle. Towards the bottom Ulrich tugged Skar's sleeve. The big man looked and saw Ulrich sliding into a short gulley that opened in the forest floor. A big pine tree had fallen perhaps the previous winter. As it went over its roots had torn a dip out of the earth, one that was already grown over by ferns. Ulrich slid into it and Skar went in after him. Both scrambled to pull ferns and bracken around them then pressed themselves as flat to the ground as they could.

Both panted as hard as they could for the few moments they had before the villagers came over the top of the ridge. Skar pressed his face into the soft loam of the forest floor, trying to hide his face and mask his heavy breathing. His mouth was filled with dry pine needles and their aroma mixed with the taste of dirt. Ears straining, he heard the cracking of branches and rustle of dried leaves cease and he knew that the villagers had come to a halt on the top of the ridge.

'I heard one of them say they were going to the fjord,' Skar heard one of the villagers say.

'They probably have a boat,' another said.

'Come on, quick,' a third villager said. 'If they make it to a boat we'll never catch them.'

General shouting broke out and the sounds of many men thrashing through the undergrowth resumed. For a few more moments Skar and Ulrich held their breaths again, then it became clear that the sounds were receding away into the forest, not coming closer.

Ulrich risked a peek over the rim of the gully.

'They fell for it,' he said.

'It never ceases to amaze me how often that trick works,' Skar said, standing up and brushing pine needles and leaves off himself. 'Shall we go back and get that bastard Vakir?'

Ulrich shook his head.

'If I were him I'd be long gone already,' he said. 'Anyway, right now it's more important we get back to Hakon and fast. I wish we did have a boat. If we did we could be sure we'd beat that mob back to the village. Now they know Hakon is a Christian they'll hang him higher than that slave in the clearing and we can kiss goodbye to Jarl Hlader's silver.'

Eight

Affreca strode along the path that went through the middle of the village. The streets of her home town of Dublin were lined with wooden-planked walkways but this was little more than a muddy track lined by the longhouses of the settlement. It was only a short walk from the ale house to the biggest longhouse that was the home of the village head man, Vemond Ragnaldsson. As he was the most important man in the district, this was where Hakon was staying while on his visit to drum up support.

Four of Jarl Sigurd's warriors stood outside, armed but bored. There was not much to worry about in Dale. They recognised Affreca and nodded to her as she walked past them and into the house. The double doors in the gable wall opened into a short entrance hall stacked with barrels of ale and food. The hall led into a long room which had a table and chairs, a fire pit in the floor, and several burning oil lamps that cast their light from tall stands.

At the table sat three men. One was middle-aged, white haired and fat, with plump rosy red cheeks that told of barrels of downed ale. He was clad in reindeer skins and wore a felt hat, even though indoors. This was Vemond the head man. The second was in the prime of life. He was dressed in the heavy cloak and sealskins of someone who had just arrived from a voyage across open seas. He had a long, drooping Saxon-style moustache like Wulfhelm. Across from him sat a young man. Affreca knew he was only sixteen winters old but he bore himself with a confidence – back straight, shoulders back – well beyond a lad of his years. He had a full blond beard and like his infamous father, Harald 'Fair Hair', first King of Norway, he was taller than most men and had shoulders like the crossbeam of a longship. This was Hakon, the new King of Norway.

All three men held drinking horns and from the delighted expressions on their faces were sharing a joke.

The steward of the head man's household who had brought the invitation to Affreca stood near the table. Seeing Affreca still wore the same clothes she wore when he had arrived in the ale house, he sniffed and looked away. Two slaves stood beside him, one holding an ale jug, but Affreca ignored them as she strode across the floor of the longhouse and tossed the dress onto the table.

Hakon and the other men looked up in surprise, their laughter dying away in their throats.

'Is this some sort of joke?' Affreca said.

'I don't think that's the proper way to address the King of Norway,' the steward said.

'I'm the daughter of the King of Dublin,' Affreca said, baring her teeth at the thrall with a glare that made him flinch. 'I'll talk to my equals any way I want to. A lesson you, as merely steward here, should perhaps learn.'

Hakon coughed.

'Please, sit down, Lady Affreca,' he said. 'Forgive the steward. We all should have more respect when we talk to you. But the way you dress, some folk might mistake you for a Valkyrie rather than a woman of royal blood.'

'Many Valkyries *are* women of royal blood,' Affreca said.

'Of course they are,' Hakon said, casting a nervous glance towards Vemond, who fortunately appeared to be more interested in his horn of ale than the conversation. 'I know that.'

Turning back to Affreca, Hakon locked eyes with her for a moment. Affreca returned his warning glare with an insolent sneer that said *I know your little secret.*

'Why did you call me here?' she said.

Hakon sighed. He stood up and gestured towards an empty seat across the table from him.

'Please, sit down,' he said. 'We have much to discuss. Thrall! Get this lady a drink.'

Affreca sat down as the slave with the ale jug came over. He was a tall gaunt man with mousy hair that looked like it had been cut by placing a bowl upside down on his head to use as a template. He was accompanied by the other thrall who bore a drinking horn. Its rim and point were covered in a gleaming metal embossed with scenes of horned weapon dancers. Affreca could tell it was only pewter polished to look like silver, but realised that this was probably one of the village head man's most valuable drinking vessels.

As the slave handed it to Affreca she looked at him for a second time, frowning. He had the hang dog look of any other thrall – drab, woollen, patched clothes and an aversion to looking anyone in the eye – but there was something else that made her look twice at the man. Affreca frowned, racking her brains as to why he looked somehow familiar.

The thrall caught her staring at him. It caused him to

fumble passing the drinking horn and it clattered onto the table.

'Idiot!' the steward shouted. He cuffed the slave across the head with the back of his hand and shot a look at Vemond that was as apologetic as it was obsequious.

'I'm sorry lords, lady,' he said, as the thrall scuttled away from the table. 'These two are the new slaves. I haven't had time to train them properly yet. They'll feel the weight of my stick, I promise you.'

Affreca lifted the fallen ale horn off the table and held it up while the slave filled it from his jug.

'I'm sorry. Perhaps the dress doesn't fit?' Hakon said, breaking Affreca's train of thought. 'Or perhaps it's not to your taste? It's very hard to get anything of decent quality out here in the back country.'

'The dress is fine. Quite nice actually,' Affreca said. 'I just don't understand why you want me to wear it.'

Hakon blushed and looked down at the table. Affreca remembered that he was still just sixteen winters old. She was only eighteen winters herself but still Hakon seemed like just a boy to her.

'This is an important occasion, Affreca,' he said. 'I thought you might like to look your best. I'm sorry there is no wine here. Ale is all there is.'

'Ale is fine by me,' Affreca said, taking a gulp from the horn. She nodded at the man with the long moustache. 'Who's the *Aenglish* man?'

'This is Godwine, emissary of King Aethelstan of Wessex,' Hakon said.

The Saxon nodded to Affreca.

'Already I don't like this,' Affreca said. She looked at her frothing horn of ale. 'If I hadn't had a few drinks in the ale house I probably would not have come. Let me guess: This is about Jorvik?'

Hakon scratched the back of his head.

'My lord Aethelstan is displeased,' Godwine said. He spoke in the Norse tongue but with the drawl of the British West Saxons. 'He does not understand why you did not go to Jorvik before summer as planned. He wants to know if perhaps the offer of the throne of Jorvik and the Kingdom of Northumberland was not enough for you?'

'Well, I was a little busy,' Affreca said, taking a drink from her ale horn. 'Perhaps you should remind your lord that I was kidnapped by Soti the Viking on my way to Jorvik? I was taken as a prisoner to the Deer's Isle off the land of the Scots. Then we had a war to fight in Orkney.'

Now it was Godwine who appeared confused. He looked at Hakon who just shrugged.

'We threw Thorfinn *Hausakljúfr* out of Orkney. Einar, his son, killed him,' Affreca said. 'Aethelstan should be pleased. Thorfinn had formed an alliance with my brother, Olaf of Dublin. That would not have been good for King Aethelstan's plans to be Emperor of Britain. Olaf has as much right to the throne of Jorvik as I have.'

'Perhaps a better one,' Hakon said. 'Olaf is a man, after all.'

'Well, that brings us to Lord Aethelstan's current thinking,' Godwine said. 'Jorvik and Northumberland continue to be a problem for him. It's nearly ten years since the boroughs of the Danelaw submitted to him but the people there remain unruly and independent minded. Many of them are still stubborn heathens.'

Hakon coughed. Vemond finally set down his ale horn and looked at the Wessex emissary with one eyebrow raised.

'You mean they worship our Gods?' the village head man said, banging his fist on the table. 'Why wouldn't they? They're the grandchildren of we Norway folk and Dane folk. Just because they live in a new land it's no reason they should abandon our Gods.'

Affreca noticed the Saxon shoot an apologetic look at Hakon that he quickly covered up. He then turned his attention back to her.

'Lord Aethelstan feels,' he said, 'that while the people of Jorvik and Northumberland have hope of one of their own folk and... faith retaking the throne – namely Olaf Guthfrithsson of Dublin – they will continue to refuse to accept his authority. He had hoped that by putting you on the throne there, they would see you as one of their own. You are, after all, of the same O'Ivar viking clan as Olaf.'

'Except I would be Aethelstan's lap dog, instead of an Irish wolf like Olaf,' Affreca said. 'Do you think the people of Jorvik are so simple they would fall for that?'

'It depends on which way you look at the world,' the Saxon said. 'From Wessex, from Dublin or from Norway. We look at it from south of the Danelaw.'

'And what way do you look at it, Hakon?' Affreca said. 'As King of Norway or as under-king of Aethelstan?'

'Affreca,' Hakon said in a sharp voice. He clasped his hands together and placed both forearms on the table. 'As we are both of royal blood I'll speak on the level with you.'

'Thank you very much,' Affreca said, leaning back in her seat and folding her arms. 'I'm so grateful.'

'There is a greater game being played here than which

clan is the most powerful,' Hakon said. 'It's not about the individual greatness of any of us: Aethelstan, Olaf, Eirik, Constantine mac Áeda of Alba, me or even Thorfinn the Skull Cleaver, Jarl of Orkney.'

At the mention of the name of Thorfinn, Affreca frowned and glanced again at the slave that had given her the ale horn. He was black-haired, sharp-featured and big-nosed. His arched eyebrows gave the impression he was surprised all the time. Affreca narrowed her eyes, trying to understand why this man continued to attract her attention.

'Thorfinn is dead,' Affreca said, taking a drink from her horn. 'Einar killed him. Now he is Jarl of Orkney.'

'Except he isn't,' Godwine said. 'Perhaps in name, but in reality Eirik Haraldsson now holds power in Orkney.'

'That's what really worries Aethelstan isn't it?' Affreca said. 'He thought he could push the vikings further away by putting first the Kingdom of Jorvik between his beloved Wessex and Norway. Then he put Hakon on the throne of Norway so he could have his own little pet viking running the homelands. What he didn't foresee was that the wolf would move closer to his door, and Eirik would jump from Norway to Orkney.'

'True, we all would have preferred it if Eirik had put up a fight in Norway – a noble last stand and died in the process,' the Saxon said. 'But as you point out, that was not the case.'

'Eirik was too practical for that,' Affreca said. 'He's not one for death and glory. And now he's sitting just to the north of Britain. A king like Eirik would appeal to the people of Jorvik and Northumberland.'

'Clever girl,' Godwine said.

Affreca clenched her teeth.

'And if Eirik forms an alliance with my brother in Dublin,' she said, 'he'll have enough warriors to take Jorvik, then Norway. Maybe all of Britain too.'

'Thankfully, Aethelstan's spies tell us, Olaf of Dublin is still smarting from his plans with Thorfinn being thwarted,' Hakon said. 'And he believes Eirik played a part in that. Also he sees Eirik as a potential rival to the throne of Jorvik. Olaf does not trust him.'

'I'm not the only clever one in the family,' Affreca said.

'We don't know how long that will last though,' the Saxon said.

Hakon turned to Vemond.

'Where is the food?' he said.

The village head man made a face and cocked his head to his steward, who nodded then hurried out of the room.

'I'd like to discuss a proposal while we eat,' Hakon said. 'My lord Aethelstan has come up with a very practical solution.'

'I think I'm going to need another drink to listen to this,' Affreca said, proffering her ale horn at the tall slave with the jug. As he refilled it with foaming golden liquid, Hakon continued.

'As we've discussed, Jorvik and Northumberland are peopled by descendants of Norse folk. They have submitted to Aethelstan but they continue to be unruly and there is always the threat that they will switch their allegiance back to Dublin. For that reason he offered to put you in power there. Now there is Eirik in Orkney, a position where he could threaten Jorvik to the south or me in Norway to the east. However, if the thrones of Jorvik and Norway were... joined, it could provide a bulwark across the northern sea.

Two kingdoms, adjacent to one another, joined by the whale road that lies between them and now a common enemy.

'Jorvik and Norway joined?' Affreca said. 'And how would that come about?'

Hakon coughed again. His cheeks flushed a deep crimson as he looked down at the table and said something that was too low to make out.

'What was that?' Affreca said. 'You're mumbling.'

'What my lord Hakon is proposing,' Godwine said. 'Is that the two thrones be joined by a marriage. Between you and him.'

Affreca slumped back in her seat and laughed.

'You're a very beautiful woman, Affreca,' Hakon said. His cheeks were as red as cherries but his words came tumbling out as if he had been rehearsing them for some time.

'And you're just a boy,' Affreca said.

'Now look here,' Hakon's embarrassment was fast turning to anger. 'I'm as much a man as anyone. I'm a king! I've led men in battle and I've killed my enemies. You could do a lot worse than me, lady.'

Affreca raised one eyebrow.

Hakon rose to his feet, opening his mouth to retort further. The Saxon got up faster, placing a hand on the young king's shoulder.

'My lord Hakon.' Godwine said. 'Let's not let emotion run away with us. Lady Affreca will see the sense of this when we tell her all the details of the offer.'

The disgruntled young Hakon let himself be guided back down into his seat by the gentle pressure of the Saxon's hand. His lip curled in a surly expression as he held his horn out to be refilled with ale. The slave with the ale jug hurried over to oblige.

'Come now,' Godwine said. 'Let's discuss this like civilised people over dinner. Vemond – where is that steward of yours with the food? Slaves – more ale for everyone.'

Affreca shot to her feet. She glared at the hawk-nosed slave.

'That's it! The steward!' she said, levelling her forefinger at the man. He flinched as if she had shot one of her arrows at him. 'I knew I'd seen you before.'

'What's going on?' Hakon demanded. He too was now back on his feet.

'That man was Thorfinn of Orkney's dróttseti,' Affreca said. 'He was the steward who ran Jarls Gard for the Skull Cleaver. He is no slave.'

There was a crash as the other slave dropped the ale jug and it shattered on the floor. Frothing ale sloshed into the straw as the slave reached inside his tunic. He pulled out a knife.

'Eirik Bloody Axe sends his regards,' the tall slave shouted. Knife raised, he charged at Hakon who stood, frozen by surprise at the table.

Affreca shot her leg out in a scything kick. She knew she was too far away to tackle the slave but hoped the length of her leg might close the distance. Her left foot just clipped the left shin of the running man. It was not enough to knock him over but he did stumble.

The slave staggered to Hakon. He placed his left hand on the table top to steady himself then turned, knife cocked, to stab the young king. Affreca lunged across the room after him. Holding the drinking horn in both hands she drove it down. The pewter-tipped point skewered through the back of the slave's left hand and into the table top beyond. The man screeched in pain and surprise. Still he tried to stab Hakon. He brought the knife down. Hakon, now recovered from the initial shock, stepped backwards, knocking his seat over. His attacker tried to lean forwards to hit him but with his other hand pinned to the table could not reach and the blade sliced through empty air. The jolt of the movement however dislodged the point of the drinking horn from the table.

The other 'slave' – the man Affreca had recognised – bolted for the door. Despite his injured hand the man with the knife went at Hakon again. Godwine drew a seax from a sheath at his waist and stepped between the would-be killer and the young king. Vemond, the sudden danger finally chasing the fog the ale had put on his mind, started shouting for help.

The man with the knife swiped at Godwine. The Saxon jumped back. Hakon lifted his seat and smashed it into the slave. He dropped the knife and staggered backwards. Before he could recover Godwine dived at him, driving his seax into the man's guts. He cried out and doubled over, both hands clutching at the wound. He dropped to his knees then pitched forward, dying, face downwards on the floor.

The second 'slave' was not a big man but he was still larger than Affreca. Ulrich, a small man himself, had spent time training with her in some of the more specialist war crafts. *If an opponent is bigger than you*, he had instructed her, *use his own weight and movement to your advantage*.

Instead of trying to stop the man charging for the door head on, Affreca let him go past her then shoved her shoulder into the back of his right shoulder. This sent him reeling sideways. He crashed into the wall, face first.

Dazed, the man collapsed to the floor. Affreca dropped on him, planting her left knee on the back of his neck.

The door burst open and Sigurd, Starkad, Surt, Wulfhelm and Kari ran in. Their eyes widened at the scene they saw before them.

'There's trouble,' Kari said.

'We know that,' Affreca said, straining to keep the man beneath her down on the floor. 'You're too late, we've dealt with it.'

'No,' Starkad said. Affreca noticed that he looked dead serious. 'There's a mob of villagers coming towards this house. They look angry.'

Nine

Einar looked up at the mountains that soared above the fjord on either side. Steep slopes covered in dark pine forest rose upwards from the water to merge into slate grey cliffs and bare rock and eventually dark, ragged peaks. Even now at the end of summer many still bore caps of snow. Far overhead an eagle turned wide, lazy loops across the sky.

'I wonder how old these mountains are, Grimnir?' he said. 'How long have they stood here? How many winters? How many generations of folk have lived and died in their shadows, while they still stand?'

'They've been here since the dawn of the world, lad,' the old man said. He sat at the back of the little boat, one hand on the tiller, guiding their course up the fjord. 'When Odin and his two brothers, Vili and Vé, killed the *jötunn* Ymir and made our world from his corpse.'

Einar chanted the words of the ancient lore.

'From Ymir's flesh the earth was created,
The inside of the skull of that ice-cold giant formed the sky above,
From his blood came the sea,
And from his bones the mountains were made.'

'And yet,' he said afterwards, 'At home in Iceland new mountains have appeared after volcanoes erupted. Whole new islands have risen from the sea.'

Grimnir raised his eyebrows.

'And who is to say,' the old man said, 'that those too were not the work of Odin? Perhaps when he killed other jötnar? Or maybe it was Thor.'

'So you believe Odin still walks the earth?' Einar said.

'Our world is in chaos,' Grimnir said. 'Everyone is at everyone else's throat. Someone must be causing all this trouble and this I do know: two of Odin's many names are *Ófnir* and *Glapsviðr*. The Inciter and the Swift to Deceive. Odin is a restless wanderer who creates unrest and stirs up strife, now here, now there, as he works his magic.'

'You sound like you disapprove of Odin's ways?' Einar said.

'I neither approve nor disapprove,' the old man said. 'I just look for the reasons for things being as they are. But if you are asking me if Odin *actually* walks the earth, with physical legs, then I would say no. But his spirit is everywhere. And its influence is obvious.'

Einar frowned. Sometimes Grimnir spoke in riddles that were way beyond his understanding.

It had taken them three days to sail the little boat north to Dale from Gandvik, hugging the coast by day then coming ashore to camp during the few hours when it got dark. They had been able to use the sail most of the way and Einar had spent a lot of the time resting and lounging around the boat. Each day he felt his strength growing and knew he was getting better and better. They saw no more sign of vikings during the journey and Einar found the greatest battles he had were against boredom and the discomfort of being damp from the nearly constant rain.

'We should be nearly there,' Grimnir said. 'I can see some smoke drifting above the trees a little further along the shore.'

'That's good,' Einar said. 'It's nearly dark. Is there a waterfall somewhere?'

He cocked an ear to the air. Grimnir did the same. A sound like the rushing of a river in full flood drifted across the water from the tree-swathed shore.

'That's not water,' the old man said. 'That's people.'

Einar listened harder and realised that the sound was actually that of many voices raised in anger or excitement.

'Do you think this means trouble?' Einar said.

'Whoever it is, they don't sound too happy,' Grimnir said. 'Let's go and see what's going on.'

They sailed on, rounding a neck of land that reached out into the fjord. Beyond it lay a little natural harbour which had a wooden jetty with six fishing boats tied up at it.

'This is definitely the right place,' Einar said, pointing to a *snekkja* that rode its anchor a little way offshore. The light, sleek longship was the vessel Ulrich's Wolf Coat crew sailed in.

On the shore was a little settlement. It consisted of a clump of longhouses gathered around a track that led parallel to the shore. There were several torches burning in brackets but the summer twilight meant it was not dark enough to require many. A miasma of smoke from cooking fires drifted above the thatch of the houses and into the trees beyond.

'What's Hakon doing in this little place?' Einar said.

'Believe it or not,' Grimnir said, 'this is the largest settlement in this district. These parts of Norway are sparse when it comes to people.'

'Well there's no shortage of people in Dale this evening by the look of it,' Einar said. Despite the late hour of the evening, there was a large crowd thronging the track through the village. They were on the move and all heading in the same direction.

'Do you think they're flocking to see Hakon?' Einar said.

'I don't know,' Grimnir said. 'But I don't like the look of this.'

It did not take long to complete the journey to the jetty and tie up the boat. By the time they did so the crowd had moved on to somewhere within the settlement. From the sound of many raised, angry voices Einar and Grimnir could tell they were still close by. The jetty and all nearby was deserted.

'Everyone in the village must be in that crowd,' Einar said.

'Let's keep the sails of the boat unfurled, eh?' Grimnir said. 'Just in case we need to get away again fast.'

They walked down the jetty, Einar feeling the strange swaying sensation that came from spending all day on a boat then stepping onto dry land. His unsteadiness was not helped by the boards of the jetty that were black, wet and slippery with moss.

As he at last stepped onto firm land at the end of the jetty, Einar caught sight of two figures coming loping out of the trees beyond the village. They came from the same direction that the crowd had swarmed from earlier. Both were wearing wolf fur cloaks.

'By the names of all the Gods!' Einar said. 'It's Ulrich and Skar. It didn't take us long to find them.'

'At least this means we're definitely in the right place,' Grimnir said. He raised a hand to wave.

'You're not dead then?' Ulrich said to Einar as he and Skar jogged over. 'Good. I'd hate to have wasted all that time training you in war crafts only for you to take the road to Hel.'

'Don't listen to this grumpy old man, lad,' Skar said, clapping Einar on the shoulder. 'He's as glad to see you back on your feet as I am.'

Ulrich looked Einar directly in the eyes.

'Are you fit again?' he said. '*Fighting* fit?'

Einar nodded, while at the same time clasping his maimed hand behind his back.

'Good,' Ulrich said. 'The crew is small enough as it is. I don't need to lose anyone else. We also have a big problem right now so let's save the reunion celebrations for later.'

'What's happening?' Grimnir said.

'The local villagers have been told Hakon is a Christian,' Ulrich said.

Grimnir blew out his cheeks.

'Hence the angry mob we saw,' he said. 'That will indeed cause trouble. Especially here. The folk here are very diligent about tradition, customs and sacrifice. A Christian King of Norway? It is unthinkable.'

'Well if we don't do something about it, Hakon will be hanging from the nearest tree,' Ulrich said. 'We may already be too late.'

They hurried off in the direction of the clamouring villagers.

'I knew you were a strong lad, Einar,' Skar said. 'Good to have you back with us.'

'How did they find out?' Einar said as he jogged along.

'Vakir told them,' Skar said.

'Vakir?' Einar said. 'He's here?'

'Don't you go running off on some personal revenge mission,' Ulrich said. 'We'll sort him out later. Right now we need to stop that crowd hanging Hakon from the nearest tree and the rest of us along with him.'

Ten

They set off down the track to the longhouse of the village head man. There they found an uneasy stand-off happening outside. The crowd of villagers was gathered in a semi-circle before the building. Jarl Sigurd's four warriors stood shoulder to shoulder before the door. They wore brynjas and helmets, had their spears at the ready and had locked their shields together to form a short wall. Sigurd, Starkad and Kari stood behind them. They had not had time to get their war gear but had their swords drawn and their wolf's head hoods pulled up. Even though outnumbered many times, the sight had been intimidating enough to make the mob pause, at least for the time being.

The village Galdr maðr with his horned helmet stood in front of the villagers, confronting the warriors barring the way in.

'We demand to see the king,' the ritual worker said. 'He has questions to answer. Bring him out here!'

Angry shouts of 'Aye' came from the rest of the crowd.

Ulrich, Skar, Einar and Grimnir joined the back of the throng. With all their attention focused on the warriors before the door, no one in the crowd gave them a second glance.

The door of the longhouse opened and a fat, ruddy faced, white-haired man dressed in reindeer skins and a felt hat came out.

'That's Vemond, the village head man,' Skar said to Einar and Grimnir from the side of his mouth.

The village head man raised and lowered both hands, as if he were trying to pat down the noise of the mob. Einar thought he looked both scared and confused, then realised he was drunk.

'Friends, friends. My own folk,' Vemond slurred when the general hubbub of the villagers had quietened enough for him to be heard. 'What is all this racket about? Solvi, our Galdr maðr, what is the meaning of all this?'

'Hakon is a Christian,' Solvi the Galdr maðr said. 'He is not fit to be king.'

'What?' Vemond looked even more confused. 'The king has been a guest in my house. Surely if he did not honour our Gods I would know this?'

'Maybe you're a Christian too, Vemond,' someone in the crowd said. 'I've heard that's how they change folk to their faith. They convert the overlords and the ordinary people are forced to follow.'

Angry murmurs circled through the crowd like eddies caused by a strong current in the fjord. Einar saw a look of fear cross Vemond's face.

'This is a very serious charge to threaten a king with,' Vemond said. 'How do you know this about him?'

'Odin himself told us!' Solvi said. He straightened his back and puffed out his chest, glaring at the head man with a look of triumph on his face.

'That was not Odin,' Ulrich spoke up.

At the sound of his voice the faces in the crowd whipped round.

'It was someone pretending to be Odin,' Ulrich said. 'He was lying to you.'

'It's them,' Solvi the Galdr maðr said, pointing his remaining ceremonial spear at Ulrich. 'The ones from the forest. They attacked the High One! They must be Christians too.'

The faces around them became angry again. Ulrich whipped up the wolf's head hood of his pelt cloak. He bared his teeth at those around him. It was enough to cause them to hesitate for a moment.

'I am an Úlfhéðinn,' Ulrich said with a snarl. 'One of Odin's own wolf warriors, initiated in the secrets of his crafts and sworn to dedicate my life to the service of the All Father. I have seen many friends die for him. Do not dare to call me a Christian.'

Einar saw the faces of the villagers in the crowd turn pale. He pulled his own wolf skin hood up. Skar did the same.

'Why would Odin duck when a mortal axe was thrown at him?' Ulrich said, pushing forward into the crowd which parted before him to let him through. Einar, Skar and Grimnir followed behind him. 'What has a God to fear from iron?'

There were nods and some 'Ayes', from those around him.

'No,' Ulrich continued. 'The man you saw in the woods was called Vakir. He is a seið maðr. A crafter of perverted magic.'

The anger in the faces now surrounding Einar and

the others returned, though now it was prompted by the dawning suspicion that they had been deceived.

'Why should we trust the words of these men?' the village Galdr maðr said. 'They are the lap dogs of Hakon. They're not even from this folk land. They're as much foreigners as he is!'

Ulrich now stood beside the Galdr maðr.

'Watch your mouth, magic worker,' he said. 'I've killed men for less.'

The Galdr maðr swallowed hard and his face fell a little.

'You dare to threaten a holy man?' he said.

'It was not a threat,' Ulrich said. 'It was a statement of fact.'

'I've never seen Hakon at the village *Hof*,' Solvi said. 'In all the time he's been here he has never been in our temple or attended one sacrifice.'

Ulrich did not reply. It was clear this was something he had no answer for. Einar could sense they were at a crucial moment. Ulrich had managed to break the mob's conviction a little. Now they were not so sure, nor were they so charged with righteous anger. Doubt had crept into their minds. The mood and opinion of the crowd was now balanced on the edge of a blade. The merest nudge could tip it in either direction.

'What rubbish this is?' Skar spoke up. 'Hakon is the son of Harald Fairhair. No king reddened more blades or sacrificed more or drank as many toast to the Gods as Harald.'

'But Hakon was brought up overseas,' the Galdr maðr said. 'In a foreign land with foreign ways.'

'But I am still Harald's son.'

A new voice made them all turn around again. Hakon himself now stood behind the wall of shields at the door of the house.

'His blood flows within me,' he said. 'You are my folk. I am your king. We should not be at each other's throats like this.'

Einar was impressed. Hakon was still just a lad – several winters younger than himself – but he spoke with such force and bore himself with such confidence that his mere presence mollified the angry mob further. The men began to look at one another, sheepish expressions on their faces, rather than meet the commanding gaze of their king.

'Solvi, we have been deceived,' one of the men in the crowd said to their religious leader. Others nodded. 'A son of Harald would not follow the Christ God.'

'Perhaps this is so…' Solvi said, taking a deep breath.

'Forgive us, lord,' another man in the crowd said to Hakon.

'No one can blame you for fervent loyalty to the Gods,' Ulrich said. 'But this has all been a mistake. You folk can be reconciled with your king once again.'

Murmurs of agreement went through the crowd with sighs of relief.

'Yes,' Solvi said slowly. His eyes slid sideways towards Hakon. 'And to show there are no hard feelings, we should share the *Bragrfull* with the king. What better way to be reconciled than we all take a drink that has been blessed by the Gods.'

Einar saw Ulrich open his mouth and hesitate once more. It was only for the briefest of moments, so short as to be hardly noticeable. Solvi, it seemed, was still not convinced so was setting a test.

'Good idea,' Ulrich then said. 'Go and bring the sacred drinking horn from the Hof. Vemond, go with him. As village head man you should say the prayers to Odin, Thor and Frey that will bless the drink. We'll wait for you in your house.'

The crowd around them cheered. Einar could sense the tension melting away and Solvi and Vemond strode off in the direction of the village temple.

'Thank the Gods for that,' Einar heard one of the men standing nearby say. 'I like the lad, Hakon. He'll make a good king. Better than that tyrant Eirik anyway. I'd have hated to have to kill him.'

As the folk relaxed the crowd dispersed into smaller groups. Ulrich pushed on to the door of the head man's house with Einar and the others in tow.

'I suggest we retire inside, lord,' Ulrich said to Hakon. Then he looked at the warriors as well. 'All of us.'

'Is that wise?' Starkad said, casting a glance at the still-assembled villagers.

Ulrich locked gazes with him and cocked his head, then went inside. Hakon and the warriors followed.

In the room beyond, Godwine stood facing the door, seax still drawn. Surt, Wulfhelm and Affreca were standing guard over a sorry looking slave who knelt on the floor, looking like he had just lost a fight. Another slave lay, dead, in a pool of blood beside him.

'Einar!' Affreca said when she saw him enter.

Her face burst out into a wide grin and Einar felt like the much absent sun had peeked out from behind the ever-present clouds and bathed him in its warmth and light. He longed to run over to her. To throw his arms around her and hug her to him, burying his face in her auburn hair.

Instead he just grinned back at her, the thought of the scorn Ulrich and the others would pour on them for such an overt display of affection holding him back.

'Where were you, Ulrich?' Hakon said in a demanding tone. 'Jarl Sigurd is paying you good silver to keep me safe. I was attacked by these secret killers here,' he nodded at the beaten slaves, 'and then had that horde of villagers outside baying for my blood.'

'It looks like my wolf pack have dealt with these killers,' Ulrich said. 'Though that crowd might still be a problem if you don't drink the Bragrfull.'

'It's a problem for me,' Hakon said. 'And Godwine as well. We cannot drink something consecrated to heathen Gods. Our souls will be in danger.'

'You must,' Ulrich said. 'It's the custom.'

Hakon rolled his eyes.

'Why should it matter what God anyone worships?' he said with a groan. 'What business is it of any man what goes on in the heart of another?'

'I think you'll find it matters a lot to these folk,' Ulrich said. 'It may be time to renounce your God, for the sake of your life, and all of ours. For the sake of the High Seat of Norway.'

'Never,' Hakon said. He straightened his back and glared at Ulrich. Einar saw the steel in Hakon's eyes and realised the lad possessed the same utter determination that had driven his father Harald to conquer all of Norway.

'Well, could you at least pretend?' Ulrich said. 'We've all

been baptised at least once so we could fight in Christian armies. It hasn't shaken my faith in the All Father.'

The door opened. Vemond held it ajar as Solvi entered, carrying a large, round metal bowl. It was either bronze or pewter and polished to gleaming. The outside of it was embossed with writhing serpents, weapon dancers, horned men and fabulous creatures. Solvi carried it with reverence, holding it before him with both hands.

He set it down on the table and Einar saw that it was filled to brimming with an amber liquid.

'Here we are, lords,' Solvi said. 'Mead, blessed by Vemond according to custom in the names of Odin, Thor and Frey.'

He closed his eyes and held his hands over the bowl, his lips moving in a silent prayer. Then he opened his eyes and lifted the bowl once more. He held it out to Hakon.

'Drink, lord,' he said. 'To Odin.'

Hakon nodded to Vemond.

'This is your village,' he said. 'You should drink first.'

A look crossed Solvi's face that suggested his suspicions were being confirmed.

'Very well,' he said, passing the bowl to Vemond.

'Odin,' the head man said, looking deep into the amber liquid. Then he took a long draught from the bowl. When he finished he set it on the table before Hakon.

'Your turn, lord,' Solvi said. 'Drink deep, in honour of the Gods.'

For several long moments the magic worker and the young king locked eyes. Then Hakon flicked his eyes towards Ulrich, who nodded to him. Einar could see the little Wolf Coat leader willing Hakon with his eyes to drink.

The young man sighed. Now all the eyes in the room were

watching, expectant. He placed both elbows on the table and leaned over the bowl. It looked as if he were smelling the contents. Einar could see that the crucial moment had come. Hakon now had to drink or refuse. There was no room for compromise.

Hakon lifted his right hand and made a gesture over the bowl. Holding his first two fingers together he pushed them forwards, drew them back towards him, then forwards and to the right and across to the left. To Einar's dismay he realised that Hakon was making the sign of the cross over the drink, the symbol of the Christ God.

He was fast. It was done in a moment, then he lifted the bowl and drank deep from the mead within.

'There,' Ulrich said quickly. He too had noticed Hakon's gesture. 'Surely you can have no more doubts about your rightful king?'

'Wait,' Solvi said. His eyes were wide and alight with the fire of righteous indignation. 'What was that? What did he do before he drank? What does that movement mean?'

Ulrich, Skar and Godwine dropped their right hands to the hilts of the knives sheathed at their waists.

'King Hakon is doing what we all do, who trust in power and strength,' Einar said. 'He blessed the bowl in the name of Thor by making the sign of his hammer over it.'

Solvi looked at Einar for a long moment. Then he nodded.

'I will drink next,' Einar said, lifting the bowl and taking a long, deep drink. He was glad to feel the strong, sweet tasting brew going down his throat and setting fire to his guts.

'Steady on, lad,' Skar said, laying a hand on his shoulder. 'Leave some for the rest of us.'

The bowl was passed around the room, each person there apart from the prisoners drinking deep of the strong mead. When it completed its circuit, the Bragrfull bowl was passed around again. After the second turn Einar felt a warm, comfortable feeling of fellowship with the others in the room that he was sure they also shared. Vemond, who had been drunk before the bowl had arrived, was now swaying on his feet and grinning like an idiot. By the third time around Einar felt they were all now firm friends.

'I hope now that Lord Hakon has put your minds at ease,' Ulrich said. 'He is just like all of us.'

Solvi and Vemond nodded.

'I am sorry we doubted you lord,' Vemond said. 'Please do not look unfavourably on the folk of this district. Let us all go to the ale house and celebrate together.'

'Of course,' Ulrich said. 'You go ahead. Perhaps you can reassure the folk of the village before we get there? Tell them Hakon has drunk the Bragrfull and there is no more need to worry. I for one would like to change into my feasting clothes. I'm sure the others do too.'

'Of course,' Vemond said. 'We'll await you in the ale house.'

Then he staggered out the door. Solvi picked up the holy drinking vessel and followed Vemond, though he did not look quite as happy as the village head man. Whether the Galdr maðr was still unconvinced or was just annoyed at being wrong, Einar could not tell.

'Let's get out of here,' Ulrich said as the door closed behind them. He turned to Skar. 'Get Roan. We need to set sail.'

'But Hakon got away with it,' Einar said.

'Do you think so?' Ulrich said. 'That Galdr maðr is not convinced and if he stirs up the villagers again there's too many of them for us to fight on our own. Come on. We're leaving out the back.'

'There's another way out?' Hakon said.

'Of course,' Ulrich said. 'Do you think I would've let you stay here if there wasn't an escape route?'

Eleven

'Those peasant bastards!' Hakon said, clenching his fist. 'How dare they humiliate me like that?'

He stood at the prow of the Wolf Coats' longship. The short time of summer darkness had finally come and they were sailing down the fjord away from Dale, leaving the village and its folk drinking in the ale house, so far unaware that their king had left them.

'I'll make them pay for this,' Hakon went on. 'I'll get a horde of warriors from Jarl Sigurd and come back here. We'll kill every last one of those impudent bastards. We'll burn that god- forsaken hole to the ground.'

The young king broke off his rant.

'Ulrich,' he said. 'Is there something you find funny about all this?'

The little Wolf Coat leader was chuckling to himself.

'I'm sorry Lord Hakon,' Ulrich said. 'It's just that I was always told that you Christians are keen that we should all forgive those who do us wrong. This mood of yours seems a little... how can I put it? Vengeful? Such emotions would make Odin proud of you.'

Hakon glared at Ulrich. His breathing was heavy and Einar could tell he was fighting with a maelstrom of emotions that were battling within him for which would win control. Einar felt sympathy for the young king. Ulrich had a talent for provoking others when they were at their most vulnerable. It was like he took pleasure in it.

'Where are we going?' Roan, the skipper who steered the longship said. His hide was so wizened by sun and wind that in the dark his skin looked as black as Surt's. 'I need to set a course.'

'What do you think, Grimnir?' Hakon said to the old man.

'Eirik has sent vikings to raid the west coast. They've already burned Frodisborg. It's not safe for you there,' Grimnir said. 'We should go north to Jarl Sigurd's realm. He has enough warriors to deter Eirik's vikings.'

'Sigurd has his own problems to deal with right now,' Hakon said, his previous emotion deflating. 'I know I was shouting about bringing his warriors down here but right now he's busy putting down a rebellion to the north of his Jarldom.'

'You said Vakir was here,' Einar said, turning to Ulrich. 'I'm not leaving without killing that bastard.'

'He's the least of our worries right now,' Ulrich said.

'He killed my mother!' Einar said. 'He preserved her severed head and used it for his filthy magic rituals. I want him dead.'

'It's hard, I know, lad,' Skar said. 'But there's a bigger game to be played here. Vakir will get what he deserves, don't worry. Right now, however, we need to work out how to stop Eirik taking Norway back.'

Einar blinked. It had not occurred to him until then that that was actually what was at stake.

'Vakir will be long gone by now, anyway,' a new voice said. 'He's probably already halfway back to Orkney.'

Everyone looked around to see who had spoken. It was the prisoner with the big nose and arched eyebrows. He sat against the side of the ship, his hands bound before him. His left eye was bruised, swollen and almost closed over from Affreca slamming him into the wall.

'Vakir is a survivor,' the man said. 'When Ragnarök comes the fire giants will burn up everything on earth. The Fenris Wolf will eat the sun and moon. All of mankind will die. There will be nothing left alive. Then that bastard will crawl out from underneath the last rock standing.'

'Who are you?' Einar said. He narrowed his eyes. 'I know you from somewhere, don't I?'

'He was your father Thorfinn's steward,' Affreca said. 'His dróttseti. He ran Jarls Gard.'

'I am Aulvir Ranaldsson,' the man said. 'And yes, I ran Jarls Gard, for a short time.'

He grunted.

'I used to look after Thorfinn's horses,' he said. 'I was good at that. I loved doing it. I wish I'd stuck at that now. But my wife thought I could do so much better. She urged me on. Pushing me to take higher and higher jobs. Now look where it's got me.'

'Dead,' Ulrich said.

'I know what you mean about Vakir,' Einar said. 'I thought I'd killed him myself. You don't think much of him? Isn't he on your side?'

'That one is more slippery than an eel,' Aulvir said. 'I've watched him for years. He served Jarl Thorfinn but when Eirik took over he switched sides faster than the blink of an eye. He knows where power lies and clings to it like a limpet.'

'The same could be said about you,' Affreca said. 'You were Thorfinn's dróttseti and now you came here to murder Hakon for Eirik.'

'Not all who follow Eirik do so willingly,' Aulvir said, a flash of anger crossing his face.

'Don't think any of this will save you, dog,' Hakon said. 'It won't be long before you're hanging from the crossbeam. I don't know why I haven't done it already. At least those peasants came at me face to face. You pretended to be a slave so you could kill me. What were you going to do when I was dead? Slink away like the cowards you are?'

Aulvir shook his head and looked down at the deck.

'Our plan was to kill you somewhere more private, true. But the young lady recognising me forced our hand,' he said. 'I thought I was ready to die. I knew when Eirik directed us to do this task there would be little chance of coming back. But when the moment came…'

'You should have fought and died like your friend did,' Ulrich said. 'At least there's a chance Odin saw what he did. Perhaps he'll be chosen to enter Valhalla. You've missed that chance. You'll die like a slave.'

'I'd prefer it if you did not glorify someone who tried to murder me as the sort of person who will get into your heaven, Ulrich,' Hakon said.

'To die performing a deed so brave you had no heed for your own life,' Ulrich said with a shrug. 'Is that not the very meaning of Valour? Is that not the very thing that Odin built his Valour Hall to honour?'

Ulrich began stroking his chin, something Einar knew the Wolf Coat leader did when he was thinking.

A look of thorough misery fell on Aulvir's face. He heaved a deep sigh as if despair was suffocating the very breath from him.

'I never was a man of action,' he said. 'I ran the stables. The household. I was probably always bound for Hel's kingdom anyway. Svein, the man who was with me, was a warrior. And yes, he died like one. But does Odin reward treachery? To me Svein was a fool. Like Vakir, he was one of Thorfinn's sworn men now eager to impress our new overlord, Eirik. He was desperate to prove how loyal he was. That cost him his life.'

'And you're different to him and Vakir?' Affreca said. 'Why are you telling us all this anyway?'

'You're going to hang me anyway. And I've no reason to help Eirik,' Aulvir said. 'I'm not here willingly. Eirik holds my daughter, Ellisif, prisoner. He knew as *westmenn*, we could pass as slaves in Norway and get close enough to Hakon that we could kill him. When I showed reluctance he told me he would have Ellisif raped and beheaded if I did not go. She's only nine winters old. A lovely little girl.'

The words caught in Aulvir's throat. He looked down at the deck for a few moments to collect himself. Then he looked up again, this time fastening his gaze on Einar.

'You armed the slaves of Orkney,' he said. 'You helped them and the Orkney natives rise up against us, their Norse masters. We thought we were superior but that night in Torhaven, surrounded by them, armed to the teeth with those Ulfbehrt swords, I saw the truth. We Norse were always just a small number of overlords holding down many others. We did it through violence, threats and the unshakeable belief that we were superior to them. But it was all pretence. Just a show. When the slaves no longer believed it, we were finished. Even if you hadn't killed Thorfinn, the jarl was finished in Orkney anyway.'

'And yet how was Eirik able to take Orkney so easily?' Einar said. 'If what you say is true, how did he manage that?'

'Eirik came to Orkney with an army of men,' Aulvir said. 'Hardened warriors and desperate vikings who know Norway had forced Eirik out and had nowhere else to go. There weren't enough to fight Hakon and Jarl Sigurd but there were more than enough of them to quell the slaves. Most of the Norse of Orkney saw him as a deliverer and joined him. The combined forces of Eirik and the Orkney Norse was too much for the thralls and natives, even armed with those swords you gave them. It was a bloodbath. There are few trees left on Orkney and all of them groaned under the weight of hanged thralls.'

'That bastard Eirik,' Einar said in a low voice.

'You let him in,' Aulvir said. There was accusation in his voice. 'You took Thorfinn away. That allowed Eirik to walk into Jarls Gard.'

Einar closed his eyes, thinking of the slaves who he had exhorted to rise up against his father. Was he now to blame for their deaths?

The ship was starting to roll over ever-larger waves as they got closer to the mouth of the fjord.

'I'll need a heading soon,' Roan said. 'Unless you want to just keep sailing out into the Western Ocean.'

'I remember your mother,' Aulvir said to Einar. 'She was a good woman. She was just Thorfinn's bed-slave but she was beautiful. She was always good to Thorfinn's servants and she did what she could to help the thralls on Orkney. You, I think, take more after your father. Certainly in looks. From what I heard the old jarl say about you, probably in character too.'

Einar frowned. He did not know what to make of this.

'Does Eirik think he can just kill me and walk straight back into Norway?' Hakon said. 'Does the fool not realise it was the folk of this land who turned against him? It was the people who threw him out! He can do away with me but they will still hate him.'

'Eirik knows all that,' Aulvir said. 'I've heard him ranting in Jarls Gard about it.'

'But he still intends to come back?' Hakon said.

Einar detected a hint of apprehension in the young king's voice.

'When the time is right, yes,' Aulvir said.

'I know he has an army and took Orkney but Norway is a much bigger fish,' Hakon said. 'He was too weak to hold on to power. That's why he had to run away. He could not take Norway back with the horde he commands.'

Ulrich snapped his fingers.

'Of course!' he said. 'So that's his game.'

'What is?' Hakon said.

'Eirik is too weak to take Norway back when it is united under you,' Ulrich said. 'But if you were dead the land could fall back into many Jarldoms and folk lands, all at odds with each other. Then he can conquer them one by one. He can take Norway one piece at a time, just like his father Harald did.'

'Like *our* father did,' Hakon said.

'And Eirik is building his strength,' Aulvir said. 'It increases all the time. More ships. More warriors.'

'My brother Olaf of Dublin doesn't support Eirik,' Affreca said. 'Aethelstan of Wessex is against him. Who is he building this army with?'

'He's sent word across the whale roads that he will pay silver for any men who will fight for him,' Aulvir said, shaking his head. 'Vikings are flocking to Orkney to join his cause. Men with no lords, outlaws and those who fight for silver and plunder. Every day more and more arrive. Olaf of Dublin is not one of them, yet, lady but Olaf of Limerick has pledged support.'

'Old Olaf Scabby-Head of Limerick?' Affreca said with a scowl. 'If he is with Eirik then my brother definitely won't join him.'

'Men like that don't fight for free,' Ulrich said. 'Eirik's a king without a country. No one is paying him taxes. Where's he getting the silver from?'

'Eirik promises booty and plunder,' Aulvir said. 'He's sending them to harry the coast of Norway to punish the folk there. Every man can keep what he steals. For the best of them, the powerful leaders and the ones who will protect Eirik as his hearthmen, he's offering them your Ulfbehrt swords. You didn't just let Eirik in, you armed his warriors.'

Einar felt as if he had been kicked hard in the guts.

'When he finds them all that is,' Aulvir said.

'What do you mean by that?' Ulrich said.

'They're hidden all over the island,' Aulvir said. 'When Eirik's army arrived the slaves scattered and hid them. Eirik has ordered Ogvald, one of Thorfinn's noblemen, to find them all.'

He shook his head.

'The hangings continue,' he said. 'Soon there will be no thralls left! But Eirik has also promised that soon he will have even better swords for those who swear the oath to follow him,' Aulvir said.

Skar and Ulrich exchanged puzzled looks.

'What nonsense is this? Ulfbehrts are the best swords in the world,' Ulrich said with a scoff. 'What could be better? And where is he going to get these miracle weapons?'

Aulvir just shrugged.

'I think I've seen one of those magic swords,' Einar said.

All eyes turned to him as he related the events that had happened at Frodisborg, including how Bersi had died when Einar's Ulfbehrt shattered.

'What Einar says is true,' Grimnir said, noting the sceptical expressions on some of the Wolf Coats' faces. 'I saw it too with my own eyes.'

Silence settled on the longship as the portent of everything that had been said sunk into the minds of all on board.

'This is not good,' Hakon said at length. 'A king who gives the gift of an Ulfbehrt sword could attract the loyalty of the best of men – jarls and *Lendmenn* – not just vikings. And if Eirik can also offer something *better*...'

'Lords, we are passing the mouth of the fjord,' Roan said. 'Where are we going?'

'The king must be taken to safety in the north,' Grimnir said. 'That's all there is to it. We should go there first.'

'Wait,' Hakon said, looking at Affreca, 'there is also the matter of our wedding.'

Twelve

'What's this?' Einar said.

Ulrich looked at Affreca.

'What is this indeed, Your Greatness?' he said. 'Members of my Wolf Coat crew cannot marry without gaining my permission first.'

'It is King Aethelstan's wish that Affreca Guthfrithsdottir and Hakon Haraldsson be married,' Godwine the Saxon said. 'They will rule Jorvik together.'

'I don't recall ever giving an answer to that proposal,' Affreca said.

'You can't marry Hakon,' Einar burst out. 'He's just a boy!'

Affreca frowned, a look of irritation crossing her face.

'We can be married when we get to Jarl Sigurd's realm,' Hakon said.

Godwine coughed and shuffled his feet.

'Lord King,' he said, 'it is my lord Aethelstan's wish that you would be married in the great Minster of Jorvik, so that the folk there can witness your union. And also that it is in the sight of God.'

Ulrich chuckled once again.

'Old Jarl Sigurd is a great man for the sacrifices,' he

said. 'He is steadfast in his honour of the Gods. If you get married in his realm he'll expect your marriage to be blessed by Thor, Freya and Frey. I think you may find yourself in a very similar situation to the one we've just got you out of.'

Hakon's mouth dropped open a little. Einar almost felt sorry for the young man caught between the competing expectations of two very powerful men on whom he relied for his kingship. Almost, but not quite.

'King Aethelstan has prepared very comfortable accommodation for the Lady Affreca in Kings Gard in Jorvik,' Godwine said. 'So she can get to know the people she will rule better and also learn what she needs to in order that her rule is successful.'

'Oh he has, has he?' Affreca said. 'King Aethelstan seems to be taking a lot for granted if he has already arranged such things without my involvement.'

'That settles it. We sail for Jorvik,' Hakon said. 'Roan, take us south.'

'No, lord,' Grimnir said. 'I must insist. For you to leave Norway at a time like this, when Eirik's vikings are raiding the western coast and there are uprisings in the North. The king cannot sail away from the country! You would be leaving the door wide open for Eirik to walk back in.'

'He's right, Lord King,' Godwine the Saxon said. 'It's also too dangerous for you to cross the northern sea at this time. We have to sail right past Orkney to get to Jorvik. What if you are captured or killed?'

'So what do I do?' Hakon said, his teeth gritted, eyes darting back and forward as if seeking for answers in the dark of the sea. For a few moments there was silence. Then Ulrich spoke.

'Lord Hakon, I have an idea,' he said.

All eyes turned towards the little Wolf Coat leader.

'We will go north now, and leave you in safety in Jarl Sigurd's realm,' he said. 'Then we will take Lady Affreca to Jorvik. When it's safe for you to do so, and Norway is secure again, you can join her there for your wedding.'

'What?!' Affreca looked as if she might burst with rage.

'Hold on, Ulrich,' Einar said. 'Affreca says she has not even accepted this proposal yet.'

Ulrich looked at both of them. So fast as to be almost imperceptible, he winked.

'I think these mysterious swords are the key to all this,' Ulrich said. 'And we have an old friend in Jorvik who might be able to tell us more about them.'

'What about Eirik?' Grimnir said. 'Do we just let him continue to raid Norway in the meantime? You cannot allow that either, Lord Hakon. Folk will not support a king not strong enough to defend them.'

'I believe we can do something about that too,' Ulrich said. 'The same applies to Eirik. If he suddenly found himself under attack at home, the place he believes is his new safe haven, Orkney, it might rattle him. He'll have to withdraw his vikings back to Orkney to defend himself or risk losing that too. As the Saxon here pointed out, we have to sail right past Orkney to get to Jorvik. We will stop on the way and give Eirik something to think about.'

'But there are only nine of you,' Hakon said. 'Ten with your skipper. Eirik has many, many vikings.'

'A small band of highly trained, dedicated warriors can often overcome whole hordes of men who are paid to fight,' Ulrich said, his face breaking out into a grin. 'Besides, when it comes to vikings, we're the most ruthless, merciless, vicious bunch of viking bastards to sail the seas.'

They all laughed, though the laughter was nervous for most.

'We should be able to cause him enough harm that he pulls his vikings back to Orkney,' Ulrich said. 'Then when we find out more about these super swords we will return there too. My Wolf Coats will hit Eirik in his lair where he is vulnerable. We will make life very difficult for him. We might even steal that hoard of Ulfbehrts back so he'll have nothing to tempt more vikings into his employ with. We've stolen them before. Why not again? That will give you time to gather your own forces.'

Ulrich's eyes had taken on a fierce, cold glitter as if he were picturing with relish in his mind the scenes of carnage and slaughter that were to come.

'I don't know,' Grimnir said. 'You'll need more than bravado if you're going to cause serious harm to Eirik.'

'What if we had someone inside Eirik's camp, though?' Ulrich said. 'Someone who could tell us what he is thinking, what he is planning, so we can stay one step ahead?'

He pointed at Aulvir.

'Lord King, Eirik believes this man is on his side,' Ulrich said. 'I ask that you show some of that Christian forgiveness you people boast of and pardon him for attempting to kill you.'

Hakon made a face.

'Then we will take him back to Orkney,' Ulrich said. 'He will be our eyes and ears within Jarls Gard.'

Hakon looked at Grimnir.

'It just might work,' the old man said, nodding. 'They

could at least cause Eirik enough problems that he pulls back his vikings. But I don't fancy your chances of getting away alive.'

'It's a brave plan,' Hakon said.

'Brave?' Grimnir said. 'Indeed it is. The odds are so far against them they have little chance of returning alive. It's brave to the point of self-sacrifice.'

Hakon straightened his back and squared up to Ulrich.

'Very well,' he said. 'We will do this as you suggest.'

Ulrich turned to face his Wolf Coats. He spread his arms to the dark skies above from which the perpetual rain had once more begun to fall.

'Ragnarök is coming,' he said. 'I was starting to think we had run out of time. That we would not get the chance to perform a deed heroic enough, so full of valour, that in dying while performing it we achieve what is the hope of all who dedicate their lives to Odin: To become members of his *Einherjar*, Odin's chosen warriors. Now here is that chance. This is our invitation to Valhalla.'

Part Two

The Northern Seas

Thirteen

Isle of Leòdhas, off Northern Scotland

The wan face of a full moon peered out from a gap in the clouds above, casting its ghostly light over the standing stones below.

One stone, shorter and rounder than the others, stood alone, slightly off-centre of a ring of eleven others that was about a hundred paces across. They were ancient, their grey faces pockmarked and scarred by untold centuries of weather. Near to the central stone was a hearth made of flagstones set in the ground on which blazed a large bonfire that cast its flickering light on the area within the stones. Beyond the light the surrounding countryside was dark. No glimmers of light emerged from the blackness. The only sounds were the crackling of the fire, the buffeting of the wind and the rush of waves crashing on a beach somewhere nearby; all testament to the remoteness of the place.

A weaving loom had been set up between the bonfire and the central stone. Its top beam rested against the standing stone and the bottom sat on the ground. The incongruous sight of this tool of everyday domestic toil in the midst of this wild, ancient place somehow enhanced the eeriness of the scene. This was intensified by how the loom had been perverted to an instrument of horror.

Instead of a tapestry, the corpse of a slave girl, her pallid skin drained to snow white by the gash that rent her throat, was stretched. Her body hung upside down between the top bar and the heddle rods. Her long hair, now crusted with her own blood that had cascaded down the loom like a red waterfall, drifted in bloodied clumps in the breeze. She was naked and the roaring fire nearby cast shadows on the lines of her ribs that stood out starkly from her flesh, witness to the life of hard work and underfeeding that had been her pathetic lot. A line of runes, painted with her drying blood, ran down the face of the central standing stone.

The girl's killer stood before the loom and stone.

Gunnhild, the former Queen of Norway, was dressed in a long, hooded dress that was so dark a blue it appeared black in the night. Little seashells, crystals and bits of glass sown into it caught the firelight so it sparkled like a clear night sky. The dress was cut so it was tight around her, revealing her lithe body beneath. Her hands were clad in piebald gloves made from the pelt of a cat. In her right hand she grasped a distaff, a stick for spinning wool. In her left she gripped a knife that was still bloody from when it cut the slave girl's throat. Her long black hair swirled from under her hood and her snow-pale skin was bathed orange in the firelight as she raised the distaff to the black sky above.

A little behind her stood the tall, scrawny figure of Vakir. He too wore a long dark robe that sparkled in the firelight.

The ring of long white hair that circled the bald top of his head blew in the wind. He bore a wood and leather chest, held before him with both arms.

Eight warriors were positioned just outside the circle. They were dressed for a fight in war gear; helmets, shields and brynjas. The moonlight that fell on them enhanced the paleness of their faces and the whites of their wide eyes as they watched with apprehension what was going on within the stones.

'Norns and *dísir*,' Gunnhild said in a loud, commanding tone. 'Mighty women who rule the air. Accept my sacrifice. Take the blood and spirit of this thrall and grant me your favour. Great *Vǫlvur* of the Northern Isles, I call on you for your guidance. I need your wisdom.'

For several long moments she stood in silence, staff held aloft. The warriors looked on, expectant.

Nothing happened.

The clouds cloaked the moon once more. Gunnhild's shoulders sagged a little and she lowered her distaff.

'Over there!' the leader of the warriors shouted. His eyes were wide, his mouth open and he was pointing to the edge of the firelight's reach in the stone circle.

A woman now stood in front of one of the standing stones. She was dressed like Gunnhild in a dark hooded cloak that reached her feet. She was much younger, however, and her hair was blonde rather than black.

The warriors hoisted shields and readied their spears.

'There's another one,' another of the warriors said.

A second woman, again in a blue robe, now stood before the next standing stone along. She was in the prime of life, around the same age as Gunnhild. Her hair was red.

The warriors started again at the sight of a third woman in blue, this one old, her face wizened by many winters and white hair tumbling around her shoulders. None of the warriors had seen any of the three newcomers step into the circle. It was as if one moment they were not there, the next they were.

'Put your weapons down,' Gunnhild said. 'These are who I have come to see.'

'The warriors must go,' the old woman said. 'Men cannot be inside the sacred circle.'

Gunnhild gestured to the spearmen to leave.

'My lady,' the lead warrior said. 'My orders, from King Eirik himself, are to keep you safe throughout this voyage. The king will have our heads if he found out we left you alone on this strange island, in this strange place, with these—'

He broke off.

'Witches?' Gunnhild finished the sentence for him. 'And I will have your heads if you don't take your weapons and go back to the ship. Wait for me there. Do not worry. I will be fine.'

The lead warrior looked dubious, but the black-haired woman held his gaze with a commanding stare for a long moment more. Then he nodded.

'Very well. Back to the ship,' he said to the other warriors. Looking far from content, they disappeared into the darkness.

Gunnhild frowned to see Vakir still stood behind her.

'You are a man, Vakir,' Gunnhild said.

'It's all right,' the oldest of the other women said. 'He can stay. We can see by his robes that he is a seið maðr. If he has partaken in the rituals of crafting *seiðr* then he is not a man in the normal sense.'

Gunnhild nodded and turned back to the others.

'Welcome Gunnhild,' the old woman said. 'Daughter of King Gutorm.'

'Welcome Gunnhild,' the woman in her prime said, 'wife of King Eirik.'

'Welcome Gunnhild,' the young woman said, 'whose sons shall be kings in their time.'

Gunnhild let out a little gasp.

'How do you know who I am?' she said, her voice little more than a breathless whisper.

The old woman made a face.

'We are the Three Wise Women of the Northern Isles,' she said. 'The Spae-Wives. We are *supposed* to know things.'

Gunnhild walked to the true centre of the circle, beside the squat stone. Vakir shuffled along behind her. The three other women came to meet her.

'Great Ladies,' Gunnhild said. 'You are famous for your wisdom and the gifts you have of foresight. Each of you are said to be the most powerful of *völva*. You are seeresses who know the past and can divine the future. Those of us of The Craft know you are also great practitioners of seiðr. I have sailed many days north to come here. Like all seekers who come to your island, I seek your wisdom and need your guidance.'

'As well as the past and future, we also know the present, Gunnhild,' the woman in her prime said. 'We have heard that Eirik is no longer King of Norway. We know he was driven out by the people. This is why you seek our guidance, is it not?'

'Otherwise, why would a queen so powerful as you,' the youngest woman said, 'so knowledgeable herself in the ways of magic, need our help?'

'Which makes us a little concerned,' the oldest woman said. 'A queen without a country may not be able to give us what we ask.'

'I have performed the ritual,' Gunnhild said, pointing towards the slaughtered corpse of the slave. 'I have made the sacrifice.'

'Blood,' the old woman said, tilting her head back and looking down her nose at Gunnhild, 'is not enough.'

Gunnhild, with a sardonic smile, nodded to Vakir. Balancing the chest he bore on his left arm, he used the long bony fingers of his right hand to unclasp the bindings then lift up the lid.

The faces of the three vǫlvur lit up both with delight and with the reflected firelight that gleamed off the hoard of silver and gold inside the chest. Vakir, head bowed, stepped forward and laid the chest at the feet of the three wise women.

'Excellent,' the old seeress said, eyeing the treasure like a starving man shown a table laden with food. 'Now we can talk.'

'You say my sons will be kings but how will that be?' Gunnhild said. 'My husband has been driven from his throne in Norway.'

'Orkney is a realm,' the youngest of the wise women said with a shrug. 'Eirik could be king of that.'

'Orkney is a bunch of islands in the northern seas that the Gods have forsaken,' Gunnhild said, sudden anger flaring in her eyes. Her lips drew back from her perfect white teeth.

'Norway is Eirik's birth rite, won for him by the sword of his father Harald. What must I do to make sure Eirik rules Norway again?'

The wise woman who was around Gunnhild's age winced and shook her head.

'It is not that simple. Eirik lost the favour of the land spirits,' she said. 'No king can rule unless the Norns, dísir and most important of all, the *landvætttir*, are on his side.'

'It was the people who drove Eirik out,' Gunnhild said. 'Treacherous bondes, low born farmers. Impudent, jumped-up peasants who think they have a say in who rules them.'

'The spirits of the land work through its king and its people, especially the ordinary folk, the people who are tied to the land,' the oldest wise woman said. 'A great king embodies the spirit of the land and the people will love him for it. They think he is a reflection of them, of their best qualities but they do not know it is the other way round and that it is actually the power of the land spirits that they are responding to. The king and the landvættir spirits are one to them. When the king falls out of favour with the landvættir and the dísir, then the people find they no longer wish to follow him. They think it is the king's fault, and in a way it is.'

'But what did Eirik do to make the spirits desert him?' Gunnhild said.

'We cannot answer that,' the wise woman in her prime said. 'Though you may know the answer in your own heart. Ask yourself, did Eirik embody the true spirit of the land and its people? Did he personify everything that it is to be a king of Norway – to *be* Norway itself – not just perform the actions of the rituals expected of a king?'

Gunnhild considered for a moment the dour, taciturn man who was her husband. A feeling of despair pricked her heart.

'Why would the land spirits favour Hakon over Eirik though?' she said. 'He does not even share our faith?'

'Perhaps,' the wise woman who was about the same age as Gunnhild said, 'it is more that their disfavour of Eirik is greater. And Hakon is a son of Harald too.'

'So how can he win the favour of the land spirits back?' Gunnhild said, her voice cracking a little. 'And so win back the High Seat of Norway.'

'Does Eirik not have other problems to consider first?' the wise woman said. 'Is he secure in Orkney?'

'Of course,' Gunnhild said. 'Who could threaten him?'

'Orkney had a jarl: Thorfinn the Skull Cleaver,' the old wise woman said. 'And Thorfinn had a son. Einar killed his father, took revenge for the death of his mother and won the Jarldom for himself, however briefly. The poets and skalds already sing songs about him. Even here on this remote island that is our home we have heard tales of Einar Thorfinnsson.'

'Who cares what poets say,' Gunnhild said with a scoff. 'Einar, Thorfinn's bastard is no threat to Eirik. He ran away like a frightened puppy when we sailed into Orkney.'

'Think carefully about what you say, Gunnhild,' the red-haired wise woman said. 'What is it that Odin teaches?'

All three wise women locked their eyes on Gunnhild and began to chant together:

'Deyr fé,
deyia frǫndr,

deyr sialfr it sama;
ec veit einn
at aldri deýr:
domr vm daþan hvern'

'Your cattle will die, the wealth you gather will be lost,' the youngest wise woman said.

'Your friends and kin will die,' the middle wise woman said.

'You yourself will die,' the old wise woman said.

'But I know of something that never dies,' the young woman said. 'And that is what folk will say about you when you are gone.'

'The reputation you leave behind,' the red-haired wise woman said. 'The tales people tell about you, about what you did. The stories sung in the halls of high lords and hovels of low born churls. That is the only thing any of us can be sure will remain of us when we are gone. And who is it who sings those songs? The poets.'

'The same poets who now sing songs about Einar say Eirik is a tyrant,' the old woman said. 'A vicious and vengeful king whose people drove him out. And they tell that tale wherever they wander. Do not dismiss the power of the skalds, my dear. We may be able to predict the future, but we cannot control it. To control the future you must first control the past. And who owns what has happened?'

'Whoever holds power,' Gunnhild said. 'Whoever sits on the High Seat can tell the folk whatever they must believe. The strength of the king's sword ensures that.'

'But do they *believe* it?' the old woman said. 'Really, in their hearts? I don't think they do. But when a poet stands with his lyre in the hall of a lord, chanting tales of Ragnar Loðbrók, Hrolf Kraki or Einar Thorfinnsson, do you think the crowd of folk listening – rapt, spellbound to his every word – care whether what he says is true or not? All they care about is hearing a great story.'

'So what is truly stronger?' the youngest wise woman said. 'The king's sword or the poet's harp? To whom does the past really belong?'

Gunnhild's mouth dropped open slightly.

'The poets,' she said in a quiet voice.

She took a few breaths; her eyes roved around the darkness beyond the stones, as if searching for something.

'But it's the three Norns who govern what *will* happen,' she said. '*Urðr*, *Verðandi*, and *Skuld*: What has happened, what is happening and what will happen.'

'What was,' the oldest wise woman said.

'What is,' the wise woman the same age as Gunnhild said.

'And what *should* be,' the youngest said. She raised her right eyebrow. 'Not necessarily *will* be.'

Gunnhild looked at each of them in turn, then she nodded.

'Wise women, give me your wisdom,' she said. 'What must I do to ensure my sons are kings in the future?'

'The king who the land spirits possess, will possess the land. The land and the people are one. Eirik must win the approval of the land spirits,' the youngest wise woman said. She spoke with surprising confidence and authority for one her age. 'Whether in Orkney, Norway or wherever he sails to. Only then will he be secure in his rule.'

'How can he do that?' Gunnhild said.

'You must determine that,' the young woman said. 'Only you will know the best path that he can take.'

'But Eirik must realise who poses the greatest threat to him,' the wise woman in her prime said. 'Einar or Hakon.'

'And you both must learn how to master the future,' the old woman said. 'And who masters the past will own the future.'

Gunnhild shook her head.

'But we can *make* the land spirits accept Eirik through seiðr,' she said. Her eyes had become hard and any previous deference was gone. 'You can help me in the ancient ritual of *Landvættir Blót*. I have been told that you can. You are the most powerful seiðr workers in the northern world. Great women, help me to perform this. I will do anything it takes to ensure my husband's seat of power. I can give you gold, slaves, whatever you want.'

The three wise women looked at each other for a moment. There were expressions of slight surprise on their faces.

'The ritual is a dangerous one,' the oldest woman said. 'It is not for the faint-hearted.'

'I have no fear,' Gunnhild said.

'It has special conditions,' the middle woman said. 'There must be no men at the ritual but your husband. Nor must there be weapons or iron of any kind. The spirits will not come otherwise.'

Gunnhild nodded.

'There must be a special sacrifice,' the youngest said. 'A virgin girl, who is nine winters old, nine being Odin's sacred number. And freeborn, not a slave.'

She shot a glance at the dead thrall draped over the stone.

'I will find such a girl,' Gunnhild said.

'And it will be *expensive*,' the oldest woman said; her eyes glittered in the firelight as she bared her teeth. 'We will need gold, much gold.'

'I can give you that,' Gunnhild said.

The three wise women looked at each other again. Then the youngest one nodded.

'Very well,' she said. 'We will come to your island at the festival *Vetr Nætr*, the Winter Nights. You must prepare a private space for us to perform the ritual. There must be no men, no iron and a young girl to sacrifice. And gold.'

'I will ensure all of that,' Gunnhild said.

'Good,' the wise woman who was in her prime said. 'Now we must go.'

The oldest and youngest of the wise women picked up the chest between them. Gunnhild and Vakir bowed their heads as all three of the seeresses withdrew across the circle of stones. They reached the edge of the firelight then were gone once more, disappearing into the darkness beyond, leaving Gunnhild and Vakir amid the windswept stones, alone apart from the corpse of the dead girl.

Gunnhild stood for a few moments in silence, frowning as she considered all that had been said to her. Then she turned to Vakir.

'Back to the ship,' she said. 'We must set sail for Orkney. There is much to do. It is not long until Vetr Nætr.'

Fourteen

Orkney

A strong wind blew over the heather, making it ripple like a purple sea. The same wind whipped white foam from the blue sea beneath short, black rock cliffs. It was raining and though that was not that unusual weather for late summer in Orkney, the wild was cold and the sky dark.

A column of riders came trotting over the hilltop heading for a stronghold that sat on the edge of the sea. The fortress itself was a round, stone building surrounded by several other buildings built both of stone and turf. Around all of them was a rampart with a wooden palisade on top and outside that was a ditch. The track that the riders approached on led up to a double gate in the rampart. As the horsemen got closer the gates swung open, revealing a small crowd of men standing waiting in nervous anticipation in a courtyard beyond.

They stood around a large, iron-bound chest that sat on the ground. Seven of the men in the courtyard were warriors. They wore helmets and leather jerkins. Their shields were painted with the horns of a white stag, the symbol of Ogvald Karisson, the nobleman whose home the fortress was. Each of them also had another symbol, the red axe of Eirik Haraldsson, freshly painted on the shield, added in wherever space there was available. Some were above the stag, some beside it, some squashed into the small space under it.

The eighth man in the courtyard, Ogvald himself, stood among his men. He was clad in expensive clothes with a big fur cloak around his shoulders, which befitted the *Lendmann*, the most important noble in Orkney under the jarl. He was just past his middle years of life and his hair and beard were as grey as the clouds that glowered above.

'It's Eirik all right,' another of his warriors said. This man stood on the rampart beside the gate. He had his right hand cupped over his eyes as he peered into the distance at the approaching column of riders. 'I can see his banner. He's got quite a war band with him.'

Ogvald swallowed hard but straightened his back, clasped his hands behind his back and puffed out his chest.

'Well he should be pleased when he sees what we have for him,' he said, nodding at the chest on the ground.

The sound of hoofs beating on the soft turf got ever louder until the column of horsemen thundered through the gates into the courtyard of the fort. The first rider was indeed Eirik's *Merkismaðr*, the man who bore the king's standard. This was a banner emblazoned with a bloody red axe, dangling from a tall pole.

The next fifteen horsemen were warriors, dressed for

battle in helmets and brynjas and with their shields at their shoulder, each one painted with the same red axe.

Eirik himself came next, his long black hair, streaked with white, streaming in the wind behind him. Eirik, like his father Harald before him, was a big man, taller than most and with a wide, barrel-like chest. He was dressed for travel rather than battle in deerskin boots, breeches and a heavy wool tunic. A long cloak of dark fur was wrapped around him.

Another twenty warriors rode into the fort behind him. Ogvald balked at the number, which easily outnumbered his own men. It was clear that Eirik was taking no chances in crossing the countryside of Orkney, though Ogvald wondered just who would be foolish or strong enough to attack him anyway.

Two more riders completed Eirik's company. One made Ogvald start further. The man was huge. If Eirik was big, this man was as taller again. He was not gangly with it. Instead the muscle-packed shoulders, chest and thighs of the man were solid and thick and the horse he was on tottered, exhausted from bearing his considerable weight across the island. He had long brown hair and a long beard cut straight across at the bottom like a shovel blade. He wore a cloak of white fur and unlike every other warrior there, the shield slung across this man's shoulder was not painted with Eirik's red axe, but with a growling bear.

The last horseman was not a surprise. He was in his middle years like Ogvald and his red hair and beard were streaked with grey. He had broad, muscle-packed shoulders but his gut stuck out like one of the many barrels of ale whose content he had drunk over the years. It was Thord

Ormsson, one of Ogvald's own oathsworn men who he had sent to Jarls Gard to tell Eirik that the chest was ready for collection.

The horsemen swirled around the courtyard, filling it with their steeds and leaving little room for anyone else. Eirik swung himself off his horse and strode over to Ogvald.

'Welcome to Steinborg, Lord Eirik,' Ogvald said. 'Welcome to my home.'

'This is quite the stronghold,' Eirik said, looking at the ramparts and the big, round stone building. 'Every bit as secure as Jarls Gard.'

'Perhaps more so, lord,' Ogvald said, his chest swelling even more from evident pride. 'Unlike Jarls Gard, there are no secret tunnels in and out of my house.'

'It's lucky that one was discovered,' Eirik said. 'I'm glad you've sworn allegiance to me, Ogvald. If you locked yourself behind these walls you'd be a hard man to get at.'

'It was built by the ancient people, long before our folk came to these islands,' Ogvald said, his enthusiasm for talking about his home melting the unease that Eirik seemed to arouse in people without much trying. 'There are whole rooms made completely of stone. Stone seats, stone tables, stone chests, even some stone beds!'

'How comfortable,' Eirik said, making a face. 'But I did not come here for a tour. How are you getting on with the task I set you? Have you found all of the Ulfbehrts yet? I saw your handiwork in the fishing port before Jarls Gard. There were a bunch of slaves strung up there. Good work.'

'I did as you commanded, lord,' Ogvald said. 'Every slave I find in possession of one of those swords is hung.'

'They've had more than enough time to hand them in of

their own accord,' Eirik said. 'If they still hold onto them we can only assume they are up to no good.'

'I hung that last lot in Torhaven like you said,' Ogvald said. 'As an example to others. There would be no point stringing them up here where no one would see them.'

'And the swords?' Eirik said.

'Here's the latest lot,' Ogvald said. With a smile and somewhat of a flourish, he bent down and unlatched the chest on the ground. He flung the lid open. Inside lay swords, each one with the name +ULFBEHRT+ inscribed in the centre of its blade.

'Very good,' Eirik said. He squatted down beside the chest and ran his fingers over the blades. Ogvald noticed Eirik's lips moving but no words came out. Then he realised he was counting the swords.

'There are ten there, lord,' Ogvald said.

'Indeed there are,' Eirik said, getting back to his feet. All around him his warriors slid from their saddles. Ogvald noticed Thord remained mounted.

'Which is strange,' Eirik continued, 'because when I counted the number of slaves hung beside the harbour in Torhaven, there were only nine of them.'

Ogvald swallowed again.

'My new friend, Thord, here, has suggested why this might be,' Eirik said, gesturing to the large-bellied man still seated on the horse.

Ogvald frowned and glared at his liegeman. He had never liked Thord. He was over-ambitious and Ogvald had always suspected he was untrustworthy. It now looked like he had been correct about that.

'Thord tells me,' Eirik said, 'that one of these swords

turned out to be in the hands of one of your slaves, Ogvald. And that man is not now hanging beside the harbour.'

Ogvald coughed. He had gone very pale. There was little point in denying the situation however.

'Lord Eirik, I am sorry,' he said, speaking fast. 'The slave was an old member of my household. He's been a good, loyal servant to the family for many years. He was not even involved in the uprising. Some of the rebels gave him the sword to hide for them.'

'But he had a sword, Ogvald,' Eirik said, as if he was speaking to a child. 'And I told you all slaves in possession of one of the swords must hang.'

Ogvald heaved a heavy sigh.

'Yes, lord,' he said. 'I am sorry for disobeying you. But I see you intend to finish the job yourself now anyway.'

The big viking in the white fur cloak had uncurled a rope that hung from the saddle-bow of his horse and was now tying it in a noose.

'Ragnald! Fetch Drest.' Ogvald said to one of his warriors who ran into the stone building. The Lendmann cast a sheepish glance at Eirik.

'In truth, lord, my wife pleaded with me to spare the slave,' he said. 'You know how it is.'

Eirik's brow furrowed and his face darkened.

'Why would I know *how it is*?' he said. 'What are you suggesting? That my wife orders me around?'

'No, of course not lord!' Ogvald said, eyes wide. Though he had heard such talk. 'I just meant... you know... happy wife, happy life... and all that.'

Ragnald returned. Now he hauled an elderly thrall by the upper arm out of the house into the courtyard. Behind him came a middle-aged woman. Her hair was bound and she wore the apron and bore a bunch of keys that showed she was the lady of the household. Her face was flushed and bore a look of agitated concern.

'Is this the woman in question?' Eirik said.

'Ogvald what is going on?' the woman said.

'Lord Eirik is displeased about me sparing the slave, Signy,' Ogvald said. 'I'm afraid Drest is going to have to hang after all.'

His wife Signy's face fell further. The big man in the white fur cloak tossed the noose up over the bar of the gate.

'You'll need another one of those, Asbjorn,' Eirik said. 'It seems it was this woman who forced Ogvald to disobey my orders. We'll hang her too.'

Ogvald's mouth dropped open. Signy's hands flew to her face in horror. Four of Eirik's warriors grabbed her and the slave, tied their hands behind them and began dragging them towards the makeshift gallows at the gate.

'Lord. No!' Ogvald said. 'Signy does not deserve this.'

His warriors looked at him for orders. They were outnumbered and while fully armed he could see the reluctance in their eyes to start a fight they would surely lose. He knew then he could not rely on them to save his wife.

'Hang me instead,' he blurted out. It was the only way he could see to get her out of the situation. 'I could not live without Signy anyway. She's been my companion in life since we were sixteen winters old.'

'Perhaps I am being cruel to part you both then,' Eirik said. Ogvald felt a wave of relief wash over him. Then Eirik continued, 'I have a better idea. We'll hang you both. Seize him.'

Three more of Eirik's men rushed to Ogvald. They grabbed him, bound his hands and hauled him to the gate. More rope was produced and before long three nooses dangled over the gate.

Ogvald's warriors tensed, readying their weapons and making a show as if to rescue their lord.

'Easy lads,' Thord said in a loud voice. 'I've everything sorted with King Eirik. I'll be taking over from Ogvald. If you stick with me I will look after you all. I swear it.'

The lead warrior, Ragnald, looked from Thord to Ogvald, who now had a noose pulled around his neck, then back to Thord. He nodded to the others and all of Ogvald's men lowered their weapons.

Drest the slave started shouting. The big viking hauled the first rope and his cries were strangled as he shot into the air, legs thrashing. A cascade of yellow piss began emptying from the bottom of his breeches, spraying in all directions as he swung and twisted at the end of the rope. The warriors below laughed and jeered.

Ogvald twisted his head, trying to see his wife. He caught a glimpse of her terrified visage, eyes wide, mouth open. Then his heart sunk as she too was lifted into the air before his eyes. The last thing he saw of her face it was already turning deep red, her eyes bulged and her tongue pushed out of her mouth.

'Congratulations on your promotion, Thord,' Eirik said to the red-haired man with the ale gut. 'You are now in charge of the task of recovering the rest of those Ulfbehrt swords.'

'I won't let you down, lord,' Thord said.

'You'd better not,' Eirik said. 'Or you'll end up like

your former lord and master here and his wife. As for you, Ogvald: Odin owns you now. Hang him, Asbjorn.'

Then the big viking hauled the rope and the world dissolved into a crimson haze.

Fifteen

Einar sucked air in through his nose, trying to brace himself for the shock to come. The sea lapped and sloshed at the prow of the longship beneath him, waiting to enfold him in its chilling, black embrace.

They had sailed north to the realm of Jarl Sigurd where they had left Hakon in the relative safety of the jarl's fortress at Hlader. Grimnir had stayed with the young king, judging that he was too old for the sort of venture the Wolf Coats were setting out on and would only slow them down. Then they had set a course south, across the rolling waves of the northern whale roads. The sleek, thin-bodied warship was honed for speed and the voyage from Norway to Orkney had taken just over two days. The snekkja was also designed for penetrating rivers as well as ocean travel, but the shallow draught that allowed that also meant crossing the open northern sea to Britain had been a rocky ride. Einar had spent most of the first day of the voyage vomiting over the side, much to the amusement of his fellow Wolf Coats.

There had been plenty of work to do on the voyage so Einar had not had much time to sit around and wonder about how prudent this expedition was. However in the quiet hours of the night nagging concerns surfaced in his heart about what they were undertaking. Could they really trust Ulrich's judgement? Would he really make the best decisions in his leadership when at times he seemed more hungry for a glorious death than for victory over Eirik?

Ulrich himself remained as inscrutable as ever. Now and then he talked with Skar in low tones near the stern but what his actual plans were remained unshared. Had he had the time, Einar would have found this infuriating rather than just irritating.

What would happen to Affreca when they got to Jorvik remained another vexing unknown for him. He had seen Ulrich talking to her as well a few times but in the short snatches of conversation he had managed to have with her she had changed the subject as soon as he had asked about it. Affreca herself appeared unconcerned about the fact that they were sailing to a city where her fate was to become Hakon's wife and a queen as well, two things she had previously expressed nothing but disdain for.

To pique him further, he saw Affreca talking to the Saxon, Godwine, several times as well. To his chagrin he had even seen her laughing with him once, as if they were sharing a joke.

Above all, Einar worried that he was no longer fit to be an Úlfhéðinn. What would Ulrich say if he knew Einar could no longer grip a sword properly?

The snekkja now rode on its anchor stone, a little way offshore from the harbour of Torhaven in Orkney, the settlement that cowered in the shadow of Jarls Gard. The Gard had once been the fortress of Einar's father, Thorfinn, but now it was the stronghold of Eirik Bloody Axe.

It was dark. They were in the midst of a short northern

night typical of summer's end that stretched from the late sunset to the early dawn. A brazier burned on the end of the stone harbour wall that jutted into the sea before the settlement and in its light Einar could see the figures of two warriors, shields slung over their backs, helmets on their heads, standing warming their hands at the fire.

Very soon, if he made it to the harbour, he would have to kill at least one of those men.

Einar was stripped to his breeches, ready for swimming. Skar had made a preparation of grease and soot from the cooking fire and Einar had smeared it all over himself. Now every part of his exposed skin from his head to his feet was covered by the black greasy concoction. Surt stood beside him, also stripped and ready for swimming. His black skin meant there was no need for the greasy cover-up to hide him in the dark. Ulrich had given them both special long seax knives in sheaths designed for swimming. Their sheaths were worn across their backs, with leather loops around the hilts to stop the knives falling out by accident as they swam.

The rest of the Wolf Coats, along with Wulfhelm the Saxon, had also covered themselves in the black paint, though they were dressed for battle. They wore brynjas, helmets and their wolf pelt cloaks, shields across their backs. The mail rings of their protective jerkins and any exposed blades were also smeared with the black grease, lest a gleam of light fell on them and gave away the position of the longship in the dark. Aulvir was huddled on the deck near Roan at the stern. He had a dark cloak wrapped around him. There were four large barrels roped together in the centre of the deck, just behind the mast.

'Are you sure they won't know we're here?' Surt said.

'They won't,' Ulrich said. 'We've been careful to stay far enough away so the light from the brazier won't fall on us. Those fools are standing beside the fire as well. Their night sight will be destroyed by that. We can see them but they can't see us.'

Beyond the brazier the harbour thronged with ships. It was full to bursting, with vessels crammed along the harbour walls, along wooden jetties and sometimes lashed alongside other ships where there was no space for them to tie up otherwise. There were a few pinpoints of light coming from the settlement itself but otherwise the shore was dark and showed no signs of life. Einar could hear waves crashing on a beach somewhere nearby and took solace from it that they were not too far offshore.

'Do those two really need to swim to the harbour?' Affreca said, flexing the string of her Finnish bow. 'I think I could maybe shoot those coast guards from here.'

'And what if you miss?' Ulrich said. 'Or just hit one of them and the other runs for help? No. The only way to do this is for someone to swim over there and take care of those warriors in person. Then the rest of us can sail in.'

Einar also suspected that this was some sort of test Ulrich was setting him. The little Wolf Coat leader had chosen him alongside Surt to swim into the harbour, even though everyone knew that Starkad was the strongest swimmer in the crew. There had been a couple of other occasions on the voyage where Ulrich had singled Einar out for some task that required heavy physical exertion, like climbing the mast or hauling on a sail rope when one came loose in a strong wind. It was like Ulrich was trying to make certain that when Einar said he was fit enough to rejoin the crew, it was indeed true.

All in all, Einar was glad to be given the knife for this task as it meant he did not have to worry about mishandling a sword with his damaged hand.

'Right you two,' Ulrich said. 'Time to get going.'

Sixteen

Einar and Surt slid themselves over the side of the ship. Einar thanked the Gods for small mercies. At least he could lower himself into the chilling water rather than the huge shock of jumping straight in. The sound of two splashes out to sea might alert the guards on the harbour wall. Going into the water at his own speed would give him a few moments to get used to the cold.

His legs went into the water and he lowered himself down until the sea came up to his waist. There was a moment of nothing then he gasped as the cold gripped him. For an instant he thought he would not be able to stick it. His gut instinct told him to haul himself back out again, but the thought of the shame that would bring upon himself made him let go his fingers from the side and sink into the water instead.

He went straight down into the blackness. The cold sea closed over his head and his teeth clenched as a tingling shock ran through his jaw. His whole body felt like it was encased in ice.

Einar kicked his feet and resurfaced. His head burst into the air and he spread his arms and legs, letting the water buoy him up as he floated on his back, trying to regain control of his breathing. One of the many crafts Ulrich and Skar had taught Affreca and Einar as new Wolf Coats had been how to survive in all sorts of harsh places, including cold water. Einar knew from that if he did not calm his racing heart and frantic panting he would die very quickly.

He closed his eyes and tried to think of something else. Something that could distract his mind from the immediate situation.

The pleasing vision of Frida, the blacksmith of Frodisborg's daughter, swam before his inner vision. She was smiling at him as she helped tie the hammer to his arm. Einar felt his heart slowing and his breathing return to something like normal. The cold no longer seemed so intense. The sensation of drifting on the surface of the sea was almost pleasant.

Another memory, this time of Frida lying dead on the ground, surfaced and Einar remembered why he was here. He flipped around and began to tread water, looking for Surt.

Surt was a little way away, also treading water, taking a deep breath as he too completed pushing away the shock of entering the cold sea. Both of them were now ready for the next challenge, which was the swim itself.

They nodded to each other and began to swim towards the harbour.

Einar judged that it was about two hundred paces from the ship to the harbour wall. Not a huge swim but not exactly a dip in the summer herring pond either. It was across open sea, with waves to contend with and nowhere to rest if tiredness became a problem. They could not take too long either. Even though they had accustomed themselves to the cold, the temperature of the water was still working on them, bringing the heat of their bodies down to its levels. They could only spend a certain amount of time in the water until it became deadly.

All in all, the best thing to do was keep moving.

As he swam, Einar was pleased to find that the greasy black paste he was smeared in to make him harder to see in the dark, also went some way to keeping the cold water away from his skin. He had worried about it washing off in the sea but Skar had told him that he had made it extra greasy so the cold water had no chance of melting it. Einar wondered briefly how he would get the stuff off when he had to but banished the thought from his mind. There was much more important things to contend with first, like still being alive when his task was complete.

He and Surt ploughed on through the waves. Further out they could afford to use strong swimming strokes, faces in the water, arms carving into the sea like windmills, legs thrashing behind them. Their splashing was hidden by the crash of waves. As they got closer to the harbour, they had to change to the quieter frog-like swimming; bellies down, arms and legs working beneath the surface.

As he swam, Einar wondered how many times he had entered this harbour? This must be the fourth time but the first time swimming. The first had been as a naive lad, barely eighteen winters old, newly outlawed from Iceland, ignorant of the fact that the tyrant who ruled from the imposing fortress of Jarls Gard nearby was in fact his own father. It was hard to believe that only two winters had passed since that day. So much had happened in the months between. Yet what had changed? For him, nothing.

He might now be an Úlfhéðinn but to the rest of the world he was still just a farmer boy from Iceland, with no gold, no land, no wife. Nothing of value. Part of a band of killers and vikings who roamed the whale roads. So many had died, whole kingdoms had changed hands, but what had it been all for?

As they got closer to the harbour wall they switched direction so as to be heading for the dark outer side of it rather than the entrance where the brazier cast its light.

When the wall came between them and the brazier it was like they were swimming in almost complete blackness. The thought of what could be lurking in the black depths beneath them crept into Einar's mind like a spider. He remembered the horrible eel creature he had fought at the skerries north of Ireland with its rows of vicious teeth. Then there was Aegir the sea god and his wife Rán who lurked in their cold, joyless hall at the bottom of the sea. The old woman his mother had paid to nurse him used to tell Einar tales of how Aegir got lonely and would prepare his hall for a feast. He brewed ale, and the froth from the ale is the froth on the surface of a choppy sea. As he worked Rán went up from the sea bottom with a net, and snared sailors on their ships above, dragging them down into the cold depths so they could share in the feast. Once down there in those unseen depths, that was the end of them.

Einar knew such tales were just lore for children, cautionary tales to keep them from playing in dangerous waters. Now however, in the darkness, with the chilling water all around, it was easy to imagine Rán's wan face below as she reached up with pale, clammy, white fingers, to pull him down to a black, hidden death below.

He was getting tired. His arms and legs began to feel like they were made of stone as they moved through the water. His breathing got heavier and more laboured with every stroke. A feeling of dread took hold in his gut at the thought that maybe Ulrich was right. Perhaps he still had not recovered enough of his strength to undertake a feat like this. He would run out of energy and sink into the darkness below.

The sound of the waves crashing on the rocks just up ahead told him that he had nearly reached the end. He could not give up now. With a shake of his head Einar gritted his teeth and renewed his efforts to complete the swim.

The last part of the swim was the most dangerous. They had to land in near complete darkness on the rocks behind the harbour wall. The waves that crashed onto them could very well smash their bodies against the stones, or just continue to suck them back out to sea again until their strength was utterly gone and there was nothing left to do but die.

Knowing he must almost be there, Einar stretched his hands out ahead of him, feeling for the stones and making sure the first thing that ran into them was not his face.

His right hand struck the hard, cold face of a rock. At the same time a wave surged him forwards. Despite his best intentions he hit the shore hard, crashing into the rocks with a force that drove the breath from his body. Most of him was out of the water and he could feel the chill of the air on his wet skin.

Almost straight away the wave began to suck him back into the sea. Einar's fingers scrabbled frantically to gain a hold on something. He could get no purchase on the slimy, seaweed covered rocks. With dismay he realised he was going to slide back into the water.

Then he felt an iron-like grip enclose his forearm. Looking up he saw Surt, already landed and higher up the rocks, using the power of his huge, muscled arms to stop Einar from going back into the sea.

The wave retreated, leaving Einar sitting on the rocks. Surt hauled him up higher, away from the reach of the waves. He had made it ashore.

Fuck you, Ulrich, Einar said to himself. *I did it.*

Seventeen

For long moments they both sat on the rocks, trying to catch their breath. Einar was astonished and concerned at how tired he was. He was very out of breath, something made worse by the fact that both he and Surt needed to control their breathing lest they alert the men standing guard on the harbour wall above. The knife strapped to his back would be useless against their spears.

Einar felt Surt grip his arm again. He looked at the other man. In the dark, surrounded by the black rocks, there was little to be seen of either of them except the whites of their eyes. All the same he could see Surt glaring at him, his look expectant, questioning. Einar realised Surt could see how tired he was. He too seemed to hold doubts about Einar's fitness for the task in hand.

Einar met his gaze. He nodded at the other man in what he hoped was a reassuring way but held up his hand to convey he just needed a few moments to recover.

Surt watched him, anxious, until Einar felt his breathing return to something near normal and his strength regathering. He started to feel the cold of the wind on his wet skin and knew they needed to get moving.

He reached up to his left shoulder and felt for the hilt

of his knife. His fingers were still numb from the cold water and he fumbled for a few moments, trying to undo the leather loops. Then they came away and he pulled the blade free. Surt too had his seax drawn. They exchanged one more look to check both were ready, then began scrambling up the rocks to the base of the harbour wall.

It was not easy. The rocks were covered with green slime that was as slippery as ice. Einar kept his feet wide and while going as fast as he could, did not go too fast as to be reckless. One slip would result in a heavy, painful fall and probable serious injury.

When they reached the bottom of the wall they waited for a few moments. Einar could now hear the crackling of the fire in the brazier and the voices of the men on the other side of the wall. It would not be an easy climb either. The wall was nearly twice the height of a man and its stones were every bit as slimy as the rocks below.

Surt patted his shoulders and Einar realised he was telling him to climb up onto his. The big man squatted and Einar clambered on. Surt powered up to his feet again. Einar reached up and planted his hands on the top of the wall. He only had one chance so did not think about it. He flexed his arms and hauled himself up onto the top of the wall, swinging his legs around in one movement so he lay on top. He had to do this to stay out of sight of the men below.

For a few moments he lay flat, trying to press himself into the stones of the wall. Below him he heard the guards talking. Their conversation was the usual complaining of men whose lot it was to stand guard in the darkest hours of the night.

'I don't see Thord down here doing a turn,' one of them said.

'If Eirik was here he'd make sure he was seen,' his companion said. 'I've never seen anyone as brown-nosed as him. Was he as bad with Thorfinn?'

'I don't think so,' the first guard said. 'But now he's taken Ogvald's rank as Lendmann he's probably keen to make sure Eirik is in no doubt where his loyalty lies.'

'This is pointless,' the second guard said. 'Who is going to raid here now? All the most dangerous vikings now work for Eirik!'

Both men laughed but Einar detected an interesting note of resentment or disapproval in it. The coast guards spoke with the burring accent of the men of Orkney. Einar listened, running his fingers up and down the knife blade. They sounded like ordinary fellows, probably decent men perhaps with families of their own. They had no idea they were living out the last moments of their lives. He swallowed, steeling himself for a task that was every bit as unpalatable as the thought of jumping into the freezing, dark sea earlier.

Surt's fingers appeared on the top of the wall. Einar had to scrabble around to help his fellow Wolf Coat. He grabbed Surt's hand and started to haul him up. He let out a gasp when he felt the full weight of the man. For a few moments he felt as if his own arms were being pulled from their sockets.

Surt's face appeared over the top of the wall. At the same time a cry of surprise came from the guards below. Einar froze, thinking they had been spotted. If that was the case they were dead men. Their only chance rested on taking these men by surprise. Even if they tried to run now the guards would skewer them with their spears, probably while they were still scrambling down the harbour wall.

'What's that?' one of the guards said. 'There's something out there!'

'It's a ship,' the other one said. 'I'm sure of it. Just beyond the light of the brazier.'

They had spotted the Wolf Coats' snekkja.

'Go,' Surt said through gritted teeth.

Einar let go of Surt's hand and rolled off the top of the harbour wall. He turned as he came down, landing on both feet behind the two guards. In the instant that followed he took in the two guards' position, both in heavy cloaks with shields across their backs, both with spears and helmets. They were looking out into the darkness beyond the harbour but both had either heard or sensed Einar come down. Already they were turning around to see what was going on.

The lessons Skar, Ulrich and the other Wolf Coats had drilled into Einar in the crafts of war meant he knew what to do without having to think. Indeed, thinking in such situations could make him hesitate enough to cause his own death.

He stepped close behind the one on his right. He slid his left hand over the top of the man's helmet. Feeling his fingers slide into the eye holes of the visor he yanked it backwards. As Einar had gambled on, the guard had the leather chinstrap of the helmet fastened. As his helmet went back the strap yanked up his chin, knocking him off balance and leaving his throat wide open. Einar brought the seax down overhand, driving the point of the blade into the exposed flesh at the base of his neck, before the protection of his mail coat began and behind his collar bone. The man had no time even to cry out as blood welled up to choke him. An instant later he was falling backwards. Einar stepped away, letting him fall to the ground.

'You bastard,' the other guard said. He was now turned around but knew he had no time to unsling his shield. Instead he gripped his spear in both hands and lunged at Einar.

Einar leapt sideways. The point of the spear went past him instead of into his belly. He brought the seax down on the shaft with all his might. To his dismay the impact of the blade on the spear shaft twisted it a little in the weakened grasp of his injured hand so instead of breaking the spear it just knocked it downwards.

The guard recovered and jabbed again. Einar jumped the other way. Again he avoided being skewered, but he wondered how long he would be able to manage that. Sooner or later the longer reach of the spear would get him. Any moment now the guard would start shouting for help as well.

A black shadow came crashing down from above. Surt had managed to get on top of the wall and now had jumped down. He smashed onto the guard, his weight flattening the man to the stones of the quay. The spear went flying from his grasp as Surt scrambled to recover himself. He set his left knee into the fallen guard's back then drove his knife into the back of his head. The blade went in under his helmet with a gut-churning crunch. The man jerked twice then went limp.

Surt climbed to his feet.

'Thanks,' Einar said.

They both stood, panting to get their breath back, watching down the quay towards the settlement beyond to see if the recent commotion brought anyone else running.

After a long few moments when everything stayed quiet, Surt nodded to Einar.

'We got away with it,' he said. 'Better let the others know.'

They both hauled the cloaks off the dead men on the quay and swept them around their own shoulders, greedy for the warmth they provided to their chilled flesh. Then Einar lifted a burning stick from the brazier and went to the end of the quay. While Surt kept watch towards the settlement Einar waved the burning brand back and forward three times, which was a signal they had agreed with Ulrich before leaving the ship.

Before long the sound of oars dipping into the sea came and the Wolf Coats' longship emerged out of the darkness. As he watched it arrive, powered by the rest of the crew who strained at the oars, Einar felt an overwhelming sense of exhaustion sweep over him. Perhaps it was the warmth of the cloak or maybe Ulrich was right to suspect he was not yet fully fit. Whatever it was, he knew he could not succumb to it yet. Their job for the night was only half complete.

Roan steered the ship into the packed harbour. The Wolf Coats pulled the oars in and lashed the snekkja to the side of one of the ships already tied up at the quay. Skar was the first off, scrambling over the deck of the other ship and up onto the quay where he took in the sight of the dead guards with the appreciation of a master craftsman assessing the work of his apprentices.

'Good work, lads,' he said. 'But get them out of sight. The last thing we need is for someone to walk past down at the settlement and wonder why the coast guards are lying down on the job. Then take those spears and stand beside the brazier as if you're them.'

Ulrich joined them just as they were tipping the corpses of the guards off the quay and into the sea beyond.

'No other trouble?' he said.

Einar shook his head.

'Was your hand all right?' Ulrich said, looking him straight in the eyes.

'Yes,' Einar said. 'Stop asking about it will you? It's fine.'

He realised that without thinking, he had put his injured hand behind his back.

'Your Princessness,' Ulrich said over his shoulder to Affreca who was climbing up onto the quay, her Finnish bow slung across her shoulder, 'please take your bow and stand guard down the quay. If you see anyone coming this way shoot them.'

Affreca nodded. As she went past, she locked eyes with Einar.

'Are you all right?' she said.

'Of course,' Einar said, quickly. 'Why wouldn't I be? I wish everyone would stop asking!'

Affreca jogged off down the quay, unslinging her bow and notching an arrow as she went.

'Right lads,' Ulrich said to the rest of his warriors on the snekkja. He did not need to shout as the quiet of the night meant his words carried to them. 'The opposition has been taken care of, so you can get to work.'

The rest of the Wolf Coats slung their shields on their backs, sheathed their weapons and began hauling the barrels that had been tied around the mast of the snekkja off the ship and onto the quay. They were heavy and the contents that sloshed around inside made them even more awkward to carry. Einar was glad his only role now was to stand and pretend to be one of the guards.

Once on the quay they broke the barrels open. The strong smell of whale oil escaped into the night air as Ulrich handed out leather buckets to everyone and they started dipping them in the oil to fill them. Once full they fanned out along the quay, throwing the oil over the nearest ships, covering furled sails and coiled ropes. When the barrels were about half empty Skar and Starkad picked them up. Carrying them between them they took one each onto the decks of the four nearest ships and set them down. Skar then lifted his boot and kicked the barrels over, sending the contents spilling in an oily slick across the boards of the decks.

When this was complete they all gathered on the quay once more. Ulrich stuck his fingers in his mouth and made a low whistle. Affreca came loping back up the quay to join them.

'Get Aulvir,' Ulrich said.

Sigurd and Kari went back to the snekkja and brought Thorfinn's steward across to the quay. Once there they bound his hands and feet.

'Do you remember what I told you?' Ulrich said to him. 'Do you know everything you are supposed to say?'

'Yes,' the dróttseti said. He puffed out his chest and looked Ulrich in the eyes. 'And you will keep your word? You will make sure my daughter is safe?'

'I will,' Ulrich said. He turned to Skar and Starkad.

'When I can. Make sure he's as far away from these ships as possible. It's going to get very warm around here.'

The burly Wolf Coats lifted Aulvir by the arms and carried him down the quay, leaving him lying in the darkness near the top of the harbour. By the time they returned everyone else had climbed back onto the snekkja. Once Skar and Starkad were aboard they pushed off again. Everyone except Ulrich and Roan took up positions on the oar benches. When there was space they ran the oars out of the ship and began to pull. The snekkja glided towards the mouth of the harbour.

Ulrich stood beside Roan at the stern, a burning brand taken from the brazier on the quay held aloft. As the dragon-carved prow of the longship reached the harbour mouth, Ulrich tossed the burning brand into the nearest ship.

Einar started at the violence of the flames that burst from the oil soaked deck. He felt a gust of warm wind wash over him as the ship exploded into fire. The flames licked up the mast and as the Wolf Coats' snekkja glided out into the darkness the flames were already jumping to the next oil-washed ship lashed beside it. In the jam-packed harbour it would not be long until the conflagration had spread to many others.

Looking backwards as he strained at his oar, Einar could see Ulrich outlined against the flames behind him, the pointed ears of his wolfskin cloak standing out against the blazing ship.

'If we had some Greek fire we could have burned Eirik's whole fleet,' Surt said. 'That's how we dealt with you norsemen when you raided al-Andalus.'

'What's Greek fire?' Einar said to Skar, who sat on the bench next to him.

'It's a terrible and very powerful weapon, lad,' the big man said as he strained at his oar. 'I saw it used in Miklagard. We called it the Dragon's Breath. The Byzantine Emperor has ships that somehow spit liquid fire that sticks to whatever it lands on and cannot be put out.'

'Well I hope you laid Aulvir well away from those burning ships,' Einar said. 'Ulrich's whole plan depends on him being taken back into Jarls Gard.'

'He'll be fine,' Skar said. 'Even if he gets a little singed, we don't want Eirik's men getting the impression we were looking after him.'

'Do you think we can trust Aulvir to do as he was told?' Einar said. 'He was my father's steward, after all. He could betray us.'

'I hope not lad,' Skar said. 'Otherwise we'll all be knocking on the door of Valhalla when we get back.'

Eighteen

Eirik 'Bloody Axe' Haraldsson sat on the four-pillared high seat that rested on the raised dais at one end of the feasting hall in Jarls Gard. Like Odin, who sat on his high seat *Hliðskjálf* where he could watch over all the worlds, from this elevated position Eirik could see everything that went on in the hall before him.

It was morning. The tables were bare, the mead benches were empty and the fire pits were full of nothing but white ash. The torches were burned out and the hall was gloomy. The air was thick with the cloying smell of cold grease and sour beer.

The high seat, and the fortress it sat within, had until recently belonged to Jarl Thorfinn of Orkney but now they were Eirik's. Though he would much have preferred to be seated on his former chair – the High Seat of Norway at his ancestral homestead of Avaldsnes – Eirik had to admit to himself that he was impressed by both. Jarls Gard was ringed by ramparts and covered the top of a promontory that was cut off from the mainland at high tide. Thorfinn's high seat was made from a polished, very dark wood that was carved with scenes of twisting beasts entwined in combat with heroes and Gods. It was a beautiful work of the highest craftsmanship.

As he stroked his long black beard with his left hand, Eirik ran his right hand in an absent-minded manner down the right-hand pillar of the high seat. The wood of the pillar was worn smooth and his fingers slid with ease over the iron heads of the God Nails hammered into it.

The God Nails were big, square nails, the type used to build ships. Each one represented an oath sworn and witnessed before the Gods. When the oath was sworn, the nail was hammered halfway into the wood and consecrated in the name of one of the Gods. When the oath was fulfilled, the nail was hammered all the way in. Each hammered-in nail represented an enemy vanquished, a land conquered, a rival killed and a promise to a God delivered.

As Eirik's fingers reached the bottom of the column of nails, they snagged on one that still half-protruded from the wood. It seemed the old Skull Cleaver Thorfinn had died leaving one oath unfulfilled.

Eirik sat back in the chair and sighed. He was a large man, tall and broad-shouldered like his father Harald Fairhair. His long black hair and beard, both of which now were streaked with white, were combed straight and smooth. He was clad in a green shirt of the finest wool which was embroidered with the shapes of twisting intertwined beasts.

'How did this happen?' he said.

Leaning on the side of the high seat was Gunnhild. The fine features of her snow-pale face were creased in anger. Unlike nearly everyone else in the hall, she showed no signs of the deference, wariness or downright fear of the former king the way the others did. Then again, she was his wife.

'Were there no guards at the harbour?' she said in a demanding tone.

'I'll deal with this, Gunnhild,' Eirik said, irritation in his voice. 'Were there no guards at the harbour?'

Aulvir sat on one of the benches of the hall. He looked a sorry sight. His feet had been freed but his hands remained bound before him. His hair was singed in several places and his face dirty with soot. A warrior in helmet and shield stood guard over him.

Thord, the new keeper of the Steinborg fortress and now responsible for keeping order in Eirik's realm, stood before the dais. Aulvir regarded him with a withering eye. He had known Thord for many years. He had been a minor landowner, little more than a bondes. Now with the death of his *hersir* in the thrall uprising and then the death of Jarl Thorfinn, he had managed to ingratiate himself with Ogvald the Lendmann. Now it seemed he had somehow replaced Ogvald and catapulted himself into Eirik's favour. As with Svein, the would-be killer who had gone with him to Norway, the speed and enthusiasm with which Thord had transferred his loyalty did not impress Aulvir.

At least Thord was an Orkneyman, though, Aulvir thought to himself. The other men who lounged around the benches of the mead hall were either vikings who had come to fight for Eirik on the promise of plunder or the few leading Norwegians who had stayed loyal to Eirik.

To Aulvir, the vikings were the worst of the worst. They were little more than pirates, outcasts and outlaws. They were men who heeded no lord but silver and no law but their own viking one. The worst of them all was the huge man they called The Bear, the one who wore the pelt of a great white arctic bear.

Aulvir glanced sideways at him. The big man sat on one of the benches nearby, his mere presence fouling the air like a noxious fart. He rested his chin on one huge fist, looking thoroughly bored by everything going on around him.

Aulvir quickly looked away again. He had seen this man kill people just because he did not like the way they looked at him. He had raped a slave in the mead hall of Jarls Gard one night, heedless of the crowd around him gathered for the feast, just because she spilled some ale while pouring it into his horn.

It all made Aulvir wonder about Eirik's character. Jarl Thorfinn was a fearsome man who did horrible deeds, sometimes even in this very hall, but he was always discrete. Such public displays of lawlessness would never have been tolerated.

It was probably a measure of how powerful the viking was, Aulvir mused. Or else how weak Eirik had become that he now had to rely on such men. The Bear had been away raiding Norway on Eirik's behalf but now he was back and the air of menace that hung around him, even when just sitting on a mead bench, put everyone on edge. Being in the same room for him was like sitting on the heath, waiting for a storm.

Another former liegeman of Thorfinn was also there. Vakir the Galdr maðr, like Aulvir, had returned from Norway. Now stripped of his guise as Odin, Vakir wore the long white embroidered robes traditional for a worker of religious customs. He was tall and painfully thin, all skin and long, angular bones. His ring of long, white hair that circled his bald head hung in lank strands down to his shoulders. Aulvir had known Vakir a long time, but still suffered a creepy feeling every time he was in the man's presence.

'There was a coast guard, Lord Eirik, of course,' Thord said. 'The raiders managed to kill them before they set the ships alight.'

'How many ships did we lose?' Eirik said.

'Three, lord,' Thord said. 'Two more damaged but repairable.'

Eirik glowered at Thord for a long moment as an uncomfortable silence descended on the hall. The former king could be gruff and taciturn at the best of times, but the Orkneymen like Aulvir were learning, when he was angry this got even worse.

'And this man was left behind?' Eirik said at length, nodding in the direction of Aulvir.

All eyes turned in the direction of the miserable former steward.

'Yes, lord,' Thord said. 'He was trussed up like a goose. This is Aulvir, the man who ran Jarls Gard for Jarl Thorfinn.'

Aulvir rose from the mead bench in respect as the king's glowering eyes turned towards him.

'I know who he is,' Eirik said, scowling. 'It was I who sent him to Norway to kill Hakon. I take it this means you failed and my runt of a half-brother still lives?'

'I am sorry, Lord Eirik,' Aulvir said, hanging his head to avoid the dark glare of the former king. 'His bodyguards were too strong for me. I did say before I left that I know how to look after horses and run a household. I am not a warrior.'

'I thought you might at least be a man,' Eirik said with a grunt. 'Was he even scratched?'

Aulvir continued to look at the floor.

'Lord at least there are now folk in Norway who know the truth about Hakon's lack of faith in the Gods,' Vakir said. 'I told the people of Dale in Fjaler this. They think the message came from Odin himself.'

'Yes, very good, Vakir,' Eirik said.

'Aulvir is lucky to be alive,' Vakir said, casting a sideways glance at the steward. 'Very lucky indeed. Hakon is protected by Úlfhéðnar.'

'What?' Eirik sat bolt upright. He turned his gaze back to Aulvir. 'And they let you live?'

'It must have been deliberate,' Gunnhild said. 'Why were you spared?'

'They said they wanted me to deliver a message to you, lord,' Aulvir said. 'They said I was to tell you – please forgive me lord, these are their words not mine – that Hakon Haraldsson, rightful King of Norway, sends his regards.'

Eirik's upper lip curled as he glowered at Aulvir. The former dróttseti felt a rush of dread in his heart.

'And they also said,' Aulvir said, feeling a shiver in his legs, 'to tell you that the wolf pack you betrayed is hunting you.'

A heavy silence descended on the hall as all eyes turned on the brooding former king.

'Ulrich,' Eirik said after a few moments. He spat the word through clenched teeth. 'I should have known that irritating little bastard was involved in all this.'

'Not Ulrich Rognisson?' Gunnhild said. 'How is he

still alive? And why is he fighting for Hakon? It makes no sense. Ulrich's love of Odin is near fanatical. Why would he protect a Christian?'

'I have a good idea, why,' Eirik said. 'His hatred of me exceeds even his love of Odin. Thor's balls! If Hakon is indeed protected by Ulrich's úlfhéðnar that will make him hard to kill. You are indeed a lucky man, Aulvir, if you came away from an encounter with them alive.'

'Very lucky indeed,' Gunnhild said, looking at Aulvir with narrowed eyes.

'Ulrich is a born killer,' Eirik said. 'And so are the rest of his merry band. I suppose this means Jarl Thorfinn's bastard son is with him too?'

Aulvir nodded.

'Einar was on the ship, lord, yes,' he said.

Gunnhild frowned.

Eirik ran his hand down the nailed pillar of the high seat once again. His movement was impulsive and he forgot about the protruding nail. When his knuckle hit it, Eirik sucked in breath through his teeth. He clenched and unclenched his fist to dispel the stinging pain.

'He killed my son,' he said, his voice little more than a growl.

'He killed your bastard son, you mean,' Gunnhild said. 'Your *real* sons are here with you in Orkney. This is the only realm you have to leave to them now. We don't need Einar with a rival claim to it.'

'This Ulrich sounds like my kind of fellow,' the Bear said with a grin. He had not got off the bench and for the first time appeared interested in the conversation going on around him. 'I'm sorry we didn't run into him in Norway.

Finally, here is someone worth going up against. Someone who can give us a decent fight.'

'Wasn't the raiding in Norway enough for you?' Eirik said. 'At least for the time being?'

The Bear made a face.

'That was just slaughtering slaves, farmers and fishermen,' he said. 'It wasn't a contest of men. Something that could test us. The lads are getting restless again already, Eirik. They're bored. You'll need to find something for them to do soon or they'll start causing trouble.'

'If Ulrich is here in Orkney there'll be plenty of trouble,' Eirik said. 'Don't worry about that. I think you and the rest of the vikings should stay here for the time being rather than returning to raiding in Norway. If Ulrich's Wolf Coats are here I'll need all my warriors to defend Orkney.'

'Fine by me. The plunder in Norway was trash anyway,' the Bear said. 'Mostly just trinkets, hack silver and old weapons. You'll need to find something to keep the boys busy, Eirik, or you might need to start handing out a few of those Ulfbehrts to stop them leaving.'

'Speaking of those swords,' Eirik said. 'How is the reclamation of them going, Thord?'

'I recovered one more yesterday, lord,' Thord said, his chest swelling. The smile on his face to show how pleased he was with himself. 'And hung the slaves involved.'

'Just one?' Eirik said.

'It was the best I could do, lord,' Thord said, looking deflated. 'I don't have a large band of men.'

'Well get more,' Eirik said. 'Ogvald was a Lendmann. He must have had plenty of sworn men.'

'That's not so easy, lord.' Thord said. 'Folk are more

concerned about preparing for the winter than with helping me find those swords. And with all the hangings there are not enough slaves to help them. The bad weather meant the harvest was poor this year and people are starting to worry about how they will get through the dark months.'

'What about us, Eirik?' Gunnhild said, consternation evident in her tone. 'Is there enough food for the people in Jarls Gard for the winter?'

'Don't worry about that, my lady,' Aulvir said. 'If I may be so bold as to speak again? Jarls Gard has plenty of supplies. Salted meat, sheaves of corn and barley. Butter and ale. Wine even. I made sure of all this.'

'You were a good steward of Jarls Gard, Aulvir. I'll give you that,' Eirik said. 'Even in the short time we've been here it's been clear to me that you were good at running an efficient household. Since we sent you to Norway the place has been chaos. You see, Gunnhild. We will be fine.'

'All right, but Eirik we should be careful,' Gunnhild said, frowning. 'The people of Norway turned against us. We don't want the people here turning against us too. We can afford to delay finding all the swords while the Orkney folk gather the final harvest and prepare for winter.'

'Very well,' Eirik said. He turned back to Thord. 'We are on an island. Take some of our ships and send out extra fishermen. Whale hunting season is here. Get men out hunting. Divert men from finding the swords for a little time if you must. We'll salt everything that's caught and give it away to the people of Orkney. Surely then they will praise my generosity?'

'They will lord,' Thord said. 'Such a brilliant idea. I'll get to work straight away.'

'And as for the lack of slaves,' Eirik said. 'You can let it be known I am taking steps to address this. I've already sent messengers to the slave markets in Ireland that Orkney needs thralls.'

'That news will be most welcome, lord,' Thord said. 'That should settle everyone's problems. The folk will praise you to the doors of Valhalla for this.'

'Except for the problem of Ulrich and his annoying crew,' Eirik said. 'He'll be after those swords too, I know it. Ogvald's fortress at Steinborg looked very secure – safer than Jarls Gard anyway which we now know has at least one secret way in so there may be more. Thord, take all the Ulfbehrts there.'

'Aye lord,' Thord said. 'Good thinking. We don't want to have to both guard the swords and hunt these rogue vikings at the same time.'

Eirik made a face. Aulvir smirked at the thought that Thord could be so obsequious that he even annoyed the person he was fawning on.

'Move the extra stores of food in Jarls Gard there too for safekeeping,' Eirik said. 'It would look bad if the ordinary folk are starving and someone sees our storehouse is crammed with food. When all this is sorted then we'll deal with Ulrich. Someday perhaps we will share some of the food with the ordinary folk as well. That will show them how generous I am too.'

'It will be done, lord,' Thord said.

'Lord, what of my daughter?' Aulvir said. He spoke in a quiet, squeaky voice that betrayed both the terror that gripped him and his determination to ask the question despite it.

Eirik grunted.

'I don't think that will be any concern of yours,' he said. 'You'll be dead soon. I don't like failure and I find it highly suspicious that Ulrich allowed you to live just to deliver a message.'

Aulvir swallowed hard.

'Eirik, we should think about this too,' Gunnhild said. 'Killing slaves is one thing but the killing of Ogvald made you look like a tyrant, which is why the Norway folk say they turned against you. Consider how a further hanging of a freeborn man could make people here regard you.'

Eirik rolled his eyes.

'Do you think we can trust him?' he said.

'No,' Gunnhild said, 'but if he's here in Jarls Gard we can watch him. Who knows what we might learn?'

Both of them looked at Aulvir, who felt like a lamb in a field who catches sight of two wolves watching it from the forest.

'Well, like I said, Jarls Gard has been a mess since he left. I haven't had a decent meal in weeks,' Eirik said with a sigh. 'Very well, Aulvir. You can have your old job back as steward of Jarls Gard.'

'And Ellisif? My daughter?' Aulvir said.

'Get the girl,' Eirik said to a nearby servant. The thrall hurried away then returned, leading a young girl with long blonde hair by the hand. Her eyes were wide and full of fear as she looked at the people in the hall. Then, spotting Aulvir, her anxiety disappeared and a big grin broke out on her face, revealing the jumble of second and baby teeth that filled her mouth.

'Father!' she cried. 'You didn't forget me after all!'

Aulvir gasped and made to run towards her as the girl strained to pull away from the grip of the thrall's hand.

Gunnhild stepped between them.

'Wait one moment,' the Queen said.

Two of Eirik's warriors moved in front of Aulvir, stopping him from coming any closer.

Gunnhild looked down at the little girl who returned the look with a pale, upturned face. Gunnhild smiled and ran her fingers under Ellisif's chin.

'You're quite young aren't you dear?' Gunnhild said, narrowing her eyes. 'What age are you?'

'She's only nine winters old, lady,' Aulvir said. 'Have pity on her.'

'Nine?' The queen repeated the word as if half talking to herself. She turned to her husband. 'You know what Eirik? I think we should move her to somewhere safe for the time being. She's the perfect age for something I'm planning. And we don't know if we can trust Aulvir here yet, so knowing we still hold his daughter will ensure he doesn't try anything silly.'

'You're not letting me go?' the little girl said. Her bottom lip trembled and fat tears began to run down her plump cheeks.

'Your daughter will be safe in Steinborg, Aulvir,' Eirik said.

'My lord, have some mercy!' Aulvir said. Tears were springing to his own eyes. 'She's just a little girl. She'll be alone and frightened there.'

'I am a mother. I understand,' Gunnhild said. 'But it's for the best. She will remain in our care for the time being, at least until we are sure we can trust you, Aulvir.'

'How long will that be?' Aulvir said, gnashing his teeth together.

'Let's say until Vetr Nætr shall we?' Gunnhild said. 'Just until the festival of Winter Nights. Not too long.'

'We'll be watching you Aulvir. Bear that in mind,' Eirik said. 'If you are in any way in league with Ulrich we'll find out. Then you're both dead men.'

Nineteen

Jorvik – Kingdom of Northumbria

The Wolf Coats' snekkja slid across the black water of the river Ouse like the water snake it was named after. It had taken a further three days to sail from Orkney to Northumberland, with the final day spent rowing inland, up the river that led to the great city of Jorvik.

The sight of a viking longship with dragon-carved prow meandering the twists and turns of the river did not provoke the same panic it might have in other parts of Britain. Einar knew that the folk who lived in the villages and territory around Jorvik were descendants of Norse people like himself and even though some of them came from families who had settled there nearly a hundred winters ago, longships were familiar and usually heralded the arrival of friends rather than viking raiders. All the same, the wolf-cloaked crew at the oars of the snekkja still raised a few wary glances from the riverbanks.

Like most cities, they had known they were getting close to Jorvik long before they could see the place. The river became progressively more clogged with filth. It stank with the refuse, rotting detritus and sewage that flowed in ever thicker slicks from the settlement upstream. The odour began to mingle with the smell of woodsmoke, ale malting and bread baking while through the trees on the riverbanks a hubbub of noise kept on rising in volume. At the same time the river was also getting congested with more and more boats either going the same way as them or else heading downstream towards the sea.

Einar had spent some time in Jorvik before. At first he had been excited by the pace of life there with so many people all crammed into one place. As he approached the city now he felt no nostalgia for his previous time spent there. The stench and overwhelming noise made him wonder how anyone could stand the place.

The river opened into a wide bend that was lined with wooden jetties. There were many ships and boats either tied up on the jetties or beached on the muddy banks of the river. People thronged the jetties, unloading or loading cargo onto the boats or just talking and making deals.

Wooden-planked walkways, *gatr*, ran up the banks from the river to the city itself. High stone walls, built by Roman Giants (Einar had learned during his previous stay there) rose above the thatched roofs of the many longhouses that lined the walkways like ribs on a backbone. The city had spilled out beyond its defences and many new houses had been built in the ground between the walls and the river.

Roan guided the snekkja into a space on one of the jetties. Once it was tied up, Skar laid the *gangr* plank from the ship side to the jetty and everyone on board began preparing to disembark.

The sound of tramping boots on the planks of the jetty made everyone turn around. A cohort of ten warriors, with shields, leather helmets and spears came stomping towards the newly docked ship. At their head was a young well-dressed man with a gleaming silver helmet. The hilt of his sword, which was sheathed just under his left armpit, glittered with many ruby garnets.

'*Wilcumian*,' he said. '*Forhwý ofercuman êower Jorvik?*'

Einar, who had lived in Jorvik for a time, understood enough of the Saxon tongue to get his meaning. His companions were different. Seeing the blank looks of those on the ship the young warrior made a face.

'Very well, I will use your tongue,' he said in Norse. 'Though you would think if you came to the Aenglish kingdom you would at least make the effort to understand our tongue. I am Beaduheard. All new arriving ships are to be searched. What is your business here in Jorvik?'

'I'll handle this,' Godwine said, striding down the gangr plank to the jetty. 'Do you not recognise me, Beaduheard? Have I been away so long?'

'Godwine? Lord Waltheolf's reeve?' the young warrior said. 'Is that you?'

'Yes,' Godwine said. 'What's going on? Why are all newcomers being searched? Has something happened?'

The young warrior motioned with his head that Godwine should come closer. He did so and the two of them then fell into a conversation in the Saxon tongue.

'You and him seem to be getting on well,' Einar said to Affreca as she gathered her belongings into a leather shoulder bag. He nodded towards Godwine.

'He has been telling me all about my new kingdom,'

Affreca said. 'What the people are like. What it will be like to live in Kings Gard. He seems to think it will impress me. He must forget I'm the daughter of a king and grew up in Dublin. Big cities are not something new to me. But he tells a funny tale or two I grant him that.'

'Does he?' Einar said. 'Well he seems pretty boring to me.'

Affreca stopped what she was doing and looked at Einar for a long moment.

'Do you realise you stick your bottom lip out when you're peeved?' she said. There was a little smile on her lips.

'Why would I be peeved?' Einar said, frowning. 'I'm not the one who's giving up everything she says she's always wanted for something she always said she didn't.'

'Meaning?' Affreca's smile disappeared and her look became a glare.

'"Peace cows" you called them,' Einar felt his cheeks flush. 'Ever since I've known you, you've pitied them and said you never wanted to be like them. You looked down on daughters of kings who accepted their fates like cattle – to be married off to resolve one of their fathers' wars to become nothing but breeding stock for other kings' sons. Those were your words, not mine.'

'And nothing has changed,' Affreca said, scowling. 'But I've also learned things and had time to think on the voyage. This city belongs to my clan. It's a Norse city. The Romans may have built it but our people made it great. The Ivarssons have ruled it for over a hundred winters until Aethelstan tricked it away from my father.'

'You hated your father,' Einar said.

'True,' Affreca said. 'And he had no love for me. But I

don't hate my blood. I honour my ancestors, the clan of Ui Imhair, the Ivarssons, whose line goes back to Ragnar Loðbrók. We have destroyed and forged kingdoms all around the northern seas. Generations of my forefathers line the benches of Odin's Valour Hall. I don't want to let them down.'

'Doesn't Odin want chaos and bloodshed?' Einar said. 'What better way to honour him and your ancestors than by being one of the Úlfheðinn?'

'What better way to honour my ancestors than to get their city back?' Affreca said. 'Jorvik is my birthright. I am entitled to rule here.'

'No one is entitled to anything in this world,' Einar said, shaking his head. 'From what I've seen of it, might makes right. Who owns what is determined by the strength of the arm that bears the sword. By the man who commands the greatest army.'

'And in a world where a woman cannot command a horde,' Affreca said. 'Or at least where custom says she cannot, then she must look for other ways to achieve what she wants.'

'Like marrying Hakon to get the throne of Jorvik?' Einar said. The anger that had risen in him felt dampened all of a sudden. He felt as though a heavy stone was tied to his heart.

Affreca tilted her head back and smiled. It was a tight-lipped expression that bore little humour and no sympathy.

'What are you two fighting about?' Ulrich's voice made them both turn around. He and Skar now stood beside them, their leather belonging bags slung over their shoulders. 'I think we have some sort of lovers' tiff here, Skar.'

Affreca let out a gasp of exasperation. Einar glared at Ulrich, consternation locking his tongue.

'Ulrich!' Wulfhelm said, approaching them.

'What is it?' Ulrich said, noting the concerned expression on the Saxon's face.

Wulfhelm came close to their little group.

'We might have a problem,' he said in a low voice. He glanced over his shoulder towards Godwine and the Saxon warriors then, noting they were still deep in conversation, turned back to Ulrich. 'I've been listening in to what they're talking about.'

'And?' Ulrich said.

'King Aethelstan is here,' Wulfhelm said.

'In Jorvik?' Ulrich said, eyebrows raised.

Wulfhelm nodded.

'This is bad news, Ulrich,' Skar said.

Einar knew this was an understatement. The last time they had seen King Aethelstan of Wessex he had sent them off on a mission they were never supposed to return alive from.

Twenty

The Saxon warriors lined up on the jetty. Their shields remained slung over their backs and they made no obvious threat but still the mood of the Wolf Coats on the ship changed. What had been excitement at arriving in a big city with the prospect of all sorts of adventures dissipated into a prickly wariness. Hands dropped to hilts of swords as wary eyes scanned the line of warriors, assessing potential attack points, men who were smaller than their companions or who looked nervous or less resolute.

'We could take them,' Skar said out of the side of his mouth to Ulrich.

'Wait,' Ulrich said. 'If Aethelstan is here then there is a chance the person we came to see is with him. Perhaps this is good. Perhaps this is Odin helping us in our quest.'

'Helping us to get hanged quicker, more like,' Skar said.

'Is one of His names not *Hangatýr*?' Ulrich said with a smile. 'God of the hanged?'

No one but Ulrich found his jest funny. Not for the first time, Einar wondered if Ulrich's desperation to achieve a glorious death before the world ended was leading him to be reckless with all of their lives. Also who was this person he had said they were here to meet? He had not mentioned this before.

The young Saxon warrior, Beaduheard, raised a horn to his lips and blew three short blasts. There came a rattling of mail and tramping of boots as another troop of warriors began making their way down the walkway towards the jetties.

'What's the matter, Godwine?' Ulrich said, his upper lip curled in a sneer. 'Afraid you don't have enough men to search our ship?'

Godwine shook his head and spread his arms in a placating gesture.

'There will be no need to search this ship,' he said. 'I have great news. King Aethelstan himself is in Jorvik. We are to proceed straight to him.'

'Great news for who?' Wulfhelm said in a mutter to those closest to him. 'I was an oathsworn warrior of Aethelstan's half-brother, the man who tried to kill him. Aethelstan exiled us all on pain of death.'

'Maybe it's better if you stay behind,' Ulrich said. 'I have a special task I need someone to do. You can be that man.'

He leaned close to Wulfhelm and muttered quick words in his ear. Einar saw the Saxon raise his eyebrows in surprise, then nod.

'But what will be my excuse for not going with them?' Wulfhelm said in a whisper.

'I don't know,' Ulrich said. 'Make something up. You're a Saxon – say you need to visit your old aunt who lives in Jorvik or something.'

'What are you two whispering about?' Godwine asked.

Ulrich turned to him.

'We were just wondering what Jorvik has done now to warrant the presence of King Aethelstan himself,' he said, wearing his most provoking of smiles.

'He has some business to attend to here in Jorvik,' Godwine said.

Ulrich and Skar exchanged meaningful glances. What that meaning was, however, remained hidden to everyone else on the ship. Einar bit his lip, trying to control the frustration at not being let into the secret of whatever Ulrich was planning.

'Let's get going,' Godwine said. 'These warriors are just here to ensure we have safe and rapid passage through the city to where the king is.'

'Ensure we don't run off, more like,' Einar said.

'Easy lads,' Ulrich said to his crew. 'This could be to our advantage. We'll go along with it. Be on your best behaviour. Try not to kill anyone unless I tell you to.'

The others nodded but no one looked too pleased with the situation. They started to gather the last of their belongings together.

'You won't need helmets, mail or shields,' Godwine said. 'Aethelstan's army is here and will make sure the streets of Jorvik are a safe place.'

Seeing the Wolf Coats hesitate, he added, 'What are you scared of? Aethelstan and Hakon are allies. You shouldn't enter a friendly city dressed for war.'

With unsure expressions, the Wolf Coats set down their personal protection and filed down the gangr plank off the ship. Roan stayed behind.

'I stay with my ship,' he said, in response to Godwine's questioning glance. 'I always stay with my ship. Someone could try to steal it. And the port master needs to be paid for the mooring.'

Godwine looked at the skipper for a long moment, as if trying to assess if the wizened little Frisian was telling the truth or not.

'Are you sure?' he said then. 'There will probably be feasting. You'll miss that.'

'Fine by me,' Roan said. 'Rich food plays havoc with my guts.'

Beaduheard stepped forward as if to run up the gangr plank but Godwine halted him by slapping the back of his left hand across his chest.

'It's all right,' he said, casting a nervous look at the Wolf Coats around him, who had once again tensed for action. 'If he wants to miss the feast that's his choice.'

'I won't be going either,' Wulfhelm said.

Godwine frowned.

'I've been stuck on a ship with these God damned Danes for days,' Wulfhelm said in his own tongue. 'I need to get away from them for a bit. And I could do with the company of a woman.'

Godwine grinned and clapped a hand on Wulfhelm's shoulder. He said something in the Saxon tongue and they both laughed. Even without the little knowledge of Saxon that Einar had gained while living in Jorvik, he could have guessed the meaning was something like *I know what you mean, friend.*

Wulfhelm trotted off down the jetty, then the rest of them set off into the city leaving Roan alone on the ship.

Einar noticed straight away that the Saxon warriors fell in before and behind Ulrich's crew. There was little doubt this was an escort, but whether it was one for prisoners or honoured guests, it was hard to tell.

They made their way up the wooden walkway from the river and into the city itself. It was less than a year since Einar had been in Jorvik but he was amazed to find that even in that short time the city had changed, spreading out even more streets and houses beyond the walls. It was late afternoon and the noise and stench that surrounded them was at first disorientating. The air was thick with smoke from fires, the smell of beer malting and the ever-present reek of piss that rose from the foul ditches that ran along the sides of the walkways between them and the shops and houses on each side. Einar tried not to look at the black sludge, heavy with all sorts of foul waste, human and animal, along with offal and other detritus of city life that flowed slowly downhill to empty into the river.

Merchants shouted to attract customers to the wares they laid out on tables in front of their wooden houses. Skar had said on the journey that in Jorvik you could buy anything your heart desired from anywhere in the world that you could imagine. Looking at the vast array of goods on sale it looked very much like he was right. Beautiful leatherwork, superb copper workings – bowls, drinking cups and all sorts of table and ritual ware – as well as other types of metalwork and cloth of all kinds from rough un-dyed grey wool cloaks brought from Iceland to the shimmering, magic-like cloth known as silk from the distant eastern lands beyond Serkland; all were on offer at one shop or the next.

There was jewellery and precious stones for sale, as well as wood and stone carvings. There were also animals on sale and the squawks and grunts of geese, chickens, ducks and pigs added to the general cacophony as buyers tried to negotiate better prices with the merchants who sat behind their tables, their scales for weighing either Saxon pennies or the hacked up pieces of silver, copper and lead used to pay for the goods.

'I like this place already,' Surt said. 'The people here don't stare at me like they've seen one of your trolls.'

'Folk come to Jorvik from all over the world to trade, Surt,' Ulrich said. 'A man with different coloured skin is not a strange sight here.'

Children ran through the crowds thronging the walkways, as if playing a game of tag. As soon as he saw them Einar dropped his hand to the purse tied to his belt. He knew well that the nimble fingers of those same children could snatch the purses of unwary passers-by without them even knowing it was gone.

As before, Einar was amazed at the sheer number of people around him in the city. He had been told once that five thousand people were crammed inside Jorvik's ancient walls. It seemed an enormous number, too big to be believed. It was more than the whole population of Iceland where he grew up. Now, right in the midst of the throng, he could well believe it.

Something else that was different from the last time Einar had been in Jorvik was the number of Saxon warriors. They had been there before, but they had been mostly guarding Kings Gard or the city walls. Today they were a visible presence throughout the streets, stationed at crossways or patrolling the streets in their red cloaks and plumed helmets. Einar surmised that the presence of so many of them was to guard Aethelstan. The surly looks the citizens of Jorvik, who were mostly of Norse descent, cast in their direction gave Jorvik an atmosphere of a city that was occupied by a foreign force.

Another difference was the direction they were heading in.

'Are we not going to Kings Gard?' Einar said. 'I would have thought that is where Aethelstan would be.'

'The king is at the Minster,' Godwine said. 'This is Holy Month. King Aethelstan is staying with the monks and hears the Mass sung every day.'

Einar knew of the building the locals called the 'Minster' but had never been inside it himself. Still it was hard to miss for anyone in Jorvik. It was a vast Christian church that sat within the largely Norse city like an island in the midst of a hostile sea.

The Saxon warriors escorted them on into the city until Einar saw the huge building rising above all the others. It was taller and longer than everything around it and made of stone, rather than wood and wattle. Its roof was covered with red tiles, rather than thatch, though here and there some had gone, revealing dark holes. Like Kings Gard, it was so tall as to invoke dizziness. It had one tower that rose well above even the huge Minster itself from which was often heard the strange metal clanging of Christian bells.

Like a fortress built to keep the heathen city dwellers out, the Minster had a palisade around it. Here there were more Saxon warriors than ever. They stood on the ramparts of the palisade, stood guard at the gate or patrolled the streets outside. King Aethelstan, it seemed to Einar, had come to the city with a small army.

'I think we can see how safe Aethelstan feels among his loyal subjects in Jorvik,' Ulrich said, surveying the ranks of warriors.

Godwine shot an irritated glance in his direction.

'Wait here,' he said, walking up to the lead warrior of the company who guarded the gate in the palisade.

While the Saxons talked in their own tongue, Einar took a look at the merchant stalls on the other side of the street. They were like the others, though he noticed a predominance of Christian artefacts, designed to attract the visitors to the big church. One stall directly opposite the gate was selling jewellery and other metalwork. The metal worker himself was casting amulets behind the stall while a blonde-haired woman – probably his wife – dealt with the customers. Einar noticed with a wry smile that the mould the craftsman poured the glowing red molten metal into had holes set in it for casting both Christian crosses and *Mjölnir*, the hammer of Thor. Business was business, it seemed, even in matters of religion.

Godwine rejoined them.

'We can go in,' he said. 'The king is in church but will be finished soon.'

He led the way through the gate in the palisade and into a courtyard beyond. Now right beside the towering building it was even more intimidating. Einar looked up at it, feeling a churning in his guts at the sight of its impossibly high walls. He could not understand how something built of stone could stand so tall. Surely the weight of it should bring it crashing down? Yet, like Kings Gard, the Minster remained standing. Einar concluded that it must have been built by the same Roman Giants who were responsible for the other stone wonders found in Britain.

The stones of the walls were washed with white paint that made the building stand out even more against the drab colours of the city around it. The tower was painted with what looked like, to Einar's surprise, scenes of torture and killing. One showed the Christian cross but there appeared to be a naked man impaled on it, his blood streaming down his arms and legs from a wound on the side of his chest. There were other pictures showing more atrocities, the bright red paint the blood was painted with making them even more lurid. Einar surmised they must be some sort of warning, designed to make anyone planning on attacking the Minster to think twice about what might happen to them.

Inside the palisade it was like stepping into another world. As the gate closed behind them it felt like the hustle and noise of the city was left outside. Even the Saxon warriors who surrounded them fell into a reverential hush. A strange calm filled the air. From somewhere inside the vast building drifted the sound of singing, the sort Einar had once heard the Christian witches known as nuns perform inside Kings Gard. It was haunting and ethereal and evoked a feeling within him as if he were distracted or in a trance. He was so captivated by the beauty of the sound he found it hard to think.

'That noise makes your skin crawl, doesn't it?' Ulrich said.

Einar shook his head as if a bucket of cold water had been dumped over it. There were closed double doors in the front of the Minster that looked about tall enough for a man on a horse to ride through. However Godwine did not take them in through these. Instead, they went around the Minster, continuing along a side wall until they came to another stone building set at right angles to the church though still attached to the main church by a short passageway. Its walls were shorter than the Minster's, though they had very tall openings in them covered with the clear, hard substance called glass. Einar marvelled at how much money the Saxons and their churches had. Glass was unbelievably expensive, so much so as to be way beyond the means of any normal household to afford even a small piece, yet here were vast boards of the stuff, reaching nearly from the ground up beyond the second storey of the stone building.

Godwine led them to the door of this building and then inside.

'We will wait for the king here,' he said, then walked off towards the other end of the room they had entered. They turned around but saw the horde of Saxon warriors who had accompanied them from the harbour had filed in behind them and spread out, blocking any thoughts of going back outside again.

Einar looked around. It was a very strange place. It was long and tall, like a vast feasting hall of a great lord, though the light that gushed in through the tall, glass-covered openings, even on a dull day like that one, illuminated the interior far more than any jarl could even dream of. The Winds' Eye, the one hole at the top of the gable wall of Norse houses was more for letting smoke out than the sun in.

Every inch of the walls was covered by shelves that were stacked full of either round rolls of what looked like parchment or else odd objects that appeared to be large leather boxes. There were tables set beneath each of the tall windows, and at each one sat one of the Christian wizards called monks, identifiable by the rough, plain wool robes they wore and their weird hairstyles where the tops of their heads had been shaved to look like they were going bald.

Einar could not understand this. The thing he most dreaded about getting old was the probability that he would one day lose his hair. What woman would even look at him then? Yet these Christians seemed to want to hasten towards that day. Ulrich said they hated life in general and perhaps this was part of their general denial of it.

Each monk sat hunched over something on the table before him. They had big feathers in their hands and seemed to be wafting them across whatever it was. Einar assumed it was some strange Christian ritual.

'It's a library!' Surt said. He was gazing around him open-mouthed, his eyes wide with surprise and delight. 'I have not been in one of these since I was in the library of the Ymir in al-Andalus.'

'You know what this is?' Einar said.

'Of course,' Surt said. 'It's a storeroom for books but more than that, it's a storeroom of wisdom. The answer to all the questions you will ever have about the world can be found within these four walls.'

Einar frowned, looking at the leather boxes and rolls of parchment and wondering how that could be. Where would the answers lie and who would speak them?

'So that's how they do it,' Ulrich said.

He was standing beside the nearest table. The young monk sitting before it was looking up at the wolfskin-clad viking with a worried expression on his face. Ulrich plucked the feather from his hand and held it up, examining the tip which had been sliced into a tapering point that was coated in a red coloured liquid. The fingers of the monk's hand were also dyed with several different colours. Einar looked and saw a rectangular piece of parchment lay on the table before the monk. It was half covered in regular, neat lines of the runes the Christians used, each one tiny and of equal size so many, many of them fitted onto the parchment.

'I've seen these before,' Ulrich said. 'The monasteries have them. They stack lots of these parchments on top of each other and bind them together with leather. That's what those things on the shelves are.'

'They are called books,' Surt said.

'One thing I learned early as a lad on viking raids,' Ulrich said, 'was that the Christians valued them more than people. If you took one of those they would pay a ransom to get it back ten times what you would get for a man, woman or child. I always wondered how they made them. It looks like this is how. They use these feather things.'

'He's copying out the wisdom held in another book,' Surt said, gesturing towards the nervous monk. 'That way the knowledge is preserved and passed on. That is why they are more valuable than gold.'

The norsemen looked at him, incomprehension in all their expressions.

'Well, it's certainly faster than carving out runes on a stone, I'll give them that,' Ulrich said. 'This could be very useful indeed.'

Ulrich spoke in an absentminded way as if there was another conversation going on inside his head. He dropped the feather and it fell onto the parchment, scattering splashes of the coloured liquid across it. The young monk cried out in what sounded like a mixture of rage and dismay. He jumped up, grabbing a rag and started trying to wipe up the spatters from the parchment.

'We have many libraries where I come from,' Surt said. 'But I did not believe such places existed in the benighted northern realms. All of a sudden I am excited to meet this King Aethelstan.'

'That's good,' Godwine said. He had walked back to rejoin them. 'Because I am now taking you to meet him. Follow me. I am to take you to the *Rex Anglorum* and Emperor of Britain.'

Twenty-One

'The king has finished prayers in the Minster,' Godwine said. 'We're to meet him in the refectory. However you must leave all your weapons here.'

'Aethelstan must have half his army here,' Ulrich said with a sneer. 'What's he scared of?'

'Treachery,' Godwine said, his tone serious.

'How do we know they'll still be here when we get back?' Skar said.

'They won't,' Godwine said. 'You will be staying here at the Minster tonight. All your belongings will be brought to a room set aside for you.'

The Wolf Coats looked at Ulrich, who shrugged.

'Very well,' he said. 'It's not like we couldn't kill Aethelstan with our bare hands if we wanted to.'

He sent a provoking grin in Godwine's direction who just shook his head.

The Wolf Coats and Surt took off their swords and knives and set them on one of the tables, then, when he was satisfied that they no longer bore arms, Godwine led them to the pair of double doors set in the wall at the far end of the library. He opened them, revealing that they led into the Minster church beyond. Einar and the others filed through into the towering space beyond with the company of warriors tramping behind them.

Einar had never been inside a building so large. He gaped at the beams of the roof that soared above, wondering how far they were from the clouds in the sky and how they even managed to stay up. The sight made him dizzy and a little nauseous. The walls were whitewashed and painted with all sorts of brightly coloured pictures, some depicting people or strange winged beings and some depicting horrible monsters and dragons that seemed to be devouring naked humans. Einar had heard all sorts of outlandish tales of just what it was the Christians believed but he had always dismissed them. His mother had been one and he could not picture that gentle woman as participating in such horrors. Looking at those paintings now, however, he began to wonder if some of those tales were not in fact true.

There were candles everywhere. The air smelled of melting bees' wax. A group of monks were standing near a stone table, singing together. The sheer enchanting beauty of the music they wove contrasted in a disconcerting way with the monsters painted on the walls.

The Wolf Coats cast greedy stares in the direction of the gold and silver treasure laid across the stone table. There was a big gold cross, studded with rubies and emeralds. A silver platter and a tall drinking goblet, made of gold and again encrusted with precious gems rested alongside the cross.

Godwine led them across the building to another door on the far wall. This he opened with a flourish and stepped aside. He nodded to the Saxon warriors and ten of them trooped past and into the room.

'Now you,' he said to Ulrich. The Wolf Coats and Surt went inside.

They entered a long room that to Einar was like the feasting hall of a noble lord except that there were painted wooden crosses on the walls. Two very long tables with benches on either side ran the entire length of the room. Here too there were many candles but their aroma was mixed with the enticing smell of food.

There was a high table on a raised dais which ran across the width of the room and at it sat three men, one of whom Einar recognised as King Aethelstan.

Einar had met Aethelstan twice before, once right here in Jorvik, and the king had not changed much since then. He was at least as tall as Einar but much more slender. He was good- looking and though not an old man, the lines on his face and the white strands that streaked the brown of his braided hair and long, Aenglish-style moustache showed he had passed many more winters on Middle Earth than Einar had. His green cloak was of the finest wool, as was his linen shirt.

The other two men at the table both wore the clothes of Christian wizards. From the amount of embroidery on their robes and the gold, gem-encrusted crosses they wore around their necks, Einar judged that they were important.

While their dress was similar, their personal appearance was very different. The man on the right was as tall as Aethelstan. While his red hair was shaved on the top in the way of Christian monks, he also had a long, braided beard. He was older than Einar but younger than Aethelstan and if it were not for the Christian robes and haircut, Einar would have said the man was Norse like himself.

His companion was much older, looking like he had lived perhaps fifty or more winters. He was shorter than most and his crown too was shaved, though it was surrounded by a thick mop of white, curly hair. Unlike nearly everyone else he was clean-shaven. Einar also saw the man wore a cross amulet on a leather thong around his neck, carved of some sort of pitch-black wood and polished until it shone. The last person Einar had seen wearing a similar black cross was the Irish monk, Michan, whom they had rescued from King Eirik's fortress at Avaldsnes.

Aethelstan looked up when the newcomers entered. For a few moments he regarded them with a cool, appraising eye as silence descended on the room. The ten Saxon warriors stood watching, hands hovering near their sword hilts.

'So, we meet again,' Aethelstan said, rising to his feet. When he did so the other two men stood up as well. 'Your Graces, we shall have to speak in the tongue of the Norse, I'm afraid. I doubt these lot know much Latin. Archbishop Wulfstan, I know that will be no problem for you, but what about you, Abbot Dub Inse?'

'I know their tongue,' the monk with the curly white hair said, though the expression on his face suggested he was not that happy with using it. He spoke with the same accent as the Irish chieftain who had once held Einar hostage.

'Let me begin by introducing the Lady Affreca, daughter of King Guthfrith of Dublin,' Aethelstan said.

He held a hand out towards Affreca, beckoning her to step forward. She did so and Einar noted the expressions of surprise on the two men in Christian robes beside Aethelstan. It was clear they had not expected a princess of the Kingdom of Dublin to be clad in breeches, a wolf pelt cloak and a leather jerkin stained with the oil of the brynja she often wore over it.

'And the others?' the red-haired monk said.

'This is Ulrich Rognisson,' Aethelstan said, gesturing towards Ulrich. 'Former liegeman of King Eirik of Norway. The others are his company of nun-murdering werewolves.'

'Úlfhéðnar?' the red-haired monk said. 'My grandmother told me tales of such warriors when I was a boy. Dangerous men indeed, but useful too.'

'Really Bishop Wulfstan,' Aethelstan shook his head, 'sometimes I wonder whose side you are really on. Among this crew you will find Einar, son of the late Jarl Thorfinn of Orkney. I believe you are responsible for your father's death?'

Einar nodded.

'And what is this?' Aethelstan said, turning to Surt. 'I see you have been joined by someone from the lands that lie far to the south. You are indeed far from home, friend. How did you fall into this bad company?'

'It's a long story, Lord King,' Surt said.

'Well if we have time I would love to hear it,' Aethelstan said, gesturing towards the other seats at the table. 'Sit down all of you. We are about to eat and there is much to discuss.'

'Patricide is a mortal sin, Lord Aethelstan,' the Irish monk said, looking at Einar. 'A father-killer, a black man and a band of werewolf warriors no doubt in the service of the Devil himself. This is a fine band of *phágánaigh*, sinners and murderers you have brought here, King Aethelstan. Do you really expect us to eat with these heathens?'

'Did our Lord Jesus not sit down and break bread with

whores, tax collectors and sinners?' Aethelstan said. 'Who are we to judge, Dub Inse?'

The monk folded his arms and put his head to the side.

'A bishop and an abbot, eh?' Ulrich said, looking from Dub Inse to Wulfstan. 'Let me assure you, it's just as distasteful for myself, a follower of Odin, to sit down with high chieftains of Christian lies.'

He ignored the glare Aethelstan shot in his direction as he took a seat at the table.

'My lady, welcome,' Aethelstan said as Affreca plonked herself down into a chair. 'I am so glad you have decided to accept Hakon's proposal.'

'I wouldn't rush to any conclusions yet, Lord King,' Affreca said. 'My being here has more to do with my interest in Jorvik than Hakon.'

'Abbot Dub Inse here is a fellow Irishman,' Aethelstan said, referring to the white-haired monk with the black cross. 'He is the head of the great monastery of Bangor. That's Bangor the Greater, in Ireland, not the one in the kingdom of the Welsh named after it. Perhaps you already know each other?'

Both Affreca and the Irishman scowled. Einar was uncertain which one of them looked more displeased.

'I've never been to the north,' Affreca said, her tone dismissive.

'Your forefathers have,' the abbot of Bangor said. 'They burned our abbey and stole its treasures. They shook the relics of the blessed Saint Comgall from its shrine. Their souls now burn in Hell for all eternity for those crimes.'

The doors of the room opened and a large group of Christian monks flowed in. They all had the same tonsured head shaving and wore the same, hooded, ground-length tunics of un-dyed wool with wide sleeves, belted at the waist with a piece of rope. Einar could not help thinking they looked like slaves and not for the first time, felt a pang of guilt at what had happened to the slaves in Orkney.

The monks settled on the benches of the other tables in the room, several of them casting wary or surprised glances at the sight of the vikings sitting beside the king at the top table. When everyone was seated, an expectant hush fell on the room.

In the silence, Einar looked around him, marvelling at the incongruity of the situation he found himself in. Here he was, a member of a crew of Norse wolf warriors dedicated to Odin, surrounded by Saxon warriors and Christian monks. They were right at the heart of what they called 'civilisation' but also completely at the mercy of Aethelstan, the most powerful king in the northern world, a man who had dedicated his life to opposing the heathen Gods Ulrich's crew represented.

He had no idea what conversation lay ahead over this meal. One thing was sure, however, they would have to watch their tongues. One wrong word and everything could go very wrong, very quickly.

Twenty-Two

The red-haired bishop, the one who Aethelstan had called Wulfstan, stood up and spread his arms wide. All the monks in the room, as well as Aethelstan and Dub Inse, closed their eyes, bowed their heads and clasped their hands together before themselves.

Bishop Wulfstan began intoning words in a tongue Einar did not understand. He felt the hairs rise on the back of his neck at the thought that they were in the midst of some sort of Christian magic ritual. Then Wulfstan spoke a final word that all the others echoed and the spell was broken. All opened their eyes, looked around and conversation started.

A monk approached with a large pewter jug.

'Wine?' Aethelstan said. 'They have excellent ale here too if you would prefer. The monks are superb brewers.'

Ulrich held up the glazed clay cup from the table before him.

'Odin only drinks wine,' he said. 'So it's fine by me.'

The monk poured ruby red liquid from his jug into all their cups. Einar would indeed have preferred ale but he did not want to say anything among such exalted company. He felt uneasy at the arrogant expression on Ulrich's face and hoped he would not continue to provoke Aethelstan too much. They were obvious opponents, but not currently overt ones, and Einar could not help but question the wisdom of antagonising the King of the Aenglish while they were in his power and at his mercy.

No doubt Ulrich thought Odin was watching him, assessing his bravery for possible admission into Valhalla. The thought made Einar even more uneasy.

'I owe you that drink, son,' Aethelstan said to him, 'for removing your father from the great game board. He was quite a player, I have to say. But totally untrustworthy. No one could be sure whose side he was ever on. Perhaps that's a lesson you should learn if you are ever to take his place.'

Einar felt as if the dark brown eyes of the king were looking deep inside him, assessing him, measuring his worth. For the first time he realised that if he had managed to hold on to his father's high seat, if Eirik had not taken it, he would now be a rival of these powerful men at the table, an opponent in the game of power, instead of a wolfskin-clad landless viking. Perhaps, with his injured hand, not even that. Was he really ready for that kind of challenge? Was he the equal of these men or was Aethelstan now looking at him and thinking: *here is no threat to me. Here is a weak man I can overcome with no effort*? On the other hand, compared to Eirik or his father Thorfinn, Aethelstan himself seemed the mildest of characters.

'You were quite a poet, as I recall,' Aethelstan said. 'Perhaps you can entertain us after dinner?'

Einar held up his maimed hand.

'Unfortunately this injury means I can no longer play the harp, Lord King,' he said. 'My little finger is gone. I cannot play the repeated low notes that support the melody.'

The king nodded. Ulrich frowned.

'If you can't play the harp,' he said, 'I'm surprised you can still wield a sword.'

'But what about that old rascal, Ayvind?' Aethelstan said. 'He was your tutor in skald craft, Einar, wasn't he? Probably drinking Hakon's household dry now, is he?'

'No, lord. After you sent us to our deaths on the quest for the Raven Banner we discovered Ayvind was sent to our ship to deceive us and act as a spy,' Ulrich said. 'So we let him go for a swim, somewhere between Britain and Norway. We haven't seen him since.'

'I see,' Aethelstan said, the smile fading from his lips.

The serving monks brought platters of food to the table. There were lots of small, round loaves of bread as well as mounds of kale, leeks, beetroot and small, purple carrots. There was also fish of all types, some boiled, some roasted and some baked in pastry.

'These monks eat well,' Ulrich said. 'I had heard life was all starving and beating yourself in these monasteries.'

'We've been eating salted fish since we left Norway,' Skar said, a rueful expression on his face. 'I would have thought at this time of year we might have got some venison. The forest teem with deer. At least some meat from the winter slaughter would be welcome.'

'This is Holy Month here in Britain,' Bishop Wulfstan said. 'We pray every day and eat only fish at this time.'

'It's holy month everywhere,' Ulrich said. 'Blood Month. The month of sacrifice. We kill the extra animals and dedicate their blood and spirits to the Gods. What puzzles me is why you supposed Christians still honour this.'

'We honour this month because it was in this month,

many years ago, that the Christian faith first came to our country,' Aethelstan said.

'That's just a story made up to justify why folk follow the customs of their ancestors,' Ulrich said. 'The Angles, Saxons, Jutes once worshipped Odin and Thor just like us. Their names are still in the days of the week you use. But now you call yourselves Aenglish and pretend it never was so. But we remember.'

Aethelstan glared at Ulrich. Einar winced.

'Perhaps, Ulrich, you should also remember where you currently sit,' the king said, a forced smile on his lips. 'Within the realm of the Aenglish. You would do well not to insult their traditions and values. I've told you before, I hate your religion and you and your crew have done great deeds of terrible infamy; however I am prepared to see past that for the time being. This is only because Godwine told me you have done great service to my foster-son, Hakon. My patience has a limit, though.'

'Hakon could do with your help now, too,' Ulrich said, seeming unfazed. 'And not just to get a wife. The last time I saw your fleet of ships it was harrying the north of Scotland. Could they sail a little further north and hit Eirik in Orkney?'

'Unfortunately the fleet has been withdrawn to the south,' Aethelstan said.

'Is Constantine defeated?' Skar said, referring to the King of Alba. 'I'd have thought that wily old Pict would have lasted longer.'

'His kingdom has been reduced to a weakened enough state that he will no longer be a threat,' Aethelstan said. 'Constantine has realised the error of his ways and sworn fealty to me.'

'So you really do rule nearly all of Britain now?' Ulrich said. 'But if the Scots are defeated then why can't you send your ships against Eirik? He's as much a danger to you in Orkney as he is to Hakon in Norway.'

'There is other pressing work to attend to,' Aethelstan said. 'Eirik's move took everyone by surprise. I need to send the fleet to the Kingdom of Brittany.'

'In the land of the Franks?' Ulrich said, shaking his head. 'Is being Emperor of Britain not enough for you?'

'Perhaps if your kind stayed in their own lands,' Aethelstan said, glaring at Ulrich, 'We would not have to fight these endless wars. The fleet is sailing to put Alan, the rightful king of Brittany, back on the throne that was stolen from him by vikings.'

'You'd better watch yourself,' Ulrich said, turning to the Irish monk. 'Or you'll be next.'

'What is an Irishman doing here in Jorvik, meeting with the King of Wessex, anyway?' Affreca said.

'Ireland is a Christian country,' Dub Inse said. 'King Aethelstan is the cornerstone of the Christian Church. He is the bulwark, the shield wall of civilisation in its struggle against the heathens. We have much of common interest. I came here to work with a very great scholar who King Aethelstan was bringing to Jorvik, however it seems the Devil has interfered in that plan.'

'You refused to meet my father when he was King of Dublin,' Affreca said with a sneer. 'Yet you will conspire with foreigners when it suits your own interests.'

Dub Inse leaned across the table, forefinger raised in her direction.

'*You* are the foreigners,' he said, eyes blazing with

vindictiveness. 'Heathens! Pagans! *Gall*. You're like rats that infest our country and some day we'll throw you out. If Lord Aethelstan can help us do that then all the better!'

'Only a Gael would call people who have lived in Ireland for two hundred years, "foreigners",' Affreca said.

'The Irish, eh?' Aethelstan said to the others, rolling his eyes and raising his eyebrows in a comical way.

'Isn't "foreigner" the meaning of the word "Welsh" in your tongue, the tongue of the Saxons, Lord King?' Ulrich said, ignoring Aethelstan's attempt to create some sort of fellow feeling. 'I'd say it takes a certain level of arrogance to call the people who have lived in a country for generations before you did, "foreigners". And by the way, aren't the people of the Kingdom of Brittany you seem to now care so much about, actually descendants of Welshmen your ancestors drove from this land?'

Aethelstan sighed. In a moment his whole demeanour changed. His face no longer held even a pretence of friendliness. The king made an almost imperceptible movement, a mere flick of his head. A moment later all ten of the Saxon warriors in the room had drawn their swords and had their points levelled on the Wolf Coats. One of them let out a loud whistle. The door burst open and many more warriors poured in. The monks looked on in surprise and horror. The Wolf Coats and Surt were surrounded by warriors, spear points pressed into their backs and chests, sword blades held across their throats. Einar looked up to see two warriors, their spears pressing into the dips between his collar bone and the bottom of his neck. Their eyes looked into his, unflinching and cold, and he knew all Aethelstan had to do was speak the order and his life would be over.

For a long moment there was complete silence. Then Aethelstan sat back in his chair.

'I think I've listened to enough of your insolence, Ulrich,' he said. His voice was flat and suddenly without any warmth or emotion. 'I've not forgotten the monastery you raided last year or the monks and nuns you murdered there. You are also heathens, like the many who spill onto our shores like a plague from the northern seas, the same folk who my family have fought for generations. I've tried to be civil with you and all you've responded with is churlish impudence and total lack of respect. I could have you all killed right now. All it will take is one word from me. By rights I should haul you outside and hang you and your bunch of barbarians from the nearest gallows, which is what I wanted to do as soon as I heard you were in Jorvik. However, Godwine tells me you saved Hakon's life and now are engaged on a voyage to attack Eirik in support of my foster-son, a deed of heroic bravery that you may lose your own lives in the course of. I cannot help Hakon as my own fleet is engaged on the expedition to Brittany so I will allow you to go on your way. However don't—'

He leaned forward across the table and fixed Ulrich with an icy stare.

'Don't *ever*,' Aethelstan went on, 'mistake my civility and good manners for weakness. And if you continue to disrespect me or these two venerable men of our Church then I will have you dragged out into the market in Jorvik and strung up like the heathen dogs you are and Hakon will just have to find another way to deal with Eirik. Now – do we understand each other?'

Ulrich nodded.

Einar knew that one of the names of Odin was *Grimr*: the masked one. Looking at Aethelstan now, Einar understood that the usual, mild-mannered mask the king usually wore had slipped off, revealing the ruthless, determined ruler beneath.

'Good,' Aethelstan said, assuming his previous congenial demeanour. 'Now let's finish our meal like civilised folk.'

He nodded to the lead man of his warriors and the tension in the room dissolved. The warriors relaxed and lowered their weapons. Ulrich reached up and pushed the tip of the blade pressed against his throat away with a disdainful finger, looking up at the warrior who held it as he did so.

'As for the Welsh you speak of,' Aethelstan said, breaking a piece of bread, 'they were an unworthy people who had fallen into sin. Five hundred years ago the Almighty Lord chose our people to inherit this land. As He sent the Assyrians to punish the sinful Children of Israel, he sent us across the northern sea to take this island and make it bloom. Cerdic, my own forefather, came here with five ships and forged a new kingdom, Wessex, guided by the hand of the Almighty. He was a heathen, yes, and the Welsh never deigned even to try to teach him or his folk the truth about the One True God. That is the crime they must bear the guilt for. God did not forget his chosen people though. He moved the blessed Pope, Gregory to send a mission to Britain to teach our people about Christ. That is why we no longer worship the idols you do.'

'Thank you for the lesson in the lore of your people,' Ulrich said. Some of his former sarcasm remained but Einar could see the little man was taken aback and he found it hard to keep a little smirk from his lips. The danger of the situation had nearly been worth it to see Ulrich taken down a peg or two.

'You're welcome,' Aethelstan said. 'Now: tell me about this voyage to Orkney you are on and how you intend to make things uncomfortable for Eirik.'

Ulrich began talking. As he listened, Einar began to realise that Ulrich did not in fact have much of a plan at all. Not for the first time he wondered if Ulrich's first intention was to find a glorious death rather than it be a potential consequence of the mission.

'Well you have guts I'll give you that,' Aethelstan said when Ulrich was finished. 'Eight of you against all of Eirik's army.'

'Fate will decree what should happen,' Ulrich said with a shrug. 'And there are nine of us, Lord King, not eight.'

'I'm afraid it will have to be eight,' Aethelstan said. 'The Lady Affreca is too important to our plans to go on this voyage. It's not likely you will return alive.'

'Suicide is a mortal sin, Lord King,' the Irishman said. 'It is not to be encouraged.'

'Affreca is part of my crew,' Ulrich said. There was a note of consternation in his voice. 'She is key to our plans. I need her and her bow.'

'The answer is no,' Aethelstan said. Einar saw the hard glint return to the king's eye.

Einar looked at Affreca. She looked confused.

'Isn't it up to her?' Ulrich said.

Aethelstan just shook his head.

'The Lady Affreca is of royal blood,' he said. 'She will understand how important it is she stays here to prepare for her marriage. She has much to learn.'

'I must insist—' Ulrich began.

'No, Ulrich, *I* must insist,' the king said. 'Or shall I get my warriors to remind you again just who is in charge here? I wish you well in your journey but the Lady Affreca will not be going on it with you.'

Einar felt a surge of sudden panic in his heart as he realised that this could be the last time he might see Affreca. He longed to say something to her, to at least say farewell even, but she was seated several places away and there were people between them.

After the meal they would part. She would stay here in Jorvik, marry Hakon and become Queen. He would sail to Orkney, perhaps to his death, perhaps not. Either way their worlds would be separated and threads of their lives that had been woven together for the last couple of years would be parted forever.

Twenty-Three

Affreca awoke, unsure of what had brought her out of sleep. She sighed. It had taken long enough to get to sleep in the first place, and now she was awake again. It was dark so must still be the middle of the night.

After the meal earlier she had been separated from the others. The Wolf Coats had been given their own room somewhere else in the Minster but Aethelstan and the bishops had balked at the idea that Affreca should not share a room with men she was not married to. The fact that she had shared a ship with the same men for most of the last year did not sway them and she had been marched off to a room on her own, accompanied by several of Aethelstan's warriors just to make sure she went where she was told to.

The room she had been assigned was set aside for wealthy guests visiting the Minster and was on the ground floor, down a short corridor near the library. To her surprise, there were maid servants waiting for her in the room. There was a tub of hot water for her to bathe in and clothes – beautiful dresses and a long linen nightgown – that were fresh and clean in comparison to the sweat-soaked, lice-ridden breeches and oil and rust smeared leather jerkin she had been wearing for the last month. After a long, luxurious soak in the washing tub the maids had combed her hair and she had pulled on the nightgown. The servants then left her as she sank into the utter comfort of the warm, soft bed that was about as far removed from the hard, continuously undulating deck of the ship she had been sleeping on as you could get.

If this was Aethelstan giving her a taste of what it would be like to rule in Jorvik then it was not too bad.

Sleep however, had not come easily. Was she really doing the right thing? The thought of ruling a kingdom that was her birthright was a strong pull, but at what cost? Would she just be a bird trapped in a golden cage? A subordinate of Hakon, her clan name of Ivarsson used to legitimise his rule to the Norse folk of the Kingdom of Jorvik? Or rather Aethelstan's rule, for he was the real power. Meanwhile Ulrich's Wolf Coats would be sailing off on glorious adventures and perhaps performing deeds the fame of which poets would sing about for generations to come. Could she really let Einar and the others go off without her?

Eventually the warmth and softness of the bed had overcome her restless mind and she had drifted off to sleep.

Now she was awake again. Why?

A tapping came from the door and she understood what had woken her. It was insistent but light, as if whoever was knocking wanted to get her attention inside the room while at the same time trying not to make too much noise.

Affreca got out of bed and padded to the door, moving carefully in the dark so as not to stub her toes. She was about to open it when a memory of Ulrich came to her. He had not just taught weapon craft, war craft and stealth craft. When times were quiet he loved to impart the wisdom of Odin. One of his pieces of advice was: *Be cautious at a doorway. Who knows what waits on the other side?*

She had no weapons and the room was too dark to find anything so instead she moved to the side of the door and flattened herself against the wall. Reaching out Affreca pulled the latch and let the door swing open.

The insistent knocking ceased and someone pushed their head through the threshold.

'Lady Affreca?' a man's voice said. He spoke in a hoarse whisper.

Affreca realised it was the red-haired monk who had earlier eaten with them.

'Bishop Wulfstan?' she said. 'What is the meaning of this? It's the middle of the night.'

'I need to talk to you,' the monk said. 'In private. Away from King Aethelstan at least. This is the only way I can think of getting you on your own. It would not be good if a bishop was found alone with a beautiful young woman in her room at night. Perhaps you could come with me for a walk outside?'

Affreca was intrigued, though still cautious. The monk did not look like much if it came to a fight, however, and she felt confident enough that she could deal with him if he tried anything.

'Very well,' she said and slipped outside to join him. The corridor had torches burning low in brackets attached to the walls which provided enough light for them to see where they were going as Wulfstan led the way to a door at the far end, then out into the cool darkness of the deserted courtyard outside. Affreca still only wore the linen nightgown and straight away regretted not lifting her jerkin as well.

'Aethelstan's warriors have finally gone to bed, I see,' she said.

'There are plenty on watch,' Wulfstan said, still speaking in a hushed whisper. 'But they guard the perimeter of the Minster. We don't have a lot of time though. The monks will be up for their first morning prayers soon.'

'Well? What's all this creeping around in the dark about?' Affreca said, hugging herself to try to keep warm.

'I had to talk to you, my lady,' the bishop said, locking eyes with her in an earnest stare. 'I need to be sure in my own conscience that you know everything about why you are here in Jorvik.'

'Go on,' Affreca said.

'You asked what the Irishman, Bishop Dub Inse was doing here,' Wulfstan said. 'Which is an astute question. He is here primarily because of your brother.'

'Olaf?' Affreca said. 'What about him?'

'Since he took over the throne of Dublin from your late father – God rest his soul – Olaf has been trying to make his mark,' Wulfstan said. 'He has either went to war with, or forged alliances with, powerful kings in Ireland and beyond.'

'I know,' Affreca said. 'He tried to marry me off to Einar's father as part of a deal with him. Luckily that didn't work or I would be a widow already.'

'The bishop of Bangor has brought news from Ireland that your brother has his eyes on the throne of Jorvik,' Bishop Wulfstan said.

'Why wouldn't he?' Affreca said. 'It rightfully belongs to the Ivarssons. Aethelstan stole it from my father.'

'You need to understand my lady,' Wulfstan said, 'that by marrying Hakon and taking the throne of Jorvik you will be putting yourself in direct conflict with your own brother. And not just a dispute. It will someday lead to open war.'

'There is no love between my brother and I,' Affreca said.

'Dub Inse says that now Eirik Bloody Axe has taken Thorfinn's realm in Orkney,' Wulfstan said, 'Olaf of Ireland and he are already planning some sort of alliance.'

Affreca recalled an observation Einar had once made around how powerful Aethelstan was just through his faith. But it was not his God that brought the advantage, it was how it gave him access to a network of allies and spies in the monks and priests who were connected throughout his own realm and that of his enemies. They all understood a common tongue: Latin. Aethelstan had no need of *spae-wives*, wizards or wise men to advise him. He knew all his opponents moves even as they made them, sometimes before.

'The other thing you must realise,' Wulfstan said, 'is that Aethelstan will insist on your baptism into our faith. Your marriage will be carried out by me, as archbishop, in the Minster.'

'I would have thought you would be pleased with that?' Affreca said.

'I am simply here to make sure you are aware of all the facts,' Wulfstan said.

'I may just be a simple girl, Bishop Wulfstan,' Affreca said, her voice heavy with sarcasm, 'but I can't help thinking there is more to this meeting than just that.'

The bishop took a swift look around to check there was no one else there, then turned back to Affreca.

'The thing is,' he said, 'I don't believe the king's plan will work. You may be an Ivarsson but Aethelstan will never allow someone of your clan to rule here in their own right, never mind that you're a woman. It would be too dangerous for him. Hakon will be the real king but the people will not accept him any more than Aethelstan. Hakon ruled here before as jarl and the folk did not take to him. The folk of Northumberland and Jorvik are a proud people, who honour their Norse forefathers. Hakon is a son of Harald Fairhair but he left Norway as a baby. He grew up in Aethelstan's court. He's as Aenglish as he is Norse and the ordinary folk see him as little more than Aethelstan's lap dog.'

'Why are you telling me all this?' Affreca said.

'It's partly for my own sake,' Wulfstan said with a heavy sigh. 'And for the sake of my congregation. Jorvik is not just the seat of my bishopric. It is my home. I was born not far from here and I have to live here. Aethelstan can troop into Jorvik surrounded by his army and impose his will through the strength of his warriors, but when he leaves and takes them with him, I will still be here, surrounded only by the monks here in the Minster. I have to run a See here and maintain a church among a folk who are unhappy as it is with their new Aenglish masters and always on the verge of rebellion. I don't need one more thing to provoke them. They have had enough provocation already and this final thing could be the last spark needed to ignite the flames.'

'Don't you think you should tell Aethelstan your thoughts on this?' Affreca said.

The bishop made a face.

'When the king believes he is right he does not always welcome other opinions,' he said.

'You mean you don't have the balls to tell him something he might not want to hear,' Affreca said.

'I don't need to anger Aethelstan,' Wulfstan said. 'The king does not fully trust me anyway, and not because of what you think. My father was Eadwulf, a Saxon thane of Northumbria but my mother was Hervor Yngvisdottir, of the line of Halfdan Ragnarsson.'

Affreca started, looking at the bishop with new eyes. Halfdan was the brother of Ivar the Boneless, the son of Ragnar who had founded her own clan. Aethelstan may have his web of priests that crossed the whale roads but there was another mesh just as strong that had been woven across the northern seas. That of blood.

'So we are cousins?' she said with a smile. 'I wonder what Ragnar Loðbrók would make of his descendant the Christian bishop?'

'Look,' Wulfstan said, 'Jorvik has only been part of Aethelstan's Kingdom of Aenglalonde for eight years. For a century before that it was ruled by Norse kings – descendants of the sons of Ragnar; Ivar, Halfdan and Ubbe. Who knows? Perhaps someday – maybe someday soon – Norse kings will rule here again.'

'And if they do, you want to make sure you are still bishop here, right?' Affreca said. 'I understand what this is all about now. This is statecraft. This is not about your church. It's about your position.'

'It's *about* avoiding war and all the hardship, pain and

evil that war unleashes,' Wulfstan said. Even in the dark Affreca could sense his angry glare.

The sound of a small bell ringing somewhere inside the Minster made them both start.

'I must go,' Wulfstan said. 'The monks will start rising soon and we can't be seen talking at this time of night. People will be suspicious. My lady, all I ask is that you give thought to what I have told you.'

'I will,' Affreca said. 'And thank you.'

The bishop nodded then hurried off back towards the Minster.

Affreca sighed as she watched him go. There was little chance of her getting back to sleep now. She needed to talk to someone and wondered if Einar was still awake.

Twenty-Four

'Einar, wake up.'

Einar opened his eyes. It was still dark. There was someone leaning over him, shaking his shoulder.

He moaned with displeasure. The warm comfort of the bed he was in had meant he had been enjoying a deep sleep for some time and this interruption was very unwelcome. He opened his mouth to ask what was going on only to find it closed straight away by a hand shoved over it.

'Shh,' the man above him said.

Einar realised it was Skar.

'Get up,' the big man said in a whisper. 'Ulrich wants you in that library place.'

Skar took his hand away from Einar's mouth and he sat up. Skar took a cover off an oil lamp that cast a soft glow around the room.

Scratching his hair, Einar looked around the second storey room they had been given and realised all the others were no longer in the beds they had been lying in when he had gone to sleep. He was the only one still there.

'What's going on? It must be the middle of the night,' he said. 'Where is everyone?'

'Quiet,' Skar whispered. 'We don't want to wake those monks up. Come on.'

With some reluctance, Einar got out of his cosy bed and pulled his breeches on. He already wore his shirt and by the time he pulled his boots on he was ready to go.

Skar set the lamp down on the floor. He pressed a finger to his lips then cocked his head to indicate that they should go. They left the sleeping room and crept out into the corridor outside. Skar looked left and right, then tiptoed down to the stairs.

Einar, wondering what all the secrecy was about, followed. He marvelled at how such a huge man as Skar still managed to move like a cat. The Wolf Coats had taught stealth craft to him and Affreca but Skar, with many years of practice more than the novices, was on another level altogether.

At the bottom of the stairs they stopped once again. Skar cupped a hand behind one ear, trying to catch any possible noises. When none came, he started off again. Einar followed.

They went outside into the courtyard. Skar placed a hand on Einar's chest to stay him as he looked left and right, both trying to see if there was anyone out there and waiting to give anyone that was there a chance to walk into view. When no one did, Skar removed his hand from Einar and set off around the edge of the courtyard, moving in a crouch, staying close to the wall rather than going straight across.

When they got to the doors of the library Skar tapped his knuckles against the wood – a series of three short knocks, then three more. In response, three more light taps came from the inside of the door. Einar knew this was a signal the

Wolf Coats used to recognise each other when in situations where any of them could not identify the other by sight.

There was a click of metal and the library door swung open a crack. Starkad was inside, peering out. He had a drawn knife in one hand.

Satisfied with who was at the door, Starkad opened it fully and let Einar and Skar in. As the door closed behind them Einar looked around. The library was mostly dark, though a couple of oil lamps placed on the floor at either end provided some illumination. Ulrich was there, but there was no sign of Sigurd, Kari or Surt.

'What's going on, Ulrich?' Einar said. He spoke in a whisper but there was anger in his voice. He had had just about enough of the little Wolf Coat's games, plots and secrets, all of which he never seemed to be a part of.

'We have a special guest coming,' Ulrich said. 'I need you to talk to him.'

'Why me?' Einar said.

'Because you have seen something none of the rest of us have,' Ulrich said.

Before Einar could ask further questions, another series of taps came from the door behind them.

'Ah,' Ulrich said. 'It looks like you're just in time.'

Starkad responded then opened the door. A company of five men entered, four of them by their own volition and the fifth very much under duress. Sigurd, Kari, Surt and, to Einar's surprise, Wulfhelm, bundled another man into the room. He had his hands bound behind him but his identity was obscured by a black sack that had been put over his head. He wore a long linen garment that looked very much like a nightshirt and an expensive one at that. Around his middle the nightshirt was stretched almost to bursting and in places it stuck to his body by sweat. Whoever he was, he was very fat.

The Wolf Coats shoved their prisoner forwards. He stumbled across the flagstones, lost his footing and fell to his knees. Einar winced as the man, hands bound behind him, crashed down onto his knees on the hard floor. To his surprise, he did not cry out. Then the muffled grunt from under the sack told him the prisoner was gagged.

'Good work, lads,' Ulrich said. 'How hard was he to snatch?'

'Not hard at all,' Kari said with a shrug. 'Wulfhelm here had watched his house all day. By the time we got there we knew how many guards he had, where they patrolled and when they changed over watch.'

They all spoke in low voices.

'We went in through the roof,' Sigurd said. 'Cut through the thatch while the household was sleeping.'

'Just like I taught you,' Skar said, folding his arms, his chest swelling with pride. 'No one ever guards the roof.'

'He was in bed, snoring away,' Surt said. 'Before he was even half awake we had him bound, gagged and back out the hole in the roof.'

'He's a heavy bastard, though,' Wulfhelm said. 'I was glad we had Surt here with us or we'd never have got him up there and out. The rest of the house never stirred. They probably won't even know he's gone 'til morning.'

'Excellent,' Ulrich said. 'How did you get him past Aethelstan's guards at the gate?'

Sigurd, Kari, Surt and Wulfhelm's expressions of excited pride turned sheepish.

TIM HODKINSON

'That was a bit more tricky,' Sigurd said, looking at the floor.

'We, erm, had to take a couple of them out,' Kari said.

Ulrich rolled his eyes, frowning.

'Are they dead?'

'No,' Wulfhelm said, quickly, 'But they'll be out of action for some time.'

'Look, Ulrich,' Sigurd said. 'I know you said to avoid hurting any of Aethelstan's men but it was impossible to get him in here without injuring at least one of them. They're everywhere. The only way we could get in without alerting them all was to knock a few out.'

'All right, all right,' Ulrich waved his hands in a placatory gesture. 'It means we won't be able to keep what we're up to a secret any more, but once we're through with him we can get going out of here anyway.'

He nodded at the prisoner.

'Speaking of secrets, Ulrich,' Einar said, 'just what are you up to?'

Ulrich turned to Einar, a smile of self-satisfaction on his face so provoking that Einar would have loved to punch him.

'Before you strike at an enemy, lad,' Ulrich said, 'you need to find out all you can about him. Now we know Eirik well. I spent ten winters keeping the bastard alive. But what we don't know about are these special swords he's offering to vikings who come to follow him.'

'We do, though,' Einar said, frowning. 'He's taken the Ulfbehrts we supplied to the slaves.'

'Yes, we know about *those* swords,' Ulrich said in a tone that sounded like he was talking to a child, which did

218

nothing to entice Einar to unclench his fist. 'But what about these other, supposedly even better swords? My entire life has been devoted to war craft and I have not heard of a sword that is superior to an Ulfbehrt. If they exist, they must be new, or a very well-kept secret. It's through the promise of supplying these swords that Eirik is regrowing his strength, so we need to know all about them. What are they? Who makes them? Where is Eirik getting them from?'

'And where do I come into all this?' Einar said.

'You've seen one of these swords,' Ulrich said. 'Which is why I need you to talk to this man.'

He swept a hand in the direction of the hooded, bound man kneeling on the library floor. The captive's chest heaved up and down as he panted for breath.

'If anyone in the world knows about these magic swords,' Ulrich said. 'It will be him.'

Twenty-Five

'Who is he?' Einar asked.

Ulrich nodded to Starkad who pulled the sack off the head of the prisoner. Underneath was a florid face, shiny with sweat and a nose the colour and shape of a ripe plum. The man's long black hair was slick with sweat and plastered to his head and cheeks. His mouth was stuffed with a ball of cloth that was tied around the back of his head to form a gag. His eyes, wide with terror, rolled around the room as he blinked repeatedly, trying to adjust from the darkness of the inside of the sack to the low lighting of the library.

As soon as Einar saw his face he recognised him.

'Ricbehrt,' he said.

'If you want to know about weapons,' Ulrich said. 'Who better to talk to than a weapon merchant? And who better than the biggest weapon merchant on the whale roads?'

The Frank who knelt before them was the richest, most infamous dealer in weapons in the known world. He had no scruples who he sold swords, axes or armour to, sometimes supplying both sides in the same war. From this trade he had grown immensely rich and able to buy and sell weapons at the highest levels of society. Kings and jarls when planning a war would come to Ricbehrt to equip their armies. He was also the original owner of the hoard of Ulfbehrt swords that were currently causing the problems in Orkney and so many had died for in the last year.

It was clear that the recognition was mutual. At the sight of the men standing before him, the weapon merchant's expression changed from fear to apoplectic fury.

'So he survived that swim then?' Einar said. 'I thought it might have killed him.'

The last time he had seen the Merchant of Death – as Ricbehrt was widely known as – they had thrown him off his own ship into the sea off the north coast of Ireland.

'Why?' Skar said, grinning. 'He's as big as a whale. Maybe he can swim like one too.'

'Didn't he work from Dublin?' Einar said.

'Guthfrith chased him out of there.' Skar said. 'When he failed to deliver that hoard of Ulfbehrt swords he promised.'

'Did he promise those swords to everyone?' Einar said, a bemused smile on his face.

'Probably,' Ulrich said. 'And he would have delivered them only to whoever could pay the most. He now does his deals here in Jorvik.'

Einar recalled that indeed he had run into the weapons dealer the last time he had been in Jorvik, just before their voyage in search of the Raven Banner had begun.

'Now, master Ricbehrt,' Ulrich said. 'We're going to remove your gag. However do not have any thoughts of calling for help. If you shout, raise your voice or make any noise except to answer my questions, Sigurd here will cut your throat and you'll never make another sound again. We know each other well enough, don't we, that you understand that this is no idle threat. Do you agree?'

Ricbehrt nodded, glaring in rage at Ulrich, snorting breaths going in and out of his nose.

'Untie the gag, Einar,' Ulrich said.

Einar bent down and began fumbling with the knot at the back of Ricbehrt's head that held the gag. The job was made more awkward due to Einar's maimed hand. After a few moments Einar got a prickly feeling and glanced over his shoulder. He saw that Ulrich was watching him, eyes narrowed.

'You're making heavy work of that, Einar,' he said.

'It's gloomy in here,' Einar said. 'It's hard to see what I'm doing.'

'Are you sure it's not because of that injury to your hand?' Ulrich said. 'Are you sure you can hold a sword all right?'

'Was there really a need for all this secrecy, Ulrich?' Einar said, keen to change the subject. 'Why couldn't you just tell me you were coming here to question Ricbehrt?'

'Odin teaches us,' Ulrich said, 'that if you need to keep something secret, you should only tell it to one person, never two. Once three people know you may as well tell everyone. We needed to take old Ricbehrt here by surprise. Do you think he'd have talked to us if he got word we were coming?'

Einar frowned, though refrained from pointing out that it was obvious many more than two people had been in on the secret, just not him. Still, Ulrich was right. Ricbehrt had good reason to hate and fear them all, as became obvious as soon as his gag was removed.

'You!' The weapon dealer spat at Ulrich. He spoke in

Norse but with the nasal accent of the Franks. 'I should have known. What is the meaning of this? How dare you pluck me from my bed in the middle of the night and drag me here against my will? When King Aethelstan hears of this you'll hang.'

'Ah, so I was right,' Ulrich said, standing up. 'Aethelstan is also here to buy weapons from you. No doubt for his invasion of Brittany? I'm amazed he still trusts you after you never delivered those Ulfbehrt swords you promised him.'

'Because you stole them!' Ricbehrt said, spittle flying from his mouth.

'Well that's all in the past now,' Ulrich said. 'Let's get down to business, shall we? We don't have much time as those guards my men knocked out might be discovered soon. We are in need of your expertise, Ricbehrt.'

'Why should I help you?' the Frank hissed.

Ulrich squatted down so they were face to face once more.

'Because, Ricbehrt,' he said, a slight smile playing across his lips, 'if you don't I'll put that gag back on, cut your balls off and leave you to bleed to death on the floor.'

Ricbehrt's puce face became a shade paler.

'But let's not let it come to such unpleasantness,' Ulrich said. 'We just want a chat and the benefit of your knowledge.'

'What about?' Ricbehrt said, his face a mask of suspicion.

'Swords. What else?' Ulrich said. 'You see we have come to hear about some wondrous blades reputed to be better than Ulfbehrts.'

'Better than Ulfbehrts?' Ricbehrt said, raising his eyebrows. 'Are you sure?'

'This lad has seen one,' Ulrich said, placing a hand on Einar's shoulder. 'Tell him about it, Einar.'

Ricbehrt's eyes swivelled toward Einar.

'So you're here too,' he said. 'The Skull Cleaver's bastard. You killed my bodyguard, Osric.'

'He was trying to kill me at the time,' Einar said. 'The sword I saw broke an Ulfbehrt in two like it was a twig. It had runes down the middle of the blade.'

'You're sure it wasn't just another Ulfbehrt?' Ricbehrt said. Even though still bristling with resentment, his words bore a little less venom and Einar could see that Ricbehrt's demeanour had changed a bit. His professional interest had been piqued.

Einar shook his head.

'The runes were different,' he said.

'Come here,' Ulrich said. 'When I saw those monks working today I knew this place was perfect for this.'

He went over to one of the tables with the feathers and parchments. Einar followed him as Sigurd and Kari hauled Ricbehrt to his feet and half-carried, half-dragged him over to the table. Skar, Surt and Wulfhelm joined them and Starkad left the door to come over and watch what was happening as well.

Ulrich took a stopper off a clay pot and dipped the point of the feather in. When he withdrew it, it glistened with coloured liquid, this one green. He held the feather out towards Einar.

'Draw what you saw,' he said, pointing with his other hand at the parchment on the table.

Einar took the feather and pushed the point onto the parchment. To his surprise a blob of green appeared around the feather tip. He dragged it across the parchment and gasped as a green line appeared, left behind by the feather.

Behind him he heard Wulfhelm suck in a sharp breath through his teeth.

'That's probably a book of the Bible you're writing over,' the Saxon said, wincing. 'Just one page of that parchment costs a nobleman's treasure hoard to make.'

Einar did his best to reproduce the runes he had seen on the sword of the big viking who wore the white bear pelt. When he was done he stepped back so Ricbehrt could have a look.

Now it was the turn of the Frank to suck his breath in through his teeth.

'You are no craftsman when it comes to drawing,' he said to Einar, 'But that looks very like what you saw was an *Inglerii.*'

'What's that?' Einar said.

Ricbehrt's eyes widened once more, this time with excitement.

'I've never seen one myself but I've heard of them,' he said. He seemed to have forgotten his current predicament as he warmed to talking about his favourite subject, which was weapons. 'Mostly only in rumours; tales of other weapon merchants and legends told by warriors and poets from distant wars. They started to appear on the market a few years ago. As you say, these swords are said to be even better than Ulfbehrts. Astonishing blades. Their steel is so subtle that it can bend in the wind like a metal whip, but so sharp and so hard it can cut through a shield or a brynja like a hot knife through butter. These swords are so amazing that they say Ingler, the smith who forges them, is a wizard or a magic dwarf.'

'Like Ulfbehrts,' Ulrich said. 'Ulfbehrt himself, their maker, is supposed to be a craftsman highly skilled in magic. Probably he's a dwarf or a wizard troll.'

'Ulrich, let me share a little secret of our trade with you,' Ricbehrt said with a little chuckle. 'Have you ever stopped to count how many Ulfbehrts there are in the world? Hundreds. Thousands maybe. Could one man make all of them himself? And those swords have been around for years too. My grandfather sold Ulfbehrts. What age would that make Ulfbehrt? And what does that tell you?'

'That Ulfbehrt must indeed be magic?' Ulrich said.

'What I'm trying to tell you, Ulrich,' Ricbehrt said, 'is that perhaps there once was a blacksmith called Ulfbehrt. But now there are whole workshops full of smiths called "Ulfbehrt" somewhere in Francia churning out those blades by the dozen. The original craftsman must have shared his secret with others. Ulfbehrt is just a title now. A type of sword rather than a real person who makes them. Merchants like me, though we know the truth, tend not to contradict the story of the wizard-smith because it lends a certain glamour to the swords and makes them more desirable.'

'Then what of these Ingleriis?' Ulrich said, the look on his face suggesting he was sceptical of what the weapon dealer had just told him. 'Are they made in some workshop somewhere? If so, where? Can you get us some?'

'Me? No. A couple of years ago I would have said yes. But not now,' Ricbehrt said with a shrug. 'They are – or at least were – very rare so could only be made by a single, highly skilled craftsman. They say that he is – or was – a

Finn or at least from somewhere in the northern reaches of Norway. How they're made is still a mystery. A few years back, if you had the money and the right contacts you could get Inglerii blades. I knew a few dealers who claimed they could get them but then the supply completely dried up. I've tried to get some myself but it's impossible.'

'Why impossible?' Ulrich said.

'Ingler, or whatever his real name was,' Ricbehrt said, 'disappeared.'

'What do you mean, "disappeared"?' Ulrich said. 'By his magic?'

'Who knows?' the weapon dealer said. 'No one can reach him. He vanished. All contact ceased. My friends in the trade who had been able to source the blades could no longer get them.'

'He probably died,' Einar said. 'This man was clearly no immortal dwarf or troll.'

'Oh, he's not dead,' Ricbehrt said.

'How can you be so sure?' Ulrich said.

'Because the swords are still being made somewhere,' Ricbehrt said. 'And you can buy them, but not from me or anyone else I know in the trade. There is only one dealer in the world who can still supply them and he won't let anyone else sell them except him. But you're wasting your time, Ulrich. You couldn't afford one. The price is greater than Aethelstan's treasure hoard.'

Skar and Ulrich exchanged looks.

'Who sells them?' Skar said.

'A merchant called Meginbraht, a Frisian who trades in Hedeby,' Ricbehrt said. A look of distaste crossed his face as he said the name. 'He's an unscrupulous bastard who'll sell anything to anyone. Slaves, animals, children, weapons, loot.'

'So says the man who sells weapons to anyone and everyone who has the silver to buy them,' Ulrich said with a wolfish smile. 'Even if he is selling to both sides in the same war.'

'There is a difference between him and I,' Ricbehrt said, straightening up as best he could and puffing out his substantial chest. 'I deal with noblemen. Men of honour. Kings, jarls, bishops and counts. Meginbraht sells the plunder of vikings. Well, one viking in particular – Asbjorn Hviti. The Bear.'

Ulrich and Ricbehrt exchanged knowing looks. Ulrich blew out his cheeks.

'You've heard of this man?' Einar said to Ulrich.

'Asbjorn Hviti Ecgtheosson? Of course,' Ulrich said. 'He's the most notorious viking warlord in the known world.'

'Worse than that fellow Soti we ran into before?' Einar said.

'Trust me,' Ulrich said. 'Compared to the Bear, Soti is like one of those pathetic monks we had dinner with tonight.'

A noise made them all look up.

Everyone in the library froze. The sound of footsteps slapping on the stone floor as well as the voices of several men talking came from the other side of the doors that led into the Minster.

'It must be matins,' Wulfhelm said in a whisper. 'The time the monks get up to begin their prayers.'

'But it's still the middle of the night!' Ulrich said. 'Is there no end to these Christians' perversity?'

Then the doors of the library from the courtyard

opened and a monk walked in. His content, unsuspecting expression changed to one of complete shock at the sight of the armed vikings and their prisoner standing in the library.

The monk let out a little yelp and spun around to run back out. As he did so he bumped straight into another figure who now stood in the doorway behind him.

It was Affreca. She was dressed in a long, flowing nightdress of white linen that looked every bit as expensive as Ricbehrt's nightwear. She looked just as surprised as the monk at the whole scene.

Affreca recovered first. Tilting her head to one side she smiled at the monk in a manner that was so radiant it even disarmed Einar who was standing about twenty paces away. The monk was thrown into confusion.

'Lady—' he began to say.

Affreca's right fist lashed out. It caught the monk on the left side of his throat just at the bottom of his neck. The man's eyes rolled up into his head and he crumpled to the floor, unconscious.

'Great hit, lass,' Skar said, grinning with evident pride. 'Just like I taught you.'

'He won't be out for long,' Affreca said. 'Get him bound and gagged fast.'

'Lady, I don't know why you are here,' Ulrich said, 'but I'm very glad to see you.'

'I couldn't sleep,' Affreca said. 'I wanted to talk to someone so I went to the room where you were supposed to be staying. When I saw you weren't there I spotted a light glowing here and thought I should take a look.'

'Lucky for us you did,' Ulrich said. 'Lucky for that monk

anyway. We probably would have had to kill him. Odin himself must have sent you.'

'There's no time to waste,' declared Ulrich. 'We need to go.'

'Where?' Einar asked.

'Back to the ship,' Ulrich said.

He pointed to Ricbehrt. Skar, Sigurd and Surt pounced on the weapons dealer again. Einar saw the expression on the fat man's face turn to pure terror.

'Wait!' he cried.

Skar shoved the gag back in Ricbehrt's mouth and pulled the hood back over his head. Sigurd bound his feet together and then he and Surt dragged the squirming weapons dealer over to the doors that led into the Minster and dumped him there.

'If nothing else he'll make a good door stop if anyone else tries to come in,' Sigurd said.

'We need to move fast,' Ulrich said. 'This place will be crawling with monks any moment and we can't afford to alert Aethelstan's men. Everyone out of here. Back to the quays. Fast.'

Affreca trailed the brown wool robe off the unconscious monk leaving him lying on the stone floor clad in only his undergarments. As she put it on herself, she caught Einar looking at her.

'I'm not running through Jorvik in the dark dressed only in a nightdress,' she said.

Einar looked a little disappointed.

They went out into the courtyard. It was still dark but the sky was beginning to grey with faint pre-dawn light. The company sneaked out of the gate in the palisade around the Minster, past Aethelstan's still unconscious guards, and out into the dark streets beyond. After a frantic dash along the slippery wooden walkways they made it back to the river where Roan lay dozing on the snekkja.

The Wolf Coats boarded the ship. Ulrich jostled Roan awake while Kari and Einar untied the mooring ropes. Then Skar and Sigurd shoved the ship away from the quay. The current took hold of the snekkja almost straight away and they began to drift downstream.

'To the oars,' Ulrich barked and the crew seated themselves on the rowing benches. Einar grabbed hold of his oar and put it in the water, as did the rest. The Wolf Coats pulled on their oars and the ship picked up speed. Roan turned the steering oar and the longship glided out into the middle of the dark brown, filthy water of the river. With every stroke of the oars the dragon-carved prow moved ever faster downstream, out towards the coast and the open sea beyond.

Ulrich stood beside the mast, in the midst of the rest of the crew on the rowing benches.

'We sail for Hedeby,' he said. 'It seems that if we want to know where these mysterious swords come from, the answer is there.'

Twenty-Six

Orkney

Three longships, their dragon-carved prows driven into the white sand, sat on the beach. Waves made impossibly blue by the white sand beneath them lapped at their sterns and sides. Each ship bristled with warriors clad in leather jerkins and ring-mailed brynjas. Their helmets gleamed even though the sky was grey and overcast. The sides of all three ships were lined with the shields of the warriors and each one was painted with the image of a yellow sword. The sails of the ships also bore this emblem.

A group of horsemen appeared on the dunes above the beach. They too were warriors, decked out in war gear like those on the ships, though each one of these men bore the red axe of Eirik Haraldsson on his shield. There were nearly forty of them, enough to match those on the ships. At the head of the column Eirik himself rode, with Thord just behind him.

They trotted down the sand hills and dismounted before the ships. At the same time a man swung himself around the prow of the middle longship and jumped down to the sand. He was broad chested and wore a polished brynja like the others, but around his shoulders was a long red cloak of the finest wool, fastened at one shoulder by a huge, round, gold brooch that was studded with rubies and other precious stones. He had the hood of the cloak pulled up.

A contingent of the warriors followed him and fanned out on the sand behind him.

'Welcome, Olaf Kollisson,' Eirik said as he strode to meet the man in the red cloak. He pointed to the yellow swords on the sails of the ships. 'I assume that's who you are by your emblem anyway.'

The man in the red cloak pulled his hood down. Eirik winced. The other man had a long black beard but his head was bald and covered all over by red lesions and pus-filled craters. The scabs and rash spilled down around his eyes and covered the top of his cheeks and points of his ears as well.

'I am indeed Olaf,' he said. He spoke the Norse tongue with the strange accent that had twisted it during the century or so it had been spoken in Ireland. Noticing the expression on Eirik's face he added, 'The Gaels call me *Amlaíb Cenncairech*. It means Olaf Scabby-Head in their tongue.'

'How rude of them,' Eirik said.

'They hate me and I hate them,' Olaf said. 'Does the sight of my skin problems offend you?'

'Not at all,' Eirik said, forcing a smile to his lips. 'I was just taken aback a little.'

'It means nothing to me,' Olaf said. 'My wives never mention it. If they did I'd have them killed.'

Both men laughed.

'So what brings the King of Limerick to my realm?' Eirik said. 'And why did you not use the harbour like everyone else?'

'Well your harbours are full, Eirik,' Olaf said. 'They appear to be jammed with the ships of all manner of unpleasant vikings.'

'I am recruiting an army for a war,' Eirik said. 'Evil men can do much good work in that area.'

'Yes, I heard you are in need of men,' Olaf said. 'Slaves too. The news has been spread far and wide. As for why I'm here, when I heard the great Eirik Bloody Axe, the son of Harald Fairhair, had come to Orkney I thought I should pay a visit to my new neighbour.'

He pointed out to sea.

'The whale road travels from Norway to Orkney in a straight line south-west,' he said. 'Then on to the north and west of Ireland – my realm – and on to Armorica then Spain. Norsemen who live along that route should be of one accord, for our own advantages. Thorfinn Hausakljúfr, your predecessor on the high seat of Orkney, was too cosy with that bastard Olaf of Dublin. Now Thorfinn is gone it makes sense to me that we should make a common cause.'

'I'm sure you're right,' Eirik said.

'I *am* right, Eirik,' Olaf said. 'And I am here to offer you an alliance. Orkney is not a large enough realm for a man like you. I know you will want to take your high seat in Norway back and to do that you need more than the rabble you have at your command at the moment. I can pledge you one hundred ships just like these ones here. Each one filled with warriors: Honourable men hardened by hundreds of battles in Ireland. Each one ready and with the gear to fight. True warriors, not viking scum. With my men you can drive Hakon back into the sea. Norway will be yours again.'

Eirik rubbed his chin.

'And what do you want in return?' he said.

Olaf smiled.

'You will then help me deal with the other Olaf and the Ivarssons of Dublin,' he said. 'Their arrogance knows no bounds. They think all of Ireland belongs to them. Well it doesn't. If it belongs to anyone it belongs to me. Once you're King of Norway again you will have a new army, the men of Norway. We will sail for Dublin together and put the Ivarssons to the sword. Then I will be King of Ireland.'

'A tempting prospect,' Eirik said, nodding. 'Come to Jarls Gard and we will discuss it further over wine and something to eat. You're the first person of quality I've had visit here in Orkney and my wife would love to meet you.'

Olaf shook his head.

'I'm sorry, I cannot stay,' he said. 'I must get back to Limerick. Every moment I am away there is a danger the Ivarssons will steal it from me. I also have other business to do in Scotland. Do we have an agreement?'

'We do,' Eirik said.

The King of Limerick held out his hand. Eirik saw that it too was covered in scabs and sores.

'Let us swear an oath then,' Olaf said. 'I swear to support you if you support me.'

Eirik swallowed then clasped the other man's forearm.

'I swear by Tyr,' he said.

'Excellent!' Olaf said, a broad grin on his face.

They both released each other's forearm. Eirik fought the urge to wipe his hand on his breeches.

'There is one other thing,' Olaf said. 'I've heard it said you are offering some very special swords to those who follow you. They're even better than Ulfbehrts I'm told?'

'That is true,' Eirik said.

'I was thinking,' Olaf said, 'to seal our agreement, perhaps you could send some of those swords for me and my chosen men? As a gesture of goodwill.'

'Of course,' Eirik said.

'Good. If you send them to me around the Winter Nights festival then I'll know you can be trusted,' Olaf said. 'And I'll start preparing those ships.'

The King of Limerick gestured to his men and they began shoving the ships back into the sea.

King Eirik and his men watched them go, then Eirik turned to Thord.

'Get me Asbjorn,' he said. 'We are going to need those swords of his.'

Twenty-Seven

Jarls Gard, Orkney

'What in the name of Odin is going on here?'

Eirik Haraldsson stood at the door of the feasting hall of Jarls Gard, astounded by the scene before him.

He had entered the hall to find a group of thralls busy at the far end on the dais where the jarl's pillared high seat was situated, commanding a view over everyone in the building. They appeared to be taking the chair apart. One of the two carved, nail-studded pillars was already taken down and the other was at an angle as the slaves worked to lower it to the floor. At the sound of the former king's angry voice and the sight of him hurrying down the hall towards them they froze.

'It's all right, Eirik,' Queen Gunnhild said, emerging from the side of the dais to intercept her husband before he started hitting people. 'They're working under my orders.'

'What are you up to?' Eirik said.

He spotted Vakir the tall, thin Galdr maðr, coming out of the shadows near the dais as well. It was daytime and the feasting hall was empty apart from the slaves, Gunnhild and Vakir.

'Eirik, I need to ask something of you,' she said.

'I'll say you do,' Eirik said. 'What are they doing with my high seat?'

'They're taking it down,' Gunnhild said. 'I need to move it to the Hof on the heath beyond Torhaven.'

'Why?' Eirik said, looking over her shoulder at the slaves.

'Eirik, I meant to tell you before but the right opportunity had not come up,' Gunnhild said. 'I have met with three wise women—'

'I'm surprised you found that many on these islands,' Eirik said. He started to smile at his own joke but the sharp look his wife gave him froze the expression before it was fully formed.

'They are the most powerful Galdr women in this part of the world,' Gunnhild said. 'They live on an island to the north. They are very wise in the lore of our faith. They know spae craft and can see the future.'

'Who are they? The Norns themselves?' Eirik said. 'How come I have never heard of them?'

'You are a man, my love,' Gunnhild said. She slid her arms around her husband's wide chest. 'You have not been taught in the arts of magic. Men fight with swords. Women fight with other crafts.'

Eirik took a deep breath in through his nose, smelling the scent that rose from Gunnhild's hair. He felt the warmth of her lithe body that was pressed against his. The effect was intoxicating.

'I visited these women to gain from their wisdom,' Gunnhild said. 'To get their guidance. I am worried about our position here in Orkney. The ordinary folk are not happy. The harvest failed. They worry about how they will make it through the winter. Many will starve.'

'Hunger brings men to heel,' Eirik said.

'Or makes them rebellious,' Gunnhild said. 'A king is supposed to provide two things: peace and plenty.'

'I'm not responsible for the bad weather,' Eirik said.

'The king and the spirits of the land should be one,' Gunnhild said. 'And the spirits of the land send the harvest. The festival of Winter Nights is coming. If there's no food on the tables we don't want the ordinary folk deciding we are to blame.'

'*I* am to blame, you mean,' Eirik said.

Gunnhild dropped their embrace.

'Eirik: Until recently you were the King of Norway,' she said. 'We have had to leave our home, our land, and flee to this group of islands the Gods have forgotten about. If this is to be your new realm then we need the spirits of the land and the Norns who govern destiny to accept and support you. The dísir and landvættir of Norway must have turned against you. Otherwise you would never have lost the realm.'

'It was the people who turned against me, Gunnhild,' he said. 'Not the ghosts or the Gods. Traitors and back-stabbing bastards. They forced me off the high seat in Norway.'

'And if you lose this high seat too then we all go with you,' Gunnhild said. 'And so will your sons. Eirik I *won't* be homeless again so soon.'

The former king and queen glared at each other for long moments. Gunnhild was just under half Eirik's age of forty-three winters, but when it came to direct confrontation with her he knew it was best to back down. Now that his father, the infamous Harald Fairhair was dead, Eirik feared no man on Middle Earth. His wife, however, scared the shit out of him. He may have been the bloody-axed tyrant who ruled with a hard hand, but she was as dangerous and deadly as the invisible spirits that lurked in the dark of the grave mounds.

'Very well,' Eirik said. 'What do you want?'

'The three wise women have sent word that they will be here soon,' Gunnhild said. 'They are coming to help me perform the ancient rite of Landvættir Blót. It is a ritual that will ensure the land spirits grant you their favour. Then you will be secure in Orkney.'

'You know I never interfere with your magic workings, dear,' Eirik said. 'You do what you need to. I take it this is why you need the high seat?'

'Yes,' Gunnhild said. 'The high seat is a symbol of the ruler of the land. The ritual will imbue it with power so whoever sits on it will receive the blessings of the land spirits and the Norns. It's not just the seat though, I need you to sit in the seat while the ritual is performed. Otherwise the power will not flow to you.'

Eirik sighed.

'I suppose I could do that, for your sake if nothing else,' he said.

'That's not all,' Gunnhild said. 'The wise women insist on certain conditions for the ritual. It must be private and away from people. They do not like the eyes of anyone who is not initiated in the crafts of magic to fall upon them. Hence we will perform it at the Hof on the heath. That temple is in the middle of nowhere so there's little chance of anyone seeing what is going on. There is something else.'

'Go on,' Eirik said.

'No men can be allowed to attend,' Gunnhild said.

'Aren't I a man, dearest?' Eirik said.

'You are the subject of the ritual,' Gunnhild said. 'So that is all right. No other males can be in the temple. Otherwise it will anger the spirits and the ritual will not work. There can be no weapons either, except the ritual ones. It is a holy place and if blood is spilt in anything but sacrifice the spirits will be angry and the ritual will not work.'

'So you want me to go to a Hof out on the heathland,' Eirik said, raising his eyebrows, 'without my warriors. With no weapons. To perform some magic ceremony while Ulrich and his wolf men are at large? It doesn't sound like the wisest of plans to me.'

'Please, my love,' Gunnhild said, her voice becoming silky as she slid her arms around her husband again. 'You will be safe. There is a hall for feasting right beside the temple. Your men can wait there. If there are any problems they will be there to protect you in moments. Besides, nothing has happened in Orkney since those ships were burned. Ulrich has probably gone back to Norway.'

Eirik looked up at the darkness gathered in the thatch above. He prayed for the strength to deny his wife what she asked for. His common sense told him that was what he should do, but when she held herself against him the way she did now he was never able to resist.

'All right,' he said and heaved a heavy sigh. 'I'll do it. But my warriors will be armed and ready in that hall. There will be no ale for them. If I signal danger they will come running right away.'

'Of course, dear,' Gunnhild said. 'But that won't be necessary. The ritual will work, the land spirits will give you their blessings and no one will be able to harm you. No one will be able to drive us away from ruling in Orkney. Not even Ulrich.'

Eirik nodded.

'There is one other, tiny thing...' Gunnhild said, giving him a coquettish look.

'What?' Eirik said.

'The wise women require a sacrifice,' Gunnhild said. 'A girl. She must be nine winters old.'

'That's why you insisted on keeping that girl of Aulvir's hostage isn't it?' Eirik said.

'I need her brought to the Hof before Winter Nights,' Gunnhild said, nodding.

'I'll see it is done,' Eirik said. 'My dear, you are positively wicked. I hope I never end up on the wrong side of you.'

'Wonderful!' Gunnhild said. She stood on her tiptoes and planted a kiss on Eirik's lips.

At that moment the door of the hall opened again. The huge, hulking figure of Asbjorn Hviti entered the hall.

'You wanted to see me, Lord Eirik?' he said in his deep booming voice.

'Yes,' Eirik said, turning to face the big viking. 'I'm going to need those special swords you said you could get me. The Ingleriis, not the Ulfbehrts. It seems word has spread about them and I'm going to need a few to secure a new alliance.'

The Bear nodded.

'I can get them for you,' he said, folding his beefy arms

across his massive chest, 'but I will warn you, they're very costly. They're worth a jarldom each.'

'I don't care about the cost,' Eirik said. 'In fact, a jarldom is what I'll offer you. Those swords will buy me the ships of Olaf of Limerick. With them I will take back Norway. Then I will no longer have need of this place. But I'll need someone solid to run it. What say I make you the new Jarl of Orkney when I'm back on the High Seat of Norway?'

Asbjorn frowned, then nodded.

'I accept,' he said.

'Good. I should warn you though, there is someone else with a claim to Orkney,' Eirik said. 'Einar, the son of Thorfinn the Skull Splitter. But if you ever run into him I've no doubt you will not have much trouble killing him.'

'I'll do it with pleasure,' the Bear said, grinning. 'I will need something more real up front, though, I'm afraid lord, rather than just promises of future ennoblement.'

'Of course,' Eirik said. He looked around, spotting the gangly Galdr maðr lurking nearby. 'And the feeling is mutual. I don't like the idea of giving you a hoard of gold and silver and watching you sail off never to be seen again, so I'll send Vakir here with you as my agent. He can bring the gold and silver to show I act in good faith. Now, when can I get my swords? They are in your fortress I assume?'

'I usually direct anyone interested in purchasing an Inglerii to a merchant who works for me,' the Bear said.

'Good,' Eirik said. 'Vakir can work out the deal with this merchant. Why can't you just take him to your fortress though?'

The Bear looked uncomfortable.

'Lord,' he said. 'I don't want anyone knowing where my

fortress is. I have much wealth stored there and I have many enemies. Several people have tried to follow me there and I've killed all of them.'

Now Vakir looked uncomfortable.

'That's sensible enough, I suppose,' Eirik said. 'I need some assurance you will fulfil your side of the bargain though.'

'Lord Eirik,' Vakir interjected, 'I am perhaps not the best person for this task. The queen may need assistance in her rituals—'

'And I need someone to make sure Asbjorn does what he says he will,' Eirik said. 'What if he disappears with my gold and I don't get my swords?'

The Bear scratched his beard.

'Very well,' he said. 'I'll tell you what. He can come with me as far as Hedeby. The merchant who works for me is there. Vakir can stay with him while I fetch the swords from my fortress. He won't have to wait long I promise.'

Vakir's face lit up.

'I did not know that the voyage would involve going to Hedeby, Lord Eirik,' he said. 'I will do it.'

'You've changed your mind quickly,' Eirik said.

'There are certain guilds of magical crafters in Hedeby I am very interested in,' Vakir said. 'I would be happy to go and meet with them.'

'Then it looks like everyone will be happy,' Eirik said. 'Now where are those slaves? Tell them to bring some wine. It's been a long day and I need a drink.'

Part Three

The Lair of the Bear

Twenty-Eight

The journey away from Jorvik was faster and harder work than their arrival. The Wolf Coats had rowed as hard as they could back down the river Ouse. The sleek design of the ship and the fact that they were going downstream meant they made swift progress. With little sleep the night before, rowing was exhausting, relentless work and Einar wondered at times if he would be able to keep going. He did though. The thought of the scorn his fellow Wolf Coats would pour on him if he gave up drove him to persevere.

The sun rose but they kept on, Ulrich always watching the river behind them for pursuing ships and the banks for horsemen.

Finally the river widened and merged into a wide estuary surrounded by low, flat land. The ship followed the course of the estuary and on out into the choppy grey sea. Once there a strong wind caught the sail, propelling them on with such power that rowing provided no extra impetus. Roan pointed the dragon-carved prow directly towards the open sea. Seeing no ships behind them and no riders on the land, Ulrich was at last satisfied that they had escaped.

'All right you can put the oars away,' he said to the

grateful crew who drew their oars in then collapsed onto the deck, utterly worn out and soaked with sweat.

As the land slipped out of sight beyond the horizon behind them, Einar felt the old lurch of unease he suffered from whenever on a ship. It was nowhere near as bad as it used to be, but he still could not say that he enjoyed sea travel like some men did.

After a short rest to recover, the crew set about preparing for the voyage ahead. They would be crossing the open seas so needed warm and waterproof clothing. From the ship's storage chests they pulled on fleece shirts and breeches, then wrestled themselves into hooded sealskin jerkins to keep the water out. They erected a long leather canopy over the deck, secured to the stern, mast and prow, to shelter the deck. Then they all huddled underneath.

Skar lit a fire on the cooking stone and boiled up some barley stew and salted fish. Despite the rank smell and bland taste, Einar found himself so ravenous that he finished his bowl in moments. Ulrich chose Starkad and Wulfhelm for the first watch then the rest crawled into leather sleeping bags and sank into deep, bone-weary sleep on the deck.

Later Einar was shaken awake by Skar to take his turn at watch. Getting up, he rolled his shoulders and rubbed his back to try to dispel the stiffness and pain from his previous exertions. It was still light, but much later in the day. They were well out to sea and there was no sign of land anywhere. Rain hissed down from the grey sky into an equally grey sea. Huge swells continually lifted and lowered the ship as a strong wind pushed the sail taut and buffeted the leather shelter as if a mighty hand was drumming on it from above.

Skar, his own watch finished, got into the warm sleeping bag Einar had just got out of and went to sleep. The rest were still asleep except for Ulrich, who stood at the steering oar, guiding the ship, and Affreca, who had just been wakened like himself. She scratched her tousled hair and began twisting it into two braids as they both walked down the deck to join Ulrich at the stern post.

'How long will the voyage take?' Einar said.

Ulrich shrugged. 'Two or three days. Maybe more, maybe less,' he said. 'It depends on the weather, the tide and the winds.'

Einar had heard folk talk of Hedeby but had never been there himself. It was a large town in the homeland of the ancient Jute tribe at the very edge of the land of the Danes. It was one of the main trading towns on the whale road that stretched across the northern seas from Dublin in the west to Hedeby in the east.

'So where did you run into this great viking, the Bear, we're looking for?' Einar said.

'I've never met him, thanks to Odin for that,' Ulrich said. 'Such men are dangerous and nothing but trouble. Don't get me wrong: I've no fear of him. But opponents like him, they are always a problem. You never come away from an encounter with them without injury or losing men. Best to steer clear of them if you can.'

'I've heard of this Asbjorn Hviti too,' Affreca said. 'The skalds in my father's drinking hall used to tell tales about him. He's reputed to be the greatest viking since Ragnar Loðbrók. He's as rich as a king and has his own private army of vikings. He has a fortress somewhere south of the land of the Geats.'

'Why is he called the Bear?' Einar said. 'Because of his name?'

'Bjorn means bear, yes,' Ulrich said. 'But that's not the only reason they call him that. He's as tall as a giant. A head taller than Skar, by all accounts. He wears the pelt of a great white bear he killed when on an expedition to the far north, beyond even the land of the Finns. They say he killed it with his bare hands.'

Einar's mouth dropped open a little. The memory of the huge viking in the white fur cloak who had destroyed Frodisborg surfaced in his mind. He smacked himself on the forehead with the heel of his left palm.

'Of course!' Einar said. 'How could I have been so stupid?'

'What are you talking about?' Affreca said.

'Remember when I told you about the big viking in Gandvik? The one with the Inglerii who nearly killed me?' Einar said. 'He wore a cloak of white fur. It must have been him: the Bear!'

Ulrich looked at Einar for a long moment.

'First you see these magic swords and now it turns out that you've met the Bear too,' he said after a time. 'And you survived. You know there are times when I wonder if you really still belong in my úlfhéðnar. Are you really good enough and have you really recovered from your sickness? Can you really wield a sword in battle with that maimed hand? Then you come out with things like this. Skar thinks Odin sent you to help guide us and maybe there is something in that.'

Einar opened his mouth but no words came out. He looked down at his injured hand. Should he admit that he really could not hold a long weapon? He knew that Ulrich would throw him out of the crew if he did. On the other hand, was he being selfish? If he dropped a sword at a crucial moment he could get one or more of the others killed.

'If Eirik Bloody Axe has allied with the Bear then Hakon is in trouble,' Ulrich said. 'We all are. Eirik could certainly have a chance of sweeping Hakon out of Norway. Maybe then he could even challenge Aethelstan.'

'Yet we're still sailing to Hedeby?' Einar said.

'Our best chance of ruining Eirik's plans is to take away his swords,' Ulrich said. 'All of them. Ulfbehrts and especially these Ingleriis. That way he can't gain more support until he can loot enough silver and gold to buy it. If we want to do that we have to go to Hedeby. Now, aren't you two supposed to be on watch?'

Einar and Affreca left Ulrich and went to the prow, one taking either side to scan the sea ahead. Not that there was much to look out for. They were far out to sea and there were no rocks or other dangers. All Einar saw were the endless, churning waves. They kept watch nevertheless as the prow rose and fell and rose again in an endless cycle, each crash into the troughs of the waves sending chilling, salty spray into their faces.

After a long time Einar finally gathered the courage to ask the question that had been burning inside him for some time.

'What about you and Hakon?' he said.

'What about it?' Affreca said.

'I thought you were going to marry him?' Einar said. 'But here you are with us on this ship.'

'Not that it is any business of yours,' Affreca said. 'But who says I don't intend to marry him?'

'If you did,' Einar said, 'I would have thought you would have stayed behind in Jorvik.'

'I've told you before, Einar,' Affreca said with a tut. 'Leave the thinking to others.'

'Did you really leave Jorvik just because you knocked that monk out?' Einar said. 'I'm sure you could have blamed us if you'd wanted to. And what about all that talk of Jorvik being your ancestral birthright?'

'I meant that,' Affreca said; the look in her eye of a sudden became hard and serious. 'One day the Ivarssons will rule Jorvik again. But if I am going to rule there, then it will be as an Ivarsson. In my own right. Not as an ornament to Hakon Haraldsson, foster-son of Aethelstan.'

Despite the bitter wind and the damp air, Einar felt a warm glow inside as if a candle had been kindled in his heart.

'What are you smiling about?' Affreca said, an irritated expression on her face.

'Nothing,' Einar said, continuing to stare towards the horizon.

Twenty-Nine

The voyage to Hedeby was longer and more uncomfortable than the one to Jorvik. The days rolled into a week as the ship pitched and rolled over the endless churning waves. The sky was dark and when it was not raining a bitter wind kept the sail taut and bit on any exposed flesh.

Einar found himself pondering how sea travel was an odd combination of boredom and the underlying terror of certain death that might lurk beneath every cold wave which battered the prow.

They sighted the coast of Denmark and began the journey around the peninsula of the Jutes. Ulrich was concerned about Danish vikings as they sailed but in the end they saw no one. As it turned out the height of excitement was when big waves sloshed over the prow, threatening to swamp the ship.

'Get those buckets and start bailing,' Ulrich bellowed at his crew. 'Or we'll all end up in Aegir's Hall beneath the waves.'

Everyone worked to clear the water off the deck, throwing bucketfuls of briny water back over the side until the deck was clear. When it was all over they stood for a moment catching their breaths.

'Did you see Ulrich?' Einar said in a quiet voice to Affreca. The Wolf Coats, aware of the danger, had worked with steady but concentrated effort but the little Wolf Coat leader had been frantic at bailing the water off the ship. 'He's so desperate not to die in any way except with a sword in his hand.'

'Well, he believes Ragnarök is coming,' Affreca said. 'There isn't much time left to claim a seat on Odin's mead bench.'

'Do you think Ragnarök is coming?' Einar said.

'How else do you explain the weather?' Affreca said with a shrug.

'I don't know,' Einar said.

They went back to their shipboard life. This consisted of sailing duties, keeping the ship afloat and on track, hauling ropes to tighten or angle the sail, making minor repairs or upkeep jobs, or, when the wind dropped, rowing. Skar also insisted on making them all row for two periods a day to improve their overall fitness. He also had them doing other exercises like carrying each other up and down the deck, squatting up and down with a crewmate on their back or running up and down the ship in an endless loop around the mast, all to keep them fit and ready for fighting. Einar welcomed the exertions, finding himself getting stronger by the day and he began to feel he had at last recovered his strength from the weak state his poisoned wound had left him in.

He went through some nervous times as well. In between all the fitness work Skar also kept the crew busy with drills and practice in war craft. As he worked on formation tactics with the others Einar was on edge, expecting a blow to knock the wooden practice sword from his injured hand and the truth would be known. His luck held however. The wooden swords were much lighter than a real one and Skar did not want anyone to get injured while on the voyage. There was no one to replace any casualties so all blows were executed in slow motion with half effort.

Even though he got away with it, it was these times that really frightened Einar. He knew it was only a matter of time before the rest of the Wolf Coats found out he could not hold a sword properly, and then what would happen? Ulrich would not let him stay as one of his úlfhéðinn. The rest of the company would not want a man who could not fight properly either. And if he was not a Wolf Coat, then what was left for him to be? He was the heir of the Jarl of Orkney, but Eirik Bloody Axe had taken that away. Even his mother's farm, his childhood home in Iceland, was just burned-out ruins now. He could still sing but who would want a skald who could not play a harp? He would be *níþ*: a nothing. A no-one.

Once the ship was joined by groups of huge sea creatures which raced along ahead and around the prow. Sometimes their blunt, strangely shaped heads rose from the water and Einar felt an uneasy feeling that the black eyes were looking straight at him. Once, one of the creatures' long, many toothed mouths opened in what looked like a smile. It almost seemed like it was laughing at him.

'Are those some sort of whale?' Einar said, standing at the prow, watching in fascination as their shiny black backs with their single fin rolled in and out of the water.

'No, those are sea swine,' Skar said.

'Why are they called that?' Einar said.

'They have a round body like a pig. Some of them are toothed like a boar and they travel in herds like swine,' the big man said. 'And they're delicious. If we didn't have other things to do I'd be tempted to get my hunting spear out today.'

Einar made a face, unsure what such meat might taste like. They ate shark and whale at home in Iceland but the idea of killing and eating those strange creatures with their intelligent eyes and happy smiles seemed almost wrong.

After rounding the top of the peninsula Roan turned the ship south. They shadowed the coast from afar for many miles. Land was a mere dark line on the horizon to the steering board side of the ship. When Ulrich judged they were nearing their destination Roan brought the ship closer to the land. After some time they entered a wide inlet, a firth, not unlike the one they had left Britain from. Then they began to sail inland. The firth was very wide and meandered for a long way. It snaked through low, flat countryside as far as the eye could see. The land was muddy brown and devoid both of trees and any signs of human habitation.

'It's just one big swamp,' Ulrich commented. 'You can understand why the Angles and the Jutes left it and went to Britain.'

At last Einar spotted a grey miasma smearing the sky ahead. It was the smoke of many fires and he knew that signalled they were heading for a settlement, and a large one at that.

The firth widened into a large bay on one side and to Einar's astonishment he saw a palisade or wooden wall running from the land out into the water, standing three or four times the height of a man. The wall extended north and south, curving towards the shore where it continued on inland, enclosing a settlement. The smoke was rising from behind it. Even though he could not see it yet, the length of the wall around it showed that the town was huge. This was even more surprising given the endless, empty wasteland of marshes they had been sailing through.

'We have heard of this place, even in al-Andalus,' Surt said. 'I remember reading in the library of the Emir the account of a traveller who came here: *Hedeby, the town at the extreme end of the world's ocean.* I can see that now. This does seem like the very far end of the world.'

A steady stream of filth and detritus began to flow past the ship, coming from the direction of the town. The prow struck the white, bloated corpse of what Einar at first thought was either a very large dog or small cow. Then he felt a thrill of shock as he realised it was the dead body of a man.

The crew stood up to watch the corpse as it bumped along the side of the ship. Einar could see the man was naked. There was a gash across his throat like purple lips below his chin and another stab wound below his right ribs. His body had bled white and his dead eyes gazed, unmoving at the sky above.

'Take a good look, lads,' Ulrich said as the body disappeared into the wake of the ship. 'And remember to keep your wits about you here. There are plenty of drinking dens in Hedeby and just as many scoundrels waiting to steal the silver of the drunk, the naive and the unwary. Now back on the oars. Head for the water gate.'

Twin towers guarded a gap in the wall that was just wide enough for a single ship to pass through. With a combination of Roan's skilful hand and shouted orders to the crew on the oars, the ship glided across the dark muddy water into position to enter through the space between the towers. As they got closer, glancing over his shoulder Einar saw that the palisade protected a harbour where ranks of jetties and quays stretched out into the water, every inch of them jammed with ships. A veritable forest of masts rose above it all and beyond them was a town, one of the biggest Einar had seen and certainly on a par with Jorvik or Dublin. Though, as he mused to himself, Jorvik and Dublin were the only other towns he had in fact seen.

The towers that guarded the entrance were wooden like the palisade. Einar spotted archers lurking on top of them, the curved tops of their bows standing up over the crenellated walls. There was a platform just above deck level around the towers and other men in war gear stood there.

'Who is king here?' Einar said to Skar, who sat beside him on the rowing bench. 'Who rules this place?'

'Hedeby?' Skar said. 'No one. Not really. Except gold, perhaps. The land around here is at the very edge of the Kingdom of the Danes, but also that of the Empire of the Franks. To the east are the Rus and the Baltic. It's a frontier trading outpost at the crossroads of the world, lad. It's outside kingdoms, that's why it's so valuable. You can buy or sell anything here, unfettered by the laws or customs of any particular king. Those kings who rule the realms that meet here allow it to exist, as long as their tribute silver keeps rolling in. And it does. Hedeby exists for one thing only – to generate wealth. Lots of it.'

'If there is no king, then who keeps order?' Einar said, eyeing the armed men on the platform beside the tower. 'Who upholds the law?'

'There's a jarl here,' Skar said. 'But he's not like other jarls. He is not responsible for sacrifices, collecting taxes or raising an army for the king. His sole responsibility is to make sure nothing interferes with the merchant's trade. He's paid to do the job too. He's not doing it for fealty or family.'

A loud clanking sound made Einar look around again. A huge chain was rising from the water on either side of the entrance. Every one of its links were huge and festooned with green lake weed and Einar marvelled at how much iron must have gone into its construction. As it tightened it formed a barrier between the two towers, effectively sealing off the harbour – and the town's – entrance and stopping the snekkja from sailing in.

'A harbour chain,' Skar said, looking at the chain with an expression of approval. 'I haven't seen one like that since I was in Miklagard.'

'Do they not want us to come in?' Einar said.

'They're just checking who we are,' Skar said. 'And making sure we pay our entrance fees.'

'Ho there.' A man on the right-hand platform was waving the ship to pull alongside. He was dressed in an expensive, saffron coloured cloak and multicoloured breeches. He was flanked on either side by warriors armed with spears and protected by shields, helmets and brynjas. Every shield was painted with a white *Fehu* rune. The archers Einar had spotted rose from above the walls at the top of the towers. They had arrows notched and they levelled their points at the Wolf Coats sitting on their oar benches.

Roan steered the snekkja to the platform beside the tower until the side bumped against it. Ulrich tossed a rope over from the prow and one of the warriors caught it. Roan threw one from the stern and soon the ship was fast to the side.

'Are you here for trade or pleasure?' the man in the saffron cloak said.

'Both, with a bit of luck,' Ulrich called back to him.

'Well, you've come to the right place,' the man on the platform said. 'You're here at the right time too; the festival begins tonight. There's plenty here to amuse you if you have enough silver or gold. Everything has a price and this is where you start paying. I am Oddi, the Master of the Company of Watchmen in Hedeby. You must pay in silver to bring your ship into harbour.'

Ulrich nodded. Like the rest of his crew he wore arm rings, a thick gold one around his right bicep and several smaller ones on his left forearm. They were mostly for decoration, except for two which were long bands of silver, coiled around his arm twice and marked in finger-width sections so that pieces that size could be broken off. Ulrich unwound a length of one of them from his forearm. He broke off several pieces, shortening the arm ring, and handed the bits up to the man in the saffron cloak.

As the Master of the Watchmen reached down to get it, Einar noticed his eyelids and upper cheeks were painted blue and ringed with black. The paint was so thick it covered any wrinkles he might have had so it was hard to tell just how old the man really was.

The Master appeared to be satisfied with the amount of silver Ulrich had handed over.

'Welcome to Hedeby,' he said. 'Have a good time while you're here. We welcome all sorts of people here. We like visitors who come and spend their gold and don't cause any fuss or harm so don't get too carried away and don't cause any trouble. My watchmen are a capable company of men. The jarl doesn't like bother and if you cause any we'll deal with it, understand?'

He made a gesture and the loud clanking began again as the chain began to descend back into the water. Einar noted the noise was coming from inside the towers and reasoned that there must be some sort of levers or wheels in them for working the chain.

When the way was clear, they loosed the ropes, hauled on the oars and the ship slid forward again, inside the palisade and into the harbour of Hedeby.

'What was with that man's face paint?' Einar said.

'Oh, you'll see all sorts of bizarre fashions here lad,' Skar said. 'Be prepared for all sorts of sights and sounds once we get into the town. You're not on the farm in Iceland now.'

The rattling and splashing of the chain rising into place again from behind told Einar that the barrier that had kept them out would now be just as effective at stopping them from leaving.

Thirty

Many long wooden quays jutted into the water. These thronged with a vast array of ships from Norse vessels – *skeiðs*, *drakkars* and many *knarrs*, the wide-bodied trading boats that plied the northern seas – to foreign ships from what origin Einar had no idea.

They found a space at one of the jetties and moored the snekkja. The docks bustled with hectic activity as crews loaded and unloaded their cargos while merchants competed to buy the best goods before they even made it to the marketplace in the town. The hurly-burly merged with the noise of the town beyond the harbour into a cacophony that, coming after a week of relative quiet on the seas, was almost overwhelming. All the activity and noise added to a general air of excitement and there soon ensued a short argument among the Wolf Coat crew over who would be left behind to guard the ship, with everyone wanting to go into the town and no one wanting to stay behind to make sure nothing happened to the gear stashed on board.

'This place is a nest of thieves and bandits,' Ulrich said. 'There's no way I'm leaving the ship unguarded and Roan can't look after it on his own.'

Unlike the others, the wizened old skipper had no desire

to go ashore, saying he had seen it all before and when you had sailed as much as he had, one town seemed very much like another.

In the end Ulrich ordered Starkad and Wulfhelm to stay behind, much to their annoyance, though they were consoled by a promise that they would be relieved before too long.

'We'll stay in sailing clothes,' Ulrich said, seeing that some of the others had started to get their best clothes from their bags. 'Leave your wolf cloaks behind.'

'Oh come on, Ulrich!' Sigurd said, stroking the fur of his cloak. 'Must we? We've been at sea for ages. There are taverns here and when a woman sees a man wearing the pelt of a wolf coat, she just can't resist him.'

'Really?' Affreca said, raising her right eyebrow. 'I've been surrounded by men in those flea-ridden pelts for months now and somehow managed to restrain myself.'

'We mustn't draw attention to ourselves,' Ulrich said. 'The arrival of a pack of Úlfhéðnar in town will cause a stir. And if men are drunk you always get at least one idiot who'll think he's hard enough to beat us in a fight. We don't need that. So you'll just have to rely on your natural charm and wit if you want to land a woman today.'

'That's what he's worried about,' Kari said.

With some reluctance, the others stored their wolf pelts in chests on the ship.

'We can bring these, though?' Sigurd said, holding up his drinking horn. It was a black horn carved with intertwining creatures and tipped with silver at the point and rim. It was sheathed like a knife in a soft leather scabbard that could be attached to his belt. 'Right, Ulrich?'

'Yes,' Ulrich said, a half-smile on his face. 'I'm not a complete tyrant. But remember what I said about not getting too drunk, all right?'

The others cheered and grabbed their own drinking horns which they attached to their belts. Then they tramped down the gangr plank and into the town.

Einar felt the now familiar sensation of slight dizziness as he transitioned from days on the rolling deck of a ship to solid ground. The feeling, combined with the noise, stench and colours of the town that swirled around him added to the general impression that he was in the heart of a confusing maelstrom.

They walked up from the docks into Hedeby. Einar was surprised at how like Dublin and Jorvik the town was in style of buildings and thoroughfares. A web of wooden-planked walkways marked out the streets that ran between the rows of buildings. A narrow stream of filthy water ran down the sides of the walkways carrying all sorts of horrible detritus away from the town and into the harbour below. The houses, huts and many merchants' shops were of the long, rectangular Norse type whose gable ends opened onto the street. Most of the buildings were shops with all manner of goods on display outside them. Barrels of salted fish, meat and whale oil were stacked beside reindeer hides, furs of all kinds and bundles of walrus and other ivory. There was jewellery, armour, weapons, reams of material and piles of leatherwork. There were even merchants selling items that Einar had no idea what they were. Alongside them cages of clucking chickens and squealing pigs added to the general chaos and noise. There were lots of merchants selling fish – fresh, smoked, dried or salted. Most of the people who thronged the walkways or sat outside their stores looked Norse, but there were also many people whose skins were of different colours or who wore strange, foreign clothes and hairstyles.

Einar noticed that many folk had their eyes painted like the Master of the Watchmen and deduced that it must be some sort of local fashion trend. He also noticed some differences to Jorvik and Dublin, in that there were no old buildings. Nothing was made of stone and the streets were laid out in very straight lines, like a fisherman's net, rather than twisting or turning to accommodate existing buildings or trackways. This, he guessed, must be testament to the fact that the town had, as Skar had told him, been placed here in the middle of these swamps where there had been no town before. Unlike Jorvik, the Romans had not first built a town that had later been extended by the Britons, then the Saxons until finally the Norse had arrived and integrated their own buildings into what was already there.

The stench of piss and woodsmoke that seemed to be everywhere was mingled with the tang of ale from the many, many taverns and ale houses they passed and as they walked up the street Einar saw several houses where men were hawking the use of naked slave girls and boys who stood shivering and empty-eyed just inside the doorways.

Outside many houses were God posts: wooden columns carved into the likeness of Thor, Odin, Frey or other foreign deities Einar did not recognise. The householders had recently sacrificed and impaled the slaughtered animals on the God posts for everyone to see. Einar passed dead rams, goats, pigs and even what looked like the haunch of a bull skewered on the holy posts.

'They really like to show off how religious they are here, don't they?' Sigurd commented.

'They're keen on decoration too,' Einar said, gesturing at the late summer marsh flowers, greenery and berries that festooned the houses and buildings.

'The Master of the Watch mentioned there was some sort of festival going on,' Surt said. 'This must all be for that.'

'It's nearly Vetr Nætr, Winter Nights,' Ulrich said. 'They must be preparing for that. They're a little early though.'

Ulrich stopped some passers-by to ask directions then they continued up the street until it opened into a wide, open marketplace. The air of festivity was enhanced here as instead of the throng of stalls and hawkers that would have been expected there, the area appeared to be being prepared for some sort of feast or celebration. A tall wooden column stood in the centre of the area that was garlanded with greenery and berries. Lines of long tables were set up all over the marketplace and even though it was afternoon, the benches alongside them were filled with people drinking ale and eating. There was much laughter and singing. Thralls hurried among the crowd, serving ale, bread and bowls of boiled fish to the revellers at the tables as musicians danced around, banging drums and playing lyres, flutes and other instruments.

'Looks like quite a party's getting started here,' Skar said.

A column of warriors marched across the square. Their shields bore the same Fehu rune as the men at the harbour but they did not bear swords or spears. Instead, each one had a heavy wooden club or cudgel.

'They must be the jarl's watchmen,' Ulrich said. 'Making sure there is no trouble.'

Unlike the Saxon warriors in Jorvik, these men seemed accepted, welcomed even by the revellers and townsfolk. Some dancing women even draped pieces of greenery over their helmets which the men, in good-natured tolerance, did not brush away.

'It'll be all fun and games well until the effects of the ale really get to work,' Skar said. 'I wouldn't like to be trying to keep this place in order later on tonight.'

'Let's just stay out of the watchmen's way anyway,' Ulrich said.

A little way on he stopped.

'We can't all arrive in a mob at this weapon dealer Meginbraht's property,' he said. 'He'll be suspicious. Skar, me and Einar will go on to see him. That looks like a busy tavern over there. The rest of you wait for us there.'

Seeing the looks of delight on their faces, he added, 'Remember the words of Odin: *A man knows less, as he drinks more*. Don't make fools of yourselves or do anything to draw attention. And *please* don't kill anyone.'

Einar looked with longing at the building Ulrich had indicated. It was big and its double front doors were open, allowing the chatter, raucous singing and the sweet smell of fresh ale cascade out, attracting even more people inside. It looked and sounded very like something he had not had very much of lately: fun.

'Why do I have to go with you?' he said.

'Because you saw the Inglerii sword,' Ulrich said. 'If this merchant has one I need you to identify it.'

The three of them continued on around the edge of the square. At one point they had to step aside as a column of chanting people, ringing bells and beating drums, danced towards them, waving their arms and singing a song Einar did not recognise. Their faces were painted garish colours and there were twigs, leaves, dandelions and moss wound into their hair. All of them, both male and female, wore long women's dresses. They carried sprigs of birch and mistletoe. Their eyes were glazed and rolling around, like someone who has drunk too much or eaten poisonous mushrooms and sees things beyond the real world around them. They seemed oblivious to Ulrich, Skar and Einar and could well have walked into them if the Wolf Coats had not moved out of their way.

'I don't think this is a Winter Nights festival, Ulrich,' Skar said as they danced past.

They reached a very large building on the far side of the marketplace which was the trading hall of a merchant. Two steps led up from the street to an extended porch that jutted out from the double doors, providing a short corridor portal. In front of that were four burly men in leather and mail who lounged on stools and a bench. They were fighting men, with scarred faces and arms, missing teeth and broken noses. Their body armour was of different kinds and styles and bore no insignia, marking them out as hired men who fought for whoever paid the most silver, rather than honourable warriors who pledged allegiance to serve a jarl or lord. At the sight of Ulrich, Skar and Einar approaching, the men on the porch stood up.

'I'm looking for Meginbraht the merchant,' Ulrich said. 'I have business to discuss with him.'

'And who are you?' a bald guard with gold rings in both earlobes said, folding his meaty arms before his chest.

'My name is Ulrich,' Ulrich said. 'We're interested in buying some swords.'

'Well you're in the right place,' the bald man said. 'We sell swords. Among other things.'

His companions chuckled.

'Swords are expensive,' the bald man said. 'Have you got silver?'

Ulrich held up his left arm with the silver rings wound around it. Skar did the same. Ulrich also produced a leather purse from inside his jerkin and shook it. The clink of metal on metal came from inside.

'Very well. Come inside,' the bald man said. 'Have a look at the goods.'

He gestured towards the doors behind him. They were open but the interior of the building was gloomy and not much could be made out.

Einar stepped forward but Ulrich laid a hand across his chest to halt him.

'This lot will just try and rip us off once we're inside and we'll never see this merchant,' he said out of the corner of his mouth. 'We need to get past them somehow.'

'Where is Meginbraht?' Ulrich said. 'I wish to deal with the rooster himself, not his chickens.'

The nasty grins disappeared from the faces of the guards.

'Watch your tongue, sea dog,' the bald man, who appeared to be the leader of the guards, said. 'Maybe we don't want your custom today after all.'

He reached down and lifted a long wooden club from beside his stool. It looked like the handle of an axe without the blade. It was well seasoned, worn shiny from use with several splashes of dark brown, dried blood on it.

His companion to his right dropped his hand to the hilt of the knife sheathed at his belt. The third guard picked up another club similar to the bald man and the last man, a barrel-chested thug with long blond hair that he wore in two braids, unsheathed a broken-backed seax that was as big as a heavy knife used for cleaving horsemeat.

'Let's go,' Ulrich said under his breath.

Einar started. For all his talk of not drawing attention to themselves, Ulrich was going to take these men – who outnumbered them, had weapons and were above them up the porch steps – on.

He felt a brief moment of panic then forced himself to calm down. In moments he would have to pitch in to whatever happened.

Ulrich stepped forward, both hands raised in a placatory gesture. Skar was on his right and Einar on his left. In his right hand he held up his leather purse.

'Look, we've got off on the wrong foot, I'm sorry—' Ulrich said.

Then he struck.

Ulrich slapped the leather purse across the face of the bald man hard. It connected with his jaw in a crack of bone. The bald man's head whipped sideways, several of his teeth came flying from his mouth and he staggered backwards then collapsed, plonking down on his backside on the porch.

Skar jumped up onto the porch, his long legs making it easy to skip the two steps. In an instant he was chest to chest with the second guard who was still in the process of drawing his knife. Skar dropped his right hand on top of the guard's, stopping him from unsheathing the blade any further. Skar head-butted the guard full in the face. The man's nose exploded in a crimson flower. He cried out, his free hand going to his smashed nose. Skar drove his left knee up into the man's groin, doubling him over with new pain. Then Skar stepped back from him and swung his other leg. His right foot connected to the guard's chin with full force and he crashed, unconscious, face first to the porch floor.

Ulrich ran up the steps. The other guard with a club came at him. He had the weapon raised behind his head, cocked for a massive swing that if it connected was likely to take the little man's head right off his shoulders.

Ulrich stepped towards him. He raised his left hand and caught the back of the guard's arm, pushing against it. The fully extended angle the guard's arm was at, and the force of Ulrich's shove, meant he just could not follow through with his swing. The man's eyes widened in disbelief that the little man before him could be preventing him from hitting him. He tried again to swing and failed again. Ulrich kicked his right leg forward. His boot connected with the guard's kneecap. The man howled with pain and fell over. He dropped his club on the way down as both hands instinctively grabbed his knee as if they could staunch the agony that had exploded there.

Ulrich stepped over him, lifted his club and cracked him over the skull with it. The guard went limp on the floor.

The man with the seax swiped at Einar. It was a huge chop designed to cut deep into the side of Einar's chest. Einar went up on his toes, arched his back and pulled his stomach in so the blade missed him. The momentum of the swing meant the guard continued to twist at his waist in a half turn.

Einar reached with his left hand and grabbed the guard's

long braids. He hauled back on them and yanked to the right at the same time, both tilting the man's head backwards and compelling him to turn further. He now faced away from Einar and swiped harmless chops at the air before him.

Einar balled his maimed right hand into a fist and brought it down as hard as he could, hitting the point on the right of the guard's throat where it reached the bottom of his neck, the same point Affreca had hit the monk in Jorvik.

At the same moment, Skar, finished with his own opponent, slammed his big fist into the chin of the guard Einar was fighting. The man's head snapped back and Einar felt him go limp.

Einar felt a thrill of triumph. They had dealt with four dangerous opponents in about as many heartbeats. To be in a fight again felt good, and a rush of relief that he had not made a mess of it flooded his chest.

'How many coins do you have in that purse?' he said to Ulrich, looking down at the shattered jaw and broken teeth of the first man Ulrich had hit.

'None,' Ulrich said. 'Just lead balls that clank like coins. It's a useful little ploy. You can take a purse many places you're not allowed to take weapons.'

'What about all that talk about not drawing attention to ourselves?' Einar said.

'I don't intend to,' Ulrich said. 'Let's get them out of sight and inside before one of those patrols of the Watch comes past.'

Einar glanced around and saw the passers-by in the street had not taken notice of the fight and no one was looking their way. Perhaps the fight had been so swift and silent that no one had seen it or perhaps Hedeby was the sort of place that when you saw something violent happen, you made sure you minded your own business in case you were next.

Einar and Ulrich grabbed an unconscious guard each by the jerkin. Skar grabbed the other two and they dragged the men off the porch and into the house through the double doors.

Once inside, they stopped. Going from the daylight outside to the gloomy interior, it took Einar's eyes a moment to adjust.

He saw that they stood in a long room that was stacked full of all sorts of goods and materials. A richly dressed man in clothes of many colours and a blue felt hat sat behind a table. He had a long black moustache under which sat a faintly amused smile.

Behind him stood six archers with their bows drawn. They had arrows notched, and the points aimed at Einar, Skar and Ulrich, two on each one.

'Don't make another move,' the man at the table said. 'And give me one good reason why I shouldn't have you shot like the dogs you are and then call the jarl's watchmen to collect your corpses.'

Thirty-One

'Because it would be murder?' Ulrich suggested.

The man at the table gave a little chuckle.

'My friend, you break into my property,' he said, 'assault my bodyguards and now no doubt intend to rob me. I am on very good terms with the watchmen. I make sure I always pay my taxes, and a little extra to ensure I am not troubled in my business. They will not worry about the deaths of three strangers, I assure you.'

He stood up.

'So what do we have here?' he said. 'You look like ordinary shipmen, sailors just off a boat. But the way you dealt with my bodyguards shows you are not simple mariners. My men were no ordinary warriors. One of them used to protect the Frankish Emperor. Another was a former hearthman of King Gorm of Denmark. They were not cheap. Yet you managed to deal with them in moments.'

'They weren't that good,' Skar said.

'Every instinct I have tells me that I should tell my archers to shoot you,' the man in the hat said. 'However I'm intrigued. You *have* come to rob me, I take it?'

'Not at all,' Ulrich said. 'We wish to do business.'

'You have a strange way of approaching it,' the man said.

'I like to get to the point quickly,' Ulrich said. 'Your men were messing me about. You are Meginbraht I take it?'

'I am,' the merchant said. 'You know my name, but do you know who I work for?'

Einar noticed the merchant's eyes flicked from Ulrich to Skar to himself to over their shoulders and back again. The smile on his face was fixed and bore little humour. Einar realised then that despite Meginbraht's supposed nonchalance, bravado and air of control of the situation, the merchant was shaken and on the lookout for another attack.

'Let me warn you my friend,' Meginbraht said. 'If you're really here to rob me it would be very foolish. The man I work for is very dangerous. Very dangerous indeed.'

'Asbjorn Hviti?' Ulrich said. 'I know all about him, don't worry. I have come from King Aethelstan of Wessex. If I were to tell you he wishes to buy swords from you would you tell your archers to relax?'

Meginbraht waved his right hand in the air as if trying to dispel a bad smell.

'I deal with kings, jarls – all sorts of nobility – all the time,' he said. 'Do you think mentioning the name of Aethelstan will make me drool like a puppy? This is all very hard to believe. Aethelstan is a great and powerful Christian king of the Saxons. You are norsemen. If there is one thing Aethelstan does not have much truck with, it's vikings. And you do not look particularly noble either. You are obviously highly accomplished in war craft but you have the look of simple sailors in your sealskins. I have to ask myself: would Aethelstan send three scruffy vikings to do his business for him?'

His bowmen remained ready. Einar saw the cold eyes at the other end of the arrows pointed at him and knew they would not hesitate to shoot if the order was given.

'We're former Úlfhéðnar of King Eirik Bloody Axe of Norway,' Ulrich said. The merchant raised his eyebrows. 'We now protect his half-brother, King Hakon. Aethelstan, his foster father, requested that Hakon send us to you to make a deal. Aethelstan is about to go to war. What better way to keep his intentions secret from his future opponents than sending the most unlikely of people to do his dealing for him?'

Meginbraht turned down the corners of his mouth.

'Perhaps,' he said. 'But I know that Aethelstan has his own pet weapon dealer. He has no need to deal with me.'

'Ricbehrt?' Ulrich said. 'We're old friends.'

Einar spotted Skar just about managing to stifle a laugh.

'It was Ricbehrt in fact who told us about you,' Ulrich went on. 'His problem is that he cannot supply what Aethelstan wants.'

'Go on,' Meginbraht said. Einar could see his expression had changed and he had a hungry look in his eyes.

'Aethelstan wishes to buy Inglerii swords,' Ulrich said. 'You're the only person who sells them. Aethelstan is the richest king in the northern world. He has given me permission to tell you that he will pay whatever price you set, provided you can supply the swords.'

Meginbraht was silent for several moments. Then he clicked his fingers. His archers lowered their bows. They still kept their arrows notched, but Einar felt the tension drain from his body.

'So the Emperor of Britain wants my special swords?'

the merchant said, shaking his head and grinning. Einar could see he was delighted at the thought of the wealth this promised.

'The Inglerii have made me rich and Asbjorn even richer. That voyage to Finnmark was the most profitable raid he ever made.'

'What voyage?' Ulrich said.

Meginbraht recovered his composure.

'Never you mind,' he said. 'But all right: I might be interested. When does Aethelstan want them however?'

'As soon as he can get them,' Ulrich said.

'That might be a problem,' Meginbraht said with a sigh. 'All the swords are spoken for at the moment. I cannot supply any more until the current order is fulfilled.'

'So you – or rather Asbjorn – can get more?' Ulrich said. 'He knows where to source them?'

'We can get you more, don't worry friend,' the merchant said. 'But there is a waiting list for them.'

'Who is the current order for?' Ulrich said. 'Aethelstan will pay more than whoever it is has ordered them. We can deal between us and leave the Bear out of it.'

'Who they are for is my business,' Meginbraht said. 'And Aethelstan could not pay me enough for me to sell you the swords behind Asbjorn's back. I'd be a dead man if I did. Asbjorn Hviti himself needs them.'

'I see,' Ulrich said. 'What if we talked to the Bear directly then? If you tell us where his fortress is, we'll go there and talk to him. We have our own ship.'

Meginbraht shook his head.

'I can't tell you that,' he said. 'Asbjorn has many enemies and much treasure. He's obsessed with keeping the location of his fortress secret. He kills anyone he even suspects of knowing where it is.'

'I know we're getting on better than a moment ago,' Ulrich said, gesturing towards Meginbraht's fallen guards who still lay on the floor. They were starting to groan and stir as consciousness began to return to their bodies. 'But you've seen what we are capable of. Have no illusions. If we want to get you we can and we will. We could come back in the night and *make* you tell us where the Bear's fortress is.'

'That would be no use, my friend,' Meginbraht said, shaking his head and smiling. 'The fact is, I don't know where it is and I don't want to. If Asbjorn thought I did then he might see me as a danger to him and that is not a position I ever want to be in.'

Ulrich looked at the merchant for several moments as if trying to make up his mind if he was telling the truth or not.

'But I'll tell you what,' Meginbraht said. 'I'm expecting a visit from someone who I might be able to ask if we could perhaps divert some of the Ingleriis to you, provided Aethelstan is prepared to pay the right price. Why don't you go and enjoy the festival for a bit? Come back later and I might have another answer for you.'

'What is this festival anyway?' Skar said. 'It's a little early for Winter Nights, isn't it?'

'It's called the Festival of Sirius, because that star is rising at this time,' Meginbraht said. 'We have many people here in Hedeby from all over the world. Many worship the *Aesir* but many worship other gods. There are a few Christians here, and we even have worshippers of the Gods of the Serks. The jarl wants a festival that everyone can join in with. That is good for business. So everyone can honour their own gods in their own way, then the whole town gathers together for celebration in the marketplace.'

'So it means nothing, then?' Ulrich said.

'It means everything,' Meginbraht said, spreading his arms wide and smiling. 'Not least for the merchants who supply wine and ale. Go along. You might even enjoy yourself.'

Ulrich sighed. He looked at the merchant, then the archers, then shrugged.

'Very well,' he said. 'We'll go and return later tonight. How likely is it you will be able to get some of the swords though?'

'I'll do my best,' Meginbraht said. 'That's all I can say.'

Ulrich led Skar and Einar out of the merchant's house once more. It was starting to get dark and torches in brackets had been lit in the streets, as well as braziers across the marketplace to provide light and heat to the revellers there. More and more people were gathering and, as ever more ale was drunk, the noise was growing louder.

'What now?' Skar said as they stood among the moving throng of people in the street outside. 'Can we go for a drink with the others?'

'Not yet,' Ulrich said. 'I wonder just who he's going to talk to. Let's find somewhere we can keep an eye on the place without him knowing for a bit and see what we learn.'

'If you don't believe him why don't we just go back in there and make him talk?' Skar said.

'Because I did that the last time and walked straight into his archers,' Ulrich said. 'You should know, Skar, sometimes you can learn more just from watching. I should have followed my own advice: Watch first, then strike. Never attack until you know as much as you can about your enemy. When the time comes to strike, you should know him better than you do your own wife.'

'I'd hate to be your wife, Ulrich,' Skar said.

Meginbraht's property was at the edge of the busy marketplace, on one side of a street that proceeded onwards inland. Ulrich, Skar and Einar went to the other side of the street where they did their best to both lose themselves in the crowd of passers-by and look like they were interested in goods offered by the merchants whose stalls and properties lined that side. With a practised tactic Skar had taught Einar and the others previously, two of them took it in turns to engage with a merchant, asking questions about his wares or haggling about the price, while the third man took the opportunity to keep a surreptitious watch on Meginbraht's house while pretending to be engaged in the conversation.

Einar took his turn but nothing of consequence happened. No one came out and no one went in. Then it was Ulrich's turn and Skar after him. After the watcher role had rotated like this three times, Einar started to get bored and found himself more interested in the goods the merchants on that side of the street were selling than the house of the merchant he was supposed to be watching.

One thing that grasped his attention in particular was a curious little bronze statue. It depicted a strange looking man sitting cross-legged on top of what looked like a large flower. His eyes were oval shaped and he was wearing some sort of pointed hat. Einar was just about to ask the merchant selling it if it was supposed to be an elf when he felt someone grasp his elbow.

Turning, he saw it was Ulrich, whose turn it was to watch Meginbraht's house.

'You should go,' Ulrich said. 'We don't need you any more.'

'What?' Einar said, frowning. 'What about the Inglerii? I thought you wanted me to identify them?'

'Yes, well he hasn't got any at the moment so we don't need you,' Ulrich said. 'Skar and I can handle this. Go and have a drink.'

'This is—' Einar started to protest further. He was confused and a little upset by Ulrich's sudden change in demeanour.

'I'm telling you to go,' Ulrich said, glaring, wide-eyed at Einar. 'Don't question my orders again.'

'Do what he says, lad,' Skar said, laying a hand on Einar's shoulder.

Einar looked at both of them, jaw gaping, astounded by the sudden change in their attitude towards him.

'All right, I'll go,' he said.

Einar turned and stomped off towards the marketplace. His confusion turning to anger and resentment that, as usual, Ulrich was dismissing him. The Wolf Coat leader's words from their discussion on the ship after leaving Jorvik – *are you really good enough and have you really recovered from your sickness?* – resurfaced in his mind.

Had Ulrich really so little faith in him?

Thirty-Two

'You were a bit hard on the lad, Ulrich,' Skar said once Einar was gone. 'What's going on?'

'I had to get him out of here quickly,' Ulrich said. 'Look down the street. Be careful though.'

He flicked his head backwards as he picked up the bronze statue Einar had been looking at and pretended to be interested in it.

Skar glanced down the street. A crowd of men, obviously together, were making their way along the wooden planking. They were a rough looking band, clad in leather jerkins and brynjas that glistened with oil for suppleness and ease of movement in combat rather than polished for show. Their faces were scarred and tattooed and they exuded an air of menace like a dark cloud around them. They led several pack horses along the street. In their midst was a huge man, a head and shoulders taller than the crowd around him. His shoulders were swathed in a cloak of white animal fur.

Skar turned back to Ulrich.

'That can only be our man the Bear,' he said in a quiet voice.

'Who else would Meginbraht be waiting to talk to?' Ulrich said. 'Did you see who was with him?'

'A bunch of rough-looking vikings,' Skar said. 'Probably his own crew.'

'Look again,' Ulrich said from the corner of his mouth.

Skar looked over his shoulder again. This time he spotted another man in the Bear's company. He was tall and painfully thin and wore a long, blue robe that reached to his feet like a woman's dress. The crown of his head was completely bald with a ring of long white hair around it that fell to his shoulders.

'Well, well,' Skar said, turning away again. 'If it isn't our old friend Vakir the seið maðr as well. What do we do?'

'Get out of the way for the time being,' Ulrich said. 'You're nearly as tall as the Bear and I don't want Vakir spotting us.'

They pushed their way through the crowd then ducked down into the gap between two of the longhouses that lined their side of the street. Skar lurked further back while Ulrich flattened himself against the wall of one of the houses close enough to the corner that he could still peer around it to watch what was going on in the street.

'I spotted him coming a way off,' Ulrich said. 'Now do you understand why we had to get Einar out of the way?'

'Yes,' Skar said. 'The hate he holds for Vakir – if Einar caught sight of him I doubt he'd be able to control the rage that Odin has blessed him with.'

'He would rush out and kill him,' Ulrich said. 'I've no doubt about it, and that would ruin everything. If we keep our heads and watch what's going on at Meginbraht's, they could lead us right to the Bear's fortress and those Inglerii swords.'

Skar cast an admiring glance at Ulrich.

'You're quite clever for someone so short,' he said with a smile.

'Did you notice something else?' Ulrich said. 'This street leads inland, away from the harbour.'

'So they didn't sail here,' Skar said. 'They must have come across the marshes.'

'It makes sense,' Ulrich said. 'If Meginbraht sells his plunder here then where the Bear keeps it mustn't be too far away. Did you hear what the merchant said about the swords as well? When they run out they can get more. So Asbjorn Hviti didn't just steal all those Ingleriis in a viking raid. The wizard blacksmith who makes them must still be alive and the Bear must have some sort of deal with him to keep making them, except now just for him. And here we go – what a surprise…'

Ulrich's tone of voice betrayed the fact that what he had just observed across the street was anything but a surprise.

'… the Bear, his men and Vakir have all just gone into Meginbraht's house.'

'What do we do now?' Skar said.

'We need to find out what they're talking about,' Ulrich said. 'We need to get in there again.'

'But how?' Skar said. 'The Bear must have ten or more men with him and he looks pretty dangerous himself. There's far too many of them for us to fight this time.'

'Nor do I want to try,' Ulrich said. 'This calls for stealth, not force. Let's see if we can find another way in. Come on.'

They walked back out into the street once more. The Bear and his crew were gone inside Meginbraht's house and the door was now closed, though six of his vikings now stood guard on the porch outside. The pack horses were tied to a post and the chests that had been strapped to their backs were gone.

Ulrich flicked his head to Skar and they walked on up the street, past the next building along from the merchant's property.

After a quick look around to check no one was watching them, the pair slunk off the street and ducked into the space between the house beside Meginbraht's and the one beside that. They crossed the length of the building until they reached the rear. There were enclosures behind the houses marked out by daub and wattle fences. Some had chickens, pigs or geese in them, some had small patches growing vegetables and all had a latrine pit surrounded by a wicker wall. Because of the way the streets of Hedeby were laid out like a net, the enclosures behind the houses on the street and Meginbraht's house were back to back with the enclosures of the buildings on the next street along. Ulrich led the way through the enclosures until they came to the large one at the back of Meginbraht's.

He and Skar scrambled over the daub and wattle fence and tramped through a patch of kale and other vegetables. There was a small door in the gable wall.

Ulrich exchanged glances with Skar then they both flattened themselves against the gable wall, one on either side of the door. Ulrich reached down and with careful fingers pulled the door open.

Nothing happened. No one shouted. No one came out.

Both Skar and Ulrich rushed in. They found themselves in a gloomy cooking room. It was very warm from the fire and there were pots and cauldrons bubbling above it. They saw a thrall, lurking behind a door on the other side of the room, his ear pressed to it. His attention was fixed on listening to whatever was going on beyond the door and he had not noticed the newcomers. Whether he was waiting for shouted orders or just being nosey, Skar did not wait to find out.

Lifting a large metal ladle from one of the cauldrons, in a couple of strides of his long legs he crossed the room. The slave just had time to catch the movement out of the corner of his eye. His mouth was opening to cry out when Skar brought the ladle down with a dull clang across the back of the slave's skull. The man's eyes rolled up into his head and he sprawled backwards across the dirt floor, knocked out cold.

Ulrich and Skar stood in silence for a few moments, ears straining for any sign they had caused enough noise to attract attention. When none came, Skar dropped to a crouch and ripped the unconscious slave's shirt apart, using it to bind his hands and gag his mouth.

They could hear the sound of voices from the other side of the door the thrall had been listening at. With bated breath Ulrich laid his hand on the latch. With agonising slowness he pushed it down, hair's breadth by hair's breadth, then pulled the door open a crack.

They found themselves with a narrow view of the opposite end of the long room they had previously talked in to Meginbraht.

There was a crowd in the other room gathered around the table: the merchant, the Bear, Vakir and the rest of the Bear's vikings as well as the merchant's archers and bodyguards. The injured men were gone. There was a chest on the table and Meginbraht was counting out silver and gold pieces from it, listing the items that he had sold on behalf of the Bear; a litany of stolen plunder from gold and silver crosses to jewellery, household goods and slaves. The big man listened, a glowering expression on his face.

'You've done well to shift all this,' he said at length. Like most very large men his voice was low and booming. 'You deserve your cut.'

'*You've* done well from plundering all this, Asbjorn,' Meginbraht said. 'This latest haul must make you richer than some jarls.'

'I have men to pay,' the Bear said, 'A fortress to run. Ships to provision. It's not all profit.'

'Now for future business,' Meginbraht said, closing the chest on the table with a flourish. 'There is a lot of interest in the Inglerii swords, as usual. I even had someone asking about them today.'

The huge viking held up a spade-like hand.

'We must fulfil the current commitment before doing anything else,' he said. 'Eirik needs my current crop of swords and it suits my own aims to make sure he gets them. Which brings me to our friend Vakir here.'

He nodded towards the seið maðr.

'He's here to take the consignment back to Orkney,' the Bear said. 'I need you to look after him here while I fetch the swords from my fortress.'

'You're leaving me here?' Vakir said, a dubious expression on his face.

'I've told you before: I don't like anyone except my most trusted men knowing where my fortress is,' Asbjorn Hviti said. 'A man like me makes many enemies in his life and the last thing I need is them finding out where I live.'

'I don't see why I cannot go with you,' Vakir said. 'Your fortress cannot be too far from here.'

'Don't worry,' the merchant said. 'He doesn't even trust me enough to let me know where it is. And you won't be on your own. We'll look after you here. Hedeby is a very hospitable place. There is much to entertain you. You can get whatever you want in this town and we are celebrating the Festival of Sirius tonight.'

'Indeed? Is it tonight?' Vakir said. He looked a little mollified and began to stroke his chin. 'I've heard of this celebration. I'm a religious man and I will admit that I am curious as to how the Gods are honoured here.'

'I can assure you, my friend,' the merchant said. 'Whatever gods you pay homage to, there are people here to honour them in their own way.'

'Tell me,' Vakir said. 'I've heard that in Hedeby there are many followers of...'

He licked his lips, his eyes flicking sideways.

'Helblindi's brother,' he finished in a quiet voice, as if he did not want too many people to overhear him. He gave a little cough.

There was a moment's silence. Meginbraht looked at the Bear. Then both men exchanged knowing smiles.

'A man of special taste's, eh?' the merchant said. 'Well my friend that is true. You will find many like-minded folk here. My men will take you to the marketplace where I am sure you will find some of Helblindi's brother's devotees.'

'Meginbraht and I have much to discuss that is of no consequence of yours anyway,' the Bear said. 'You will stay here in Hedeby and I will return in time with the Ingleriis, then you can take them back to Eirik.'

In the cooking room, Skar looked at Ulrich and mouthed the words *Helblindi's brother?*

Ulrich shrugged.

'Until then, then,' Vakir said, a lewd grin breaking out across his face. Then two of Meginbraht's bowmen led him outside through the front door.

Skar leaned very close to Ulrich.

'Should we follow him?' he said in a breathless whisper, directly into Ulrich's ear. 'What if he runs into Einar?'

Ulrich shook his head.

'We have to take that risk,' he whispered back. 'We stay here and keep listening. We've got to find where the Bear's fortress is.'

After Vakir had gone, the merchant produced a wine jug and poured two horns full, one for himself and one for the big viking.

'Fucking pervert,' the Bear said in a growl, glaring at the door Vakir had left by and taking a swig from his drinking horn. 'He makes my flesh creep. I'd swear Eirik only sent him with me to get him out of his own way.'

'Are you sure you can't make more Ingleriis any faster?' the merchant said. 'Honestly, I could sell ten times the number you currently supply, even at their sky-high price.'

The Bear sighed.

'It's limited to what one man can make,' he said.

'What if we get more blacksmiths?' Meginbraht said. 'Wouldn't that speed things up?'

'Smiths are not exactly easy to come across,' the Bear said. 'It's a trade handed down father to son and the son inherits the father's forge. There don't tend to be spare ones wandering the countryside. Besides, these swords are made in a very special process and that stubborn fool Ingler refuses to share it.'

'I'm sure you could make him,' the merchant said.

'I'm sure I could,' the Bear said. 'But I must be careful how much pressure I put on him. He's shrewd as a fox that one and bloody minded too. If the time comes when I must make him tell me then I'll do it, but I risk him doing something stupid like killing himself and then we'll all lose out.'

'I see what you mean,' Meginbraht said. 'Best not kill the goose that lays the golden eggs, eh?'

'At least not until the goose is no longer able to lay those eggs,' the Bear said. 'Then he will make a fine supper. Speaking of supper, have you got anything to eat?'

In the cooking room, Ulrich and Skar exchanged glances.

'*Time to go*,' Ulrich mouthed at Skar.

The big man hoisted the bound, gagged and unconscious thrall over his shoulder and he and Ulrich hurried out the back door.

Thirty-Three

After leaving Ulrich and Skar, a highly disgruntled Einar stomped off to the marketplace, intending to return to the tavern they had left the rest of the crew at and drink his fill of ale, wine, mead or whatever else was on offer there.

Fuck you, Ulrich, he thought to himself. I'm going to enjoy myself whatever your orders.

As he walked towards the laughter, chatter and general merriment that was coming from the festival site, he had to step aside as a company of the jarl's watchmen came hurrying in the opposite direction. They were trailing the limp bodies of two unconscious men along the street whose faces were little more than bloody pulp. The sticks and clubs of the watchmen, as well as their boots, were spattered with blood. It was clear that even though some of the watchmen still wore the flowers and greenery they had allowed revellers to deck them with, their tolerance for any behaviour that got out of hand was all gone.

The festival was now in full swing. The tables that lined the market square were jammed with people drinking and singing. Some people were dancing around as musicians went around the tables, entertaining the revellers. The murk of late evening had descended and the whole scene was lit by torches burning in raised brackets or braziers dotted around the area.

Einar skirted around the party until he came to the tavern he was looking for. It was a long- house like the others but had large double doors like a jarl's hall. As Einar went in, two drunk men came stumbling out, clinging to each other for support like drowning swimmers. Einar avoided them and went inside, relishing the fug of warm air and ale fumes that filled the air.

The tavern was packed and very noisy. People crowded the tables or stood around, talking and drinking from ale horns. Slaves rushed to and fro, serving ale and dried or salted fish to the customers. There was a roaring fire at one end of the room. Einar pushed through the crowd of drinkers, looking for his crewmates.

There was no sign of them however. He felt a moment's panic at the realisation that he was alone in a foreign city, then reasoned that it was not the first time. The rest of the Wolf Coats had in all probability gone on to somewhere else or joined the festivities outside and if he failed to find them he could always just go back to the ship. He went over to the long serving table. A bald man with a scarred head stood behind it, arms folded, a peeved expression on his face. Einar guessed he was the owner of the tavern.

'Have you seen a bunch of men in sailing clothes?' Einar said, raising his voice to be heard above the chatter and laughter of the tavern patrons. 'They were in here earlier. I'm trying to catch up with them.'

The tavern owner raised an eyebrow. Einar realised how stupid his question must sound. The tavern and the town were both awash with folk who had just come off ships.

'One has black skin,' he said. 'There's a young woman with them. She's very beautiful.'

'If you buy a drink I'll tell you,' the tavern owner said.

'Ale, please,' Einar said, remembering his raging thirst.

He pulled a little piece of hack silver from his purse and laid it on the table. The tavern owner lifted a ladle and dipped it in an open barrel of ale, then poured the frothing amber liquid into a drinking horn, which he then handed to Einar.

'So did you see my friends or not?' Einar said.

'No,' the tavern owner said.

Einar shook his head and turned away. He took a long, appreciative drink from the horn as he leaned back against the serving table and took a look around the room.

'So it's really true,' a voice said from nearby. 'No matter where you sail in the world, you will run into an Icelander.'

Einar turned and saw a group of young men standing nearby. They were dressed in shaggy cloaks of un-dyed wool and plain tunics and breeches, clothes which looked very plain compared to the riot of colours the other patrons of the tavern wore. For a moment Einar peered at them. There was something familiar about several of them but he could not quite work out why. They were looking at him, lopsided grins on their faces.

Then he realised who they were. Einar could scarcely believe it. Here he was in a tavern in a town at the far end of the world and some of his old friends from Midfjord, his home district in Iceland, were standing before him.

'Ulli! Kikkur!' Einar cried, rushing over to join them. 'Hegg! You're here too? What are you doing here?'

There was much joyous hugging and slaps on the back

and arm clasping. From their flushed faces and inane grins he could tell the lads had been drinking for some time and were many horns of ale ahead of him. They were all around the same age, Einar's peers from the old homeland and had known each other all their lives. Einar felt a strange pang at the sight of them. Being surrounded once more by familiar old faces gave him a sudden longing for home.

'We're all part of Gunnar's crew now,' Kikkur said. 'He sailed with Bjarni just after you first left Iceland. He made so much wealth he's now got his own longship. We joined his crew and we've been voyaging with him for most of the last year.'

'You must have had some adventures,' Einar said.

'We've been all over the world,' Ulli said. 'But nothing like what you've been up to.'

'I heard you're an Úlfhéðinn now,' Hegg said, his expression and tone of voice tinged with awe. 'And you killed a dragon in Scotland.'

Einar blushed but felt a thrill of excitement at the thought that his former teammates from the Midfjord *knattleikr* team, his peers from his home in Iceland, the lads he had grown up with, now held him in such high regard.

'It was a very big dog, I'm afraid,' he said. 'Not a dragon. Let me get you all a drink, eh?'

He waved to the bald-headed tavern keeper who tramped over, a large jug of ale in his arms.

'You lot better behave,' he said as he refilled their drinking horns. 'You're getting very noisy and I don't want any trouble in my ale house.'

'We're just old friends having a laugh,' Ulli said.

'That's what they all say,' the tavern keeper said. 'Next

thing they're fighting with the rest of the customers and the place is wrecked. You suet-munchers from Iceland are the worst for that.'

Some of the happy smiles dissipated from the faces of Einar's old friends.

'If we did decide to turn nasty, friend,' Kikkur said. 'What do you think you could do about it?'

'I'll call the Watch,' the tavern owner said. 'They'll sort you out, don't worry. So don't even think about it.'

He filled the last ale horn and went back to the serving table.

'Miserable old bastard,' Ulli said.

'It's the same everywhere we sail when people find out you're from Iceland,' Kikkur said. 'Suet-munchers, sausage-boilers, sheep-shaggers. They think we're all just bumpkins.'

'If we decided to cause trouble in here he'd soon know about it,' Hegg said. 'Especially with an Úlfhéðinn among us now.'

'All the same,' Einar said, 'I saw those watchmen dragging a couple of drunks away from the festival. It looks like they don't mess around.'

'They really don't,' Kikkur said. 'They won't allow any trouble at all. As soon as anyone even looks like they're going to fight or their partying gets out of hand they go in hard.'

'I heard the jarl doesn't allow any trouble at the festival,' Ulli said. 'It brings a lot of wealth to Hedeby and if there's any trouble it might put people off coming next year.'

'Yet they do nothing about the Loki lovers,' Hegg said, an expression of indignation crossing his face. 'As soon as a few lads get a bit boisterous the Watch pile in, clubs drawn.

But those deviants dance around the whole town and no one bats an eyelid.'

'They're mostly wealthy folk, that's why,' Kikkur said. 'And after all; it is their festival.'

'Who are you talking about?' Einar said, thinking he had misheard.

'You must have seen them?' Ulli said. 'They prance about in dresses, both women and men, faces painted, decked with moss and marsh flowers. They worship Loki.'

Einar's jaw dropped open a little. Loki lived with the Aesir gods in Asgard but whether he was on the side of good or not was very hard to say. He was the son of a jötunn and a goddess and this dual nature meant he sometimes did good and sometimes evil. He was brother to the terrifying jötnars Helblindi and Býleistr. He had helped Odin and Thor in a few adventures but he had killed Baldur, the terrible deed that would eventually lead to the end of the world, the Ragnarök. Loki was also both the father and the mother of the monsters who would bring destruction on that day of doom: *Jörmungander*, the huge serpent that will rise from the sea and battle to the death with Thor. Fenrir the wolf who will devour the sun and Odin himself, and Hel, the horrible, half-rotting queen whose army of the unworthy dead would overwhelm Middle Earth. Why anyone would want to worship a creature like that was beyond him.

'How is this their festival?' Einar said. 'I was told this is the Festival of Sirius?'

'Sirius is just the name the Franks use for the star we call *Lokabrenna*,' Kikkur said. 'Loki's Torch.'

'And they really worship Loki?' Einar said.

'So they claim, but they're also full of magic mushrooms

and the bitter herbs that steal your mind away,' Ulli said with a shrug. 'In my opinion the whole thing is just an excuse to shag anything – women, men...'

'Horses,' Hegg said.

They all dissolved into raucous laughter. Though there was some truth in his comment, as Loki had once taken the form of a mare to distract a magical horse of a jötunn. The stallion had mounted him and Loki had later birthed a magical foal, Sleipnir, the eight-legged horse of Odin.

'Still,' Ulli said. 'It's a great excuse for a party, eh?'

'How's the knattleikr team doing this year?' Einar said.

'Not great,' Kikkur said, taking a drink. 'With all of us gone overseas they've lost the best players. The younger lads just aren't tough enough. They let the Vididal boys push them around too much.'

'Not like when we had old Einar here, eh?' Ulli said, clapping a hand on Einar's shoulder. 'Remember when he punched the face off Audun Hrappsson?'

They all laughed again, though Einar's mirth was bittersweet. It was that moment of rage that had ended up with him being outlawed from Iceland and set him on the journey on the whale road that had led to where he was now. How different would his life be now if he had been able to keep his temper that day? Would he still be living back home in Iceland or would he just have ended up leaving anyway like the lads who stood around him? Would his mother still be alive?

Then again, he would also never have met Affreca. He would not now be the rightful Jarl of Orkney.

Skar had told him several times that he believed the rage that took hold of Einar was sent by Odin himself. Perhaps it was indeed the old one-eyed God who had sent it that day during the ball game on the ice. A little nudge to set him on the path he was on now. But was it Einar's path, or the one Odin wanted him to take for his own, ever inscrutable reasons?

'I'm sorry about what happened to your mother, Einar,' Kikkur said, becoming quite sombre. 'It was a shocking deed. Cold, cowardly murder and nothing else. I only wish some of us had been there to protect her. It would never have happened.'

'Still,' Ulli said. 'I bet you made the bastard who did it pay for his crime, eh?'

'Of course he did!' Hegg said. 'An Icelander always avenges the killing of his relatives, never mind what an Úlfhéðinn would do for the killing of his own mother! What did you do to him, Einar?'

'I thought I'd killed him,' Einar said with a shrug. 'I really did. But the bastard somehow survived.'

An awkward silence fell on the little band of lads for a few moments. Then Kikkur said, 'Still. You'll get him next time, I'm sure. What about some more ale?'

The ice broke again and they fell to talking about old times, reminiscing about funny stories and catching up on what had happened to all of them since they had last been together. As the ale flowed, Einar felt the resentment of Ulrich and the strains of his life melting away. It was comforting to be surrounded once more with folk he had known all his life. People who knew the places he knew, who spoke the same way as he did, not just with the same accent but with the same quirky words used only in Iceland. The feeling, combined with the ale, made him forget he was supposed to be trying to find his crewmates. His heart began to ache a little for his homeland.

'If you were travelling you'll have missed the volcano in Iceland earlier this year then,' Einar said. 'That must've done some damage to the south. I was back there and had to leave just as it erupted. I hope everyone was all right.'

'We heard about that too,' Ulli said. 'Your fame has spread wherever there are Icelanders in the world. You killed Jarl Thorfinn – threw him into the volcano!'

Einar blushed again. At the same time he felt a little shiver run down his spine as he remembered the horror of that battle to the death with his own father. A memory of the hulking figure of Thorfinn the Skull Cleaver, his outline a black silhouette against the rivers of fire that flowed behind him as he prepared to strike, surfaced in his mind. At the same time he clenched and unclenched his injured hand.

'It must have been a huge volcano,' Hegg said. 'The weather's terrible even this far south. I notice the bread isn't as abundant as it should be here. Folk are hoarding for the winter already.'

'What do you mean?' Einar said. 'What's the volcano got to do with the weather?'

'Didn't your old folk ever tell you?' Hegg said, then his expression changed to one of understanding. 'Oh, I forgot, your mother was a foreigner wasn't she? Irish I think? And your father was... well.'

He shrugged.

'All the old folk in Iceland used to talk of how the *fimbulwinter* follows a volcano,' Ulli said.

'My grandmother told me the last time that volcano erupted,' Hegg said, 'a long time ago when she was very young, there was no summer for two years afterwards. It was like the volcano somehow stopped summer coming.'

Einar frowned. If this was true then Ulrich was wrong. The world was not ending. Ragnarök was not coming. Part of him hoped it was not correct because if Ulrich got them all killed on some last mad dash for glory because he thought there was no time left, then they would be going to the graves for nothing.

'Shall we have more ale?' Einar said, noticing the drinking horns were empty again.

'I want another drink but I don't fancy giving that miserable bastard any more custom,' Hegg said, cocking his head towards the tavern owner who was standing behind the serving table, his meaty arms folded across his chest, glowering at them.

'This isn't the only tavern in the town,' Ulli said. 'And there's plenty of ale being served at the festival outside.'

'Plenty of girls too,' Kikkur said.

They all cheered.

'Come on,' Hegg said. 'Let's go.'

Full of ale and good cheer, the band of happy lads shoved their drinking horns into their belts and strode out into the night outside.

For a moment they stood in the threshold, looking at the revelry going on outside.

'Here come a bunch of Loki lovers, lads,' Ulli said. 'Watch your arses.'

They all laughed.

Einar looked and saw a column of the same odd-looking folk he had seen earlier come dancing along the street. Like before, they all wore long women's dresses, both men and women. They chanted, rang bells and beat drums as they danced with strange, jerky movements. Their eyes were glazed and wild.

Then he froze.

He could hardly believe his own eyes. Prancing along at the end of the column was a tall, stick-thin figure. He had a bald crown that was surrounded by a ring of long white hair.

It was Vakir.

Thirty-Four

Einar felt a sensation like ice-cold water being poured down his spine. All his mirth and good feeling vanished. Everything around him appeared to be bathed in a strange ochre hue that had nothing to do with the flickering torchlight of the marketplace. He breathed in and out through his nose, sparking a prickling feeling like pins and needles through his shoulders and neck.

The rage was coming. He could do nothing about it, he knew.

Nor did he want to. If Odin really did send this anger then he must also have placed both Einar and Vakir in this place at the same time. Odin was asking a question: What was Einar going to do now?

All the doubts, second guesses and overthinking that usually caused him to procrastinate vanished. There was only deep, cold rage. Einar no longer cared if he lived or died. All he felt was an overwhelming lust to maim, destroy and kill the man who had murdered his mother.

Then he was running. He neither screamed, shouted or roared. In total silence he bolted away from his friends and pounded over the wooden-planked walkway of the street.

He was aware of frightened faces passing before him but was intent on just Vakir.

The Galdr maðr caught sight of Einar. His eyes were wide and he fumbled to draw a knife from his belt. Einar was aware of movement from the corner of his eye. There were others – a couple of burly men like the ones he had seen earlier at the merchant's house – were running towards him. He knew they were on course to stop him getting to Vakir.

Then Hegg, Kikkur and Ulli were by his side. They tackled the other men and all of them went down in a heap of punches and kicks in the street. Einar kept going. The world seemed to have slowed down around him. He was moving at a normal rate but to Einar it seemed that everyone else was moving slowly, like people trying to run through deep water.

Vakir had his knife drawn now. He brandished it before himself like someone holding a holy talisman to ward off an evil creature, rather than defending himself against a trained warrior. Einar just swatted Vakir's slim right wrist aside with a sweep of his left hand, taking the blade out of the way with it.

With his other hand, Einar ripped his drinking horn from its sheath on his belt. Grasping it by the wide end he raised it above his head. He brought it down, stabbing the pewter-capped tip into Vakir's flesh at the left side of the base of his neck. At the same time he barged his left shoulder and head into the Galdr maðr.

Once, when he was twelve winters old, Einar had travelled with his mother and their household to a *Dísablót* feast at one of the neighbouring farms. His mother had forgotten a haunch of ham she was supposed to bring and had sent

Einar back to fetch it, dismissing his protests of fear at the prospect of crossing the dark countryside on his own. He had been crossing a barley field, his heart full of terror at what trolls, witches, dark elves or the dreadful walking dead, the *draugr*, may be lurking in the darkness.

Halfway across the field his heart had frozen at the sight of a strange figure in white, rising about the barley ahead. Then in panic he had charged the figure, only to find it was just a scarecrow. Instead of a jarring impact he had just gone sprawling through the arrangement of sticks and sheets like there was nothing there.

Einar found himself experiencing the same feeling as he crashed into Vakir. It was like running into a bundle of sticks wrapped in a sheet. The Galdr maðr flew backwards, landing flat on his back on the wooden planks in the street. Einar fell on top of him. The grip of his maimed hand failed. The top of the drinking horn twisted away from his grasp, leaving the pointed end embedded about the depth of a finger in Vakir's throat.

Vakir's eyes bulged and his mouth opened and closed in frantic motion. He was saying something but to Einar it felt as though he spoke in a different tongue. His words meant nothing to him. Einar pushed himself back up, kneeling on the Galdr maðr, one leg on either side of his chest.

He grabbed the drinking horn, this time with both hands. This time there would be no mistake. Vakir would die. Einar wrenched the horn out of Vakir's wound. As soon as the tip was free it unleashed a huge spurt of hot, red blood that sprayed across Einar's chest and face.

Einar stabbed down again with the drinking horn. This time he drove it into Vakir's screaming mouth. He felt it breaking teeth and grinding against bone then he pulled it up again. Einar stabbed again, this time putting it into Vakir's staring left eye. The tip exploded the Galdr maðr's eyeball and crunched through the bone that held it in place, powering on into his skull and the brain within it. Vakir's body jerked and bucked beneath Einar for a moment with surprising power for such a slight-built man. Then he went still, a torrent of his life's blood gushing from the three gory holes driven into his head and neck.

This time Vakir was dead for sure. Unlike the last time Einar and he had clashed, this time he would not be returning.

Einar looked up. The air was filled with the coppery smell of blood. He could feel it hot and sticky across his face. He was surrounded by people staring at him, frozen in horror. Kikkur, Ulli and Hegg were still fighting with one of the merchant's men, having managed to knock one of them out.

Then horns and whistles were blowing. There was shouting and six of the Hedeby watchmen came charging onto the scene.

'What's going on here?' one of them shouted.

'Murder!' a woman in the dress of the Loki worshippers shouted. She was pointing at Einar. 'He just ran up and killed one of our people. With no reason!'

The watchmen hefted their shields and readied their clubs. They split into two groups, three going for Einar and six for the other Icelanders. They had their shields linked in a wall formation. Einar knew their intention was to slam their shields into him then pummel him with their clubs.

Einar jumped to his feet and ran straight at them. Just as they braced their shoulders for his impact Einar threw himself to the ground. He rolled side over side, barrelling under their shields and scything their legs from beneath them.

The watchmen went sprawling forwards, falling on their own shields, while Einar rolled back to his feet. Ignoring the men he had knocked over he charged at the other watchmen who were attacking his friends. He was now behind them and smashed with all his weight into their backs, disrupting their shield wall and sending another two to the ground.

Hegg, Ulli and Kikkur tore into the other four watchmen. The struggle became a brawl with men exchanging punches and kicks, locked in desperate grapples with each other while their feet skidded on the wooden boards that lined the street.

More horns blew and the shouting around them became a torrent of noise. Then the watchmen were no longer fighting with them but were fighting to get away. They freed themselves and withdrew, back-pedalling away with their shields held before them.

All of a sudden the noise around them abated. Einar, Hegg, Ulli and Kikkur looked around them and saw many more watchmen had arrived on the scene and they now formed a complete ring of Fehu-painted shields around them. Unlike their previous comrades, they did not charge straight in. Instead they stood rigid, shields locked. There was no way out.

The four old friends stood, panting, their breath rising in clouds into the night air as they looked around at the shields that encircled them.

'I don't know who that fellow you killed was, Einar,' Hegg said. 'But I hope you did. And that he deserved it.'

Einar could feel his initial rage draining from him, leaving his body feeling cold and a little shivery. No one had landed a blow on him but he felt a vague confusion as if someone had hit him on the head.

He looked sideways at Hegg.

'Of course I knew him,' Einar said. 'And he deserved it all right. Don't worry about that.'

'That's all right then,' Hegg said. 'I'm glad we helped you.'

Einar felt a stab in his heart. He felt no remorse at the death of Vakir – none at all – but he knew that his impetuous assault had landed not just himself in trouble now but his friends as well.

Two of the watchmen parted and into the ring stepped Oddi, the master of the Hedeby Watch. He still wore his saffron cloak and he looked a lot less happy than the last time Einar had seen him when he allowed them to enter the harbour.

Oddi glared at them, hands on hips, looking at Hegg, Ulli, Kikkur and finally Einar in turn. He shook his head.

'Why is it?' he said, 'that you foreigners can't come here to our town, drink some ale and just enjoy yourself? Why does it always have to end in violence?'

He looked at the corpse of Vakir which lay flat on his back, steam from the blood that covered him rising into the night air.

'Well, you've done it now,' he said. 'Fighting is one thing, but murder is another.'

'What do we do, lord?' one of the watchmen forming the ring of shields said.

'They'll have to go to the jarl for judgement,' Oddi said.

'But sir—' the watchman said. 'It's the Festival of Sirius.'

'It's *murder*,' Oddi shouted. 'A man is dead! They have to go to the jarl. Now.'

He turned back to Einar.

'It's probably too late to ask you to behave like civilised folk,' Oddi said, 'But are you going to come along with us to the jarl quietly or are we going to have to beat the shit out of you first and drag you there?'

Einar looked around at the ring of shields. Skar and Ulrich had taught him to look for weaknesses – the men who were out of line, the ones who did not hold their shields properly, the ones who were less disciplined than their fellows who would provide any potential chink in the defence of the shield wall. He saw none, however. A quick count of the number of legs he could see under the shields, divided by two, told him there was about forty of them. They were outnumbered ten to one.

Einar looked at his friends. The other lads shrugged. There was no other option, apart from being beaten to a pulp. Skar and Ulrich had taught him another lesson: *Sell your life for the highest price. Only die when you have to. There will come a time when you have no choice but to go out fighting, but until then, always seek for a way out.*

Perhaps a way out of this would come yet, Einar thought. He raised his hands and nodded to Oddi.

'Sensible choice,' the Master of the Watch said with a smile. He signalled to his men and they moved in, tightening the ring around Einar and his friends.

Einar raised his hands and his fellow Icelanders did the same. The shield wall closed in around them. Their formation turned into the twin columns of an escort, preparing to shepherd the troublemakers away from the marketplace. Einar and the others turned around with reluctance to face in the direction they wanted them to go.

At the last moment, when they were mere paces away, the watchmen braced their shields, raised their clubs and attacked.

Einar found himself forced to the ground by the pressure of shields as blows from the watchmen's clubs rained down on his head. He curled into a ball, raising his hands to protect his head. As he did so the watchmen began beating his knees, elbows and sides. As he dropped his hands to protect his body they turned their attention to his skull again.

At the same time, he felt hands working on his ankles. They bound them together with leather straps. Then many hands grasped his arms and forced them behind him. They too were tied.

Before long, Hegg, Ulli and Kikkur were bound just like him. Then they were all hoisted on poles carried between two watchmen each, slung through the binds of their ankles and wrists.

'Where are you taking us?' Einar said, twisting his head to the side so he could see Oddi who marched along beside him.

'You're going to see the jarl,' the Master of the Watch said, without making eye contact. 'You're going to face justice and pay for your crimes.'

Thirty-Five

Suspended from the pole by his arms and legs, Einar was jostled and jolted across the marketplace. Every lurching step by the men carrying the pole sent shocks of pain through his shoulders and thighs. He felt like a dead boar being carried home from a successful hunt.

They travelled away from the marketplace and along a street that headed inland from the harbour, then turned into another street, passing amused revellers who grinned and pointed at these fools who had got on the wrong side of the watchmen. Eventually they came to another open space a little smaller than the marketplace. In the centre of this area was a very large hall. It was long and narrow and its arched, shingled roof that almost came all the way down to the ground made it look a little like an upturned longship sitting in the midst of the town.

The company of watchmen halted and Einar and the others were dumped without ceremony on the ground. The sound of revelry – singing, laughter and good-natured chatter – emanated through the walls of the feasting hall along with a delicious aroma of roasted meat and fresh ale.

'Don't try anything,' one of the watchmen growled in

Einar's ear as several of them withdrew the carrying poles then hauled Einar to his feet.

Another watchman went up to the big double doors of the feasting hall. He knocked on them then had a brief conversation with the person who opened one. The door closed again and the watchman returned to his comrades.

'There's quite the party going on in there,' he said. 'The jarl's not going to be happy about this.'

'I don't care if he's happy or not,' Oddi said. 'This is serious. It's his responsibility to deal with it.'

After a little wait the doors of the hall opened again and a man strode out. He looked to have lived perhaps thirty-five or forty winters and he was dressed in clothes expensive enough to rival King Aethelstan's. His feet were clad in the finest of deerskin boots and his legs were wrapped in soft woollen breeches. His shirt shimmered blue in the torchlight and Einar guessed it was probably made of the magical silk material. A cloak of the purest red wool was fastened at his left shoulder by a circular gold brooch about the size of Einar's fist and studded with rubies and garnets. The braids of his hair and beard appeared to have been wound with a thread made of gold and like Oddi and many other denizens of Hedeby, there was thick paint around his eyes. The faint flush on his cheeks showed he had been drinking ale. Or by the look of him, Einar reasoned, more likely wine.

At the sight of him the watchmen all stiffened, straightening their backs and puffing out their chests.

'Stand up straight for the jarl,' one of the watchmen holding Einar hissed in his ear. Another one prodded Einar in the back with his club.

'What's going on, Oddi?' the newcomer, who Einar realised must be the Jarl of Hedeby, said in a demanding tone. 'I'm entertaining important guests.'

'There's been a killing, lord,' Oddi said. 'One of the followers of Loki. An out-of-towner.'

The jarl rolled his eyes.

'A drunken fight?' he said. 'I can never understand why can't people just enjoy themselves without falling out.'

'No, lord,' Oddi said. 'From what witnesses say it was unprovoked murder.'

'And you couldn't deal with this yourself, Oddi?' the jarl said. 'You know I'm hosting a Festival of Sirius feast for all the most important of people both in town and from abroad tonight.'

Einar tutted to himself. It seemed that sitting at benches in the open air of the marketplace, crammed in, cheek by jowl, with the ordinary folk was not something the rich and privileged went in for.

'Lord, it's our duty to report such a serious crime to you,' Oddi said. 'This will require the most severe form of justice. The Watch is not permitted to serve that.'

The jarl sighed. He looked at Einar and the other prisoners.

'Who are they?' he said.

'They're out-of-towners too,' Oddi said. 'Icelanders, I believe.'

'Look, I have two kings, a Frankish count, four jarls and some of the richest merchants in the northern world to entertain in there,' the jarl said, cocking his head towards his feasting hall. 'As well as their entourages. And if that wasn't enough my damned skald has picked this of all times to get sick. I don't have time for this now. Hang this lot straight away so I can get back to the feast.'

Oddi saluted the jarl and the watchmen tightened their grip on the prisoners. One of them produced a length of rope from a leather satchel and began forming a noose. Einar felt a surge of panic and dismay. Could he really be about to die? If Odin had really brought this all about what perverse game was he playing?

'Wait!' Hegg said. 'You can't do this.'

'Why not?' the jarl said. 'I'm Jarl here. I can do what I want, within the Law.'

'That's just it, it's unlawful,' Hegg said. 'We have the right to a proper trial. Where is your Law Speaker? He should hear the witnesses. We are entitled to present our own side of the story. Only then can judgement be pronounced.'

The jarl gave a little chuckle.

'You Icelanders are all the same,' he said. 'Always harping on about the Law and how important it is. What is it with you suet-munchers that you are so obsessed with legal matters?'

'Because we're all free men,' Kikkur said. 'We have no kings, no jarls, so all we have to hold the folk together is the Law.'

'Our land was built on the Law,' Hegg said. 'It's the most important thing there is. Without Law we would be savages enslaved to the whims of tyrants.'

Einar nodded. All Icelanders had these sentiments drummed into them from a very early age.

'Well let me tell you something,' the jarl said. 'Here things are different. Here *I* am the Law. I am the Jarl, the Law Speaker and the Judge, and this is my judgement.

Oddi – hang these sheep-shaggers so I can get back to my guests!'

Einar braced himself, stiffening his resolve. If this really was the end then he would meet it showing as little fear as he could. One of the watchmen was already hauling a noose over Hegg's head.

'Hold on,' Hegg said. 'Did you say your skald is sick?'

'I did,' the jarl said. 'He's hoarse as a duck. The rascal probably ruined his throat drinking. What of it?'

'As you said, we Icelanders are famous for our respect for the Law,' Hegg said. 'But we are also famous for our poets.'

'True,' the jarl said with a shrug. 'Icelandic skalds are said to be the greatest in the world. What of it?'

'Well if you hang us tonight,' Hegg said. 'Then you'll be hanging one of the greatest poets in Iceland. Do you want to be known as the jarl who did that?'

The jarl frowned. As did Einar.

'What do you mean?' the jarl said.

'Einar here is one of the best poets I've ever heard sing,' Hegg said.

'Is this true?' the jarl said to Einar.

Einar's mouth opened. He did not know what to say.

'He is,' Kikkur said. 'I've never heard anyone better. This is Einar Unnsson. He's famous.'

Einar clenched and unclenched his maimed hand. He could sing, but he could no longer, as was expected of a skald, play a harp or lyre to accompany his tales. He also doubted this supposed fame in Iceland spread much beyond Midfjord where he had grown up.

The jarl looked at him for a long moment through

narrowed eyes. Behind him the door of the hall burst open. Another richly dressed man leaned out. He looked very drunk and clung on to the doorpost to stop himself spilling out into the street.

'Jarl Kar,' the man slurred. 'What's going on? We're all waiting in here. People are getting bored.'

'Just coming, your highness,' the jarl said over his shoulder, a fixed grin on his face. He turned to one of the watchmen.

'Go and get Hvin,' he said.

The watchman trotted off into the jarl's feasting hall.

A few moments later he returned, accompanied by a short man with grey hair. As soon as he came into the cool night air the grey-haired man was wracked by a bout of coughing.

'This is Hvin, my skald,' the jarl said. 'Hvin, have you ever heard of a poet called Einar Unnsson?'

The skald squinted upwards, as if the answer lay somewhere in the dark sky above. His face was also very red and the fumes of ale that wafted from him would have knocked out a bear.

'No, lord,' he said, his voice cracking. 'I can't say I have. There's an Einar Thorfinnsson who's supposed to be very good. He was a pupil of Ayvind Finnsson, King Hakon's skald.'

'That's me,' Einar said. 'Unn was my mother. My father was Thorfinn Hausakljúfr, the Jarl of Orkney.'

'Really?' the jarl said. 'And how is the old Skull Cleaver these days?'

'He's dead,' Einar said. 'I killed him.'

The jarl winced.

'Is killing people some sort of habit of yours?' he said. 'What sort of a maniac are you?'

'If this is indeed Einar Thorfinnsson,' the skald croaked. 'Then he is supposed to be one of the best skalds on Middle Earth right now. So they say anyway.'

Einar's head spun with amazement.

'Look, if you're as good as they say you are then this could get me out of a hole,' the jarl said. 'I'll tell you what. If you entertain the guests at my feast then I won't hang you tonight after all. You'll get a proper trial in the morning.'

'What about my friends?' Einar said. 'I won't do it unless they get the same.'

'Very well,' the jarl said. 'But first I want to see if you really are any good. Go and get your lyre, Hvin. The rest of you, untie the prisoners.'

The skald staggered off back towards the hall and the other Icelanders, now freed, gathered round Einar in a happy bunch.

'You got us into it but you'll get us out again,' Kikkur said, slapping Einar on the shoulder.

'Don't get too optimistic yet,' Einar said from the corner of his mouth as he held up his damaged hand. 'I can sing but with this I don't know how to play anymore.'

'Well you'd better learn, and fast,' Hegg said.

Hvin was already returning from the hall, now with a lyre in his unsteady hands. He handed it to Einar.

'Be careful with that, Icelander,' he slurred in his hoarse voice. 'It's expensive. You're not handling a sheep now.'

'Right. Off you go.' the jarl said. 'Chant us something good. I always liked the *Krákumál*. Do you know it?'

Einar took the lyre, aware to his sudden embarrassment

that his hands were trembling. He took a long, deep breath through his nose, trying to calm his pounding heart. His mind raced as he tried to work out what to do. The normal way to play was for his left hand to pluck lower strings to create a rhythm while his right picked out the melody. However with his missing finger on his right hand he would not be able to hit most of the upper notes.

A strange idea came to him. If he swapped hands and played the melody with his left instead then he could cover all of the required notes. The rhythm, plucked with one finger less than was required, would have to be more deliberate and forceful, dropping notes he could not pick. It would be difficult, but not impossible, almost like the old childhood trick of trying to rub your belly while patting your head at the same time.

He looked around at the expectant faces of his friends, knowing that if he failed in this they were all dead men.

There was nothing else for it.

He started to play. The first few notes came out in the right way but the effort of thinking which fingers to use when made him doubt he would be able to sing at the same time. Then he plucked the wrong string. His right middle finger hit the note it was used to playing instead of the opposite one his left would normally play. He saw the less than impressed expression on the face of the jarl and his heart sank. He kept on playing but the music sounded clumsy as he fought against his own hands which seemed determined to play the way they were used to instead of the way he needed them to now.

Odin, Einar, is inspiration.

For some reason Einar found himself recalling the words

of his old tutor, Ayvind, the man who had betrayed him and he had left to die a lonely death in the cold seas of the northern whale road. The memory of a lesson one morning in Jorvik surfaced in his mind. He remembered the older skald leaning towards him, his eyes bleary and red rimmed, the smell of the night before's wine on his breath.

The berserker who is overcome by fury on the battlefield – Ayvind had said. *The man at the feast from whom wine steals his reason, the trance the skald goes into when performing to a hall full of people hanging on his every word, his every note. When a person's mind slips from its normal way of thinking and ascends to a higher state of awareness, it is Odin who is possessing him and letting the mead of* Suttungr *flow through their veins. To be a great poet, Einar, you must let him in.*

Einar closed his eyes. He cleared his mind, thinking of nothing, waiting for the old, weird feeling of entrancement that used to take hold of him when he chanted or composed poetry – at least at the times when it really flowed from him, almost like he was not the creator, just a conduit for the words and music. A deep sensation of calm flooded his chest. He closed his eyes and began to move his fingers across the strings. The music started to flow like a stream in spring as the ice that has bound it through the winter begins to melt – how he was doing it he could not question. He knew if he stopped to think about it, it would break the spell and he would no longer be able to do it.

With his hands changed around and the missing finger on his right, the notes he plucked somehow had more power, more of a driving rhythm that stirred the heart and ignited a fire deep within his spirit.

Without further thought he opened his mouth and the words of the song flowed from him. Einar chanted the words, supposedly composed by Ragnar Loðbrók himself as he lay dying of his wounds.

'Very good.'

The jarl's voice interrupted Einar and he opened his eyes. He saw everyone around him was gazing at him, rapt by the spell his song had cast on them. Hvin's face bore a look of someone stunned while at the same time a little resentful.

'I think I've heard enough,' the jarl said. 'It's safe to say you're as good a poet as you're reputed to be. My feast is saved. In you go. There are important guests waiting to be entertained. As a reward tomorrow you'll get the fair trial you requested.'

Hegg, Kikkur and Ulli all clapped Einar on the back.

'I knew you could save our necks,' Ulli said, grinning.

Einar shrugged. He could scarcely believe it himself. A deep sense of excitement sparked in his chest. He may no longer be able to wield a sword like a true warrior but at least he was still a skald. He was *something* after all.

Then he remembered the predicament they were all still in.

'I've saved them for now,' he said. 'If the verdict of the trial tomorrow is guilty we'll still end up with our necks stretched.'

Thirty-Six

Einar was woken by having a bucket of cold water hurled over him. Shivering, he opened his eyes to see one of the men of the Watch standing over him, an empty pale in his hands and a grin on his face.

'Right you lot,' he said. 'Up you get. It's time for your trial.'

Einar groaned. It felt like he had only just crawled into bed.

After proving his skill the night before, the jarl had taken him into his hall where a magnificent feast was in full swing. Many richly dressed guests in multicoloured clothes sat at long benches. There were people from all over the world there with lots of different, foreign clothing and hair and beard styles but the one thing they all had in common was wealth. This was the elite of the folk in Hedeby, here for the festival. Gold and silver dripped from every neck and arm.

The tables strained with the weight of fish, bread and jugs of wine and ale. If folk were hoarding food in Hedeby in expectation of a hard winter, there was no sign of it at the jarl's feast. As he entered, Einar felt all the eyes in the room turn towards him in expectation.

He was led up onto the dais at the front of the hall and

told to sing. Einar began with the *Haustlǫng*, the Long Autumn, both because he thought it was appropriate to the time of year and because it featured Loki, which might please any of his followers who might be in the hall.

As the night progressed Einar chanted many more songs. He found a deep joy that he could still play and sing, something that he thought he would never do again thanks to the injury to his hand. The more he played the more used he became to his new way of plucking the strings and his audience appeared to like the new rhythmic way he played.

Six burly members of the Watch stood guard around him so he had no chance of running away, but the evening was far from unpleasant. He was even given a few horns of wine to help his voice. The feast went on late into the night and Einar played until everyone was too drunk to take notice of him any more. The audience broke up into a chaotic babble that consisted of multiple different conversations, raucous laughter or groups of folk singing their own songs. At that point the watchmen escorted Einar out of the hall and down the street to a building near the marketplace that seemed to be being used as a temporary prison for the duration of the festival. It was in fact a horse pen which had had wooden cages built into it which were now crammed with drunks, thieves, brawlers, swindlers and all the other people whose behaviour during the festival had brought the attention of the watchmen. Many of the prisoners bore black eyes, cut heads or missing teeth from the none-too gentle manner in which the watchmen had stamped out any trouble as soon as it began.

They threw Einar inside. As the door closed he found a space to lie down in the filthy straw that lined the ground and fell into a half-drunk, half-exhausted sleep. The last thought that crossed his mind was the disappointment that just as he had rediscovered he could still play music, he might, in the morning, end up being hung after all.

Now the moment of truth had arrived. Soaked, his head hurting from the wine and stiff from sleeping on the ground, Einar dusted himself down, tried to remove as much of the filthy straw from his hair as he could and in general make himself look as little like a crazed murderer as possible.

Outside his cage, Einar found Ulli, Hegg and Kikkur waiting. They looked like they had had as rough a night as he had. The watchmen formed up around them, then they were all prodded, kicked and marched down the street back to the jarl's hall once more.

Hedeby had the look of a place where a great party had happened the night before. It was untidy, dishevelled and hushed, as if the whole town were hiding indoors, nursing sore heads.

Now in daylight, Einar saw that in the space in front of the jarl's feasting hall there was a long, low mound raised about half the height of a man above the flat street level. Einar could tell that this was where trials and other legal judgements took place. It was the same all over the northern world; legal cases and disputes were heard on a raised mound or artificial platform on appointed days throughout the year.

A crowd of onlookers had gathered but it was not the usual throng that would have been expected on a court day, probably due to the number of people in town still in bed. It seemed the rulers of Hedeby were keen to get all justice required in cases of misbehaviour during the festival dispensed as fast as possible, to send the clear message to foreigners that nothing would be allowed to disrupt the trade of the town.

One criminal had already paid the ultimate price for his crimes. The freshly hung corpse of a man dangled from a gallows beside the mound. The man twisted in the wind, his blood-filled eyes bulged from his strangled face, which was almost black with trapped blood. His tongue protruded from his mouth while his breeches were sodden with unleashed piss.

Einar swallowed. How long would it be until he was swinging from the same gallows? If this was to be his fate he just hoped he could hold onto the contents of his bladder.

A queue of miscreants waited below the judging mound. They looked like the same sort who Einar had left behind in the temporary festival jail. Mostly men, though there were a few women, most with black eyes, bruises and a look like the morning daylight was hurting their eyes. The watchmen were lined alongside them, shields ready, looking like they were just itching for any excuse to unleash their cudgels.

The jarl himself was slouched in a high-backed wooden seat. He was bleary-eyed and scowling, looking as hung over and glad to be there as everyone else. Oddi stood beside him. Einar imagined that the jarl's mood would mean he would probably not be too inclined to be merciful in his judgements that morning.

They stood in line as the cases before them were heard. It was a litany of drunken brawls, accidental injuries and some thefts. Oddi recited the charges against each one, then the jarl listened to evidence presented by the watchmen and any witnesses who had been rounded up. He heard the pleas of the accused and sometimes, for those who had Law Speakers to represent them, the pleas presented on their behalf. Then judgement was passed. For those folk who sustained injuries, compensation payments were agreed – a piece of silver for a lost tooth, two for a broken bone – which the guilty parties paid. Some were sentenced to ordeals to be carried out at a later time, some were outlawed and exiled from the town. The jarl was particularly harsh to three young lads of about eleven winters, caught stealing from out-of-towners who had drunk too much, sentencing them to be sold as slaves in the marketplace. To Einar's increasing dismay it seemed that no one was ever found innocent.

After some time it was Einar and the others' turn. The jarl watched them with his bloodshot eyes as they were led up onto the platform by the watchmen.

'Ah, the poet,' the jarl said. 'Oddi send someone to fetch Meginbraht. His case is starting.'

There was a delay while a watchman pushed through the crowd then went running off down the street. After a short time he returned, now accompanied by the merchant, Meginbraht. Alongside him stalked the hulking figure of Asbjorn Hviti, also known as the Bear. Einar stared at the huge man whose shoulders were wrapped in a cloak of white fur, feeling an involuntary shudder at the memory of him charging towards their shield wall in Frodisborg, smashing men out of the way like they were midges.

'Let's get on with it,' the jarl said.

'Who will represent you in the court?' Oddi said to Einar and the others. 'Have you a Law Speaker or will you do it yourself?'

Einar, Ulli, Hegg and Kikkur looked at each other and shrugged.

'I will be speaking on their behalf, lord.'

A new voice from the crowd made everyone turn around. A small figure in a grey, shaggy cloak of un-dyed wool with the hood up, was pushing his way to the front.

'Show your face before you come up here,' Oddi said.

The newcomer pulled his hood down and Einar saw, as he had suspected from the sound of his voice, that it was Ulrich.

Ulrich clambered up onto the court mound.

'My name is Grim,' Ulrich said. 'One of these men is part of my crew. I know the Law, so I will speak in their defence.'

Einar, a questioning expression on his face, mouthed to Ulrich: *you know the law?*

Ulrich winked at Einar. The other Icelanders looked at Einar who returned a nod that he hoped was reassuring.

'I heard you'd gotten yourself into trouble, lad,' Ulrich said out of the corner of his mouth. 'It was the talk of the town in all the taverns last night. A crazed Icelander murdered some poor innocent bastard. But this could still go well for us.'

'So you're an out-of-towner as well?' the jarl said. 'You're not another suet-muncher Icelander, are you?'

'No, lord,' Ulrich said. 'I'm a Norwegian.'

'This man came to me yesterday, lord,' Meginbraht said, an indignant expression on his face. 'He claimed to be an agent of King Aethelstan, Emperor of Britain. He wanted to buy swords.'

'Is this true?' the jarl said to Ulrich.

Ulrich bowed his head.

'Well don't think throwing the names of important kings or nobles around here will hold any sway,' the jarl said. 'I had three kings at my feast last night. That sort of thing doesn't impress me.'

'Nor should it, lord,' Ulrich said. 'The only thing that should matter here is that justice is done and seen to be done.'

'Good,' the jarl said. 'Because I intend to make an example of anyone who comes to our town and thinks they can cause trouble, as a warning to others who might think of doing the same in the future.'

Oddi announced the charges to the court: That Einar wilfully murdered a man in an unprovoked attack. That Ulli, Kikkur and Hegg helped him in that crime and that when the watchmen tried to apprehend them they resisted and caused injuries.

'And who is the victim here?' the jarl said.

'His name was Vakir, lord,' Meginbraht said. 'He was a Galdr maðr of King Eirik Bloody Axe of Norway. He was an important customer of mine and the man I act as a factor for, Asbjorn Ecgtheosson. Vakir was dealing with us on behalf of King Eirik.'

All eyes turned to the big man in the white fur cloak. Most folk looked away again quickly.

'So the injured party here in terms of who requires justice or compensation would be King Eirik,' the jarl said, sucking in air through his teeth and shooting a censorious glance at Einar. 'Well as he's not here I take it you will be taking that role?'

'Yes, lord,' Meginbraht said.

'Then you should come to the court as well,' the jarl said.

The merchant and the viking lumbered up onto the judgement mound. As he got closer, Einar was aware that the Bear was looking at him, a curious expression on his face.

There followed the testimonies of several eyewitnesses. A woman from the followers of Loki, still wearing her face paint, robes and greenery from the night before, two other bystanders from the festival, one of the men Meginbraht had sent to the marketplace with Vakir and two members of the Watch. All told the same tale – that Vakir had sought out the followers of Loki, asking to be part of their ritual celebrations that night. He had said that he had some specific magical role he wanted to play – something that was quickly glossed over by the court before too many details were revealed. He had joined them at the festival site then out of the blue Einar had run out of a tavern, attacked and killed him in a most brutal manner.

'This seems pretty clear cut to me,' the jarl said. 'Have you anything to say in their defence, Grim? If so I'd be very surprised.'

'Grim' clasped his hands behind his back, then walked up and down, looking at the ground, then the sky. His lips moved as if he were having a silent conversation with himself. Then he spun around, his right forefinger raised, to face the jarl again.

'Firstly,' Ulrich said, 'I wish to address the matter of the three young men who were not involved in the actual killing. Lord, these others were merely helping their old friend out. Yes, they may have attacked Meginbraht's men or a few of the watchmen, but if any of us saw a friend in trouble, would we not do the same?'

He spread his arms wide and turned to the watching crowd, nodding at them as if to try to glean support.

'Their friend was in trouble because he had just murdered someone,' Oddi said. 'And they attacked members of the Watch. *My* men. They're as guilty as Einar. Enough of this. Let's move on. Einar should hang.'

The jarl nodded. Ulrich sighed and dropped his arms.

'Very well,' he said. 'However the word "unprovoked" has been used a lot in describing these events. I wish to take exception with that.'

'Well what would you call it when a man runs up to a complete stranger in the street and kills them?' Oddi said. 'If that's not unprovoked I don't know what is.'

'Well, let's see about that,' Ulrich said. 'I would like to ask this lovely lady…'

He pointed to the follower of Loki who had testified earlier.

'… when Einar attacked the victim, did he look like a normal man, in full possession of his senses?'

'No,' the woman shook her head, as if trying to dispel the horrific memory from her head. 'He looked like he was in a trance, or possessed by some violent rage.'

'Ah!' Ulrich's forefinger was raised again. 'And what I ask you – I ask everyone – would have caused such a reaction in this young man?'

'He's clearly a violent menace,' Oddi said. 'He should be put down like a rabid dog. He must hang.'

The Bear was still looking at Einar. His eyes were narrowed and he was stroking his chin. It made Einar uncomfortable, but he also had the feeling there was curiosity rather than outright animosity in the viking's eyes.

'I know you from somewhere, don't I?' the Bear said.

'Please: no side conversations,' the jarl said. 'This is a court of law.'

'Einar,' Ulrich said. Einar tore his eyes away from the hypnotic gaze of Asbjorn Hviti and looked at Ulrich. 'Did you know the dead man?'

'Yes,' Einar said. 'He killed my mother.'

Gasps came from the watching crowd and a bubble of excited chatter rose.

'Quiet! Quiet!' Oddi shouted. The members of the Watch readied their cudgels but the prattling subsided again as folk turned their attention back to the court.

'So you see, lord,' Ulrich said, addressing the jarl directly, 'this was not the unprovoked action of a deranged berserker. In fact this young man had a serious grievance against the victim.'

'He still murdered him in the middle of my town,' the jarl said.

'Lord I wish everyone would stop using that word, *murder*,' Ulrich said, a pained expression on his face. 'As you know, in our laws murder is when someone secretly kills someone else then hides the body and does not admit to the crime. On the other hand, if someone admits to a killing in an open space, then he is liable but only for man-slaying, not murder. Murder is a different crime. It is shameful, underhand and unmanly, even *ergi*. Now I don't think, after all we have heard from the witnesses, that anyone can say Einar attempted in any way to conceal the killing of Vakir. Indeed, he did it very openly.'

'But he did not publicly announce his responsibility,' Oddi said. 'So it's still murder.'

TIM HODKINSON

'Perhaps,' Ulrich said. He strode over to lay a hand on Einar's shoulder. 'But who is to say what this young lad intended to do, had not the watchmen of Hedeby charged in to attack him?'

'What?!' Oddi said. His face darkened.

'Einar, I ask you, before all these people,' Ulrich said. 'Did you intend to admit your responsibility in the killing of Vakir in public?'

'Say yes,' he added out of the corner of his mouth.

'I did,' Einar said in a loud voice.

'If only the watchmen had not been so hasty last night,' Ulrich said, addressing the crowd now, shaking his head and with an expression of disappointment on his face. 'Then this young man would not be standing before you all this morning, charged with the terrible crime of murder.'

'You're accusing *my* men—' Oddi said. His face darkened and it seemed that indignation stopped further words coming out of his mouth for a moment.

'Lord, I put it to you,' Ulrich said, speaking to the jarl. 'Einar is not a murderer. He killed Vakir, yes, but by manslaying. Therefore he should not hang. He has the right to pay the offended party compensation, and only if they do not accept it should he suffer a different sort of justice.'

'He has a point, Oddi,' the jarl said. 'And I for one would prefer not to be known as the jarl who hung a famous skald. However, the weregild of the Galdr maðr of a king will be substantial, and if you don't mind me saying so, you don't look like any of you could afford it.'

'Lord, with respect to everyone,' Ulrich said. 'Eirik is no longer a king. The people of Norway ousted him. He rules in Orkney but that is as a cuckoo in the nest of the rightful jarl, who is none other than young Einar here. You see now the lad had plenty of provocation in this act. I hope you will set the compensation price with that in mind.'

'Asbjorn and I are the injured party here,' Meginbraht said. 'Eirik is a valued customer. This is very embarrassing. We must be recompensed.'

The jarl sighed and leaned back in his chair. He pulled the hood of his fine wool cloak up over his head and sat for a few moments, as if he were trying to blot out the world around him. Then he pulled his hood down again.

'Oddi what would the compensation normally be?'

'Lord, I—' Oddi began to protest.

'I've heard enough of this!' The jarl cut him off. 'There are a lot more cases to hear this morning and I'm dying of a hangover here. We'll move to judgement.'

Oddi named the figure. It was substantial but Einar felt a wave of relief. He could not cover it by himself but Ulrich had enough silver wrapped around his arm to pay the blood price.

'Would you accept that in recompense?' the jarl said to Meginbraht.

The merchant looked at the Bear for approval, who nodded.

'We would, lord,' Meginbraht said.

'Very well,' the jarl said.

'Einar can you pay this?' Ulrich said.

'Not by myself,' Einar said, surprised. 'But perhaps if my *friends* help me out...'

He looked pointedly at the silver and gold rings on Ulrich's arm.

'Can you?' Ulrich ignored Einar's signal and looked at

Hegg, Ulli and Kikkur instead. 'You are liable as well in this. Can you pay your own contribution and give extra to help Einar?'

All three shook their heads.

'I have nothing,' Hegg said. 'None of us do. We won't get our share of the voyage profits until we return home to Iceland.'

'That is unfortunate,' Ulrich said, shaking his head. Einar glared at him in indignation. Was he really not going to help him out in this time of desperate need?

'We demand justice!' Meginbraht said. 'If he can't pay then he has to be punished in some way. Hung, blinded or lose a limb.'

'Lord, if I may suggest an alternative,' Ulrich said. 'The sum requested is for the life of one man. It is recompense for the time on Middle Earth that was taken away from him by his early death. As these lads cannot pay it with silver, how about they pay with their own lives and time? I suggest they are enslaved to Asbjorn Hviti and pay their debt that way.'

'What?' Einar grabbed Ulrich by the arm. 'Wait one moment—'

Ulrich pulled himself away as the jarl looked at the big viking.

'I have plenty of slaves,' the Bear said, shaking his head. 'I've no need for more.'

'He's a really good skald,' the jarl said. 'I can vouch for that.'

The Bear laughed.

'I have *absolutely* no need for poets,' he said. 'You should hang him. But before you do, there is something I need to find out.'

He looked directly at Einar again.

'Where do I know you from?' he said.

Einar straightened his back and met his glare.

'We fought each other in Frodisborg,' Einar said. 'When you raided it.'

A crooked smile of recognition crossed the Bear's face.

'Ah! That's it,' he said. 'The hammer man! You were lucky that day. I should have killed you. Tell me something though. That was a blacksmith's hammer you wielded. Do you know anything about smithing or did you just think you were Thor?'

'Poetry is not the only craft Einar here knows,' Ulrich said while Einar was still opening his mouth to answer. 'He was apprenticed to one of the greatest blacksmith's in Norway. He is highly skilled in all types of metalworking. It would be a real shame and a waste of talent to hang such a man.'

'Why are you here lad?' the Bear said to Einar. 'Are you following me?'

'Believe me,' Einar said. 'After what you did to Frodisborg, you are the last person I would want to see again. I joined a ship's crew and just happened to end up here at the same time as you.'

The Bear looked at Einar for a long moment, then he turned to the jarl.

'I have changed my mind,' he said. 'As it happens I am in need of a smith. I will accept the offer.'

'Good,' the jarl said. 'Then at last we can move on. These

men are now thralls. They are your property to do as you will with them. That is the judgement of the court.'

'I only want Einar and one other,' the Bear said. He pointed at Hegg. 'He will do.'

'What will we do with the other two?' Oddi said.

'I don't care,' the Bear said with a shrug.

'You could let them go, lord?' Ulrich suggested. 'They were not really involved anyway.'

'Whatever,' the jarl said, waving his hand in the air as if he was wafting the whole matter away like a bad smell. Ulli and Kikkur looked relieved.

'What do you think you're doing, Ulrich?' Einar said in an agitated whisper to Ulrich as the watchmen advanced towards him. 'You could easily have paid that fine for me.'

'Sorry lad,' Ulrich said in a voice meant for everyone else to hear. 'That amount of silver would barely cover my fee for representing you in court. Look on the bright side – I saved you from the gallows. But you've been a good crew member. Let me give you some last advice.'

Ulrich threw an arm around Einar's shoulders and leaned his head close.

'We need to find where the Bear's fortress is,' he whispered through clenched teeth. 'I'm counting on him taking you there and then we'll have a man on the inside. We'll follow and you find a way to let us in. Use this to help us track you. Remember what we taught you about leaving a trail.'

Einar felt Ulrich's other hand push something into the pocket of his jerkin.

'What are you saying to him?' Oddi said, noticing Ulrich's muttering.

'Just saying goodbye,' Ulrich said, taking his arm away and stepping away from Einar.

'That's good,' the Bear said, grasping Einar by the forearm with one huge hand. 'Because where he's going, you won't ever see him again.'

Thirty-Seven

Einar and Hegg were shoved and herded through the streets back to Meginbraht's property. There they waited outside, surrounded by a taciturn and surly band of the Bear's vikings while Asbjorn and the merchant did some final business inside.

While they waited, the vikings fitted iron slave collars around the necks of the prisoners. As it closed around his throat, Einar felt a shiver run down his spine that had nothing to do with the cold of the iron. There were two long chains connected to the collar, one that connected him to Hegg and the other to their new masters. It stopped him running away and was also a clear signal, if one was needed, that his freedom was now gone.

Once the collars were fitted the vikings lost interest in the new slaves as they could not run away. They began rolling dice and gambling among themselves. Einar took the opportunity to see what Ulrich had slipped into his pocket. It was a leather pouch that rattled as Einar took it out. Pulling the drawstrings apart he saw that it was filled with lots of what looked like white pebbles. The bag was too light for that, however and picking one he realised they were not stones but pieces of white ivory. It looked like

Ulrich had chopped up a large horn or walrus tusk and filled the bag with the chips.

From the tracking and trailing craft Skar and Ulrich had taught him, Einar knew what he was supposed to do. The trick would be doing it without getting caught.

'How come you know that big man?' Hegg said.

Einar told him the whole story. When he was finished Hegg blew out his cheeks.

'That's quite a tale,' he said.

'I'm sorry I've got you into this, Hegg,' Einar said. 'You and the others. At least they let them go.'

'Don't be stupid, Einar,' Hegg said with a grin. 'We were all on the same knattleikr team. If one of us is in trouble we all pile in. That's just how it is. And when we're overseas, us Icelanders have to stick together. You'd have done the same for me.'

Einar nodded. He would have.

'We'll find a way out of this, I'm sure. The only thing that worries me now is what they're going to do with us,' Hegg said. 'This Bear seems to need a blacksmith though so you're all right. What's he going to do with me though?'

'That's worrying me too,' Einar said. 'And I'm not as all right as you think. I did smithing in Frodisborg but it was only because I had a special hammer and strap. When the Bear finds that out he may decide he has no use for me after all.'

At that moment the Bear came out of the merchant's house lugging a heavy chest in both hands. The clinking and rattling that came from it told Einar there was a lot of loose metal inside and he surmised that this was the profits from the plunder the merchant had sold on the big viking's behalf. His warriors jumped to their feet and untied their pack horses. The chest was strapped across the back of one of them then the chains attached to Einar and Hegg's slave collars were fastened to the horses' bridles. The Bear grunted 'let's go' and they all set off.

To Einar's surprise they did not head in the direction of the harbour. In fact they went in the complete opposite direction, following the wooden-planked walkway further into the town. There was a river running through Hedeby and they crossed this using a bridge. On the other side they kept going until they reached the palisaded rampart that ringed the town, protecting it. There was a gate in the rampart guarded by watchmen, who opened it letting the little company leave. As they went through the gate Einar dropped a piece of ivory in as surreptitious a way as he could manage. To his relief none of the others noticed.

The countryside beyond the walls of Hedeby was bleak. It was flat as far as the eye could see, waterlogged and empty. A wooden track, not unlike the ones that lined the streets of the town continued on across the bog in a straight line. The planks floated on the sodden moss and peat, providing a way for folk to cross the treacherous heath in relative safety.

They trekked on along the walkway for a long time. Einar had no need to drop many of the ivory markers. Skar had taught him that when laying a trail there was no need to leave markers all the time if the route was straight, which the walkway was. It was enough to leave one every two thousand paces or so, unless the route changed, and then you drop one at the turn or deviation.

He did his best to keep count as they went along but it was not always possible to drop a marker at exactly two thousand steps. Sometimes there was too much chance of being caught by the Bear and his men so he had to wait until they were otherwise occupied looking away or paying attention to something else before he managed to drop a piece of ivory on or between the slimy boards underfoot.

On either side and in front of them lay wide fens and mires. Mists drifted over black, noisome pools. The air was filled with the reek of rotting vegetation and stagnant water. Dry reeds hissed and rattled in the breeze, nearly the only noise in the strange, silent wilderness.

The iron collar was uncomfortable. It was not too tight to actually restrict his breathing, but Einar found the weight and feel of the cold metal, slick with his sweat and the damp of the air, somehow still stifling.

All the while the Bear kept looking over his shoulder, watching the trackway behind them for any sign of someone following. If Ulrich and the others were in pursuit, Einar reasoned, they must not be following too closely, otherwise the Bear or one of his warriors would spot them.

After a long time walking, the land around them looked a little drier and they came to a point where a track that was little more than an animal path intersected with the planked walkway heading east to west across the peat hags.

The company turned off the main walkway onto the little path in the westward direction. Einar managed to drop a piece of ivory on the planks as he stepped off them but did not dare to drop another on the track as he saw that one of the Bear's warriors was watching him.

They set off along the little track, Einar hoping that the one marker on the walkway would be enough for the Wolf Coats following to know they had changed direction.

They continued on along the track that threaded its way across the vast fen, through an endless network of pools, mires and winding, half-strangled watercourses. The only green was the scum of weed on the dark surfaces of the waters and the carpets of moss that coated parts of the bog. Dead grass and rotting reeds loomed in the ever thicker mists that swirled around them. Einar managed to drop a few more ivory markers on the way, fervently hoping now that the Wolf Coats would not have decided to go east when they left the planked walkway.

The light began to fade with the sinking sun and the Bear called a halt.

'I don't want to walk into a bog by accident in the dark,' he said. 'We'll camp here.'

They built a camp on an area of dry ground as darkness closed in. Lighting a fire the Bear and his men began roasting fresh meat they had brought from Hedeby and boiling barley in a black iron cauldron. Einar and Hegg were given some of the barley while the rest ate the meat and broke open a few leather goatskins filled with wine.

Einar knew any chance to mix with the others would end in a contemptuous reaction, if not violence, so he and Hegg kept themselves apart. The others had leather tents and sleeping bags but as slaves he and Hegg were expected to sleep on the ground in the open. As it turned out the spongy moss that covered the ground was quite comfortable, however that did not help with the dank cold that closed in as the fire dwindled.

Tiredness overcame them however and they managed to drift off for a little.

'Einar!'

The urgent voice of Hegg whispering his name woke Einar late into the night. Bleary-eyed, he looked at the other Icelander who was sitting up and staring out into the darkness.

'Look,' Hegg said. 'There's something out there.'

Einar peered into the black emptiness around them. At first he saw nothing. Then lights appeared. He rubbed his eyes, thinking he was perhaps imagining them. The lights were gone. Then he caught another out of the corner of his left eye, a wisp of pale glow that faded away fast. Others appeared soon after. Some looked like dimly shining smoke but others were like misty flames flickering above unseen candles. Sometimes they twisted like luminous sheets being shaken out by hidden hands then vanished.

'Do you think it's your friends coming after us?' Hegg said.

'I doubt it,' Einar said. 'They will be silent. You won't even know they are here until they're right beside you. And I fear we've lost them in these swamps anyway.'

They watched the strange lights for a time more. They never got any closer or further away.

'If we weren't chained up I'd go and see what's going on,' Hegg said.

'I wouldn't advise that,' Einar said.

The booming voice of the Bear made them whip their heads around. The last glow of the fire's embers showed the silhouette of the big man standing outside one of the tents. Einar's heart plunged in his chest. Had the Bear overheard him talking about Ulrich and the others?

Asbjorn walked a little way from the tents and began fumbling with his breeches. A moment later a stream of piss began to jet from his loins into a nearby pool. Einar relaxed a little. The Bear had only got up to empty his bladder.

'Those lights are corpse candles,' the big man said. 'The folk here in the marshlands say they're held by the ghosts of people who drowned in the bogs. Their spirits are trapped in the meres and they're angry about that and jealous of the living, so they waft those lights to try to entice folk to follow them. But they just lead them to their deaths, drowned out there in the bogs.'

He fastened his breeches.

'I have much work for you to do when we get to my fortress,' he said. 'So don't go wandering off following ghosts.'

With that, the Bear went back to his tent. Einar did not sleep another wink.

In the morning they were surrounded by thick fog. The sun that peered through it was like a ghost of itself, a pale, round, smeared disc that gave no colour or warmth. The Bear and his men got their fire going again and fried some salted pork for themselves. Einar and Hegg were given a couple of scraps of stale bread dipped in the pork fat.

Then they were off again, moving along the small track which meandered along the drier ground, skirting pools and meres with surfaces like black, polished metal, disturbed only by long-legged insects and water beetles.

They walked until the sun was high overhead and Einar noticed the ground beneath their feet was getting more spongey and waterlogged once more.

Out of the mist loomed wooden posts, standing like a line of scarecrows in the gloom. As they got closer Einar saw that they were on the edge of a broad lake or wide river.

A rickety, slime-covered wooden jetty with rotting boards, several of which were missing, jutted out into the waters. Two long skiffs were tied to the jetty and unlike it, the boats were in a well- maintained condition.

The chest of loot was taken off the horse and placed into one of the boats. Both animals were then tethered to a post while the company started to clamber into the skiffs. Einar realised with rising panic that once on the water, from then on he would no longer be able to leave any tracking markers for the Wolf Coats to follow.

One of the Bear's men shoved him towards the boats. Einar stumbled forwards. Recognising a timely opportunity, he exaggerated the effects of the push and fell to his knees on the slippery boards of the jetty. As the Bear's men laughed, Einar lodged a piece of ivory between two of the boards then struggled back to his feet again and finished climbing into one of the boats. Einar and Hegg were put on the oars of the skiff they were in and both boats pushed off from the jetty and out into the wider water.

'Are you just going to leave them there?' Einar said, nodding towards the horses left behind on the bank.

'We have an arrangement with some folk,' one of the Bear's men said. 'Now shut up and row.'

They slid across the surface of the dark, flat water. Surrounded by the thick mist, it was impossible for Einar to work out where they were though he suspected it was a wide lake as he could see no sign of banks on either side of them. How the Bear knew where they were going he had no idea, though the big man often looked up at the pale circle of the sun above so was probably judging which way was north based on its position.

After a while on the boats, a dark shape loomed in the mist up ahead. As they got closer Einar saw that it was an island. A fortress was built on it. It was circular, with stone walls that almost came to the water's edge. There was a long jetty that came out from a heavy iron-bound door in the wall. There were several boats tied to the jetty, three like the shallow-bottomed marsh skiff Einar currently rode in, but also a viking longship. That was a sea-going vessel and it told Einar that there must also be a way into this lake from the fjord they had travelled to Hedeby along.

The Bear stood up, lifted a horn to his lips and blew several blasts on it. It was a particular pattern of short and long notes, which told Einar this was a signal. The boats pulled up to the jetty and once moored, all those on board disembarked and made their way along to the door. The Bear lifted a mighty fist and hammered on it. Like his horn blasts, this was not just random rapping. Instead he beat out a distinct sequence of beats on the wood.

There came a rattling of bolts. After that the heavy fortified door swung open with a creak of its hinges. Two men in brynjas and helmets stood inside.

'Welcome home, lord,' one of them said.

The Bear just grunted and stepped inside. The others followed and Einar and Hegg were half-led, half-pulled into a gloomy room on the other side of the door. As they went in, Einar saw that the stone walls were as thick as the length of a man's arm.

As the door closed behind him Einar noticed the air inside the room stank with an unpleasant musky smell that had a strong taint of piss in it. He wondered how clean the habits of the denizens of the Bear's fortress were. This was not unusual. Whenever a band of men all live together some standards tended to slip. There was something else as well, like the fug of a sheep's wool that has been out on the heath in wet weather.

The thought came to him also that surrounded by the water and with these redoubtable stone walls, the fortress was as impregnable as Jarls Gard in Orkney. How Ulrich and the others would ever find a way in was beyond him. That was if they even found their way to it in the first place.

Then came a noise that chilled him to the bone.

Thirty-Eight

On the far side of the room they stood in was another fortified door. It looked every bit as formidable as the one they had just come through, if not more so. It was made of stout wood with strips of iron and leather to strengthen it. There was a thick wooden bar across the back of it as well as three large iron bolts as big as sword blades to hold it closed.

It was from behind the second door that the sound came.

There was a deafening roar. Some huge, angry animal was behind the door. Then something struck the door, hard, making it rattle on its hinges despite its considerable weight. Einar saw the vikings around him flinch. The door held but then came a sound like claws scratching on the other side of it, making the door buck and shudder even more. There was another hoarse roar which was followed by some husky panting.

Unlike everyone else in the room, the Bear was smiling.

'He knows I'm home,' he said. 'He must have missed me.'

Einar felt a chill of horror as he watched the door bounce and buck with the battering it was getting from the other side. Whatever creature was behind it was huge and very angry. It was no dog. Even a great battle hound like the one he had killed at Cathair Aile was not big or strong enough to deliver such a pounding to a heavy, iron-bound door like the one here. Einar prayed to Thor that the door was strong enough to hold whatever it was on the other side back.

'Come along,' the Bear said, raising his booming voice to be heard over the roaring and scraping of claws. 'There is much work to do. The silver must go into my hoard. To the feasting hall.'

Einar and Hegg were shoved out of the room into a corridor that led to the right. In the gloom they found a spiral staircase that twisted upwards towards the roof high above.

The fortress was the strangest construction Einar had ever been in. The outer walls were made of stone, built in what seemed like a perfect circle. Like some of the buildings in Jorvik it had three stories, at least as far as Einar could judge as they passed two doors as they wound their way up the stairs.

'This place was built by the Romans many years ago,' the Bear said, noticing Einar and Hegg's wondering gazes around them. 'This land was beyond their empire and this was a trading outpost of theirs, like Hedeby is now. They needed to be safe so they built it strong, using magic knowledge we know nothing of today. When I found this place out here in the meres and marshes it was in disrepair but I made it habitable. More than that. I've added some extras. It's the perfect place for a man like me and my men to hide out.'

Einar could tell the Bear was proud of his lair and liked the opportunity to show it off, even if it was only to a couple of slaves. He probably did not get much chance to do it very often.

At the top of the staircase they came to another door which opened into a long room. There were torches burning in brackets in the walls providing light as there were no windows. Two long tables ran the length of the room, with benches on either side. At one end of the room was a high seat with tall wooden pillars on either side. There was a smell of cold grease and beer and Einar judged this to be the feasting hall mentioned by the Bear. He was starving but knew any hope that they had been brought there to eat would be a forlorn one.

It did not take long for that to be verified.

'Father!'

A young lad came running across the room towards the Bear. His resemblance to the big viking was obvious. The same blond hair and large frame. The same broad shoulders and long, thick legs. He was like a smaller version of Asbjorn Hviti.

'Erling!' the Bear cried.

The boy and the viking embraced. When they parted, the Bear, grinning, ruffled the boy's hair while the lad looked up at him with adoring eyes.

'You've been away so long,' the boy said. 'I'm so glad you're back.'

'It's good to be home,' Asbjorn said. He turned to Einar and Hegg, his huge chest swollen with evident pride. 'This is my son, Erling. The apple does not fall far from the tree in his case. Can you believe he's only ten winters old?'

Einar's eyes widened. The boy was indeed like his father,

in size at least. Had the Bear not told him the lad's actual age Einar would have judged him to be fifteen or sixteen.

'Now,' the Bear said. 'Let me introduce you to my other pride and joy.'

They were prodded and pushed to the far end of the room, the end opposite where the high seat was. Their feet echoed on the wooden floorboards as they crossed the room. As they got closer, Einar saw that there was a hole in the floor. It was round and lined with stone, reminding Einar of a well, though much wider than any he had ever seen. A stench like rotting meat mixed with musky fur rose from the hole. Attached to the floor near the hole was a large windlass which had an iron chain wrapped around it. The chain led across the floor and down into the hole.

Just before they reached the edge, a loud roar like the one they had heard downstairs echoed from the pit. Einar stopped, frozen by the terrific noise. The Bear seemed unfazed.

'Take the collars off,' he said to his men.

Einar felt relief as the iron slave collar was unclasped and removed from his throat. The Bear was standing on the edge of the pit now.

'This was some sort of chimney the Roman's used. They came here to trade but also smelted bog iron,' he said. 'As you'll see I've put it to better use. It makes a perfect home for my little pet.'

He gestured for them to come closer. Two of the Bear's men shoved them in the back to reinforce the message. Einar felt huge misgivings but at the same time an overwhelming desire to know what lay down the round hole. He and Hegg stepped forward.

Hegg swore. Einar gasped.

The stone-lined hole in the floor was a pit that went all the way down to the ground floor. At the bottom of it was an enormous bear. It was far bigger than any bear Einar had ever seen and its fur was white rather than brown or black. It had an iron collar around its neck, not unlike the ones just removed from Hegg and Einar. The other end of the chain attached to the windlass was connected to the bear's collar.

At the sight of the men at the top of the shaft the beast snarled and gnashed huge, yellowed fangs. It reared on its hind legs, stretching to its full height, trying to leap up out of the hole. Einar and Hegg flinched back as the bear's claws scrabbled on the stones but even though it reached up past the first floor of the building, it could not get out. It continued to snarl and roar, its black eyes gleaming with hatred.

'Magnificent, isn't he?' Asbjorn Hviti said. He stroked the white fur cloak he wore around his shoulders. 'This cloak was once his mother. I came across them on a voyage far to the frozen north, beyond the land of the Finns. He was just a cub then. The bear bitch defended him like you would expect any mother would her child. When I killed her I took her skin and caged him. I brought him here. I've raised him like my own son. I've made him what he is today. Right lads, send the silver down.'

Two of Asbjorn's men threaded rope through the handles of the chest full of Meginbraht's profits. They began to lower it into the pit. When it was just over halfway down the white furred bear leapt up at it. Its claws grabbed the chest and swotted it against the wall. It shattered, spilling the hacked gold, silver and other precious contents all over the floor of the pit. Einar then noticed the bear below did not stand on a stone floor. It was on a mound of treasure. Rubies, garnets, gold chalices, crosses, silver pieces, chains of gold; a vast pile of riches. The bear's back claws slipped and slid among a fortune that was the equivalent of the treasure hoard of a king.

'They say dragons love to guard treasure,' Asbjorn Hviti said. 'But who needs a dragon when I have him? He keeps my wealth safe from any greedy hands who would try to steal it away from me. Now. You. The blacksmith. I want you to do something for me.'

'Look——' Einar said, raising his hands.

The Bear stepped forward and grabbed Hegg by the scruff of his neck in one, huge hand. He swept his arm forward, propelling Hegg towards the pit. Einar started forward to catch his friend but two of Asbjorn's men grabbed him and held him back. Hegg only had time to cry out with surprise before he was toppling over the edge of the hole. Then he was falling, head first, down towards the waiting white bear below. His cry of surprise turned to a scream of terror.

With a snarl the creature reached up and swiped its paw, catching Hegg across the side of his head while he was still falling. The terrible claws took off most of his face in one go, leaving an awful, bloody hole behind. The bear sunk its fangs into his shoulder at the base of his neck as it raked his torso with both claws. Hegg's stomach was ripped open, unleashing a waterfall of intestines that uncurled and fell onto the treasure below. It bit again, this time taking off

Hegg's left arm. Before Einar's horrified gaze, what was left of Hegg's body fell apart under the onslaught of the bear's claws and teeth, dropping to the floor in several chunks of bloody meat. Then the remains disappeared under the bulk of the creature, its white fur now streaked and splashed with red, as it crouched over them, gorging on the remains. Hegg's cries were no longer. He was very dead and the only noises were an unpleasant crunching of bones and tearing of flesh that sounded like someone ripping wet cloth.

'Looks like he was hungry. No wonder he was so angry,' Asbjorn Hviti said.

The boy, Erling was laughing. To Einar's shock it was not at his father's comment but at what he was watching in the pit below. What sort of a monster was this child?

Einar took a deep breath trying to quell the horror and panic that swirled in his heart. Was he next?

'So this was what you meant when you said you had a use for us?' Einar said.

He tried to make his voice sound as unconcerned as he could but was aware that it was more high-pitched than usual. He called to mind great heroes and how they responded to certain death with a witty quip or defiant gesture. Gunnar Gjukisson when thrown in a snake pit had asked for a harp and played it as he died. Ragnar Loðbrók had composed the Krákumál as he lay in a similar pit dying. If Einar was thrown into this pit, he would not even have time to shout a curse before the creature at the bottom of it tore him limb from limb.

'For your friend, yes,' Asbjorn Hviti said. 'Bjarki – that's what I call my little pet down there – needs to taste human flesh every now and again so he retains the hunger for it. For you, well that depends.'

'Depends on what?' Einar said.

'I'm a strong man,' the Bear said. 'I can make most people do things that I want. A simple threat is usually enough to get them moving. There are some others however, that need more persuasion. They are stubborn, or principled or have some other reason to refuse to obey my orders. They are almost always someone with some sort of craft or talent. They try to hold out and often do for a time. Sometimes even after torture. These people are few and far between but I suspect you are one of them.'

Einar swallowed. He was not sure he was one of those folk at all.

'The thing is,' the Bear said, 'In the end most of even those people end up giving in anyway. There are a very few who will actually die rather than give in, but either way, it's all a tiresome waste of time and effort. So I've learned to get straight to the point. I confront them with what will happen to them if they refuse to do what I want and they make the choice there and then. Do they comply or do they die? Those with the guts to do so chose death but most give in. You now have that choice.'

'You haven't told me what you want me to do yet,' Einar said. 'It can't just be blacksmith work.'

'Part of it is, actually,' the Bear said. 'I have a blacksmith who works for me. He is a very special smith with particular skills. He makes very special swords that make me a lot of wealth. I've managed to persuade him to work for me but he will not share the secret of how they are made. He's one of those folk who will die rather than reveal it.'

'Isn't your strategy then to kill someone like that?' Einar said.

'I *need* the secret of how he makes the swords,' the Bear said with a sarcastic smile. 'I need to make more. If he is dead then I can't do that unless I learn how to make them. He knows this. When I have him watched, the bastard just stops working and I can't afford delays. When I threaten him he just dares me to go ahead. He's a tough old bird I'll give him that. Anyway he has become a mountain and I am the storm. We are at a standstill.'

'So what's this to do with me?' Einar said.

'You're a blacksmith,' Asbjorn Hviti said. 'Like him. And you're a slave like him too. I will tell him I've bought you to help him forge the swords. We need to speed up their making. He will trust you. And you will learn the secret of how those swords are created, then you'll tell it to me.'

'And if I refuse?' Einar said.

The Bear pointed to the pit, his smile turning to a grin. As if prompted, the great white bear in the pit let out a roar.

'You will join your friend down there,' Asbjorn Hviti said. 'I trust you have no illusions about what will happen then?'

'What's to stop me learning this secret but refusing to tell you as well?' Einar said. Almost as soon as he spoke the words he felt like slapping himself on the forehead, admonishing himself for revealing what might have been his only way of escape.

'Then you'll still go down the pit with Bjarki,' Asbjorn

Hviti said. 'I'll have gained nothing but lost nothing either. It's your choice.'

Einar knew he had no choice but to comply with the will of Asbjorn. This was not made any more palatable by the fact that the big man knew this, which he made obvious with a smile of mixed triumph and contempt. Einar felt like his blood was boiling. Anger at the killing of Hegg mixed with humiliation at being forced to do the will of his killer. And not just Hegg either. Frida, Bersi and all those innocent people in Frodisborg slaughtered by Asbjorn's vikings. Part of him longed to tell the Bear to go and fuck himself, even at the cost of meeting the same horrific end as Hegg.

Then a recollection of something Ulrich and Skar had both taught him resurfaced in his mind: *Sometimes you have to lose a battle to win the war*. If he swallowed his pride now and let go his thirst for revenge for Hegg for a time, perhaps it would give Ulrich and the others time to find him and find a way into the fortress. Then Asbjorn's time would come and they would give Eirik another bloody nose too. He had to keep control of himself.

Einar heaved a heavy sigh and looked at the floor.

'I'll do it,' he said.

'Excellent!' the Bear said. 'When I recognised you were a blacksmith I knew Odin had sent you to help me solve this problem. Or perhaps it was Loki, given that it was at the festival in his honour.'

Einar paled. His knowledge of blacksmithing was the one thing to save his life but his maimed hand meant he could not carry out the work properly. It would only be a matter of time before the Bear found out. He may have escaped death but it was only temporary. This was exactly the sort of cruel mischief Loki would play. He would think it a fine joke.

'Come along,' Asbjorn Hviti said. 'I shall introduce you to Ingler, the greatest smith in the world.'

Thirty-Nine

'I think we've lost him,' Skar said.

They were trekking along the wooden walkway through the bogs, following the trail of ivory pieces Einar had dropped.

'I hope not,' Ulrich said. 'That ivory he's using to lay the trail cost me a fortune in the marketplace. The horn it came from was a real work of art. It was a shame to smash it up.'

Ulrich had wanted to wait as long as was responsible before setting out from Hedeby. The marshland was so flat that if anyone in the group they were trailing had looked around it would be easy to spot someone following behind them. So they had first returned to the ship to get their wolf pelt cloaks and other special gear that could be of use when crossing bogs and meres, then they had waited until much later in the afternoon before setting out.

The flatness of the countryside turned out to be of advantage to them. Not long after they left the gates of Hedeby Sigurd had noticed someone was following them from a distance. The Wolf Coats ducked off the path to one side of the marsh. They hid a little way off the path, crouching in the soft moss behind some peat hags, careful not to end up sunk in the bog. Sigurd, Skar and Kari had then crawled on their bellies back to the walkway, rolled across it and off to the opposite side.

After a short while a company of ten men in war gear came tramping along the path. When they got to the spot where the Wolf Coats had left it, they stopped, turning towards where Ulrich and the others crouched in the mere.

'We know you're there. We saw you leave the path,' one of the men shouted. Ulrich recognised one of the men from Meginbraht's house, now decked out in helmet, shield and brynja.

Ulrich, Starkad, Wulfhelm and Surt stood up.

'Meginbraht pays the watchmen at the gate to tell him who comes and goes,' the merchant's warrior said. 'We knew you'd left just after you walked out the gate. Where do you think you're off to?'

'We're just out for a stroll,' Ulrich said. 'Enjoying this lovely countryside.'

The warrior on the path narrowed his eyes.

'Where's the rest of you?' he said. 'Where's the girl and the big man?'

'Right behind you,' Ulrich said.

The men on the walkway whirled around but it was already too late. The three Wolf Coats on that side had been inching their way back towards the walkway, blades drawn. Now they sprang to their feet and attacked.

Skar, Sigurd and Kari each cut a man down as he was still half turned. Affreca rose from behind a peat hag, bow drawn, and shot another of the men on the walkway. Ulrich, Starkad, Wulfhelm and Surt were already running forward and killed another four while they were still trying to work out which way to turn. The last two of Meginbraht's men were killed in as many moments.

'That should teach those nosey bastards to mind their own business,' Ulrich said, wiping a spray of blood from his face. 'Sink the bodies in the bog and let's get going.'

They had then continued on until they had gone so far that Skar thought they had lost Einar's trail.

'That's about four thousand paces since the last marker,' Skar said. 'Either we missed one or they turned off the path somewhere.'

'Or Einar was caught dropping them,' Surt said.

'Right. Turn around,' Ulrich said. 'We walk back again. Everyone keep your eyes open for more of them until we reach four thousand paces.'

They returned the way they had come, each of them scanning the boards beneath them for any sign of an ivory piece until they arrived back at the spot where the last one was dropped.

'There's a track going east to west,' Starkad said, pointing to the line that crossed the walkway with a sweep of his arm. 'They might have turned off here.'

'But in which direction?' Wulfhelm said.

'We split,' Ulrich said. 'Affreca, Starkad, Wulfhelm and Kari follow the track east for three thousand paces. The rest of us will go west. Then turn and meet back here. With luck one of us will spot another marker.'

It was Sigurd, sharp eyed as always, who spotted the next marker dropped by Einar on the westward track. They returned to the wooden walkway and waited for the others to come back, then they all headed west.

As the daylight began to fade, they spotted an orange glow through the rising mist ahead.

'They've made camp for the night,' Ulrich said. 'We're getting too close. We'll find somewhere to stop for the night ourselves and follow in the morning.'

'Why don't we just kill the Bear and his men while they sleep?' Affreca said. 'And rescue Einar tonight?'

Ulrich rolled his eyes.

'Because I want to know where the Bear's hideout is, your worshipfulness,' he said with an exasperated sigh. 'We're after those swords, remember?'

They spent an uncomfortable, damp night on the moss. Then in the morning, when Ulrich judged the Bear's company had had enough time to get on their way, they took up the trail again.

They kept going until the trail ran out at the rickety wooden jetty on the edge of a wider expanse of water that disappeared into the mist. The Bear's two pack horses stood, standing patiently, tied to the post near the water's edge.

'Do you think it's a lake or a river?' Sigurd said.

'There's a lot of rushes around the edge,' Wulfhelm said. 'I'd say it was a lake.'

'The trail ends here, Ulrich,' Skar said. 'They must have taken a boat from here. Even if we had a boat ourselves, we'd never find them in this fog. What do we do now?'

Ulrich rubbed his chin, looking around at the empty jetty, the reeds and the water.

He clicked his fingers, then pointed to the horses.

'Do you think the Bear has so many horses he can just leave a couple behind?' he said.

'Maybe he does,' Affreca said. 'A man like him doesn't

care about people or animals. He probably just leaves them here to die.'

'Perhaps,' Ulrich said. 'But even if that's true, the next time he needs to carry a load of loot to Hedeby for Meginbraht to sell, he'll need to have new ones waiting here when he gets off his boat.'

'So what are you saying?' Skar said.

'I think there is someone who looks after his horses for him,' Ulrich said.

'Out here?' Starkad said, looking around at the mist and bogs.

'Find somewhere out of sight,' Ulrich said. 'We'll wait and see who comes along.'

'We can't waste any more time, Ulrich!' Affreca said. 'Einar could be in danger. The Bear could have killed him already!'

'Now why would he do that?' Ulrich said. 'He needs a blacksmith, doesn't he?'

'I hope you're right,' Affreca said.

They found a place amid the tall reeds that allowed them to watch the jetty without being seen themselves.

After a long while the sound of steady splashes reached their ears. Through the mist a weird figure loomed. It looked like half a person and half some sort of huge insect. It seemed to have four very long legs that allowed it to wade through the water while keeping its body dry. Surt gasped. Affreca rubbed her eyes and the rest of the Wolf Coats grasped their weapons, thinking some strange marsh monster was approaching. Then the newcomer walked up out of the water beside the jetty and they all saw that it was a man wearing a pair of long stilts and holding very long poles in each of his hands to balance himself. Once out of the water he dropped the poles and jumped down off the stilts.

The man was a wild-looking fellow, with long bushy hair and beard to match. He walked to the post and began to untether the horses.

'Stay here,' Ulrich said in a whisper to the others. Then he stood up himself.

'Hello friend,' he said. 'Are those your horses?'

The man froze. He looked sideways at Ulrich like someone caught doing something they should not be doing.

'Em... yes,' he said. He spoke the Norse tongue with the thick accent of the Danes.

'You need two horses?' Ulrich said.

'Who's to say what I need?' the other man said. 'I live here. You come into the marshes and start questioning if a man owns his own horses? Who are you, stranger? What is your business here?'

'I'm looking for a famous viking known as The Bear,' Ulrich said. 'Asbjorn Hviti. He lives somewhere near here. Have you heard of him perhaps?'

The man's eyes widened.

'I've never heard of him,' he said.

'Are you sure?' Ulrich said. 'He's a big man. Wears a cloak of white fur.'

'No, no. I'm quite sure,' the man with the unkempt hair said, shaking his head in a furious manner. 'Now I am a busy man. I need to go about my work.'

He completed untethering the horses then slung the stilts and poles across the back of one of them.

'That's useful gear,' Ulrich said, pointing to the stilts.

'Best way to get about in the marshes,' the man said in a gruff voice. 'Quickest anyway. If you don't have horses to mind. Listen, stranger—'

He fixed Ulrich with a steady gaze.

'This is a dangerous place for those who don't know it,' he said. 'People disappear here all the time. Those foolish enough to go wandering off the path soon find themselves in trouble. We marsh folk live here. We know this land well and all its dangers. If I were you I'd go back to town before something bad happens to you. Understand?'

With that he turned and led the horses off down the track the Wolf Coats had arrived by.

A few moments later the Wolf Coats emerged from the reeds.

'You realise he's lying, don't you?' Skar said.

'Of course,' Ulrich said. 'Sigurd and Kari, follow him. See where he goes. Don't get too close. If it looks like he's spotted you just leave him alone and get back here.'

The two Wolf Coats nodded and loped off across the marsh.

'Now we wait,' Ulrich said.

They lounged in the moss and reeds for some time as the day wore on. The mists lifted a little, growing thinner and more transparent. Far above, the sun was high and showed a ghostly outline through the vapours. The company saw that they were indeed on the shore of a large lake which the bog merged with, through a sea of tall, pale brown reeds.

After a while Sigurd and Kari returned.

'Well?' Ulrich said.

'We followed him down the track,' Sigurd said. 'Not far along it he turned off and headed across the moss.'

'I didn't see any other tracks,' Skar said.

'He knew where he was going,' Kari said. 'There is a track, a very faint one, but you would only find it if you knew it was there. We followed him until he came to some sort of village. It wasn't a big place, no more than half a dozen huts and a big hall or something but it was half in and half out of the water; built on a platform that sat on columns that went down into the lake.'

'Sounds like a typical marsh dweller village,' Skar said. 'They're a strange folk. They exist on whatever fish live in lakes like this, and birds or their eggs. They keep themselves to themselves and don't like outsiders.'

'The perfect folk you'd want to live among if you didn't want anyone from the real world to know where you were,' Ulrich said. 'Was there any sign of the Bear?'

Sigurd shook his head.

'No,' he said. 'But there was a commotion when our man arrived back. I could hear a lot of shouting and there were a few people running around.'

'Good,' Ulrich said. 'With any luck we won't have too long to wait then. Starkad, Skar, I want you two to prepare a little surprise. The rest of us will hide back in the reeds.'

The little Wolf Coat leader outlined his plan and they all took up the positions as he ordered.

After a while the sound of oars, dipping in the water came from the lake. Then a long, flat bottomed boat, designed for skimming across marshes, appeared from the mist. There was a man rowing and a young boy at the steering oar. As it got closer they could see the man at the oars was the same marsh dweller who had earlier collected the horses.

As the boat went past the end of the jetty a hand reached

up out of the water and grabbed the side of the vessel. Skar, a knife gripped in his teeth, had been lurking just under the surface waiting for the boat to pass. At the same time Starkad reached up from the other side and grabbed that side. Their weights counterbalancing each other, both Wolf Coats hauled themselves on board the skiff in a moment. The man and the boy in it had no time to react before they found they had Starkad and Skar's knives at their throats.

'What do you want?' the marsh dweller said.

'Take it in,' Skar said, flicking his head towards the jetty, where Ulrich now stood.

'You again?' the man with the wild hair said as his boat bumped against the wooden jetty. 'I thought I told you to get out of here. Well, if you can't take good advice then that's your own lookout.'

'Hello again my friend,' Ulrich said, stepping into the boat. 'I wanted to give you the chance to rethink your answer from the last time we talked. You see, I think you really do know where the Bear's fortress is. Not only that but you work for him. I suspect you keep an eye on the place while he is away on viking raids. And you make sure he has horses available when he needs to transport his plunder to Hedeby for sale. Today, when you found me nosing around, asking about the Bear, you were anxious to warn him and my guess is that you're on your way to do that now.'

The marsh dweller, impassive, returned Ulrich's gaze but said nothing.

'I want you to take me and my friends along with you,' Ulrich said. 'I need to know where the Bear's fortress is.'

The man grunted.

'Never,' he said. 'The Bear would kill me if I did. He'll

burn our village to the ground and feed me to his pet. Do you think I'm stupid?'

Ulrich smiled.

'And I,' he said, running a finger along the blade of his knife, 'Will kill you if you don't. Then we'll go and burn your village to the ground and kill everyone in it. You see, it's what will happen either way. The only thing I don't have is a pet, but some of my men can be real animals at times. So you may as well deal with the most pressing danger, which is us, here and now.'

A look of consternation came across the marsh dweller's face.

'Is this your son?' Ulrich said, running his knife blade down the young lad's face. 'I think we will start with him.'

'Wait!' the marsh dweller said, holding up a hand. 'All right, all right. I'll show you where it is.'

'Wise choice,' Ulrich said, signalling to the others waiting in the reeds to get into the boat. 'Now let's get going.'

Forty

Einar was taken down the stairs again to the place he had first entered the Bear's fortress. As they passed the inner fortified door the beast on the other side sensed their presence and launched another all-out assault on the door. Again it bucked and rattled as the fearsome roaring of the white bear behind it battered their ears but to Einar's relief, the door still held firm. The snarls brought back memories of Hegg's horrific fate and Einar felt a feeling like cold water running down his spine.

Despite this, he considered the position of the door. It could not be at the bottom of the pit he had looked down at the bear from. That was towards the other side of the building, which meant there must be some sort of passage that led from the base of the pit to this door.

Asbjorn Hviti led the way out of the fortress using the door they had entered by.

'Are we leaving so soon?' Einar said.

'We're not going far, don't worry,' the Bear said.

Outside they got back into the boat they had arrived in and pushed off, moving away from the round fortress. Without Hegg, the second oar was taken by one of the Bear's men. They rowed around the island, following its edge. The mist was a lot thinner now and Einar saw that there was another little island not far away. Unlike the regular stone circle of the fortress, this one was more chaotic. It was surrounded by a wattle fence which encircled a collection of huts, including a round, thatched building in the middle. The unmistakable clang of metal hammering on metal came from inside while thick grey smoke rose through a hole in the thatch. There were several chickens perched on the roofs of the huts, watching the approaching boat with their unblinking eyes.

They docked the boat at a small jetty and clambered out. Two more of the Bear's warriors stood guard at a gate in the wattle fence. They nodded to Asbjorn Hviti as he approached and he, Einar and Asbjorn's son, Erling, passed through the gate into a sort of yard. It was covered in filthy straw and chicken shit. There seemed to be chickens everywhere, clucking and pecking at the earth.

'Does this Ingler like eggs?' Einar said, pushing one away from his foot.

'It's one of the special conditions he insisted on that I agreed to,' the Bear said. 'He wanted lots of chickens. He claims he needs lots of eggs to keep his strength up. Who knows though? He's a strange fellow.'

'He's mad, father,' Erling said. 'Mad and smelly. I don't know why we have to keep him.'

Einar saw a face at the door of the round building. It was a young boy with skin so pale he seemed luminous in the gloomy interior. At the sight of the Bear's son the eyes of the boy inside the door widened with something that Einar recognised as fear.

The Bear spotted the boy too.

'Tell your father we are here to see him,' Asbjorn Hviti said and the young lad's face disappeared again.

He led the way to the doorway.

'You first,' the Bear said to Einar.

The doorway was low and the interior dark, but the warm air and smell of hot metal and smoke told Einar straight away that this was a blacksmith's forge. He went inside and immediately he began to cough. The air inside was foul, not just with the odour of charcoal smoke and metal slag that was usual to a forge but there was something else in the air, an almost acidic stench that made Einar gag when he drew in breath. It was also gloomy. Einar waited for a moment while his eyes adjusted to the semi-dark.

When they did, his bottom jaw dropped open a little. It was a large, round room. The forge fire was on a raised platform in the middle, glowing orange with waves of heat emanating from it. Nearby was a long trough filled with water. There was an anvil and normal blacksmithing tools but also lots of strange devices and models that Einar could not identify. There were tongs and hammers but they had been modified for some unknown purpose. There was a little metal model of a wagon that looked like it could roll by itself. There were boxes and chests, and what looked like an iron face mask. There was war gear – helmets, shields, brynjas and other types of protection – but no weapons except for seven sword blades, yet to have handles fitted, which stood propped up against the wall.

Beside the forge stood a man with a hammer in his hand. Einar had never seen an elf, but if he had then this man would fit the description. He was short and slight, which was surprising for a blacksmith, who tended to be large, burly men. His long, very black hair was tied back in a ponytail. He had a pointed beard beneath his chin and long moustache to match. His eyes were very narrow, like someone who spent a lot of time squinting against very bright sun on snow. They were a very pale grey-blue. Seeing the newcomers enter, he set down his hammer and turned towards them. His clothes were a uniform blue wool, both jerkin and breeches, and his front was covered by the customary leather apron of a blacksmith. On his head he wore a pointed cap of white felt.

The boy he had seen earlier stood near the bellows. His hair was so blond it was almost white and he had the same pale eyes as the smith. Einar judged he was perhaps ten or eleven winters old. A noise made Einar look around and he spotted another young boy who looked very similar but a few years younger, so probably a brother.

'I've brought you some help, Ingler,' the Bear said, a smile forced onto his lips. He laid a massive hand on Einar's shoulder. 'This is Einar Thorfinnsson. He is both a blacksmith and a poet.'

The smith's upper lip curled into a sneer.

'I don't need any more help, Asbjorn.' he said. He spoke Norse but with the accent of the Finns or Laps of the far north. 'I have my sons, Witege and Waldere.'

'If you don't need help, then why can't you make the swords any faster?' the Bear said, his smile gone.

'Some things just take a certain amount of time, Asbjorn,' Ingler said. 'It takes nine months for one woman to birth a baby. You cannot birth the same baby in one month with nine women. These swords are works of art. You can't just bash them out.'

'Well you'd better start, Ingler,' the Bear said. 'I have customers waiting. Important ones. I'm giving you extra help so get to work.'

'I won't work with one of your spies watching me,' Ingler said. 'Surely you've learned that by now.'

'This fellow is a smith, like you,' the Bear said. 'He is not my spy. He was enthralled to me by a court in Hedeby in recompense for a murder he carried out. There's no reason for you to suspect him. He's as much a slave as you are.'

The blacksmith cast a sideways glance at Einar and pursed his lips.

'So *you* say,' he said.

'Is this not correct?' the Bear said to Einar.

'It is,' Einar said. 'Though it wasn't murder. I rightfully killed the man who murdered my mother. My friend and I were enslaved by the jarl as we couldn't pay the weregild. This man brought us here. He threw my friend to that white bear of his in the pit. It tore Hegg apart. *That* was murder.'

The Bear let out a growl of exasperation. He swung his left hand, backhanding Einar across the side of the head. Einar, who was not expecting it, went reeling sideways. The big man then swung his leg in a roundhouse kick that drove his boot into Einar's guts and all the breath from his body. Einar felt like he had been kicked by a horse. He doubled over then sank to his knees, fighting hard not to vomit.

'I've had enough of arguing with slaves!' the big man

said through clenched teeth. 'All of you better remember who the master is here. Get to work and start making more swords. And if you don't want to work with this man, Ingler, then perhaps I should let one of your boys play with Bjarki? Perhaps then you'll appreciate an extra pair of hands.'

The two boys ran to their father who threw his arms around them. With one last hostile glare Asbjorn turned and left the forge. His son took a moment to cast an intimidating glare at everyone then he followed out the door.

Einar was still on his knees, gasping for breath. After a few moments he recovered enough to struggle back to his feet. The others made no move to help him.

'Are you all right?' Ingler said. His tone of voice suggested he cared little either way.

'Just winded,' Einar said.

'So you're a blacksmith are you?' Ingler said.

'I worked for one for a time,' Einar said through gasps. 'I know the basic craft.'

'So you're not an actual smith, then?' Ingler said.

'No,' Einar said. 'But I didn't want to tell him that. My life depended on me being a blacksmith. It still does.'

Ingler looked at him for a long moment through even more narrowed eyes.

'I suppose there is some work I can put you to,' he said.

'So can I stay here and work with you?' Einar said.

'I don't think there's much choice about that,' Ingler said. 'Don't expect me to trust you though. There are certain secrets I won't tell you.'

'I may as well level with you,' Einar said, looking into the pale eyes of the smith, searching for some sort of fellow feeling. 'The Bear did not just put me in here to help you out. He wants me to find out how the swords are made.'

'You expect me to be surprised by this?' Ingler said. 'I'm not as stupid as he seems to think I am. I may as well level with you as well: I won't tell you that anyway. Many folk have died for that secret and it's the last bargaining piece I have to deal with Asbjorn. Provided you're useful I will give you work but you won't learn the secret of how the swords are made. Now I know that is what your life depends on but that isn't my problem. I have my sons to worry about. I did not get you into this situation. The Norns who weave our fates put you here. They can be really vindictive bitches sometimes.'

'All right,' Einar said, wondering at the same time how long the Bear's patience would last if Einar did not soon find out and pass on how the swords were made. 'As long as we speed up the making of these swords I guess.'

The smith chuckled and shook his head.

'Perhaps you did not hear me when I said there are certain tasks that take certain lengths of time?' he said. 'The Bear will just have to learn patience.'

'You hate him?' Einar said.

'I have good reason to,' Ingler said.

'He cannot sell these swords if you don't make them for him,' Einar said. 'Why do you do it? Like you said, you have a winning bargaining piece.'

'Unfortunately so does he,' Ingler said. He ruffled the hair of the boys who stood on either side of him. 'In fact he has *two* of them. When I first came here I had three sons with me.'

His eyes became glassy and hard.

'I'm sorry to hear that,' Einar said.

'It wasn't your fault,' Ingler said. 'Like I said: The Norns are bitches. Now grab that hammer. There is work to be done.'

Forty-One

'**Y**ou can beat out a sword blade can't you?' Ingler said. Einar nodded.

'Well let's see how good a job you make of this one,' the smith said. To Einar's surprise he picked up a pair of crutches, placed them under his arms and shuffled towards the fire. His legs were straight and stiff and he moved with difficulty, as if in pain and with little control of his limbs. When he was halfway to the forge he looked around and saw Einar watching him.

Ingler stopped, bent over and pulled the left leg of his breeches up. There was a thick scar across the back of the smith's leg just above his knee. It stood out against his flesh like a thick, purple rope. There was another across the back of his ankle.

'When he captured me, Asbjorn slit my hamstrings and the sinews between my ankle and calf muscles,' the smith said. 'It's the same on both legs. He did it so that I could not run away. It's a brutal but effective tactic. It saves him having to have me guarded all the time. Now: the sword.'

Three rods of iron, laid two side by side and one on top, bound with wire, were poked into the fire of the forge. They had been there for some time and glowed cherry red. Einar took the tongs and twisted the rods together to form a bar. Then it went back into the fire. After a time he took it out again and began beating it flat with the hammer. All the while Ingler watched him, arms folded, his already narrow eyes even narrower.

It was hard work and took a long time. Unlike the specially adapted hammer he had used in Frodisborg, the one Ingler had provided had a full length handle so Einar had to grip it halfway along it. This meant it took extra effort to swing and several times it twisted in the weakened grip of his maimed hand. He wondered if the same solution he had worked out for playing the lyre – to switch hands – would work with the hammer too. However when he tried it he found that his left hand was too clumsy and the hammer head missed the heated metal as often as it struck it. There was nothing else to it but do it the hard way.

By the time he had beaten the iron into a flat blade Einar was sweating and out of breath. He took it to the trough. As he dipped the hot metal in the water it hissed and bubbled, unleashing a cloud of steam. Then he held it up, watching as the flickering firelight in the forge shimmered across the surface. He handed it to Ingler.

The blacksmith examined the new sword with an appraising eye. He ran his fingers along it. He held it up to eye level, looking down the blade to assess straightness. Then he made a face.

'You made hard work of that,' Ingler said. 'You're not holding the hammer right. Is it because of the missing parts of your hand?'

'Yes,' Einar said, holding up his injured right hand. 'I used to use a special hammer with a short shaft.'

'So I'm not the only cripple here,' the blacksmith said. 'Was it an accident?'

'No, it was deliberate,' Einar said, and told the smith the whole story of the duel fought against his own father above a river of lava in Iceland; how Jarl Thorfinn the Skull Cleaver had severed his little finger and part of his palm, and how he had then sent the jarl screaming to his death in the fires below.

'That's quite a tale. You must be quite the warrior,' Ingler said. He handed the blade back to Einar. 'The sword is shit though.'

Einar frowned.

'Take it outside and file it down,' the blacksmith said.

'What?!' Einar said.

'File it down,' Ingler said. 'There's a file and a metal knife over there. We can reuse the metal when you're done.'

'Why not just melt it?' Einar said.

'Are you questioning me?' Ingler said. 'I am the master here, remember? So you do what I say. Or do you want me to tell Asbjorn you're no use to me with that maimed hand?'

Einar shook his head.

'Then off you go. Outside. I want that blade turned to metal shavings. The whole thing, understand?' Ingler said. 'And I have my own work to do in here that I don't want you watching.'

Still incredulous, Einar lifted the file, took the sword blade and left the forge. As soon as he left the forge he heard a bolt rattle on the inside and knew Ingler had locked him out while he did whatever his secret work was.

Outside he found a three-legged stool near the door. He plonked himself down on it, convinced he had just been given a pointless task for the sole purpose of getting him out of the way. Then another thought came over him. For the first time in as long as he could remember he was alone and had some time to himself. He was out of the heat and stench inside the forge in the cool afternoon air. Who knew when – if ever – he would be in this situation again. He may as well enjoy it while it lasted.

He began to file down the sword he had worked so hard to forge.

Einar worked on filing the sword all day. There was little else he could do anyway. A quick tour of the yard outside told him that there was no opportunity of escape. Ingler's island was ringed by a fence and though there was little chance of the hobbled blacksmith going anywhere, now Einar was there the Bear had tasked four of his men with guard duty. They took it in turns to patrol the outside of the fence so even if Einar managed to climb it, one of them would catch him before he managed to swim very far.

So Einar contented himself to sit on the stool, running the file down the blade, shaving off curls of metal that fell on the ground before him into a little pile. With the mist gone he could see now that the Bear's islands sat on a wide lake surrounded by tall reeds and bullrushes. It was very quiet apart from the lapping of the water and the occasional cries of marsh birds.

Now that he was away from the immediate threat of the Bear and the hostile suspicion of Ingler, as well as the foul stench inside the forge, Einar found a certain sense of peace descend on him. As the chickens pecked and scratched around him he chanted *kviða* and *drápa* to them, practising the poems and sagas. Now he knew he could play the lyre again he found his old delight in the skaldic art had returned.

Later on, however, as the sun began to dip, black thoughts clouded his happiness. He was starting to doubt if the Wolf Coats would ever find him in the vast watery wilderness of the marshlands. Ingler was intent that he should not find out the secret of how the swords were made, nor would he speed up making them. Unless he found some way to escape, the most likely future for him would be that Asbjorn Hviti would feed him to his pet bear like he did to Hegg.

The chickens seemed to be everywhere. They were on the roofs of the huts and all around the enclosure. They pecked around his stool and one hopped onto his foot at one point. There were quite a few dead ones as well, lying in heaps of rotting feathers here and there around the yard and adding to the general stink of the place. One thing was sure, Ingler was not using the chickens' eggs. Einar could see them lying around uncollected everywhere. On the occasions he got up to walk around and stretch his legs Einar's boots crunched on other eggs under the filthy straw of the yard. Many of them had been there a long time as the terrible smell that rose from the broken shells told him.

It took the rest of the day for Einar to reduce the sword to a heap of metal shavings. It was difficult enough work without the file slipping now and then from his injured right hand but in the end he was done. As it started to get dark he stood up and knocked on the door of the forge. After a rattling of bolts the door opened a little and Einar could see the older one of the boys peering out with his earnest expression, like someone who had grown old before his time.

'Tell your father I'm done,' Einar said.

The boy disappeared from the door. Einar could hear a short conversation going on inside then the lad returned with a leather bucket, a small shovel and a broom.

'Father says to put the metal into this,' he said, holding them out.

Einar took them and went back to his heap of shavings. When the bucket was full he brought it back to the door and handed it to the boy who took it, then opened the door wide.

'Father says you can come in,' he said.

Einar stepped into the gloomy forge. Almost straight away he coughed and thought he was going to choke again. The stench from earlier was much worse now and the air seemed thick and heavy with it. Einar's eyes started to water and he wondered if it was from coughing or the foul air.

'By Thor's balls what are you burning in here?' Einar said through wheezes. 'Shit?'

Ingler was sitting near the forge on a stool just like the one Einar had sat on outside. His useless legs were stretched out before him and his pointed felt hat was a little askew. He had a bemused smile on his face and his eyes seemed bleary. At first Einar thought the fumes of the forge had befuddled his mind but then he spotted the clay cup in his hand and the jug near his stool. At Einar's question the blacksmith fell into a fit of wheezing giggles.

'I'm glad you find this so amusing,' Einar said.

'Sit down, sit down,' Ingler said, waving his hand towards another stool. 'It's just something you said. I mean no harm. Join me for a drink.'

Einar sat down and Ingler handed him another cup. Einar noticed it was far from clean but said nothing.

'You'll like this,' Ingler said, his words slurring a little. He picked up the clay jug and stood up, unsteady and swaying. He limped on his damaged legs a couple of steps. Einar stood up and met him to save him the effort. He held up his cup and Ingler sloshed some dark red liquid into it from the jug.

'It's a special concoction of my own,' he said. 'One of the few concessions I got from Asbjorn. I insist he supplies me with red wine from south-western Francia. I doubt very much that it actually comes from south-western Francia but it's the right colour. After I do what I do with it, it doesn't matter anyway.'

Einar took a drink. His eyes widened as it burned like fire down his throat. His heart began to race and a fierce joy spread through his chest.

'Have you ever tasted anything like that?' Ingler said.

'I know a wise man called Grimnir,' Einar said, in a breathless tone. 'He used to boil mead and produce a drink that tastes a bit like this from the steam.'

Ingler pursed his lips. He looked a little disappointed.

'That's what I do,' he said. He pointed to a large copper kettle that now sat over the forge fire. A long metal pipe came from the top of it, rising straight towards the roof then bending back towards the floor. The end of it sat over the top of another clay jug and a light pink liquid dripped from the pipe into it.

'So you are wiser than you look,' Ingler said. 'Have you travelled much?'

'I come from Iceland and I've been to Norway, Ireland, Britain, Orkney and now the land of the Danes,' Einar said, feeling a sudden pride swelling his chest.

'Not bad for someone your age,' the smith said, refilling his own cup with more of the fiery liquid. 'Though by your age I'd been to Miklagard, Serkland and I'd sailed the great middle sea. Rome, that was quite a spot.'

'Is that where you learned how to make the swords?' Einar said, remembering the amazing stone buildings like Kings Gard in Jorvik, which had been built by the Roman wizards many centuries ago.

'No,' Ingler said. 'I learned that in a place called Damascus in Serkland.'

'I've never heard of it,' Einar said.

'I'd be surprised if you had,' the smith said. 'You got the sword filed down? Good work. Must have been difficult with that hand of yours.'

'Nothing is easy with this,' Einar said, flexing his maimed hand.

'Witege,' Ingler said, calling to the eldest of his sons. 'The chickens need to be fed.'

The boy emerged from the gloom with a bucket filled with grains and went outside.

Einar took another drink from his cup.

'It seems such a waste of a perfectly good sword,' Einar said. 'To file it down like that.'

'I'm a perfectionist, lad,' Ingler said. 'That's why the swords are so good.'

'You weren't just making life hard for me?' Einar said. 'And what's with all the chickens?'

'I like eggs,' Ingler said.

'You don't seem to eat many,' Einar said. 'They're lying all over the place out there.'

Ingler just chuckled and tapped the side of his nose.

'That's all my business, young man,' he said. 'I thought I made it clear I wouldn't let you spy on me for Asbjorn.'

Einar sighed and held out his now empty cup for a refill. He could already feel the warm glow in his stomach and a slight fuzziness in his head from what he had drunk. Ingler's brew was harsh on the throat but he wanted more.

'It helps the pain, doesn't it?' the smith said, his grin fading a little as he poured more of the drink out for Einar. 'I drink it every night. It helps me forget about my cares. Otherwise I'd never get to sleep. The thoughts and memories torment me.'

'I can imagine,' Einar said. 'It must be hard having a son killed by the man who also made you lame.'

'A son, a wife and a daughter,' Ingler said. He was staring at the floor as if he could scarcely believe it himself. 'My house. Everything. I used to live in Finnmark, far north of Norway. That's where I'm from. After my travels I settled down and put what I learned to good use. I became rich from what I made. The fame of my swords spread wide. I thought the Gods and the Norns had blessed me. But it was a curse.'

He shook his head, his shoulders slumped.

'My fame reached the ears of Asbjorn Hviti,' he said. 'And he decided that if he made me his slave he could become rich from the swords I made. One morning his ships arrived. He didn't even try to negotiate. I might have done a deal with him! But he just attacked. Burned my beautiful house. Raped my wife. Killed her. Did the same to my beautiful daughter. Took me and my three sons here to be his slaves.'

Einar did not know what to say. The door to the yard opened and Witege returned, his bucket empty after feeding the chickens.

'But I do not sell my labour cheap,' the smith said. He now spoke through clenched teeth. He looked up at Einar. His eyes glistened but they were hard and angry. 'I resist him any way I can. I push back. I do what I can to annoy him, thwart him.'

His face fell again.

'But that cost my eldest son his life,' he said. 'Asbjorn lost patience and threw poor Egil to that bear of his. He says he'll do the same to the others if I push him too far again.'

A little gasp made Einar look around. He caught sight of the younger boy, Waldere, staring wide-eyed with horror as he listened to his drunken father's ramblings from the semi-darkness at the back of the hut.

'Asbjorn is quite a bastard,' Einar said.

'The worst,' Ingler said. He spat the words through gritted teeth. 'And his son is just as bad. That arrogant little shit torments us every opportunity he gets.'

'I hate him,' Witege said.

Einar surmised that as someone the same age as him, Ingler's eldest son probably got special attention from the much bigger lad of Asbjorn's.

'There is no wife?' Einar said.

'He killed her,' Ingler said. 'Drowned her in the bog because she annoyed him one night. The son doesn't give a shit. He idolises his father so much.'

'You've been through a terrible time. I see that,' Einar said. Desperate to change the topic for the sake of the boys listening, he continued, 'But let us talk of better days, eh? Tell me of your travels. What is Miklagard like? It must have been amazing to be there.'

Ingler's narrow eyes widened. His smile returned at the memories that flooded into his head.

'Indeed it was,' he said. 'It's the greatest city in the world. The Kings of the Greeks, who rule there, had the most amazing toy. It was a person but all made of metal. It could move its arms and legs like a real human being but it was not one. It was an astounding feat of craftsmanship.'

They drank and talked long into the night. Ingler told Einar about his travels, the amazing things he had seen and learned, how he had perfected his blacksmithing skills and even learned new ones from the peoples far to the east and the south, with dusky skins, strange gods and different customs. He spoke in particular of the beauty of the women and the wealth of the kings.

Much later, now very drunk, Einar got up off his stool and swayed on unsteady legs.

'I need a piss,' he replied to Ingler's questioning look.

'There's an outhouse across the yard,' the blacksmith said.

Einar staggered out of the forge into the dark. Outside the cool, fresh night air hit him, making him dizzy for a moment. He stood for a moment steadying himself as the door of the forge banged shut behind him. There was some ghostly wisps of mist floating across the water but high in the sky above was a bright full moon, bathing everywhere in a silver light so bright that it cast faint shadows.

Einar found the outhouse by the stench of it. It was so dark inside that he was unsure if he managed to piss into the cesspit or not and suspected as he started to return to the forge that he had probably just added to the smell of the place.

Something caught his eye.

Einar stopped, frowning. What had it been? It was something in the hill of chicken dung that sat at the edge of the yard. Then he saw it again. There was something glinting in the moonlight.

He walked over and took another look. He blinked. It was like many tiny stars were winking among the mound of dung. Einar squatted down and poked at one with his finger. Pulling it out he was surprised to see it was a metal shaving, just like one of the many he had created that afternoon when filing down the sword blade.

He stood up, anger rushing into his heart. Was Ingler just messing with him after all? Had he set him a pointless task then tossed away the fruits of his labour? Not just tossed it away but threw it in the pile of chicken shit?

Einar strode back to the forge and pulled the door open, intending to confront Ingler and tell him he was not the fool the smith clearly took him for. Inside, however, he saw Ingler had fallen asleep while he had been outside. The blacksmith still sat on his stool, but was slumped against the wall, a gentle snore wheezing in and out from his nose. Einar briefly considered shaking him awake then sighed, the anger inside him draining away. What would be the point?

He found himself a spot to lie down near the warmth of the fire and went to sleep.

Forty-Two

'If this is our path to Valhalla,' Affreca said with a sigh, 'I never thought it would be so boring.'

She pulled her hood up and hunched her shoulders to try to dispel the dank discomfort of her wet clothes and stiff muscles.

'You know what Ulrich teaches,' Starkad said. '*Watch first. Never attack until you know as much as you can about your enemy. You should know him better than you do your own wife before you strike. That way nothing will come as a surprise.*'

Affreca, Starkad and Wulfhelm were lying on their bellies in a clump of reeds on a tiny little island not that far away from the island which the Bear's fortress was built on. The marsh dweller had led them through the fog along a wide, meandering river that opened into a broad lake. There they came across the Bear's fortress. It had been too risky to approach directly in broad daylight so they had found somewhere to hide in the reeds and bullrushes that ringed the edges of the marsh lake. After nightfall they had ventured out again to survey the area.

The Bear guarded his fortress well, however, and there were burning torches and braziers on the jetty and the roof of the round stone building to chase away the darkness and illuminate anyone coming close. There were warriors on the roof as well, keeping watch, the fire of the torches glinting on their helmets and brynjas.

They had spotted this little islet, however. It was a tiny patch of reed-covered land, not much bigger than the size of a wagon, set in the water just beyond the light cast by the Bear's torches.

Ulrich had ordered Affreca, Wulfhelm and Starkad to swim over to it under the cover of the darkness and set a watch on the fortress to see what they could learn. They were told to count how many warriors guarded the island, what were their habits and could any way in be identified. Now, as the sun rose they were in a prime spot to see what was going on, which turned out to be not very much. Their biggest problem, apart from the discomfort of wet clothes and not being able to stand up, was boredom.

Affreca tutted.

'What would Ulrich know about wives?' she said. 'He spends his life in the company of men. I pity the woman who ends up as his bride.'

They spoke in low voices, each of them aware that sound could travel far and fast across water.

'He was married once,' Starkad said.

'What?' Affreca said. Both Wulfhelm and she turned to look at Starkad, expressions of genuine surprise on their faces.

'It was before I became a Wolf Coat,' he said. 'When Ulrich was young. Skar told me about it once. Ulrich never speaks of her so no one really knows the truth of it. Something happened to her and she died.'

'She probably killed herself,' Affreca said. 'That's what I would do if I had to share a bed with him.'

'Wait,' Starkad said, holding up a hand. 'Something's happening.'

The heavily fortified door in the fortress was opening. It swung inwards revealing a dark interior.

'There's something moving in there,' Affreca said, narrowing her eyes as she peered across the water.

A thunderous roar echoed from the darkness within the fortress.

'Blood of Christ!' Wulfhelm said.

They all froze in shock at the sight of a great white bear that came loping out through the door of the fortress. It roved its large head to the left and the right, as if looking to see if anyone was there, then padded down the wooden jetty. When the bear reached the end it jumped off into the lake with a huge splash.

'It's coming for us!' Wulfhelm said, starting to push himself up from his belly.

'Stay where you are,' Starkad said, laying a hand on the Saxon's forearm. 'Look at its neck.'

Affreca and Wulfhelm looked at the bear that was now swimming in the water, its head above the surface. There was an iron collar around its neck and a long chain trailed from it back into the doorway of the fortress.

'What is it?' Wulfhelm said. 'I've never seen a creature so huge.'

'It looks like a bear but it's white,' Affreca said.

'It's a bear all right,' Starkad said. 'It's from the very far north, beyond Thule, where it is all ice and snow all year round. They're dangerous bastards. I've never seen one this far south.'

'What's it doing?' Affreca said.

'Looks like it's having a swim,' Starkad said. 'They're good swimmers and eat fish and seals up in the icy north. Maybe this is how they exercise it. It's not like you could take it for a walk. It would bite your head off.'

They watched as the great creature dived and ducked in the water. It could only go so far from the fortress before it reached the limit of the chain which snapped taut, stopping the creature from getting away any further. After a long time splashing and diving it clambered back out of the water, now with a large fish in its mouth, and began to stalk up and down outside the fortress door.

The sound of a metallic clanking came from deep within the fortress walls. The chain began running back inside the doorway until it once more drew taut. The great bear roared and strained against the pull but it was unable to stop itself being dragged back through the door by the chain and into the fortress beyond. Once it disappeared from sight there came a loud boom of a heavy door being slammed shut. Then the outer door of the fortress was closed as well.

'So that's how they get it back in then,' Starkad said. 'I was wondering if some idiot might have to try to walk it in or something. There must be a winch or windlass inside somewhere. It must be quite a strong one at that to reel that beast in. It must be like fishing for a whale with a rod and line.'

'We should tell Ulrich,' Affreca said. 'I think this is important.'

'Agreed,' Starkad said. 'But we have to wait until dark or they'll see us leaving this island.'

The rest of the day was uneventful. The white bear did not emerge from the door again nor was there any sign of Asbjorn Hviti, the man known as the Bear. As it turned out they did not have to wait until it was completely dark before they left the islet. As it wore on towards evening thick fog rolled in from the surrounding marshes once more and stole across the surface of the lake, obscuring the fortress from view but also hiding the three watchers on the island from the gaze of any of the Bear's warriors who might be looking that way.

Affreca, Starkad and Wulfhelm slid into the water at the back of the islet and set off back across the lake. They swam slowly, with methodical, deliberate strokes to minimise splashing and noise.

After a while they made it to the far shore and clambered out among the reeds. Dripping with dank lake water, they made their way back to the camp where the rest of the Wolf Coats were hiding.

Ulrich and the others listened while they told them what had happened at the lake.

'This is interesting,' Ulrich said, stroking his chin. 'Very interesting indeed.'

'Anything happen here?' Affreca said.

'Not much,' Ulrich said. 'Except our guests' friends came looking for them. We hid and they didn't find us.'

The marsh dweller and his son were still captives. He had professed to hating the Bear and only helping him out because of the threats he levelled at the village. Ulrich was sceptical and judged that the relationship between the viking and the villagers was probably more one of mutual benefit. They looked out for Asbjorn Hviti and he provided them with things they needed and protection from unwanted outsiders. Nor did Ulrich trust that the man's professed hatred of the Bear would not be so great that the marsh dweller would not run straight to him as soon as they let him go.

Still, there was no pressing reasons for the Wolf Coats to kill their prisoners, and it seemed also that the marsh dweller and his son had spent the time Affreca and the others were watching the Bear's fort showing the Wolf Coats how to catch water fowl, where fish could be caught and other crafts that were essential to surviving in the wetlands.

Ulrich had devoured all this new knowledge with relish.

'This is yet another type of country we can now fight in,' he said, looking around at the reeds, moss and bogs. 'There are few now that we do not know.'

'Have you ever been in the desert?' Surt said.

'I've never heard of "the desert",' Ulrich said.

'Try to imagine the very opposite of this place,' Surt said. 'Endless plains of burning sand. No water anywhere. No life and a sun so hot it burns your skin wherever it falls on.'

'Remind me never to go there,' Ulrich said. He turned back to Affreca. 'Do you want something to eat?'

The company had dug a little tunnel in the marshy ground and somehow got a fire going in it. The smoke dissipated into the earth covering so none rose above the reeds to give away their position, though now the fog had come in they may as well not have gone to the bother. There were two fish sizzling on sticks in the embers.

'Yes, I'm starving,' Affreca said, eyeing the fish with relish.

'There was no sign of Einar?' Ulrich said.

She shook her head.

'That doesn't bode well,' Ulrich said. 'He's enslaved but I'd hoped he might have some freedom to roam around at least. He knows we're following him so I would have expected some signal from him or at least for him to show himself.'

'There was nothing,' Affreca said. She looked very pale all of a sudden. 'You don't think he might be dead?'

'I don't know,' Ulrich said. 'But I don't think we can wait about much longer. We need to find a way into that fortress. Preferably one that doesn't end up with us getting eaten by that big white bear.'

Forty-Three

The after-effects of Ingler's drink from the night before meant that Einar woke that morning with a sore head and a mouth that felt like it had been stuffed by the wool of a long dead sheep. At first he thought the pounding that assaulted his senses was inside his head but then realised that Ingler was already up and hammering away at a red-hot sword blade. Orange sparks fountained in every direction with every hammer blow.

He struggled to his feet, rubbing his temples.

'You're up early,' he said. 'Don't you have a hangover? That drink of yours is lethal.'

'You just need more practice, lad,' the blacksmith said. 'Like me. I drink it every night. There's work to be done. We can't lie about all day or Asbjorn won't get his precious swords made.'

'What do you want me to do?' Einar said.

'I want you to beat out another sword blade,' Ingler said. 'Just like yesterday.'

A long bar of metal lay glowing in the fire.

'Well if you don't mind waiting for me to get it done,' Einar said, holding up his injured hand, 'then I'll get to work.'

'About that,' Ingler said. 'I have something for you.'

The blacksmith tried to lean over to pick up something that rested on the anvil. With his stiff legs he looked like he was going to fall over and Einar moved to help him, but Ingler managed to lift the item before Einar made it over to him.

'When I saw your hand I was reminded of two things,' Ingler said. 'First: The thunder God.'

'Thor?' Einar said.

'*Öku* we call him in the lands north of Norway,' Ingler said.

Einar had heard some old folk in Iceland use the name *Öku-Thor* but he had thought that was something to do with the chariot *Thos* rode across the top of the sky, the rumbling of its wheels making the sound men call thunder.

'Like we blacksmiths,' Ingler said, 'Öku-Thor wields a hammer. But when the Dwarves were making that hammer one of them was bitten by a fly. Distracted, he ended up making the handle of the hammer too short. That fly, so they say, was really Loki in disguise.'

'Loki is the cause of much mischief,' Einar said, thinking more of his own predicament than anything else.

'But Mjölnir, that hammer, is a very powerful weapon,' Ingler said. 'So powerful no one could wield it.'

'Except Thor,' Einar said.

Ingler smiled and held up a forefinger.

'Not even Öku-Thor,' he said, shaking his head. 'Were you not taught the words of the High One? The wisdom of the one-eyed?'

Einar knew he spoke of Odin. He did not want to also say that Ulrich never ceased from preaching his words but he racked his brain trying to remember some of them that would be relevant to this. Nothing came to mind.

'These were the words of Hárr the High One when he spoke to Gangleri,' Ingler said. '*Thor has a third great treasure, his Járngreipr, his iron gauntlets. He cannot do without them when he wields his hammer-shaft.* When I saw you holding that hammer yesterday and you said you used one with a shorter shaft that old tale came back to me. What you need, my friend, is a járngreipr.'

He held up the item he had picked up from the anvil. Einar saw that it was a metal glove, the kind some warriors wore into battle. It was the shape of a mitten but made of leather covered with rings of mail. Unlike the standard battle glove, however, this one had been modified. The bottom end of the glove, where the ring and little finger would usually go in, had been replaced by two thick strips of iron that came from where the back of the hand would be and curved around to form hooks that almost touched the palm. A hoop of leather was fastened to the front and back at the base of the metal strips and there was another strap that fastened the glove around the wearer's wrist.

'I also once met a man in Miklagard who had a problem like you,' Ingler said. 'He was a great warrior but he had lost a few fingers and could no longer wield a sword properly. He had a special glove made like this one. So this morning, while you were snoring, I knocked this one up for you.'

He handed the glove to Einar. Einar slid his hand into it. He was surprised by the feel that it was lined with some sort of soft fur and that it fitted so well. There was even some sort of padding at the bottom edge that filled out the space where his little finger and the right side of his palm had been.

'I added those hooks so you'll be able to grip things better. And there's cats' skin inside,' Ingler said, smiling and evidently pleased with his own work. 'May as well be comfortable. And I did my best to fit it to your hand. You were out cold and didn't notice.'

Einar frowned, wondering both how long Ingler had been working on it and that he had not woken with whatever he was doing to his hand. Had there been something else in that drink last night that had made his sleep so deep?

'Try that hammer now,' Ingler said. 'Hold it properly this time.'

With tentative movements, Einar picked up the hammer with his left hand. He slid it into his gloved right hand and the metal hooks clasped around the shaft the way his finger and the bottom of his palm would have before he lost them.

Einar gasped, closing the rest of his fingers around the shaft and taking a few short swipes in the air. It felt almost like normal.

'The strap will hold it in place,' Ingler said. 'You can do that with one hand.'

Using his left hand, Einar pulled the leather hoop up and around the hooks, securing the hammer-shaft in his grip.

With a whoop of joy, Einar swung the hammer overhead, bringing it down in a ringing blow onto the anvil. To his delight the shaft did not slip or twist from his grasp and he held it just as firm after the blow landed as before he brought it down.

Waves of relief and excitement surged through Einar's heart. If he could wield a hammer again then he could wield a sword. He no longer needed to worry about being thrown out of Ulrich's Wolf Coat crew.

'This is amazing!' Einar said. 'I don't know how to thank you.'

'I didn't do it for your sake, lad,' Ingler said with a sardonic grunt. 'You just weren't much use to me with that gammy hand. Now you can work much faster, I hope. Speaking of which…'

He pointed to the glowing metal bar in the fire.

Einar set to work battering the iron flat filled with a fierce joy. He relished the effort now the hammer fitted in his grip and from all the overcompensating it had been doing his right arm was stronger than ever. The forge rang with the loud clanging of the hammer on metal. Sparks flew in all directions as the glowing metal flattened and spread into the recognisable shape of a blade. When he finished and dipped the hot metal into the hissing, bubbling water trough he reckoned he had finished the job in about half the time it had taken him the day before, if not less.

'There you go,' he said, handing the sword blade to Ingler while beaming with pride. 'What about that?'

The smith took the blade. As he did the day before, he began to examine it with utmost care and his experienced eye. He ran his fingers along its length. He held it up to eye level and peered down the blade. He hefted it to assess how balanced it was. Then he made the same face as yesterday.

'You've finished it a lot quicker,' Ingler said, handing the new sword back to Einar. 'Which is good. But the blade still isn't good enough. Not for an Inglerii anyway. Take it outside and file it down to shavings like the one you did yesterday.'

Einar's mouth dropped open.

'What?' he said. Then he shook his head. 'Piss off. I won't do it.'

'What do you mean, you won't do it?' Ingler said. 'You made such a good job of it yesterday. And you're supposed to do what I say, remember?'

'I saw the filings in the dung hill last night,' Einar said, his face reddening. 'You're just telling me to do this to get me out of the way while you do whatever it is you do in here.'

'I've actually given you a vital task in the process,' Ingler said. The expression on his face was so hurt and self-righteous that Einar felt sorry he had said anything. He was still not convinced Ingler was not trying to get rid of him however.

'Perhaps I should take my iron gripper back?' Ingler said. 'Perhaps you don't deserve my help after all.'

Both men glared at each other for a moment, then Einar rolled his eyes.

'All right, I'll do it,' he said.

Einar put the sword under his arm, grabbed the file and went outside. As he closed the door behind him he heard the rattle of the bolt as Ingler locked the door.

With a sigh Einar sat down on the stool and began to file the sword he had worked so hard to forge back into little strips of curled, shiny metal shavings.

As with the day before, Einar found himself slipping into a sort of trance as he worked. His mind wandered, reciting poems in his head and testing his memory to see if he still remembered all of them.

Excitement grew in his heart at the thought that he could now both play the harp and hold a sword again. He felt complete once more. His old self. He could take his place among the úlfhéðnar without being plagued by self-doubt. He could prove to Ulrich he was still good enough to be part of the wolf pack. He was someone again. He was no longer níþ.

As the day wore on Einar heard the bolts rattle and the door of the forge opened. Ingler's eldest son, Witege, came out. He carried a piece of wood with a roasted chicken on it which he set down beside Einar.

'My father sends this for you to eat,' the boy said.

Einar realised he was starving. He pulled the carcass apart and shoved meat into his mouth. It tasted amazing.

'This is delicious,' Einar said, juice running down his chin. 'Thank you.'

'It's all we ever eat,' the boy said with a shrug. 'There's so many of them and they die all the time.'

'Why's that?' Einar said, chewing on a mouthful of meat.

'Probably because of the feed—' the boy began to speak, then he stopped. He met Einar's gaze for a moment, then said, 'I have to go back to work.'

The boy turned and hurried back into the forge. The sound of the door shutting behind him was quickly followed by the noise of the bolts locking it.

Einar frowned and went back to eating. When the chicken was finished he returned to work.

Later on the door opened again and both boys came out, the younger one struggling to carry a shovel and Witege bearing a large bucket. Without looking at Einar they went over to the mound of chicken dung. They shovelled dung into the bucket and when it was full, both of them lifted it between them and staggered back into the forge.

Einar scratched his head. All this had to add up somehow. He recalled the metal shavings he had seen in the dunghill the night before. Surely they were not going to pick them out again? It would be too laborious. What was the point anyway?

Perhaps Ingler really was mad? Perhaps the murder of half his family then his enslavement, combined with the torture that left him crippled for life had been too much for his mind to bear.

Einar looked down at the metal glove that covered his right hand. It did not look like the work of a madman.

Still puzzled, he went back to work. Over the course of the day the boys came out several more times to collect buckets of chicken shit which they took back inside.

The fog of the marshes rose again and soon the sun was obscured behind its ghostly cloak. The lake and the surroundings disappeared from view again.

As evening drew in Einar finished his work of shaving the sword down. He got up and knocked on the door of the forge. Witege let him in and Einar told Ingler that he had finished.

As with the day before, the air in the forge was foul. It stank so much Einar's eyes watered and he knew it could not be just from the lack of fresh air with the door closed. He also saw the bucket of dung was empty.

'It's been a hard day,' Ingler said holding out a dirty clay cup brimming with his deadly brew. 'We deserve a drink.'

The smith's face was flushed red and Einar guessed he had had a few cups himself already. Einar took off his new glove and pushed it into his belt. He took the cup and drank a swig, wincing as the liquid burned its way down his throat and set fire to his belly.

'Are you using the chicken shit to fuel the fire?' he said, looking at Ingler with a raised eyebrow.

The blacksmith smiled and did his nose-tapping gesture.

'Please, lad,' he said. 'Don't try to guess my secrets.'

Ingler produced another roast chicken from a spit suspended over the forge fire.

'Sit,' he said. 'Let's eat.'

They spent some time eating and drinking more of the strong brew. The shadows of the evening closed in and the gloomy forge became Stygian dark, apart from the glow of the ever-lit fire. After some time Ingler ordered his sons to feed the chickens and the two boys went outside, this time carrying another bucket filled with grains.

Their father leaned over to pick up his jug of fiery drink. As he poured another two cups Einar let his eyes roam over the various bits and pieces scattered across Ingler's work benches. He spotted what looked like a metal bird's wing and picked it up. Turning it over in his hands he saw that it was indeed a metal wing, almost perfect with iron bones and steel feathers like they were the real thing. Near to it lay the bones and feathers of a real chicken's wing which Einar guessed must have been the model for it. The bones flexed and the feathers moved, just like a bird's would when it flapped its wings.

'Did you make this?' Einar said.

'I did,' Ingler said. 'It was part of an idea I had to escape once. I thought maybe I could build a pair of wings and fly off this island. That was a trial piece to test the idea.'

'It's amazing,' Einar said. 'Just like the real thing.'

'It didn't work,' Ingler said. 'There must be more to it than how all the pieces fit together.'

'You really must be the greatest blacksmith in the world,' Einar said, still looking with disbelief at the metal wing he held.

'If I am,' Ingler said, making a face. 'It hasn't done me much good.'

They were interrupted by the sound of raised voices outside. It was Ingler's sons and they sounded in distress. Einar saw the look of panic and dismay on the blacksmith's face as he struggled to get to his feet.

'It's that little bastard, Asbjorn's son, I'll bet,' Ingler said, moving stiff-legged towards the door as fast as he was able to. 'Why can't he just leave my boys alone?'

Einar threw open the door of the forge. In the evening gloom outside they saw Witege lying on his back on the ground. Erling was straddling him, raining punches down on the boy beneath him. He laughed with delight at Witege's squeals of pain and humiliation. Ingler's other son stood nearby, hands cupped beneath his squashed and bleeding nose. The bucket of chicken feed lay spilled on the ground beside him.

Einar strode over to the fighting boys. He just had time to notice that there were metal shavings mixed with the chicken feed before he reached them. What new madness was this?

'Get off him,' he said, grabbing hold of a handful of Erling's cloak and dragging him to his feet.

The boy glared at Einar, a look of utter outrage on his face.

'How dare you touch me, slave,' he said. 'My father will hear of this.'

'What do you think you're doing?' Einar said.

'I'm helping my father find out what he wants to know,' Erling said. 'Those weaklings know their father's secrets and I'll get it out of them if I have to beat one of them to death.'

He planted both hands on Einar's chest and shoved. He was a big lad and Einar, caught off guard, let go of his cloak and stumbled backwards a few steps.

Erling turned and drove a vicious kick into the side of the prone Witege's ribs.

'You little bastard,' shouted Ingler, who by now had managed to limp over. Einar saw the blacksmith had the file he had used to reduce the swords to shavings gripped in one fist.

'Piss off, cripple,' Erling said.

'Ingler, no—' Einar said.

The blacksmith swung the file. It caught the boy across the side of the head with a crack, sending him reeling sideways.

Einar was surprised how quickly Erling recovered. He did not fall over but instead touched his fingers to his head where blood was already starting to dribble from a cut. He looked at Ingler, his mouth opening and closing without words coming out, literally speechless with rage.

'We're in trouble now,' Einar said.

'What's going on here?'

A new booming voice made them all turn around.

Erling's father, the Bear, had arrived.

Forty-Four

The huge viking stood at the gate in the wattle fence, flanked on both sides by four of his warriors. He glared at the scene before him in the yard.

Einar bit his lip. They were in a serious situation now. He looked around to see if there was anything that could be used as a weapon but the only thing that came close was the file the Ingler still gripped in his right hand.

The Bear strode into the yard. His warriors came with him.

'Are you all right, son?' he said.

'Father, this slave struck me,' Erling said.

'He'll regret that, don't you worry,' Asbjorn said.

'He was beating my son,' Ingler said. 'What do you expect me to do? Stand by and watch?'

The Bear took a deep breath, his face turning very pale. Einar felt his heart sink. The Bear's barely controlled rage was palpable.

'I came here to see what progress you have made in making my swords,' he said, his voice little more than a growl. 'Now you have some help I was expecting there to be many more ready for me. But instead I find this.'

'I was trying to force the worms to tell me their secrets,

father,' Erling said. 'Then we can make them ourselves and feed all these slaves to Bjarki.'

'How many swords have you made, Ingler?' the Bear said.

'Go and see for yourself,' Ingler said.

The Bear stalked across the yard and went into the forge. A few moments later he came back out. His face was pale and his eyes danced from side to side. He was breathing hard through his nose. He held two sheathed swords in one large hand.

'Two?' Asbjorn said. His voice was thick as if his suppressed rage was choking his throat. 'Is this some sort of joke? You've finished two? And there are only four unfinished blades in there. When I got here yesterday there were seven.'

He let out a roar and ran forwards. Ingler tried to raise the file to defend himself but Asbjorn just batted it aside with the back of one hand. He balled his other hand into a fist and smashed it into the blacksmith's face.

Ingler went flying backwards. His crutches flew in different directions as he crashed into the straw on the ground and rolled head over heels to come to rest flat on his back. Ingler's two boys rushed over to him and crouched beside his prone body. After a moment the smith waved them away with his hand and sat up. He spat to the side then looked down at the puddle of his own blood and one of his teeth that had landed in the middle of it.

'I've had enough of this nonsense,' the Bear said. 'Call the others. We'll bring them to the feasting hall. It's time I applied some more encouragement.'

The warriors unslung their shields, hefted their spears

and advanced into the yard. For the moment, Einar knew there was little he could do. Ingler, a cripple, would not be much use in a fight so it would be just him, unarmed against four men in full war gear and the Bear himself. And these were not Hedeby's watchmen armed with just clubs and sticks. They were hardened vikings, their spear points sharp and deadly, and would not hesitate to kill him if the need arose. The best thing would be to go along with whatever they wanted and hope that an opportunity to escape might arise.

Two of the warriors seized Ingler and dragged him between them out of the yard, his paralysed legs trailing behind him. The other two forced Einar out of the yard at spear point while Erling took great delight in booting and shoving Ingler's two sons along behind. Once outside the fence they were all forced into the boat the Bear had come over in.

They rowed back to the main island. Arriving at the jetty, the four prisoners were manhandled out of the boats and propelled down the jetty to the fortified door of the Bear's fortress.

Asbjorn thumped out the same sequence of knocks on the door that he had used when they had first arrived at the fortress. The door was opened from the inside and they all went in.

Ingler, his sons and Einar were marched up the spiral staircase to the feasting hall. Einar felt a sense of cold dread spread through his guts at the sight of the round, stone-lined hole at the far end. As soon as they entered the room he could hear a snuffling noise from the pit and could smell the musky scent of the creature that lurked down there.

'Bring them over,' Ingler said.

His warriors shoved Einar and the boys down the hall until they came to the pit. Dragging Ingler, they dumped him on the ground beside Einar. The smith, a trickle of blood still running from the side of his mouth from the Bear's punch, began to struggle to get up. Einar reached his arm under the blacksmith's and hauled him up to his feet.

Then the warriors behind them each snaked an arm around the throats of each one of the prisoners. Einar felt the prick of a knife point being prodded into his back. Asbjorn Hviti propped the two finished Inglerii swords up against the windlass that the captive bear's chain was wound around. Then he turned to his prisoners.

'What are you going to do?' Ingler said. His voice trembled in fear of the answer.

'It should be no mystery to you,' Asbjorn said. 'I warned you this would happen if you didn't do what I ask you. If you didn't make more swords.'

'Please, don't do this,' Ingler said. All his previous insolence and defiance were gone.

'Erling. Pick one of the boys,' the Bear said.

A huge roar came from the pit as if the beast at the bottom of it knew what was going on above.

Ingler's younger son began to cry. Erling grinned.

'Witege,' he said.

The elder boy spat in the direction of Erling. Einar was surprised at how composed the boy was considering the situation he was in. Did he not realise what was about to happen? He felt a lump in his throat at the thought that someone so young could be so brave.

'*Please*,' Ingler said. 'I will make more swords. I will make them faster. I swear to you—'

'You had your chance,' the Bear said.

He grabbed Ingler's eldest boy by the arm. Witege finally cried out and tried to struggle but there was little the boy could do against the huge power of the big viking.

Ingler tried to pull away from the warrior behind him but was hauled back straight away.

Using both hands, Asbjorn Hviti lifted Witege above his head. The terror finally overcame the boy and he screamed. The noise mixed with the roaring of the bear and a high-pitched whining Ingler now made.

'He sounds like a dog, father,' Erling said.

The Bear hurled the boy into the pit.

Einar had once seen a goatskin full to the brim with red wine burst by accident. The red liquid inside had exploded in every direction, showering the surroundings with crimson rain. He was reminded of that as, unable to tear his eyes away, Einar watched as the beast in the hole ripped Witege to pieces. The creature clamped its huge jaws around the boy's head while it grasped his body with its fore claws. Witege's scream ceased mid cry. The boy just seemed to fall apart in the mighty grip of the white bear. His blood burst from a hundred ruptured vessels and splattered over the walls of the pit. His insides toppled over the treasure heaped on the ground at the bottom.

The only consolation Einar could think of was that, horrific as it was, at least the boy's end was quick.

Sated by the blood and meat, the creature in the pit's roaring ceased. Asbjorn Hviti stood glaring down at the carnage, his breath panting in and out of his nose. None of his men said a word. Ingler's high-pitched whine had descended into forlorn sobs.

The loudest sounds came from Erling, who stood at the edge of the pit, watching the beast below feasting and as he did so he laughed. Einar looked at the boy and his father and thought of the old saying that an apple does not fall far from the tree.

'Now,' Asbjorn said. 'Perhaps you will stop trying to make a fool of me. You understand how serious I am.'

'I knew how serious you were when you killed Egil,' Ingler said in a broken voice. He stood, head bowed, his hair hanging around his face. 'You didn't have to do that.'

'Well now you perhaps finally realise that you are my slave,' Asbjorn said. 'You will go back to work now. You will work harder, faster, than you have been. You will teach this other slave, Einar, how to make the swords and you will make me more Ingleriis. Do you understand, or do I have to throw your last remaining son in the pit as well?'

Ingler raised his hands in a placatory gesture, as if trying to ward off even the idea of that happening. He shook his head.

'Take them back to his workshop,' Asbjorn said.

Einar felt them relax. The arm was removed from his throat though he still felt the dagger at his back. The man holding Ingler did the same.

Then Ingler let out a shout. He threw himself forwards, lurching for a few steps on his stiff, crippled legs. For an instant Einar thought he was going to throw himself into the pit after his son. However there was someone between him and the edge of the hole. Erling.

The boy just had time to notice Ingler stumbling towards

him before the blacksmith thumped into him. Ingler shoved him with both hands, sending the lad reeling sideways. Erling was a big lad and Ingler could not push him far but the few steps he did were enough.

As his right foot stepped into thin air above the bear's pit Erling realised what was happening. His expression of delight changed to abject terror. He let out a high-pitched scream as his arms windmilled in the air for a few moments. Asbjorn dived towards him. It was too late. The boy was already falling.

The creature in the pit roared with delight at having another meal thrown to it so soon. It clamped its jaws across Erling's left thigh and tore his leg off with one huge bite. Blood gushed from the severed stump and the creature then ripped into his torso. In as many moments the boy was dead, the many parts of his body scattered and mixed up with the bones of previous victims and the remains of Witege that littered the bottom of the pit.

Now Asbjorn was roaring as loudly as the bear had. He was on his hands and knees at the edge of the pit, glaring in horror into the hole in the floor as if unable to believe what he had just witnessed, but at the same time knowing he would never be able to forget the sight.

'Now we are starting to get even, Asbjorn,' Ingler said. His face bore a malevolent grin.

'You...' Asbjorn said, his voice little more than a growl. He rose to his full height, glaring with abject malice at Ingler. Even his own men looked intimidated by the sight. They did not move, either from fear of their own master or from shock at what Ingler had just done.

'Though we've a long way to go yet,' Ingler said. 'You killed my wife, my daughter and two of my sons.'

Einar winced. Ingler seemed oblivious to the fact that taunting the big man would only make whatever was to come a lot worse.

Asbjorn stomped towards Ingler. His movements were deliberate and slow, as if rage was making his legs as stiff as the blacksmith's. Not for the first time Einar was reminded when he looked at the big viking of an actual bear trying to walk on its hind legs.

'How dare you,' Asbjorn said. His voice was choked with rage. 'How dare you think you are equal to me. Revenge is not for slaves. But I will take a terrible revenge on you. You are going to die. It will be very slow. Very painful. You will not know agony like it.'

Einar realised the Bear's stiff movements and hoarse voice came from a supreme effort to hold himself back from slaughtering the blacksmith there and then. The only thing that was stopping him doing that was the desire to make Ingler's end as unpleasant and agonising as possible.

'What about your precious swords?' Einar said. 'If you kill him you won't be able to make any more.'

Asbjorn turned to Einar. His expression suggested he had forgotten Einar was there until he had spoken. Einar regretted opening his mouth.

'He will tell me the secret of the swords,' Asbjorn said, pointing at Ingler. 'He has no idea what awaits him. A world of pain. In the end he *will* talk. They always do. And if not, he still has one son left...'

'What are you going to do?' Ingler said. 'Throw him to

your bear as well? What sort of man lets a beast do his dirty work? Perhaps you are not enough of a man yourself?'

Einar sucked breath in through his teeth. Did Ingler not realise he was only making things much, much worse? Could he not see the big viking was barely able to restrain himself?

Ingler spat with contempt.

'He's nothing,' he said. 'Just a bully. Without his men and his animal he's nothing. He thinks he can be a jarl but he wasn't even noble born. He's the son of a low born farmer. A bonded labourer.'

Einar shook his head. The blacksmith was sealing his own fate.

'Shut your mouth, slave,' Asbjorn said.

He swiped his hand, backhanding Ingler across the face. The blacksmith stumbled sideways and fell to the floor.

'Look how far I've risen,' the Bear said. 'And how far you've fallen. I remember that fancy house you lived in, before I burned it to the ground. I remember your beautiful wife. All gone. All taken away by me when I made you a slave. And know this. These swords I made you make for me, will make me a jarl!'

'Oh, you've risen far,' Ingler said, wiping away blood that now dribbled from his nose. His voice brimmed with sarcasm. 'You've gone from the son of a farmer to the lord of a bog. King Nothing. No wife. No family. No realm and now…'

He looked up at the big viking who towered over him and smiled.

'No son,' he said.

Asbjorn let out a huge roar. Einar could see in his eyes

that the supreme effort of self-control was no longer enough to hold back his rage. He grabbed one of the Inglerii swords from where it rested against the windlass and ripped it from its sheath. He swung it back, hovering over the blacksmith on the floor, preparing to bring it down in a mighty chop.

'I was surprised how much Erling squealed when he met your pet,' Ingler said. Einar could not believe he was still taunting the big man. 'My son was much braver.'

Asbjorn's eyes rolled around in his head as if rage had taken over the mind behind them. His arms tensed. He was about to bring the death blow down. Then he stopped.

'Your son…?' the viking said, speaking through clenched teeth.

An evil, deranged grin spread across his face. He half turned and instead of striking Ingler brought the sword down on his remaining son.

The boy never had a chance even to realise what was happening. The blade bisected him from crown to navel. He was dead in an instant. Einar froze, mouth agape. How much more horror was there going to be before this all ended?

'There!' Asbjorn said, grinning at Ingler. 'Now you have no family either. You have nothing. And soon you will have no life. And *I* will be Jarl of Orkney.'

'What?' Einar said. Despite the situation he could not help himself.

'Eirik has no desire to be king there,' Asbjorn said. 'He thinks it is beneath him. When he returns to the throne in Norway he has promised me the high seat in Orkney provided I keep supplying him with these swords.'

The sound of laughter made them both look around. To

Einar's absolute astonishment the sound came from Ingler who was still lying on the ground, now rocking himself back and forth in some sort of insane mirth. Einar could only judge that it had all been too much for him and he had finally lost his mind.

'What's so funny, slave?' Asbjorn said.

'You fool. You'll never learn the secret of how the swords are made now,' Ingler said, his laughter subsiding. 'The one thing I was worried about was that if you tortured me my son Waldere would not be able to help himself and he would tell you. He cannot do that now.'

Asbjorn turned his head, the grin on his face becoming fixed, to look at the butchered corpse of the boy.

'You were so easy to taunt into killing him,' Ingler said. 'My main worry was that you'd throw him to the bear too, but you didn't have the character – the breeding – to restrain yourself.'

'You will rue these words, Ingler,' Asbjorn said through clenched teeth. 'I will make you sorry for everything you have done today. You will take days to die. The torture will be so bad you'll beg me to let you tell me the secret of the swords. This I swear before Odin himself.'

'That won't happen,' Ingler said. 'Goodbye, Asbjorn. I'll see you again in Hel's kingdom.'

The blacksmith rolled sideways over the edge of the pit.

Einar blinked. Ingler was gone in a moment, disappearing down the shaft. Then there came the roaring of the bear and the sound of tearing flesh. Astonished, Einar realised Ingler made no sound whatsoever as the bear tore him apart.

Silence once more descended on the room. Everyone stared in shock at the bloody scene at the bottom of the pit.

The only sound was Asbjorn's heavy breathing. Einar took a deep, shuddering breath as he tried to dispel the shock and horror in his heart.

Ingler had met his fate like the heroes of old: Ragnar, Gunnar or King Volsung himself. Einar realised he now needed to steel himself for whatever fate awaited him.

Then a bang came from the bottom of the pit. The beast within it roared. The windlass began rattling and spinning ever faster as the chain on it was dragged down into the pit. Einar looked over the edge and saw that the bear was somehow gone.

The sound of many voices shouting in surprise and terror came up from below. It was not Ingler. He was already long dead.

'Someone has let the bear out,' Asbjorn said to his men. 'Get down there and find out what's going on!'

Forty-Five

There was barely enough room on the little island for the six Wolf Coats, Surt and Wulfhelm. They had made preparations in their little camp in the reed beds as darkness began to fall. They had taken the soot from their fire and mixed it with grease then smeared their faces, hands and bodies with the black concoction. They tied up the marsh dweller and his son, then put war gear in goatskin bags to protect it from the water. Then they pulled on their wolfskin cloaks, slipped into the lake and swam out to the little islet Affreca and the others had watched the fortress from earlier.

For a while they lay on their bellies watching the fortress, assessing whether or not it was safe to go any further. The fortress appeared a hazy bulk in the fog. As the darkness fell the Bear's warriors lit their beacons and torches on the roof once more but they were fuzzy blurs in the mist and their light did not stretch far across the water.

'This is good,' Ulrich said in a quiet voice. 'This mist will cover our approach.'

'There's someone coming,' Starkad hissed.

They all froze, lowering their heads further in case they showed at all above the surrounding reeds. The sound of angry raised voices then the splash of oars dipping in water reached their ears. As they watched, a boat came rowing around the island and docked at the jetty.

'It's Einar,' Affreca said, seeing he was in the boat. 'He's alive.'

'Shh!' Ulrich whispered, impatience in his voice. 'They might hear us.'

The Wolf Coats watched while Asbjorn Hviti, four of his men – two of whom dragged a black-haired man between them – three young boys and Einar got out of the boat and went to the door.

Asbjorn rapped on the door and it was opened.

Affreca saw Ulrich exchange glances with Skar. Both of them smiled.

When the party entered the fortress and the door closed again, Ulrich turned to the others.

'Did you hear the way the big man knocked on the door?' he said. 'That's some sort of signal. It tells the man inside to open the door. That's our way in. Let's go.'

'Those men on the roof though, Ulrich,' Skar said. 'Fog or no fog, they're bound to spot us as soon as we reach that jetty. We'll have to find a way in through that door fast or they'll drop spears on us while we're still climbing out of the water. At the very least they'll raise the alarm.'

'Your worshipfulness,' Ulrich said to Affreca, 'I don't suppose you might be able to do something about those guards on the roof?'

Affreca looked at the fortress. The moon was rising in the sky above but its light was diffused through the haze of the fog. The men on the roof were very hard to make out and as they moved back and forth they were only really visible when they walked in front of the braziers that sat on the roof and came between the fire and her line of sight. She watched for a few moments more, observing the pattern of the guards' movements, then nodded.

'I think I can,' she said. 'But I'll need to hit them nearly at the same time.'

She pulled apart the metal clasps that sealed the top of the goatskin bag she had carried across the lake then pulled out her Finnish bow. She notched an arrow to the powerful weapon while still lying on her front and half drew the string.

'It won't be easy,' she said, still watching the men as they moved across the roof.

'My lady,' Ulrich said. 'If it was easy, I wouldn't ask a princess like you to do it.'

Affreca's mouth curled in a wry smile.

She watched a little longer, her lips moving as she counted the moments.

The moment she had been waiting for arrived. Both men walked in front of the fires at the same time.

Affreca sprung up to her feet. In one movement she drew the bow fully, raised it to her eye and shot the arrow. It hit the guard on the right somewhere on the chest. He let out a short cry as Affreca was already notching a second arrow. The other warrior on the roof froze, shocked for a moment at the sight of his comrade, collapsing to his knees, the feathered end of an arrow protruding from his chest.

Then Affreca's second arrow came whistling out of the fog and he too was dead. The arrow transfixed his neck and he fell backwards into the gloom.

'Go,' Ulrich said.

All of the company dived into the water and powered

towards the fortress. There was no time for stealth now, just a headlong dash to reach the fortress before another warrior appeared on the roof, came out the door, or discovered their dead friends.

Arriving at the jetty they hauled themselves from the water and paused for a moment to pull their weapons from their goatskin bags.

A terrible roar made them all freeze.

'That was the bear,' Wulfhelm said. 'The real one I mean, not the viking. Ulrich, that thing is in there waiting for us.'

'Then we'll need to take care,' Ulrich said. 'Come on. There's no time to waste.'

They ran to the fortified door in the fortress wall. There they divided into two groups, each one flattening themselves to the wall on either side of the door. Ulrich, who was closest to the left of the door, did a quick check that they were all ready. Then he held up his fist and knocked, copying the pattern of raps Asbjorn had made earlier.

A wicked smile spread across his face as the sound of rattling bolts came from within. With a creak of hinges the door opened a crack.

Skar came round from the right and kicked the door wide open. The bear's warrior who was on the other side of it went stumbling backwards, arms flailing to try to regain his balance. The rest of the Wolf Coats rushed into the doorway and in an instant the viking was dead, his throat cut across by Kari's seax.

The room beyond the door had a torch burning in a wall bracket. By its light they could see another of the Bear's men, eyes wide with surprise and terror, fumbling in panic to draw his sword. Skar brought his axe down on the man's head and he crumpled to the floor as if all the bones in his body had dissolved, his lifeblood spilling into a crimson pool around him.

For a moment they stood in silence, looking around them and assessing where they now stood. They were in an empty room with one door leading off to the right and another, much heavier door, fortified like the exterior door they had just come through, leading straight ahead.

Starkad closed the door they had come in by.

'Fasten it,' Ulrich ordered. 'We don't want anyone coming in behind us and giving us any surprises.'

Starkad nodded, drawing the bolts in the back of the door into position to lock it.

'Well we're in,' Skar said. 'What now?'

The sound of angry shouting drifted from somewhere in the depths of the building.

'At least there's no sign of that damned white creature,' Wulfhelm said, making a little involuntary shudder at both the memory of it and the thought that the huge bear lurked somewhere inside the fortress.

Ulrich looked at the big inner door, running his hand over the metal bands and leather coating that added strength to it.

'Why would you fortify a door *inside* a building?' he said as if speaking to himself.

'It must be because of that bear,' Skar said. 'They probably keep it out here somewhere, between the outer and this inner door, where it will eat anyone who tries to get in. Asbjorn Hviti and his men remain safe, protected behind this inner door.'

Everyone looked around, eyes wide, searching for any

sign that the huge white beast might be somewhere around, just waiting to pounce.

'Well if Asbjorn's safe in there then we should join him, Ulrich,' Wulfhelm said. 'We stand a better chance fighting men than that white monster. That thing could rip us all to shreds in moments.'

'Agreed,' Ulrich said, 'Let's get this door open.'

He pulled back the great bolts that fastened the door closed while Skar slid away a heavy wooden beam that also ensured it stayed closed from its brackets. Then Ulrich and Skar both heaved the heavy door open.

The first thing that hit them was the smell. The stench of rotting meat, the coppery tang of fresh blood and the odour of piss, shit and wet animal fur that wafted out from behind the door wrinkled their noses.

A dark corridor led away from the door. It was black and they could see nothing in it. At the other end though was a chamber on which light fell from above, coming down what looked like some sort of shaft that led upwards. The bulk of a huge creature sat on what seemed to be a mound of gold and silver in the midst of the chamber. The beast was hunched over, a lump of bloodied meat in its paws, munching on it with relish. It stopped and looked around, the pitch-black eyes fixing on the group of Wolf Coats standing in the open doorway.

'Oh shit,' Skar said. 'How wrong could I have been?'

The great white bear dropped the meat and lunged towards the passageway.

'Shut the door,' Ulrich shouted.

All of them fought to shove the door closed once more but in their haste got in each other's way. The bear, now mere paces away, roared. Even if they managed to get the door closed Affreca could see there was no time to slide the bolts home, never mind put the bar back. The huge creature would smash the door open again and they would all be dead.

'Run!' she shouted.

The others did not need telling twice. There would be no time to unlock the outer door either. Surt wrenched open the side door and they all piled through it in panic.

There was a tremendous crash behind them as the bear smashed the fortified inner door wide open and ran into the room beyond.

Sigurd lost his footing, tripped and fell. The others coming behind him sprawled over him, all of them going down in a jumbled heap.

Affreca heard the scrabbling of the bear's claws on the stone floor behind her. Skar was on top of her, his weight pinning her down. She managed to twist her head and saw the huge creature lumbering through the doorway after them. Terror froze her as she realised there was no chance of getting away now.

The creature leapt forward. Both its front paws landed on the heap of Wolf Coats behind the door. They all grunted and gasped at the huge weight suddenly on top of them. Affreca smelled the stench of its dirty fur and felt its hot, rancid breath. The pressure bearing down on her was unbearable. She could not breath. For a moment the world around her appeared to grow dim.

Then the weight was gone.

Sucking in a huge breath, Affreca looked up and saw the bear too was gone. It was loping up a spiral staircase that led up towards the roof, the long chain attached to the collar on its neck rattling behind it.

The Wolf Coats, Surt and Wulfhelm disentangled themselves from each other and scrambled to their feet.

'It seems our white furry friend is looking for someone else,' Skar said. 'Thanks be to Odin.'

'Where do you think it's going?' Affreca said.

'I don't know,' Ulrich said. 'But I wouldn't like to be wherever that is.'

Forty-Six

Einar knew this would be his only chance. The Bear and his men were distracted and looking either down the pit or towards the doorway at the far end of the hall.

He stamped his right foot backwards, feeling his heel connect with the shin of the man behind him. The viking cried out in pain. Einar dipped, twisted and drove his elbow into the man's ribs as hard as he could muster. Despite the metal rings protecting the man's torso, Einar felt something give under them and the warrior cried out again.

Einar did not wait to see what damage he had done. He tore forwards, away from whatever blade the man held and would bring to bear on him when he recovered. He dived for the nearby windlass and grabbed the remaining sheathed Inglerii sword that rested against it.

A huge roar came from the pit. It echoed up the side walls but at the same time appeared to be receding. Wherever the creature down there had gone it seemed it was getting further away. The chain was being dragged into the pit at a tremendous rate, which could only mean the creature was running away somewhere. Wherever it was going, however, Einar could see it would not get much further. There was very little of the chain attached to the bear's collar left wound around the spinning windlass.

Einar pulled the special glove Ingler had made him from his belt and shoved his hand into it. He looked up and saw most of Asbjorn's men looking around them in total confusion. The man who had been behind him was now on his knees, hugging his injured ribs but one of the warriors had run after Einar. He was mere steps away, his sword drawn and raised to strike.

The Inglerii was fastened into its sheath by two leather straps over the pommel. He did not have time to unbutton them and draw it before the man was on him.

There was a hook set into the floor on the other side of the windlass. The last link of the chain was looped over it. This would act as the final stop when the entire length of the chain was completely played out, preventing the bear from going any further away.

Einar shoved his foot under the chain and popped the loop free so it was no longer attached. He crouched, grabbed a loop of the loose chain and came up again, slashing it before him like a whip just as the Bear's warrior was bringing his sword down to strike.

With a rattle of metal the chain wrapped itself around the warrior's blade. At almost the same moment the chain reached its limit and wound off the end of the windlass. The end of the chain, now wrapped around the sword instead of the hook in the floor, kept running into the pit, ripping the blade out of the warrior's grasp as it went. The sword pinged against the stones around the rim then disappeared down the hole.

Einar pulled the straps off the pommel. He grabbed the

sword handle with his iron gauntlet, letting the end slide into the hooks at the bottom end, then ripped the Inglerii out of its sheath. The Bear's warrior drew a long-bladed seax knife at the same time. Einar felt a sensation of ferocious delight at how the sword rested as normal in his grasp, even without him having time to fix the leather straps. There was no ungainliness, it was perfectly balanced and under his total control. He was ready for war once more.

Einar struck with the sword, catching his opponent across the forearm. The blade cut through the metal rings of his brynja like it was made of wool. It parted the flesh and the bone beneath then was through the other side. The man's lower arm, severed halfway down, his hand still clutching the handle of his seax, clattered to the floor. He screeched, grabbing the severed stump with his other hand, sinking to his knees as hot blood spurted into the air.

Einar blinked. Even though he had seen the Inglerii used before, the effectiveness of the blade was still stunning.

Then he looked around. Asbjorn Hviti had now drawn his own Inglerii. His other three remaining men also had their swords drawn and were advancing towards him. Not only was he outnumbered but he was yet again facing Asbjorn himself, a warrior who had just been too powerful for him the last time they fought.

The Bear came charging forward. Einar swept his sword in a strike aimed to cut the big man's legs from under him. With surprising dexterity for one so large, Asbjorn jumped into the air and Einar's blade sliced through nothing but air.

The big viking landed on his feet. He barged his shoulder into Einar's chest, sending him flying backwards to crash to the floor, flat on his back, all the breath driven from his body.

Einar looked up and saw Asbjorn looming over him. The viking was grinning with triumph as he raised his Inglerii sword above his head with both hands. Einar knew when he brought it down the blow would be every bit as devastating as the one that had sliced Ingler's son Waldere in half.

The door at the far end of the hall shattered in an explosion of splintered wood. The big white bear came crashing through.

Asbjorn's warriors cried out in confusion and terror. They began running in every direction. Asbjorn himself was distracted for a moment, then turned his attention back to Einar intent on finishing him.

The white beast ignored Asbjorn's men and instead made straight for Asbjorn. In two great bounds it had loped across the room and reared up onto his back legs. It wrapped its forepaws around his body and sunk its great jaws into his left shoulder, tearing a huge chunk of flesh and bone away in one terrible bite.

Asbjorn cried out as blood erupted from the wound. He tried to stab upwards with the sword but the bear's claws were already sunk deep into the flesh of his chest. The bear pulled them back, ripping deep bloody furrows in his body. The big viking's cry turned to a gurgle as blood welled up his throat and gushed out of his mouth. His strength left him and he collapsed to his knees under the weight of the great beast behind him. The bear sank its teeth into the side of his neck and Einar saw the light of life fade from Asbjorn's eyes.

Einar rolled sideways as Asbjorn Hviti fell forwards, the white bear still on his back, landing face forwards in the exact spot Einar had been.

Einar did not wait to see what happened next. He rolled

over and then over the edge of the pit. Reaching up he caught the rim for a moment, hanging by his hands rather than fall straight down. The drop was too far to do that. Then there was a tearing, ripping sound above him and a waterfall of Asbjorn's hot blood flooded over the rim of the pit and cascaded around him.

Einar let go. He dropped to the bottom of the pit, landing hard on the mound of bones and treasure below. He rolled to break the fall then rose to his feet. He saw a short tunnel leading away from the bottom of the pit. The door at the far end was open and light from a torch burned in the room beyond.

As he had hoped, this was the way out.

He scrambled down the tunnel. He felt coins, bones and something squidgy he did not want to think about slide away from under his feet. Then he burst into the room at the other end.

He found he was in the entrance room to the fort. Now he understood how the bear had got to the door to rattle it in such a threatening way every time they had passed through this room.

Several figures appeared in the doorway that led to the spiral staircase. Einar tensed, expecting more of the Bear's warriors to come rushing in.

Instead, Affreca did. Her face lit up when she saw him.

'Einar!' she said. 'We've come to rescue you.'

'Good work,' Einar said as the rest of the Wolf Coat crew came into the room behind her. 'Thanks. Now we need to get out of here. Fast.'

Forty-Seven

They fled Asbjorn's fortress pursued by the sound of the roars of the great white bear. They ran down the jetty and jumped into the boats tied up there. Then they were rowing hard across the lake and away from the fortress.

As they did so the last three survivors of Asbjorn's vikings came spilling out of the fortress door in panic. The boats gone they jumped into the lake and started to swim for whatever safety they could get to.

'Let them go,' Ulrich said. 'Without Asbjorn to lead them they're no danger to us.'

Back at the Wolf Coats' temporary camp they gathered the remainder of their belongings and untied the marsh dweller and his son.

'What do we do with them?' Sigurd said, running his finger along his knife.

'Let them go,' Ulrich said. 'It doesn't matter now.'

'The Bear is dead?' the marsh dweller said.

'Very,' Einar said.

The man looked relieved.

'We never liked him,' he said. 'He forced us to help him. We lived in fear of what he might do to us if we didn't.'

'Well you don't need to worry any more,' Ulrich said.

'You are going back to the town?' the marsh dweller said.

'As soon as it's light enough to,' Ulrich said. 'I don't want to fall into a bog in the dark.'

'I can guide you across the marsh through the night if you want,' the marsh dweller said. 'I know the safe paths.'

'That would be good,' Einar said. 'I'd rather not stay too close to that fortress now the white bear isn't chained up any more.'

'There's a king's fortune in gold and silver in that fortress,' Wulfhelm said. 'From what Einar tells us all the profit of Asbjorn Hviti's viking raids is at the bottom of the bear's pit. If we took it we'd all be very rich men.'

'And women,' Affreca said.

'Well if that big white bear stays in the fort then it can guard the treasure for us,' Ulrich said. 'Until we come back. Right now we have other business to attend to.'

So they set off, trekking across the marshland until, early the next day, they arrived back outside the palisaded rampart of Hedeby. Ulrich used the last of one of his arm rings to purchase re-entry to the town at the gate. They hurried across Hedeby to the harbour before any of the jarl's or Meginbraht's men could relay the message that they were back, jumped aboard the snekkja and pushed out to sea.

They rowed out of Hedeby's water gate and raised the sail. Able to retire from the oars, most of the rest of the crew began to make preparations for some long overdue sleep. They unfurled leather sleeping bags and found places to lie on the deck. Skar got a fire going on the cooking stone and began to seethe some beef as the others gathered around for something to eat before they retired to their sleeping bags.

'So, Ulrich; I'm wondering,' Skar said, as he poked the bobbing meat with his knife. 'As we're leaving, did we win?'

'What do you mean?' Ulrich said.

'Well, we didn't get the Inglerii swords,' Skar said. 'Isn't that why we came here in the first place?'

'We came here to stop Eirik getting the swords,' Ulrich said. 'Which we've achieved. No one got the Inglerii swords. And we will take the Ulfbehrts back. When Eirik has no swords he will be nothing. Níð.'

'And now no one ever will know why those Ingleriis are such great swords,' Einar said. 'The secret of how they were made died with Ingler.'

'You really have no idea, even from spending a couple of days working with him?' Affreca said.

'He just had me doing useless tasks to get me out of the way while he did the real work,' Einar said with a shrug.

He went on to describe the forging then filing down of the swords.

'Asbjorn thought the chickens had something to do with it, but I think Ingler was just crazy,' he said when he had finished. 'What had happened to him had twisted his mind. It looked like he was feeding the metal shavings to the chickens and burning their dung in the forge. Does that sound like the work of a sane person to you?'

'It sounds like the work of someone who knew how to make Damascus steel,' Surt said.

All eyes turned to the black-skinned man. He returned their looks with one of slight surprise.

'You mean you don't know?' he said, frowning. Then a look of realisation dawned on his face. 'Of course you don't! The iron of your swords in the north of the world is so much more inferior. Why do you think the swords of al-Andalus or of Syria – Serkland as you call it – are so superior to your uncouth weapons? We purify the iron.'

'Ingler said he had visited a city called Damascus,' Einar said.

'Well he must have learned there how they make high quality steel,' Surt said.

'We purify iron too when we make swords,' Einar said. 'The impurities come out as slag in the forge.'

'My people found a way to purify the metal even further,' Surt said. 'Except we used ostriches instead of chickens. It's much more efficient.'

'What are ostriches?' Ulrich said.

Surt rolled his eyes.

'Sometimes I forget I swim in a sea of ignorance here,' he said. 'Ostriches are like very big chickens. Very big. The sword is forged, which takes the initial slag from the metal, as you know. Then the sword is filed down to shavings and mixed with bird feed. The shavings with the purer metal glitter brighter in the feed and it attracts the birds' eyes. They peck the shinier shavings and leave the more impure ones. Then they pass them in their dung. You could sit and sort them by hand but why do that when the birds can do it for you? It's much quicker and they are better at it, too. There are also qualities in the bird dung that further encourages the impurity to bubble out of the metal when it goes back into the forge. You repeat the process until the metal is as pure as you can get it. The only problem is that it takes a lot more iron to make one sword as so much of it ends up being discarded.'

'So that's why there were seven sword blades in Ingler's

forge when I arrived but only four two days later,' Einar said.

Ulrich looked at Surt.

'So you knew about this all along?' he said. 'And you didn't say anything?'

'No one asked me,' Surt said. 'Anyway, who would have thought someone in this savage north would know how to purify steel like civilised people?'

'At least there's one thing,' Skar said. 'If we can work out a way to kill that bear we can come back here someday, take Asbjorn's hoard and live like kings.'

'And,' Einar said, 'I now know how to make the best swords in the world. I could become a very rich man.'

He glanced towards Affreca.

'That did Ingler a lot of good,' Affreca said.

'What's with this strange glove you have now, Einar?' Ulrich said, pointing at the metal mitt pushed behind Einar's belt. 'And why do you have only one?'

Einar held up his injured hand.

'You were right all along, Ulrich,' he said with a sigh. 'The wound my father gave me left me unable to play the harp or hold a sword properly. But on this journey I've learned how to play again and Ingler made this so I can wield a sword, hammer, axe or any long weapon just like before I was injured. I'm just as effective a crew member as I was before.'

Ulrich looked Einar in the eyes for a long moment.

'Really?' he said.

'Really,' Einar said.

'Well that's good,' Ulrich said. 'Because this isn't over yet and we'll need every man we have. We sail for Orkney.

Ragnarök is coming. Winter Nights is nearly here and we still have a little girl to save and a hoard of swords to steal.'

Part Four

Winter Nights

Forty-Eight

Orkney

Day of the Winter Nights festival

'This is insane, Ulrich,' Einar said.

He sent a nervous glance around the busy tavern then took a long drink from the horn of ale he grasped in his left hand.

'Relax,' Ulrich said, leaning back against the wall. 'No one knows us here.'

Wind and weather had conspired to make the voyage back to Orkney longer than they had hoped and at one point Skar had questioned the wisdom of returning at all. Ulrich had insisted however, on the ground that if Ragnarök did come, he did not want to be explaining to Odin why he had not fulfilled the last oath he had made to Aulvir. So they battled the waves north until in the end they made it back to Orkney.

Einar and Ulrich now sat at a bench near the back wall of the busy tavern in Torhaven. It was farthest from the fire so less folk chose to sit near them. Despite being mid-day the place was half full. Drinkers were plonked on most of the benches and tables. The fire blazed to allow patrons soaked by the dreary rain outside to dry themselves a little. The resultant fug of warm wet wool mingled with smoke from the fire and the herby aroma of the black cauldron full of stew that bubbled away over the flames and the sour scent of ale.

Both Einar and Ulrich had swapped their wolf pelt cloaks for Surt and Wulfhelm's less conspicuous plain woollen ones. They were hunched over a couple of horns filled with foaming ale and bowls of steaming stew. Most of the time they kept their heads down as if in conspiratorial conversation but every now and again they looked up to scan the others in the room for any potential danger. Something which, Einar mused, aptly described most of the men around them in the tavern.

The atmosphere of the tavern was one of brooding menace. The other benches were filled by a motley collection of burly men. Most of them had skin tanned to the colour of leather by the sun and wind, telling of years spent on the open waves of the whale roads. Many were covered with tattoos: black lines that either swirled like whirlpools across their arms or branched like twigs or the imprint of birds' feet up their necks and in some cases across their faces. They were of all ages from young lads to men in their midlife but all of them were lean and fit. Their muscled bodies told of long days spent at the oars of ships or hacking with weapons in the training yard. All bore some signs of a violent life:

scars; bent noses; swollen ears; or missing teeth. These were not poor men, either. Most wore thick rings of silver or gold around bulging arms. The many rings on their fingers rattled against their ale horns. Their beards and hair were braided through little toggles made of silver or ivory.

Thankfully, the others stuck to their own conversations and ale and ignored the couple sitting by the wall.

'Have you ever seen such a bunch of dangerous looking bastards?' Ulrich said quietly. His tone was almost wistful. 'By Odin's holy spear! What I could do with a couple of crews of vikings like these.'

'It's what Eirik intends to do with them that worries me,' Einar said. 'I wouldn't like to get on the wrong side of them.'

'You could always sing to them,' Ulrich said, a mischievous smile crossing his lips. 'Many a poet has saved his own skin with a few well-chanted poems.'

Einar scowled.

They sat in silence for a moment, then Ulrich made a face.

'This stew is disgusting,' he said. 'It tastes like boiled grass.'

'It probably is,' Einar said. 'With the bad weather I would say everyone is hoarding what meat they have for the winter.'

'At least the ale is decent,' Ulrich said, taking a swig from his horn. 'It's got a flavour like nothing I've tasted before.'

'It's special to Orkney,' Einar said. 'They use heather to brew it. Whatever the weather, that's one thing there's never a shortage of here.'

There was another short silence, then Einar said:

'Do you think he'll turn up?'

'Aulvir?' Ulrich pursed his lips. 'If Eirik believed his story, then yes. If not, then no. He's dead.'

'Then so are we,' Einar said, taking a quick glance around.

When they had left Aulvir tied up on the harbour quay, his task – provided Eirik believed his story – was that he should spend his days finding out what was going on inside Jarls Gard and as much about Eirik's plans as possible. Ulrich had in particular tasked the steward with finding out where the Ulfbehrts were being stored and how the Wolf Coats could get them. The Wolf Coats then needed to reconnect with him in order to get this information.

Aulvir had already told them that the secret tunnel into Jarls Gard they had previously used to get in and out of the fortress had been discovered by Eirik and sealed off, so Ulrich's plan was that Aulvir should find an excuse to leave Jarls Gard and meet them outside. As none of the Wolf Coats were very familiar with Orkney, and it needed to be somewhere nearby, Ulrich had suggested one place he did know: the tavern in Torhaven.

The tavern door opened, causing most heads in the room to turn. Several of the vikings dropped hands to the hilts of knives or swords in instinctive movements. When they saw who stood in the threshold however, they all relaxed again and went back to their own drinks and conversations. This man was no threat. He was young but had been through a hard time. His clothes were rough wool and marked him out as a thrall. He was tall but scrawny and his lank blond hair hung limp around his head, while his patchy beard dripped from gaunt cheeks beneath hollow eyes that spoke of endless pain. He was supported by two wooden crutches beneath his armpits and he struggled to both manage to hold the door open and manoeuvre himself through it. As he was a slave, no one moved to help him.

Seeing him trying to limp through the door, Einar cursed and spun round so he faced away from the newcomer. He knew it was already too late – the thrall had looked directly at him.

'I know who that is,' he said in a low voice. 'He's an Irish slave called Mealshechlin from Jarls Gard. I knew this was a mistake Ulrich! It's too risky.'

'Careful,' the little Wolf Coat leader said out of the corner of his mouth. 'Don't draw attention to us. Do you think he might recognise you?'

'He helped me get into the feasting hall of Jarls Gard when I came to try to kill my father,' Einar said. 'Reluctantly it has to be said, by lending me his clothes. We tried to talk him into escaping with the other slaves that night but he refused. It looks like he's paid a heavy price for that. He was a young, fit man last time I saw him.'

For a moment Mealshechlin stood peering around the room as his eyes became accustomed to the smoky gloom after the daylight outside. Then he spotted Einar and Ulrich.

'He's seen us,' Ulrich said, his hand dropping to the hilt of his seax knife. 'He's coming over.'

Einar slid his right hand into his iron gauntlet and braced himself, waiting for the shout of accusation then the inevitable onslaught from the others in the room. Could Ulrich and he fight them off? It was doubtful. He looked around the room again. Their only hope would be to escape. Was there another way out apart from the door?

The expected commotion did not happen, however. Instead the slave half-shuffled, half-limped across to where they sat, his crutches scraping through the hay that covered the hard- packed dirt floor. He moved stiff legged, as though everything from his knees down barely worked.

'I thought it was you,' he said to Einar when he at last made it to the table. He spoke in a low voice. 'Einar Thorfinnsson. And you must be the wolf warrior they call Ulrich?'

Ulrich nodded.

'I have a message from Aulvir,' the Irishman said. 'He cannot get away. So he sent me instead.'

'Sit down then,' Ulrich said, though he did not move his hand away from the hilt of his knife.

Einar moved aside to make room for Mealshechlin on the bench beside him. The Irishman tottered for a moment, trying to move himself off his crutches and onto the seat without falling on his face. Unable to sit any longer, Einar half rose, caught him by the elbow and guided him onto the bench.

When they were both seated the thrall cast a grateful glance in his direction.

'Thanks,' he said, speaking the Norse tongue with the lilting accent of the Irish.

Einar shook his head.

'It's you who should be thanked,' he said. 'This is very dangerous for you. You don't need to help us like this. You've clearly suffered enough already.'

Mealshechlin looked around the room then back at Einar and Ulrich.

'Now aren't you two a pair of fine fellows?' he said, a half-grin on his face. 'Sitting here in the tavern surrounded by King Eirik's men, right under the nose of Eirik himself up there in Jarls Gard. You must be mad! Or stupid.'

'Mad, maybe,' Ulrich said. 'But we're not stupid. These men may be in Eirik's pay but they're as much strangers here as we are. They've no idea who the men at the next table are, never mind us. So provided we don't draw attention to ourselves we should be fine.'

'Aye,' the Irish slave's expression became grim. 'Eirik is desperate to rebuild his strength. He's sent word across the whale roads that he will pay silver for any men who will fight for him. Vikings are flocking here to join his cause. Look at these lot in here. The scum of the sea are gathering in Orkney.'

Einar leaned forward on his elbows.

'What happened to Aulvir?' he said.

'Eirik and Gunnhild don't trust him,' the slave said. 'He's watched all the time so there was no way he would be able to get away from Jarls Gard without them sending someone to follow him. So he sent me. He knew I know what you look like, Einar, and he knows I can be trusted. He's a clever old bastard I'll give him that. He's back running the household at Jarls Gard and needs fish ordered from the harbour. It's the perfect excuse for him to send me down here to buy it. I can come and go without suspicion. No one suspects a cripple of being up to much. You lot are late, by the way. Aulvir expected you a week ago. I've been coming here every day since. We were starting to think you weren't coming.'

'The weather,' Ulrich said.

'Good job fish needs to be bought fresh every day,' Mealshechlin said. 'So I can keep coming.'

'Why does Aulvir trust you?' Ulrich said.

'Your friend slit my hamstrings,' Mealshechlin said,

looking him straight in the eye. 'I'll never walk properly again. Because of that I've vowed I'll do whatever I can to make my overlords' lives a misery.'

'Atli betrayed my company as well,' Ulrich said, referring to the renegade Wolf Coat who had almost been the death of them all. 'He was no friend of ours.'

'He was working for Eirik though,' Mealshechlin said. 'And Eirik is the root of all this misery. We slaves would have all been free if he had not sailed into the harbour with his army. I want that bastard dead as much as you. If we ever want to get rid of Eirik you're the only hope right now.'

'Don't get carried away,' Ulrich said. 'There's only nine of us. We're not strong enough to take Eirik on directly.'

'You can make life uncomfortable for him though,' Mealshechlin said. 'I've heard him talking with his wife. He's only here because he had nowhere else to go when he had to flee Norway. He's not committed to Orkney and he's ruling by terror. People are scared of him and he's not liked.'

'Does he never learn?' Ulrich said with a derisive snort. 'That's what got him kicked out of Norway.'

Einar looked at the Irishman, remembering the cruelty inflicted on Ingler too.

'If I ever take back the high seat of Orkney,' he said. 'I will outlaw this savage practice. No one will ever have their sinews cut again. Whoever does it will be hanged.'

'That's very commendable,' Mealshechlin said. 'But it won't do me much good.'

'What message does Aulvir send to us?' Ulrich said. 'And what else can you tell us about Eirik? What's he up to?'

The Irish thrall told them everything that had happened since they had burned the ships in the harbour.

'So the rest of the Ulfbehrt swords are in this Steinborg fort,' Ulrich said. 'That's where we will need to go first.'

'You'll need to go fast, if you want those swords,' Mealshechlin said. 'Eirik has formed an alliance with that leprous bastard Olaf, king of the norsemen of Limerick. He promised him some of those special swords. To be sent when the Winter Nights festival comes. That's tonight. When Vakir did not return from Hedeby and there was no sign of Asbjorn Hviti, Eirik decided to send Olaf half the Ulfbehrts in Steinborg instead.'

Ulrich stroked his chin.

'Olaf is promising Eirik warriors and ships, no doubt,' he said.

'The rumours are that Scabby-Head can send Eirik enough men to take back Norway,' Mealshechlin said. 'Then they will turn on Ireland, I've little doubt about that.'

'And they're moving the swords today?' Ulrich said.

'Tonight,' Mealshechlin said.

'Then we need to take them today,' Ulrich said.

'Good luck with that,' the Irish thrall said. 'Steinborg is the most secure fortress in Orkney. More formidable even than Jarls Gard.'

As he was talking a group of men came into the tavern. Unlike the others they were not warriors but dressed in sealskins and furs. They carried long spears and two of them had very long-bladed knives tucked into their belts.

'Watch out,' Mealshechlin said. 'That lot are locals, not vikings. They might recognise you.'

Einar looked away, trying to not look suspicious at the same time. He had recognised the men's implements however.

'Are those whale hunters?' he said, remembering the sea swine creature he had seen in the sea on the way to Hedeby.

Mealshechlin nodded.

'Thord, Eirik's new right-hand man, has ordered all able-bodied men to go fishing,' he said. 'The harvest was poor because of the bad weather and everyone is worried about food for the winter. Someone spotted a great herd of whales out to sea yesterday and men have been sailing after them ever since.'

'Did Aulvir find out where his daughter is?' Einar said. 'He told us Eirik is holding her hostage.'

Mealshechlin looked downcast.

'That terrible woman, Queen Gunnhild, has taken her to a heathen temple out on the heaths,' he said. 'I fear for her life. Three frightening women arrived last night – witches every one of them or I'm a donkey – and they all set off for the temple. They took the wee girl with them. Eirik's there too. They took the very high seat from the hall in Jarls Gard. They're going to use it all in some awful devil worship. Some pagan blasphemy!'

'You don't honour our Gods, do you?' Ulrich said, a wry smile on his lips. 'So Eirik will be there and engaged in a ritual? The chances are he won't be armed then either. It's a pity.'

'What do you mean?' Einar said.

'Well it might have been a good opportunity to get at him when he's vulnerable,' Ulrich said. 'But the swords have to remain the priority. We go for them. Anyway, I wouldn't want to anger the Gods or the spirits myself by interfering in a holy ritual. We might bring bad luck down on ourselves.'

'But they are going to kill the girl!' Einar said.

'That's too bad,' Ulrich said. 'In war there are always casualties. To go after Eirik tonight would be too risky. Too uncertain. And we can't do both. So we must make hard choices and do what is most likely to bring victory in the long run. We go after the swords.'

'And what was all that talk on the ship about not wanting to be an oath breaker?' Einar said. 'Have you forgotten what you said then?'

'Odin tells us that we can break oaths when there is no other choice,' Ulrich said.

'When did he say that?' Einar said. 'That sounds like the word of someone trying to weasel out of their own threats.'

Ulrich glared at him for a long moment.

'Well, what do you suggest?' Ulrich said at last. 'We can't do both.'

'Maybe we can,' Einar said. 'I have an idea...'

Forty-Nine

The twelve riders stopped on the brow of the hill, looking down over the ness below. The sea, which was as cold and clear as the air appeared black and green due to the infinitely twisting forest of seaweed that swirled beneath its surface. The water churned to foam as it washed over the dark rocks of the promontory and across the short beach whose sand was so light a yellow to be almost white. The sun was sinking behind a steel-grey cloak of clouds and evening gloom was stealing in from the heaths and the mountains.

At their highest reach, the waves lapped the wide crescent-shaped tail of a dead whale. The rest of its vast, glistening-black body stretched away across the sand. Countless seabirds hovered in the air or settled on the giant corpse, jostling each other for position on the mountain of carrion. Their cries sounded as if they mourned the death of the great beast, but this was belied by the enthusiasm with which they tucked into so great a feast.

'You see, Lord Thord? It's there just like I said,' one of the horsemen, a balding, scrawny man in an ill-fitting woollen cloak said, pointing at the huge corpse on the beach below. He grinned, revealing gums with more teeth missing than present.

'Good work, Stein,' Thord, said. 'Once that beast is carved up and salted there'll be enough meat to keep us all going through the winter.'

All of the riders made involuntary glances at the dark, glowering sky from which a steady drizzle fell.

'This weather is unnatural,' Gairmund, another of Thord's men said. 'With the failed harvest many will starve before the year is out.'

'But not us, lads,' Thord said. 'You picked the right man as your leader. I told you I'd look after you. The Gods have shown their favour and given us this gift. I'll make sure every one of you gets a fair share of the meat. After I take mine, of course. That's your reward for supporting me. All our families will live to see next spring.'

The others cheered, but the rain somehow distorted the sound to be desultory.

'That's if Ragnarök doesn't come first,' Gairmund said. He tried to make it sound like a black joke, but the tone of his voice betrayed his real feelings.

'Tell those thralls to hurry up with the wagon,' Thord said, turning to look over his shoulder. Four slaves were struggling up the hill behind them, pushing and pulling a wooden four-wheeled cart over the uneven, heather-choked ground to catch up with the horsemen. 'The rest of you: Let's get down there and start cutting. We need this beast carved up and back to the fortress as soon as possible. Eirik wants those Ulfbehrts packed and sent to the harbour tonight.'

He brandished his flensing knife and kicked his heels. His horse started off down the hill and the others trotted after him, leaving the thralls who had just struggled up to the summit looking on in dismay.

The company of horsemen came to a halt before the whale carcass and dismounted. They cast grins and gazes on the mound of blubber and flesh like ravenous wolves spotting a flock of new lambs. They carried axes, saws and long-bladed knives on shafts. Behind them the slaves dragging the wagon to put it in came trundling down the hillside.

The men set to work, using their blades to slice into the white blubber of the whale and peal it away from the dark meat beneath. Soon the pale sand was stained red as rivulets of blood trickled down into the sea.

'Lord Thord, look at this,' Gairmund said after a short time.

Thord and the others stopped cutting and looked around. Gairmund was standing at the tail of the whale that the waves lapped around. There was a rope tied around it, with the rest trailing off into the sea.

'This whale didn't wash up on this beach by accident,' Gairmund said, lifting the rope and trailing it through his hands. 'Someone towed it here.'

'Look up there,' Stein said. He raised his long-bladed flensing knife and pointed at the slope they had ridden down. Three men were walking down towards them. They all wore cloaks of animal fur around their shoulders. They were the pelts of wolves. The beasts' heads formed their hoods, which were pulled up so the pointed ears stood up above the wearer's head.

'Who are they?' Thord said.

'I don't know, lord,' Stein said. 'I don't recognise them with their hoods up.'

'Well if they think they're taking any of my whale they'd

better think again,' Thord said. 'Let's show them who's in charge round here.'

'You men,' Thord shouted to the three strangers. 'Who are you? What do you want?'

One of the men in the wolfskin cloaks pulled down his hood. He was short, slightly built and balding.

'Who wants to know?' he said.

'I'm Thord Ormsson,' the leader of the horsemen said as he walked back up the beach. 'I am Lendmann here now, in case you haven't heard yet. So this is my whale. You needn't think we'll share any of it.'

'Who says it's yours?' the man in the fur cloak said.

Thord swiped the long, curved knife through the air before him.

'Me and my men here outnumber you more than three to one,' he said. 'That should be more than enough I'd say to prove this meat is ours.'

The newcomer seemed unimpressed.

'I am Ulrich,' he said. 'Son of Rogni. I am the leader of King Eirik's Úlfhéðnar company. A company he betrayed.'

Thord narrowed his eyes. The rest of his men all stopped work. They looked at each other, the expressions on their faces a mixture of surprise and confusion.

'So you're the bastards who have caused such upheaval?' Thord said. 'Einar Thorfinnsson is part of your crew isn't he? Things were just fine here until he started interfering – freeing slaves and overthrowing the jarl. Who knows where things would have gone if King Eirik had not taken charge of Orkney. We swear our oaths directly to King Eirik.'

Ulrich's upper lip twisted into a snarl.

'You swear your oaths to a cuckoo,' he said. 'A king with

no country. The people of Norway threw Eirik out and so he's come here, taking that which doesn't belong to him. Einar Thorfinnsson is rightful jarl here.'

'There is no jarl here any longer. And Eirik Haraldsson is the rightful King of Norway,' Thord said, glancing over his shoulder. It was as if he was worried Eirik Bloody Axe might somehow be watching and he wanted to make sure Eirik heard his declaration of loyalty. 'Orkney is ruled by Norway. We must obey him.'

'And cowards like you pledge him your support,' Ulrich said.

'You expect any different?' Thord said. 'Eirik is powerful. He has many warriors. If we support him he looks after us. Einar freed the slaves. He armed them with Ulfbehrt swords! Thank the Gods Eirik put down their rebellion and restored the rightful order of things.'

'I see you found our rope,' Ulrich said, nodding towards Gairmund who still held it in both hands. 'We borrowed this dead beast from some hunters we came across at the harbour and brought it here. Well, when I say *borrowed*, it would be more honest to say "stole".'

'Why?' Thord said, his expression a mixture of incredulity and confusion.

'We needed something to coax you out of that fortress of yours,' Ulrich said. 'We want a word with you and I was told Steinborg is impregnable.'

'A word about what?' Thord said.

'About those Ulfbehrts,' Einar said. 'We want them back.' Thord grunted.

'Those swords are each worth the price of a chest of gold,'

he said. 'You think I would just hand them over? Besides, King Eirik is sending them to Limerick tonight.'

He turned to his own men.

'This is a double bounty today lads,' Thord said, his evil grin spreading from ear to ear. 'First the whale and now the Norns of fate has delivered an enemy of the king right into our hands. Eirik will pay good silver when I send him the head of this bastard Ulrich.'

'That head belongs to me,' Ulrich said. 'If you want it you'll have to take it.'

Thord threw back his head and laughed.

'You have some nerve little man, I'll give you that,' he said. 'As Lendmann here I can call on one hundred men, armed warriors with swords and spears, to fight for me. You denigrate the king's name but what have you got? Where is your horde of warriors?'

Ulrich smiled. He flicked the wolfskin cloak away from his left shoulder, revealing a shining brynja beneath. His right hand dropped to the hilt of a sword sheathed high on his left side.

'Allow me to introduce them,' he said.

Fifty

Ulrich put his forefingers into his mouth and blasted out a short whistle. A figure rose up from the gorse about halfway down the slope that Thord and his men had ridden down to the beach. It was a woman. Like Ulrich she wore the wolf pelt cloak around her shoulders. The head hood was down revealing skin so pale it seemed pure white. Her red-gold hair was tied in a short braid. A pair of very dark eyebrows arched over eyes so green which would not have looked out of place on a cat. Those eyes peered unflinchingly down the shaft of an arrow that was notched on her fully drawn bow and aimed at Thord.

'A girl with a bow?' the Lendmann said with a guffaw. 'Really?'

'That girl with the bow could put an arrow through your eye at three times the distance she is from you now,' Einar said. 'This is Affreca Guthfrithsdottir, of the clan of Ivar the Boneless, rulers of the Kingdom of Dublin.'

Thord was just opening his mouth for a further jibe when Affreca loosed her fingers. His words froze in his throat as her arrow whizzed through his hair, barely a finger's breadth from his scalp. In a moment she had another arrow notched, the bow drawn and aimed once more at Thord. With a slow, deliberate movement she lowered her aim a fraction so no one was in any doubt where the next arrow would strike.

'Perhaps we should just leave the whale, lord?' Stein said out of the corner of his mouth.

As if in response to his words, two more figures stood up, this time from the heather at the top of the slope. Silhouetted against the sky behind them, it was clear they all wore the pelts of wolves with the pointed ears of the creatures standing up above their heads.

'They were mere paces from where we stopped at the top of the hill,' Stein said, his face creased with confusion. 'How did we not see them?'

'They're Úlfhéðnar,' Gairmund said, his voice little more than a hoarse whisper. His eyes were wide with dawning terror. 'Such men can move like ghosts.'

For the first time Thord's expression of arrogance and confrontation turned to consternation.

'We can't fight Wolf Coats, lord,' Stein said.

Thord rolled his eyes. His jaw muscles bunched as he gnashed his teeth together.

'We still outnumber them!' the Lendmann said. 'What sort of cowards are you?'

'Hand over the swords and there won't be a fight,' Ulrich said.

Thord shrugged. His expression became pained like he had just bitten a sour berry.

'All right, all right,' he said, holding his arms wide. He took a step closer to Einar. 'Let's talk about this.'

Ulrich nodded, relaxing his grip on his sword pommel.

'If we can avoid unnecessary bloodshed then all the better,' he said.

'Look,' Thord said in a conciliatory tone, taking a step closer to Einar. 'Eirik is powerful. He will kill me if I hand over those swords. Now you come with master warriors and demand the opposite? What are we to do? We're simple folk here. All we want is to gather this meat so our families can survive the winter. This strange weather means the harvest will fail this year—'

Ulrich opened his mouth to respond when Thord scythed his flensing knife, its blade long as a short sword, through the air, a strike aimed directly at Ulrich's throat.

On instinct, Ulrich dropped to a crouch. He felt a rush of air as Thord's knife just missed taking off the top of his skull like he was opening a boiled egg.

Ulrich drove himself back up to a standing position, powering his left shoulder into Thord's stomach, sending him staggering backwards.

A blood-curdling roar made Ulrich glance upward. One of Thord's men who had been standing on top of the whale cutting a long strip of blubber away, launched himself through the air, knife gripped in one hand, diving straight for him.

A brief whizzing sound ended in a thump as Affreca's arrow hit the flying man while still in the air. His roar ceased abruptly and he plummeted like a rock onto the sand, already stone dead.

Ulrich had to jump sideways to avoid being hit by the falling body. Thord, his balance recovered after Ulrich's shove took advantage, sidestepped around Ulrich then turned to swing his knife again. Ulrich cursed, understanding straight away what he was up to. By moving in that direction Thord had placed Ulrich between himself and Affreca. She could not shoot Thord without risking hitting Ulrich.

Gairmund dropped the rope and ran up the beach at Skar, knife raised above his head to strike. Without deigning to draw his own sword, Skar caught Gairmund by the wrist of his knife hand with his own right hand. Teeth gritted, Gairmund strained with all his might but was unable to push the knife any further. Skar balled his left hand into a fist and powered it into the other man's exposed stomach. Gairmund let out a gasp as all the wind was driven from his body. He doubled over, released his grip on his knife and dropped to his knees. Skar drove his knee up into Gairmund's chin. The Orkneyman's head snapped back, his eyes rolled up and he fell backwards, unconscious, onto the sand.

Ulrich pulled his sword from its sheath. Despite the dreary weather the blade gleamed like lightening, the weak sunlight flashing over the pattern-welded metal like countless steel snakes writhing together.

Thord's eyes widened.

'You have an Ulfbehrt,' Thord said, recognising the sword. 'Well, don't think I'm that impressed.'

He drew his own sword from its sheath. Ulrich saw that it bore the runes INGLERII on the blade.

'Eirik gave one of these to his most trusted men,' Thord said. 'Ulfbehrts are a good sword. But this is much better.'

He shouted over his shoulder to his men:

'Get them lads! They have more of the swords the king wants!'

Ulrich did not have time to see how Thord's men reacted as the Lendmann lunged at him with the sword. The blade was aimed at Ulrich's throat. Ulrich swiped his sword upwards, deflecting the blow with a ringing clang of clashing metal.

Ulrich stepped back to create space as Thord advanced on him again, holding up the Inglerii before him like a torch or some kind of talisman.

'The silver King Eirik will give me for killing you will just add to the pleasure I'll take in doing the deed,' he said. 'Your sword is no match for mine. Prepare to die.'

Ulrich stood, feet shoulder-width apart, waiting for the coming attack.

Thord lunged, driving the point of his sword at Ulrich's guts. Ulrich spun on his left foot, making a fast half turn so he was no longer in the way of the blade which was now behind him. Thord blinked. It was like Ulrich had vanished from in front of him. He halted his charge, feet churning in the sand.

Both men were now almost back to back. This time with his sword pommel gripped in both hands, Ulrich continued his turn, swinging the sword across his body at waist height. It jolted as it scythed into Thord's side, just above his left hip. Thord screamed as the blade sliced through his flesh, only stopping when it hit his backbone.

Ulrich wrenched his sword free of the huge wound and the Lendmann collapsed face first onto the beach. He made one last groan as his blood gushed across the sand to mingle with that of the whale. His now sightless eyes gazed, unblinking, out at the endless wastes of the sea.

'You see now,' Ulrich said to the corpse, 'the sword doesn't make the difference. It's the man who wields it.'

Ulrich, panting from the sudden exertion, looked around to see where the next threat would come from.

There was none. The sight of three of their number –

including their lord – falling in as many moments, along with two well-placed arrows from Affreca and the sheer menacing presence of Skar, Starkad, Sigurd and Kari, now brandishing drawn Ulfbehrt swords as well, had been enough to knock any further fight from the rest of Thord's men. They stood in a semi-circle, watching Ulrich and the others with wary eyes.

'Thord was a fool to fight Wolf Coats,' the one called Stein said. 'He's not been our Lendmann long. It seems we chose badly when we chose him to lead us. We'll do better next time.'

Ulrich looked at him for a long moment.

'Lord, we know where your swords are,' Stein said, quickly. 'Spare us any more bloodshed and we will get them for you. I'll go and get them now.'

Ulrich shook his head.

'No,' he said. 'I trust those thralls over there more than you. But you will help us. We're all going back to Steinborg. You're going to get those swords as planned. Say you are taking them to the harbour as you were ordered. We will be waiting just over the top of the hill on the way out of the fortress and you'll hand them over to us. Have you got that?'

'Yes, lord,' Stein said. 'But what will we say about Thord?'

'Tell them Eirik sent for him or something,' Ulrich said. 'I don't know. Make something up. Whatever you like but it better work. What's your name?'

'Stein, lord.'

'Well, Stein,' Ulrich said. 'Do as I tell you and you will make the world a better place. Don't do as I tell you and we'll hunt you down, and kill you. Then we'll kill all your family and burn your homes. Do you doubt me when I say this?'

'No, lord,' Stein said, accompanied by a vigorous shaking of his head.

'Good,' Ulrich said. 'Now go and get me my swords.'

Fifty-One

The little girl, Ellisif, shuffled in a languid dance to the incessant beating of the drums. Her eyes were vacant, the lids heavy and the snatches of song mumbled through her half-smiling lips betrayed her state of confused bliss. The strong drink laden with a concoction of intoxicating herbs had robbed her of all care, which was a blessing. She had no idea that what was happening around her was all aimed at bringing to an end her short life on Middle Earth.

A few paces behind her hovered the oldest of the Three Wise Women of the Northern Isles. She wore a long black robe. Its hood was raised, throwing the top half of her face into shadow. She held one pale, scrawny arm behind her back, concealing a long-bladed, wicked-sharp knife clutched in her bony fist.

In contrast to the bliss of the slave girl, Eirik 'Bloody Axe' Haraldsson, looked distinctly uncomfortable with what was going on around him. He sat on the four-pillared high seat of Jarls Gard, now transported to the temple out on the wilds of the heath. He was clad in a long, white robe that was embroidered with twisting, curling dragons and other beasts; the vestments a king wore when taking part in a religious ceremony. His long hair and beard were combed straight and smooth. The flickering light of the fire that blazed before him deepened the shadows of the creases his frown sank into his forehead.

Before Eirik in his high seat blazed a large bonfire in a stone hearth set in the floor of the Hof, the building that was used for the worship of the Aesir. The flames cast a baleful light on the wooden walls and upwards across three statues, pillars carved from single stout pine trees, each the image of a God. These stood around Eirik's pillared seat as if gathering around him in support. The statue on the right depicted Thor with his stark, glaring eyes, his hammer grasped before him in huge fists. Behind the high seat stood Odin, his one eye gazing down on the scene before him. The third statue, which was on the left of the seat, was hewn into the image of Freyr – the God whose name meant *the Lord* – with his huge, erect member. All three idols glistened with holy oil in the firelight.

The second of the witch women, the one who was in her prime of life, held a large jar of the holy oil. She dipped a cloth into it and rubbed it into the wood of the statues, muttering prayers and spells as she did so.

The youngest wise woman was stripped to her waist. She thumped a goatskin drum in rhythms that no doubt made sense to her but in no way seemed coordinated. Her eyes were glazed and empty, staring at the visions that her inner mind conjured. She had drunk from the same concoction of mead, bitter herbs and mushrooms as the girl who would be the sacrifice and it had driven out her rational mind. Her inner spirits swirled and soared around and above, hovering in the dark like a screaming Valkyrie above a battlefield, watching with fierce delight.

Gunnhild, also dressed in a long black robe, stood before the high seat. The little seashells, crystals and bits of glass sown into the material of her hooded dress swirled and swayed with her movements. They caught the firelight and her dress sparkled like the night sky. She wore black-and-white fur gloves of softest cats' skin and in her right hand grasped a distaff, a stick for spinning wool.

'Norns, dísir and landvættir,' Gunnhild shouted to the darkness that hovered beyond the reach of the firelight above. 'We call on you. Take the blood we are about to spill in return for your favour.'

Eirik shifted in his seat.

'Is this all really necessary, my love?' he said.

Gunnhild scowled and gave an explosive sigh.

'We've been through all this, Eirik,' she said. 'The answer is yes.'

'I know,' Eirik said. 'But now I'm actually here I'm not comfortable surrounded only by women without weapons or my trusted warriors. I don't think it's safe.'

'This is a holy place,' Gunnhild said. 'It's a house of the Gods. You know that weapons are forbidden by custom here lest blood be spilled in anger rather than in a spirit of sacrifice. Bringing a weapon into this holy place will enrage the spirits. And the magic we weave is sacred to women. We cannot allow men inside the temple.'

'*I* am a man,' Eirik said.

'And *I* am your wife,' Gunnhild said, a hard glint in her blue eyes. 'So I'm under no illusion about that. But you are the object of our spell tonight and are under our protection as our invited guest.'

'Ulrich is still out there somewhere,' Eirik said, looking

around as if he expected to see someone lurking in the shadows where the firelight failed to reach the walls.

Gunnhild let out a loud tut.

'Ulrich's werewolves are as dangerous to you as flies to a stallion, Eirik,' she said. 'They cause annoyance but no real harm. And as for the few *Orkneyingas* who won't accept that you are now their ruler, when this ritual works its power they will soon realise any opposition to us is futile.'

'I'd worry less if I had a few of my warriors in here with me,' Eirik said.

'Perhaps you lost your balls when you lost the throne of Norway, Eirik,' Gunnhild said. Her nose wrinkled and her upper lip drew into a snarl. 'There are over a hundred of your men in the feasting hall across the heath. They're a mere stone's throw away. If anything happens they will come running. Now let us proceed with this ceremony before we end up kicked out of a second realm! Try to be more grateful, Eirik. I am doing this for you, after all.'

Gunnhild raised her distaff again. The drumming increased to a thunder. Eirik winced at the cacophony.

The old woman in black stepped forward, moving closer to the oblivious little girl. She raised the knife above her head. The polished blade gleamed in the firelight.

Some sixth sense made Ellisif turn around. The blissful expression disappeared from her face as her looming fate became apparent. Her mouth dropped open in dismay.

Then the doors crashed open.

Fifty-Two

Einar Thorfinnsson stood in the entrance of the Hof, silhouetted against the dark of night outside. Warm air and the clatter of frantic drumming flowed out from inside.

He stepped through the portal, looking round at the scene before him. He saw the slave girl, flinching before the old woman with the raised knife. Beyond her was the blazing fire.

Gunnhild turned to see what was happening. Her eyes flashed with rage at the sight of the intruders and her lips curled into a snarl. The woman who had been oiling the statues started to her feet, clutching her jar of holy oil to her chest. Eirik Bloody Axe rose from the high seat. Even the befuddled mind of the drumming woman realised there was something wrong and her rhythm faltered into silence.

Above it all, the imposing statues of the Gods, their oiled wood gleaming in the firelight, loomed like watching giants.

On Einar's left, the Saxon Wulfhelm came through the doors. On his right, Surt strode into the temple. All three were clad in mail brynjas and helmets that glittered in the light of the flames. Einar's dark wolfskin curled around his shoulders. He wore his iron glove, the járngreipr, over his injured right hand. He and Wulfhelm bore unsheathed swords while Surt carried a spear with a long, leaf-shaped blade.

At the sight of the dark skin of Surt's part-exposed face and arms, the young woman on the drums wailed in terror.

'Our spells have summoned a jötunn,' she said, her voice breathless with terror.

The crone with the knife ignored the intruders. She bared her teeth, her knuckles whitened and her arms tensed as she moved to stab the little girl before her.

Surt lunged forward, launching his spear. The weapon shot over the temple floor. Its blade hit the old woman on the left side. It ploughed through her body and burst from the opposite side of her chest. She stiffened, back arched in pain, her mouth working soundlessly. The knife fell from her grasp as a torrent of blood gushed up from her mouth. Then she collapsed.

The stunned silence was broken by a piercing scream from Gunnhild. She sounded as much outraged as she was astonished.

'Men are in this sacred space,' she said, her voice choked with rage. 'And now you've shed blood in anger as well! This is terrible.'

Eirik laid a hand on Gunnhild's shoulder and pulled her back, pushing her behind him. Shaking her head in stunned disbelief at the disrespectful intrusion to the Gods' house, Eirik's normally overbearing wife complied without protest.

The former king cast a cold gaze over the three newcomers, then he pushed his shoulders back and drew himself up to his full height, which, like all the sons of Harald, was taller than most men.

'What's the meaning of this?' he said in a commanding

voice. 'This is a temple of the Gods and you have interrupted a sacred ceremony. You barge in where men are not supposed to be, with weapons drawn and your faces hidden behind helmet visors. I am a king. How dare you show such disrespect? What is your business?'

'You're in my seat,' Einar said, gesturing with his sword to the pillared high seat behind Eirik.

Ignoring Einar, Eirik turned his gaze to Surt.

'I know you. Your face may be hidden by your visor but you cannot hide your black skin, my friend,' he said. 'You are my *blámaðr*.'

'I'm not anyone's anything any more,' Surt said through clenched teeth.

'It can speak!' Eirik said, his eyebrows raised in mock astonishment. 'I always knew you could understand us, but I believed it was in the way my dogs understand my commands. I thought like them you were no more than a beast, incapable of speaking our tongue. This is interesting. Very interesting indeed.'

He moved his gaze to Einar, then Wulfhelm.

'And who are these other two? These brave warriors too cowardly to show me their faces,' he said. 'No doubt you're part of Ulrich's band of rogue vikings who have caused trouble in my realm?'

Einar snorted.

'*Your* realm?' he said, pulling off his helmet. His blond hair tumbled around his shoulders. 'You're a king without a country. Your own people threw you out of Norway and you've come here and set your thieving arse on the high seat that by birthright is mine.'

'Ah!' Eirik said, pointing his right forefinger at Einar. 'I know you now. You're Thorfinn the Skull Cleaver's bastard son. As I recall you're the son of his bed-slave. That makes you little more than a base born *thrall*, not the heir of a jarl. A treacherous jarl at that. Thorfinn was nothing but a fool who thought he could outwit me.'

'And yet I killed Thorfinn,' Einar said. 'And I sat in that seat, however briefly. It belongs in Jarls Gard, yet you have dragged it to this temple out on the heath, away from the protection of the Gard's walls. Who is really the fool here?'

'It's central to our ritual. The Norns will bless it and bless Eirik who sits on it as the new ruler here,' Gunnhild said, poking her head around her husband's shoulder. 'It's symbolic of power. Who sits on this high seat rules this land.'

'Yes,' Einar said. 'We heard you were coming down to this temple here to perform seiðr.'

'It is not seiðr!' Eirik said, his voice a growl. 'I would never indulge in such unmanly magic.'

'Why then do you hide away in here, surrounded only by women?' Einar said, a mischievous smile on his lips. 'Without your warriors? Perhaps there was something going on you didn't want them to see?'

'My warriors are not far away, don't you worry,' Eirik said. 'They will be here in moments.'

'Really?' Wulfhelm spoke for the first time. 'Only when we walked past that feasting hall nearby it sounded very like they were all in there getting drunk. Granted it's only a short distance away but the way they were singing I doubt many of them could manage to stagger over here in a hurry.'

'Thorfinn's bastard, my blámaðr and the Saxon,' Eirik

said. 'That can only mean Ulrich Rognisson and his band of úlfhéðnar are not far away. Where is the little shit?'

'You know Ulrich,' Einar said. 'He's a religious man. He doesn't want to call down the Gods' wrath by spilling blood in a temple.'

'But he's happy for someone else to do it for him,' Eirik said, narrowing his eyes. 'Same old Ulrich.'

'That,' Einar continued, 'and we have other pressing work that needs done tonight as well. My Wolf Coat brethren are engaged in that.'

'Including the Dubliner, no doubt?' the former king said. 'Guthfrith's bitch of a daughter.'

'What do you want?' Gunnhild said. Her voice was thick and slightly hoarse, as if she already knew the answer.

'We heard, lady, that your husband was leaving the protection of Jarls Gard,' Einar said. 'To travel down to this sacred Hof out on the heath, and your men had been ordered that they could not be with you during a secret ritual; well we thought it was an opportunity not to be missed. We are here to take the girl. You won't sacrifice her tonight.'

'Oh, you heard this, did you?' Eirik said, raising an eyebrow. 'Let me guess who from? Her father no doubt. I knew we couldn't trust Aulvir.'

Einar smiled.

'You're not as popular here in Orkney as you might think you are,' he said. 'There are many who would be happy to see you gone. And as you are here, alone and weaponless, we can make that happen.'

'Very good,' Eirik said. 'I'll deal with the traitor Aulvir later.'

'I also hear that you are looking for these swords,' Einar

said. He held up his weapon so Eirik could get a better look. The firelight shimmered across its blade and the runes set into it that spelled the unmistakable name of INGLERII. 'Let me bring this one to you now and show you just how good it is. There will be no *later* for you, Eirik.'

'Very good,' Eirik said. 'But you are wrong on several counts.'

'Really?' Einar said. His knuckles white around his sword hilt he began striding towards the king.

'I am not weaponless,' Eirik said.

The king whirled around. He thrust his hand under the cushion on the high seat and when he turned around again, it now grasped a sword, its naked blade gleaming in the firelight. As the flames danced across the metal, Einar saw it too had runes embedded in the blade. They spelled INGLERII too.

'Nor am I without help,' Eirik said. This time Eirik reached inside the loose white robes he wore and pulled out a horn. He put it to his lips and began to blow. Loud blasts blared across the Hof.

'It's a signal!' Surt shouted. 'He's calling his men.'

Fifty-Three

Two warriors ran out from behind the effigies of the Gods. They wore brynjas and helmets but were wrapped in dark cloaks that had helped them hide in the gloom.

'You had armed men hidden in here?! You brought a weapon into the sacred space?!' Gunnhild said, glaring in angry disbelief at the blade in her husband's fist. 'You fool! You might just have ruined everything.'

'I might just have saved our lives, dear,' Eirik said, gritting his teeth and taking up a ready stance. 'Run. Get out of here. Go for the back door and run to the hall. Get the rest of my men. We can hold this rabble until the rest get here.'

Einar's fast walk became a charge. Wulfhelm ran after him, sprinting across the floor of the temple towards the blazing fire and the royal couple. Surt ran towards the fallen priestess to retrieve his spear.

Gunnhild backed away, then turned and fled towards the back of the temple, disappearing into the gloom beyond the towering statues.

The two cloaked warriors ran in front of Eirik, coming between Einar and the former king, the fire and the high seat. One bore a sword and the other an axe. Both had shields painted with the bloody red axe of Eirik. Einar could see that the one with the axe had eyes which were wide and rolling as he came forward. His teeth were clenched so hard the muscles at the top of his jaw stood out like balls. Einar deduced that he was one of the king's berserkers, handpicked men blessed by Odin with divine rage. Such men knew no fear and were perfect for dangerous tasks like guarding the king alone.

The berserker ran straight at Einar. His mouth opened and he let out a roar as he charged forward, shield first, axe raised. Einar kept running himself. He had both hands to his left side, close to his waist, gripping his sword hilt. As they were about to meet the berserker raised his axe even higher, preparing to strike it down on Einar in an almighty blow designed to cleave him asunder.

Einar swept his sword up and across his body. It scythed over the top of the berserker's shield and smashed into the armpit of his raised right arm. The Inglerii's wicked-sharp blade shattered the iron rings of the man's brynja and hewed through the flesh beneath. The berserker's axe arm stopped dead as Einar's sword parted his sinews and bone, almost severing his entire right shoulder from his chest before it stopped, its momentum spent, just under his collarbone. His angry shout became a high-pitched wail. Jets of blood squirted out from the massive tear in his body. His near-severed arm rotated backwards at an impossible angle, the axe dropping from his unfeeling hand. Then the berserker's knees collapsed and he fell backwards to die on the floor.

Einar stood for a moment looking down at the dead man at his feet. As he wiped away the hot blood that was splashed across his face with the back of his hand, he thought how the Inglerii had such devastating effect; that in the hands of a trained warrior, as he now was, they almost made a fight unfair.

Then he recalled what was going on around him. He turned and saw that the second warrior was confronting Wulfhelm. Eirik still stood before the high seat, his own sword brandished before him. The path to Eirik for Einar was clear. He sucked in air through his nose and ran towards the king.

As Einar ran past him, Eirik's other warrior slashed his sword at Wulfhelm. The Saxon stopped the blow with his own blade. Then he rotated his sword, pushing his opponent's weapon out of the way. Wulfhelm lunged forward, driving the point of his sword into the other man's face. With a cry Eirik's second warrior fell dying to the floor.

Einar reached Eirik. He swung his sword in an overhead arc aimed at the centre of Eirik's head. Eirik countered the blow with his own blade, halting it mid-air before it clove his skull in two.

Sparks showered from the point where the two weapons met. Einar withdrew his weapon to strike again and saw to his consternation that there was a nick in the blade.

With speed that took Einar by surprise, Eirik turned his defensive block into an attack. He swept his blade in a reverse arc, perfectly aimed to strike the top of Einar's arm. If it landed and parted the metal rings of Einar's brynja – which the Inglerii could do with ease – it would sever his left arm at the shoulder.

Einar countered with his own sword. The clang of metal rang out as the blades met again.

Eirik glanced around and saw Surt was mere paces away and Wulfhelm just behind him. Instead of striking back at

Einar he grasped with his free hand for the black-robed woman who stood nearby. She still clutched the jar of sacred oil to her chest as if it was the most precious thing in the world to her.

'Give me that,' Eirik shouted, trying to pull the jar away from her.

'No,' the woman said, fear in her eyes. 'It is holy oil, blessed by the Gods.'

With a frustrated roar Eirik grabbed her by the shoulder and hurled her forwards towards the blazing fire in the hearth before the high seat. As she stumbled forwards, Eirik lifted his right boot and planted a kick on her behind, propelling her faster.

The woman fell, face first, her jar of precious oil dropping from her grasp as she went down. The clay vessel smashed on the stones that formed the hearth and the contents gushed out in every direction.

Einar heard a loud whoosh. He felt a blast of hot air billow around him as the fire ignited the oil. A sheet of flame rose from the hearth, spreading in every direction and engulfing the fallen priestess. The heat made him crouch, hands up to protect his face. Surt and Wulfhelm threw themselves to the floor to avoid the scorching wave of air.

When it passed Einar looked up, wondering why he was not dead. Eirik, however, was running into the murky shadows beyond the statues in the same direction his wife had gone.

The priestess, now a screaming mass of blazing fire, got to her feet. Blind with terror and agony she charged, waving her burning arms, straight into Einar. Some of the flames jumped onto Einar's cloak and he smelled his own hair burning. The woman bounced off him and stumbled sideways into Surt who was just getting himself up off the floor.

Wulfhelm jumped to his feet, ripped off his cloak and cast it over both Surt and the burning woman, wrapping it round them to smother the flames. Einar patted out the burning patches on his wolf pelt and hair, grabbed his sword from the floor and ran after Eirik.

A rivulet of burning oil dribbled across the floor from the fire. It touched the base of the oil-covered statue of Frey and the towering wooden sculpture erupted into flames. The youngest of the Wise Women, her mind still confused by the herbal drink, first howled then whimpered in horror at the sight of the burning God.

Shielding his face from this new blast of heat with his raised right arm, Einar ran into the middle of the three pillars of the Gods. The flames that engulfed Frey drove away the shadows at the back of the temple and Einar saw that there was a door in the back wall. It was open to the dark of night outside and there was no sign of Eirik or Gunnhild.

'Einar,' Surt called to him. He stopped and turned back. Wulfhelm and Surt, now no longer burning, stood beside the fast-spreading fire.

'They've got away,' Surt said. 'We need to go too before Eirik gets to his men in the hall.'

Einar hesitated, glancing round at the open doorway once more. He cursed. Surt was right.

Einar ran back to rejoin the others. As he was about to pass his father's high seat he stopped. He braced his shoulder against the back of it.

'What are you doing?' Wulfhelm shouted above the ever louder roaring of the flames.

'If I can't have it, no one will,' Einar said. He heaved, straining his thighs, sending the chair toppling forwards into the conflagration burning across the hearth and floor.

Then he ran over to the little girl who was standing, bewildered by all that was going on around her and heaved her over his shoulder.

'Let's go,' he said.

They ran for the door they had entered by. Behind them the burning statue of Frey toppled sideways into the statue of Odin. Also covered in oil, it too burst into flames. Tongues of fire spread across the floor and began to lick upwards towards the thatch above.

As he ran into the night outside, Einar felt a shiver that was not all to do with the chilled air. They had spilled blood and burned a holy place.

The Gods would not be happy.

Fifty-Four

The Hof Gunnhild had chosen to work her ritual in was on a heath some distance from any settlements. She had picked the place as it was remote, the sort of place the spirits of the land liked to frequent, where they could go undisturbed by human beings with their noise and mess. There were only two buildings, the temple itself and a long hall about three hundred paces away, used for ceremonial feasts and *sumbl*, the ritual drinking sessions. All around was in darkness apart from the glow of burning torches set in brackets above the door of the hall.

Einar, the little girl still over his shoulder, ran across the heather as fast as he could go. It was a race for who would get to the hall first – Surt, Wulfhelm and he or Eirik and Gunnhild. He knew the king and queen were somewhere in the darkness of that wind-blasted heath too. Eirik still had his sword and the noise of his oathsworn warriors, enjoying their ale in the feasting hall, drifted through the night. From the noise they made it was obvious that once Eirik reached his men, Einar and the others would be hopelessly outnumbered.

Einar raced on, his heart pounding in his chest. In the darkness he could easily plunge his foot into a hole and the next thing he would feel would be explosive agony as his leg bone shattered. Or he could run blindly into one of the bottomless bog pools that lay all around, ready to suck the unwary down to a black, slimy death.

As they neared the hall his heart sank. He heard the sound of a fist hammering on the wooden door at the gable end. Eirik and Gunnhild's voices, shouting for help, came drifting through the dark. Then he heard shouts from the warriors guarding the entrance to the hall and the rattling of the doors opening. Einar looked around, wondering if he should abandon Ulrich's plan and run into the dark. At any moment Eirik's warriors would come flooding out to search for them.

'Up,' Surt spoke one word. It was enough. They all understood.

The roof of the hall sloped from its apex at the centre down to a height at the side walls that was just over the top of their heads. Surt scrambled up onto the roof, then turned and held his hand out. Einar lifted the girl up and Surt took her up onto the roof. Then Einar and Wulfhelm clambered up onto the roof and they all crawled up as far as they could.

Once up on the roof they lay flat on their bellies, pushing themselves into the thatch.

'If we run now they'll catch us for sure,' Surt hissed. 'We need to wait for the right time. Now shh!'

Beneath them the sound of raised voices filled the night. Light began to flood the darkness as men came from the hall with burning torches and whale oil lamps. Across the heath flames were starting to break through the roof of the burning Hof.

'Vikings tried to kill me,' Eirik's voice rose above the clamour. 'It's Ulrich and his Wolf Coats. They won't have got far. Spread out and search the heath. I want them found. I want their heads brought to me. The man who brings them will get an Ulfbehrt sword in reward.'

'Get your weapons! Brynjas and shields,' another voice commanded. 'Form a defensive circle around the hall. Lord King, I knew it was a mistake to let you go alone to the temple. Please go inside the hall. We'll stop anyone getting to you.'

'My wife will go in, but I will not,' Eirik said. 'I'll be staying out here with you men. Leave a contingent inside to protect her. I want to see those bastards caught and dead once and for all.'

Einar heard the thump of many feet running this way and that across the soft turf. There were many voices now, all speaking in the low, unexcited tones of men accustomed to dangerous situations. These were not, after all, warriors who had taken so much ale that they could not do their jobs. Soon their voices were coming from all around as Eirik's men circled the hall, facing outwards against the dark.

Einar and the others were totally surrounded and hopelessly outnumbered. If he reached down from the roof he could probably touch one of them on the helmet. All it would take was for someone to look up and they would be discovered. Then they would be dead. Einar sent a silent prayer to the Gods that no one would look up.

'Quickly,' Eirik shouted. 'Start moving outwards. Stay as close together as you can but search every step of this heath. They're out there somewhere. I want them found.'

Einar lay flat on his face, his left cheek pressed against the roof. He watched as the line of men came into view. Their helmets and mail brynjas glittered in the light of the burning torches that were held by every tenth man in the line. They advanced at a steady pace out into the darkness that surrounded the hall, holding their formation as they went. They did not dawdle but they also moved slowly enough to make a thorough search of the heath around them.

A rattle of latches and bolts told Einar the doors of the hall had been closed and barred. The circle of torches got ever wider as Eirik's warriors expanded their search outwards from the hall. When they were perhaps a hundred paces away in every direction, Einar heard suppressed sniggers from the others lying alongside him.

'Ulrich was right,' Wulfhelm said in a whisper. 'He knew Eirik would do that. *Eirik never learns*, he had said. *Without me to council him in the arts of war it's no wonder he lost Norway.*'

'We need to make sure we aren't here when they come back, though,' Einar whispered. 'Their line is getting so stretched now it'll be child's play for us to slip through it.'

Einar looked again and saw that the torches that marked every tenth man or so in the circle of iron, which had started out perhaps fifteen paces apart, were now twenty-five or thirty paces apart. As the circle got ever bigger the gaps between each warrior and the next got ever wider.

'Come on,' he said, sliding off the roof and dropping to the ground with as much noise as a cat would make. The others followed him down and they gathered in a tight group around him.

'We need you to keep quiet, do you understand?' Einar said to Ellisif.

The little girl nodded.

'Good,' he said. 'We'll keep low and go through the dark. When we get to about where they are now stop and wait for them to give up and start coming back. They're too far apart now, their night eyes will be destroyed by the light of those torches and they think they've already searched the area behind them so they won't be looking out for us. Keep down, stay quiet and they should just walk straight past us. Once we've got past we head cross-country and meet back at the ship.'

They all nodded. Einar pulled his wolf skin hood over his helmet, covering any gleam of metal that might give him away. The others pulled their hoods up as well, crouched low and set off into the dark towards the encircling ring of now far-off torches.

It all went as Einar said.

Before long they were away from Eirik and his warriors and running across the heath on their way to the ship.

Fifty-Five

The ship was waiting in the harbour below Torhaven. With the red axe of Eirik painted on its sail, Roan had sailed it into the harbour as brazenly as Einar and Ulrich had walked into the tavern earlier. Among all the other ships brought by strangers to Orkney no one knew whether the Wolf Coats' ship belonged there or not.

When Einar, Surt, Wulfhelm and the little girl got there Ulrich and the others were already waiting for them. Several chests of Ulfbehrt swords rested on the deck.

There was someone else there as well: Aulvir.

The reunion between the dróttseti and his daughter was heart-warming, though as the girl was still under the bewildering influence of the herbal drink the witches had given her, most of the enthusiastic crying was by Aulvir.

'Mealshechlin told me what you were planning,' he said to Einar. 'With Eirik and Gunnhild away at the Hof and Thord busy there was no one to stop me just walking out of Jarls Gard.'

'What about the Irishman?' Einar said. 'Will he be all right?'

'He wants to stay,' Aulvir said. 'And Eirik does not know he helped us. He will be all right.'

'And we may need someone inside Eirik's house in the future,' Skar said. 'So he'll be useful.'

Ulrich chuckled.

'This was almost too easy,' he said. 'I nearly feel sorry for Eirik.'

'I'm glad you think so,' Einar said. 'I was quite sure we nearly got killed several times.'

They untied the ship and pushed it out into the dark waters. Before long they were sailing away into the night.

'What now?' Affreca said.

'We'll sail south, at least at first,' Ulrich said. 'Eirik will assume we went north and send ships that way. When it's safe to we will turn and head back to Norway.'

'So we stay on Hakon's side?' Skar said.

'He is still far from secure on the High Seat of Norway.' Ulrich said. 'He still needs our help.'

'He's still a Christian,' Skar said.

'And Eirik follows Odin,' Einar said. 'I'm learning that men's faiths do not seem to influence what they think in their hearts. Perhaps we can persuade Hakon to see the truth someday.'

'And what about you?' Einar said to Affreca.

'What about me?' she said.

'What about what you said about reclaiming Jorvik for the Ivarssons?' Einar said. 'Then ruling there as queen. Is that still in your future?'

'Who knows what the Norns are weaving for us,' Affreca said. 'Though if the choice is that or sailing the whale road with this band of renegade vikings, having all sorts of adventures and seeing who knows what sights, it's really no choice at all, is it?'

'And what of Ragnarök?' Skar said. 'What about our chance to win glory and be chosen to join Odin's Einherjar?'

Ulrich looked up at the dark sky. Rain was starting to fall yet again.

'It seems that Ragnarök has not come,' he said. 'Yet. But don't worry. This means we still have the chance to do great deeds. When the chance comes, we will grab it with both hands. We will achieve feats that will echo in eternity. The great heroes will sing of our exploits on the mead benches of Valhalla.'

About the Author

TIM HODKINSON grew up in Northern Ireland where the rugged coast and call of the Atlantic Ocean led to a lifelong fascination with vikings and a degree in Medieval English and Old Norse Literature. Apart from Old Norse sagas, Tim's more recent writing heroes include Ben Kane, Giles Kristian, Bernard Cornwell, George R. R. Martin and Lee Child. After several years living in New Hampshire, USA, Tim has returned to Northern Ireland, where he lives with his wife and children.

Follow Tim on: @TimHodkinson
www.timhodkinson.blogspot.com